M

The Daguerreotype

The
Daguerreotype
• a novel •

Patrick Gregory

SYRACUSE UNIVERSITY PRESS

Syracuse University Press
Syracuse, New York 13244–5160

First Edition 2004
04 05 06 07 08 09   6 5 4 3 2 1

The paper used in this publication meets the minimum
requirements of American National Standard for Information
Sciences—Permanence of Paper for Printed Library Materials,
ANSI Z39.48–1984.∞™

Library of Congress Cataloging-in-Publication Data
Gregory, Patrick (Patrick Bolton).
  The daguerreotype : a novel / Patrick Gregory.— 1st ed.
    p. cm.
  ISBN 0-8156-0825-X (hardcover (cloth) : alk. paper)
  1. United States—Emigration and immigration—Fiction. 2.
England—Emigration and immigration—Fiction. 3. British
Americans—Fiction. 4. Women immigrants—Fiction. I. Title.
PS3607.R49D34 2004
813'.6—dc22

2004004155

Manufactured in the United States of America

 *For Justina*

Patrick Gregory was born in New York City and now lives in Northampton, Massachusetts, and South Halifax, Vermont. *The Daguerreotype* is his first novel.

Contents

The Daguerreotype

London, 1849

SHE AWOKE EARLY THAT MORNING. The sunlight reached across the pillow to touch her cheek with welcoming warmth, and as she opened her eyes, the coverlet seemed awash with brightness. Overhead, golden motes danced in the resplendent air.

The other girls were still adrift in sleep. The room was absolutely quiet, except for the faint wheeze of Lillian's asthmatic breathing two beds away and the distant rattle of carriage wheels from somewhere outside, perhaps as far away as Highgate Hill.

She lay there, dazzled by the sheer glory of the sunlight. Her bed was the only one in the room to receive the early morning rays of the sun; Miss Shaw had awarded the bed to her as the best scholar in the school. Dear Miss Shaw! She need not have done that. After all, Caroline Talbot was the daughter of a baronet and had a proper claim to preferment, but Miss Shaw had decided to give it to a scholar instead. Elizabeth's heart leaped up at the thought of such goodness, such nobility of spirit. Some people found Miss Shaw cold, distant, but beneath the headmistress's severe manner Elizabeth perceived a passionate sense of justice, and it came to her as an exhilarating revelation that moral rectitude and high-mindedness were not incompatible with kindness. This discovery, made quite on her own, had filled Elizabeth with hopefulness and a comforting sense of maturity.

The sunlight sang out silently, proclaiming the new day. The awareness suddenly swelled within her that there was indeed something special about it. Today was her birthday.

She closed her eyes to savor the plenitude of her years; folding her arms solemnly, she felt the ripe fullness of her breasts under the cotton nightgown. Hastily she launched into her morning prayer, asking the Lord's blessings for herself, for her dear papa, and for good, noble-spirited Miss Shaw. On opening her eyes again, her attention was caught by an unfamiliar object on her bedside table: a small leather case, dark crimson in color, with two delicate brass latches on one side. She sat up in bed, her eyes bright with excitement, and cautiously, ceremoniously took the object in her hand. On the cover of the case, stamped in gold letters, was the legend: *Adelaide Gallery / Strand / Claudet's Daguerreotype Process.* She undid the latches with tender care so as not to scratch the leather with her nail and lifted the lid.

At first she saw nothing but a shimmering blackness; it was like peering through a window at night into a darkened room or gazing into a deep, shadowy well. Then, on tilting the object ever so slightly in the palm of her hand, the image suddenly sprang into view—so very suddenly and so very lifelike in its lineaments—that she gave a gasp, and exclaimed under her breath in rapture and surprise, "Papa!"

He was seated bolt upright, a book held open before him, and looking out at her with that strained and slightly quizzical expression that he commonly wore when interrupted in his reading. As always, he was clean-shaven, with neatly trimmed side-whiskers, and fastidiously dressed in a black frock coat, with a precisely knotted black cravat revealing a small, discreet triangle of white shirtfront. The almost coquettish primness of his attire was agreeably offset by the disarray of his thick black hair, which stood out from his head in unruly tufts. There was about his features an air of intense intelligence, poised, as it seemed, on the verge of decision, or of doubt. And in his gaze Elizabeth discerned a hint of pain, of terrible vulnerability— a lingering memory of his irretrievable loss.

She lifted the image to her lips, and as she did so, she noticed an inscription, written on a small slip of white paper in a firm, familiar hand and pasted on the red-velvet lining of the inside cover of the case: "To my beloved daughter, Elizabeth, on her seventeenth birthday, April 10th, 1849, from her father, John Gow."

Her heart was too full, it would surely burst! She placed a hand over it to quell the tumult and lay back in bed, the case resting before her, crimson and gold on the white coverlet.

But how had it gotten here, to her bedside? The miraculous nature of its appearance, along with the magical quality of the image, added to the gift's splendor. She clasped the case to her heart and pondered the mystery. Surely her father had not placed it there. No male presence was ever allowed beyond the aseptic confines of the downstairs sitting room. The truth shone in upon her: her father had brought it to Miss Shaw, and the two of them had conspired to have it placed on her bedside while she slept. Yes, that was how it had happened. Elizabeth could imagine them conversing earnestly together: Miss Shaw very erect, her hands clasped loosely in front of her; her father leaning slightly toward her on his walking stick, his tall black hat held before him, his manner formal, even a trifle ceremonious, but softened somewhat by the intimate subject of their talk. Then, with her eyes tightly closed, Elizabeth could see Miss Shaw gliding slowly through the moonlit hall, the case—a deep, dark crimson, the color of Tuscany roses—held in one hand, while the other hand lightly gripped her skirts to keep them from rustling. She saw her pause beside the bed and, bending down, carefully deposit the precious object on the little table alongside the bone-handled hairbrush and the leather-bound Book of Common Prayer, then, with a quick backward glance at the sleeping girl—a glance solemn, and stately, and full of calm reassurance—slip away into the shadows.

How beautiful of her!

Elizabeth's happiness was complete. She thought to herself: this is the happiest day of my life; I shall never be happier than I am now, at this very moment. Her eyes filled with tears, and she was weeping quietly when the morning bell rang.

London, 1850

SHE STOOD IN THE DOORWAY, UNPERCEIVED.

The breakfast room was on the ground floor, at the back of the house, adjacent to the kitchen. It overlooked a narrow strip of lawn, which ended abruptly at a brick wall, bordered by scraggly hedges; above the wall loomed the unadorned backs of a long row of late-Georgian townhouses. The room had a vaguely subterranean air about it and gave off the faint, pervasive smells of mildew, coal gas, and broiled kippers (a combination of odors that Elizabeth was to associate ever after with London, childhood, and familial intimacy).

Her father was seated at the breakfast table, gazing disconsolately at the remains of a boiled egg. An unfolded letter lay abandoned before him amidst the breakfast things. The slump of his shoulders, the slackness of his usually alert and nervously expressive features, told her at a glance that he was in one of his moods. These "absences" (as she chose to call them to herself) had become more frequent of late. When she was younger, they had filled her with dread, and she had reacted to them either by fleeing his presence to nurse her anxieties in private or by trying to divert his attention with some childish gesture of affection—throwing her arms around his neck or climbing onto his lap. In the past couple of years her anguish had been touched by pity, by a new sense of protectiveness.

"What is it, Papa?" She spoke quietly so as not to startle him.

He looked up at her, an expression of consternation passing fleetingly across his face. Then he smiled wanly. "Good morning, my dear."

"Something's the matter, isn't it?"

"What an alert little creature you are, my Bess!"

She hated it when he addressed her in those tones, as if she were still a

· 4 ·

child. It increased her sense of isolation from him, made him seem remote and helpless.

His gaze drifted to the letter. "Some disappointing news, I'm afraid."

"Not from Edinburgh?"

"Yes, from Edinburgh. I am sorry, my dear."

"But Papa, I don't understand. Whatever happened?" She moved toward him, instinctively.

"They decided to give the chair to Dr. Kincaid instead. And that, my dear, is *that.*"

"Oh Papa, how could they? It is horribly unjust! They assured you of the appointment." As she let control of her emotions slip from her, she was relieved to see her father assume control of his own.

"Such matters are never assured, Bess. No promises were made, no treaties signed, and we have only ourselves to blame if we count on things that we have no right to count on. Obviously Lord Landsdowne was particularly anxious to see Dr. Kincaid secure the position, and his influence on the committee was decisive."

"But you are the far better candidate. It *is* unjust."

"Thank you, my dear, it is kind of you to say so. And strictly *entre nous,* I do rather think that I have the slight edge. But Dr. Kincaid has done some very creditable work, Bess, and there is ample room for a lively discussion on the subject of our relative merits. Moreover, one cannot overlook the role of patronage in the whole affair. But the decision has been made, and there is no undoing it. So let us not waste our time bemoaning the choice or indulging in self-pity. That would only serve to make a bad situation worse."

His voice was calm, and he reached out to take her hand firmly in his. A moment ago she had trembled at his distress; now she found herself irritated by his composure. She detested that brave-little-boy look on his face. She knew it was noble of him to be so stoic, but sometimes she wished that he would give in to—no, not senseless rage, but something like righteous indignation. Such an outburst would at least clear the air. As it was, they were both forced to find consolation in empty gestures and platitudinous phrases.

She bent over him and folded her arms around his neck. She clung to him silently, not quite sure whether she was comforter or comforted, not wanting to hear more of his noble sentiments or look into his sorrow-stricken eyes. Finally she asked calmly, "And what will you do now, Papa?"

"Oh, I shall, I suppose, continue on much as I am at present, here in London. Of course, there is little chance of advancement as things now stand. At least not in the immediate future. But I have my research to do. And in some respects it is easier to do the work here than in Scotland, where I would have to set up a new laboratory, establish new routines, and depend a great deal on correspondence. Down there I would not be able to compare notes with Braddock on a daily basis or have dear old Mrs. Murphy to clean up after me. Yet . . ." The sentence hung in midair, and Elizabeth, sensing a resurgence of emotion, clung tighter to him, hoping to absorb some of his misery.

"Are you terribly disappointed, Papa?"

"The appointment would certainly have simplified things. It would have made our circumstances more comfortable and secure. And then, my dear, I confess that it would have given me enormous pleasure to overhear you tell one of your well-born school friends that your father had been appointed to the chair of Natural Philosophy at Edinburgh University."

"Oh, Papa!"

"There, there, my dear." She let him comfort her, sensing that this was what he wanted now. "It is not the end of the world, it is not the end of anything, except perhaps of some foolish, fantastical dreams of glory. So let them go. Begone vain images, depart from us! There, you see, they are quite vanished. Come, Bess, no more mourning. I have my work to do; we both have our work to do. That is what matters most. The moral here is abundantly plain, and if you were still a little girl, I would have you put it into one of those exquisite samplers that you used to make for me and your dear mama. It would read something like this: PLACE NOT YOUR FAITH IN THE EFFORTS OF OTHERS. I would have you decorate it with a mortuary willow, as an emblem of dead hopes and stillborn dreams, and we would have it nicely framed in black walnut, like Aunt Emma's portrait, and hang it right over there, above the sideboard, so that we would see it every morning along with our breakfast egg and take heed."

The terrible wounded look had gone out of his eyes, and he gazed back at her reassuringly, yet she sensed the depth of his disappointment, and a feeling of great pity welled up in her, accompanied by a desire, almost physical in nature, to protect him from that insidious despair that, even in the best of times, always seemed to hover near him.

As a child she had viewed her father as a paragon of courage and moral rectitude, and as a firm bulwark between herself and the dangers of the outside world. Her love for him then had been tinged with awe, for in his presence it was impossible not to be aware of her own enormous limitations, her many imperfections of character. He was not, however, a stern taskmaster as far as others were concerned, and it seemed to her that the melancholy gaze that he occasionally cast about him served to dissolve the wickedness that he saw there and turn it into remorse. As far as she was concerned, a sorrowful glance from him had always been more chastening than a tongue-lashing.

In recent months her vision of him had changed. It was not that she found him any less virtuous or meritorious, but she had grown increasingly aware of his vulnerability to the world, of the fragility of his defenses. Whether this altered perception was due to some change in him or in herself, she could not say. What she knew, however, was that their relationship had undergone a great transformation, had become increasingly, and sometimes for her bewilderingly, complex. She was often uncertain what role to adopt with him, fluctuating haphazardly between that of daughter, mother, wife— and always miserably conscious of the fact that she really did not know how any of these roles was to be properly played. The one thing that seemed clear to her was that she must teach herself to be more attentive to his moods and learn to anticipate them. She must learn to be less self-centered, less selfish.

Now, with the bad news from Edinburgh, she felt a glow of satisfaction at the thought that shortly, in a few weeks' time, she would no longer be a financial burden to him—or, at least, far less one than heretofore. She would indeed need a few new items of clothing, certainly a warm winter coat; there was no way around that. And undoubtedly a couple of pieces of sensible luggage. But beyond those few purchases, the venture would cost him nothing, and in a year's time she would be earning money of her own. She would even be able to make a contribution, however modest, to their joint household expenses. Given the uncertain nature of their present circumstances, that thought was especially gratifying. Yet it would now be harder than ever to leave him alone, even if only for a few months.

Barely three weeks ago, just two days before graduation, Miss Shaw had invited Elizabeth to come by her chambers that afternoon for "a little talk." Elizabeth had understood that it was a question of the headmistress's customary farewell conversation with each of the departing students, and she had looked forward to the encounter with a sharp pang of pleasure, edged with curiosity and fear. The girls had often speculated among themselves about the precise nature of these talks, excitedly exchanging opinions, warnings, and advice. The boldest of them even ventured to propose the sort of expression one should frame on one's face upon entering the sacred chambers; and there was much general discussion of what one should do with one's hands.

Jenny reported, with wide eyes and tremulous voice, that last year she had seen a girl departing in tears from Miss Shaw's chambers following one such interview, and this led several members of the group to elaborate on the well-worn belief that the headmistress used the occasion to present each student with a candid and detailed summary of her strengths and weaknesses. The theory was alternately challenged and affirmed by those who pointed out that Miss Shaw always avoided "personalities" in her dealings with students—one faction asserting that she would never "lower herself" to speak of individual failings or misdemeanors (or for that matter deign to keep them in her memory after the appropriate punishment or admonition had been promptly administered); the other faction proposing that she reserved these final and private meetings for the express purpose of dealing with intensely personal matters, and that it was then, as one of this faction declared in a vehement whisper, that you discovered that she had missed *absolutely nothing,* which statement provoked a moment of awestruck silence.

Sarah Barnes—who had spent part of her childhood in India, was a year older than the others, and affected a world-weary aloofness—blandly stated that Miss Shaw probably took this opportunity to warn the young ladies about the dangers of men; and Jenny, who was a perfect goose, indignantly protested that she did not see how *that* could have reduced Priscilla Gibson to tears—which caused everyone, including Elizabeth, to burst out laughing. Elizabeth had then felt obliged to bring the conversation to a close by saying that Priscilla Gibson's tears seemed perfectly natural to her and that in all probability she had been weeping because she had been overcome at the thought of bidding a final farewell to the school and to Miss Shaw.

"Now isn't that just like you, Elizabeth Gow!" drawled Sarah Barnes in her faintly superior tone of voice. Then, as if talking to herself, she added, "What nonsense!" and departed from the group with a slow, sad shake of her head.

Miss Shaw motioned her to a chair with a brisk, businesslike gesture. There was, Elizabeth noted with vague disappointment, something preoccupied about the headmistress's manner. The occasion promised to be neither ceremonial nor sentimental.

"As you have heard, Elizabeth, Mlle Desrosiers is leaving us to return to France. Her mother is gravely ill, and Mademoiselle has perceived, quite correctly I believe, that her primary duty is to be with her mother, who has no one to look after her. So it is that the world, the real world, sometimes manages to penetrate our peaceful cloister." She paused to look searchingly at Elizabeth, who gazed back at her with uncomprehending eyes. "Her departure," she continued, "leaves us without a teacher of French. In thinking of her replacement, you came to mind . . ."

"Oh, Miss Shaw, I . . ."

"Please, Elizabeth, do not interrupt. Let me finish what I have to say, and then we shall discuss the matter together.

"You, as I say, came to mind because you have displayed an aptitude for the language and because it seems to me that you have the makings of good teacher—though I might be wrong about that. Also, I was aware that you would be looking for employment on leaving here.

"However, Mlle Desrosiers is a native speaker of good family background; her French is naturally fluent, and her accent excellent. You, however, are less than proficient in the language, and your accent is, well, naturally that of an English schoolgirl. On further consideration, I found that I could not face with equanimity such a drastic decline in the quality of our French instruction at the school. In addition, there was the matter of your complete lack of experience as a teacher.

"Therefore, Elizabeth, I took it upon myself to write to an old friend of mine, Pasteur Mignard, who is the director of the École Protestante at Lausanne. A few years ago—shortly before your time—his daughter came here for a year to teach French and to refine her English. It seemed to me that a similar arrangement might be suitable for you, if, by chance, the École should have an opening. I did not mention the subject to you because I thought it highly unlikely that such an opening would indeed exist. And, frankly, I could not contemplate employing you without additional training of that kind.

"I heard from the *pasteur* last week. As luck would have it, he was on the point of seeking an additional English instructor. His daughter, Cécile, who studied with us and now teaches at the École, is expecting a child this autumn, and a temporary instructor will be needed until she is through with her confinement and has regained her strength. Of course, it is not a question of offering you a salary; but the *pasteur* will provide room and board and will pay half of your travel expenses. I will undertake to pay the other half. Such are the terms he and I agreed upon. Please—let me finish.

"If you accept the proposal, it will mean long hours of hard work, but at the end of the year you will have acquired valuable experience as a teacher— though you will find that young Swiss ladies are less whimsical and more diligent than their English counterparts—and you should greatly improve your command of spoken French. As I understand it, no one at the École speaks English, except, of course, Mlle Cécile—or rather, Mme Berthelot as she now is—and you will not be expected to speak any English at all outside the classroom, save perhaps on special occasions.

"I need only add that the *pasteur* is an eminent pedagogue and a thoroughly trustworthy person. I have known him since my own schooldays, when he was living in Geneva. He and his family will, I am sure, keep your well-being in mind during your stay with them. They are not, of course, Church of England, but they have agreed that you may attend Sunday services at the legation chapel. During the week you will be expected to attend morning and evening services at the École.

"At the end of your time in Lausanne, if the *pasteur*'s report on you is satisfactory—and I fully expect that it will be, or I would not have put myself to all this bother—I shall offer you a place at the school on a probationary basis—provided of course that nothing unforeseen happens in the interim, that Cook does not burn the place down in a frenzy of forgetfulness, or I decide to enter a religious order out of complete despair at the worldly inclinations of my pupils. . . .

"Since I shall be obliged to add the teaching of French to my other duties during the coming year, I will undoubtedly be most eager to have you back here and will be disposed to look on whatever shortcomings you may still possess with a lenient eye.

"There now, Elizabeth, I have almost finished my little speech. Do please stop fidgeting and permit me a few more words, if you please.

"After receiving Pasteur Mignard's letter, I waited almost a week before broaching the matter with you because I wanted the time to think things over. I do not expect an immediate response from you. In fact, I do not desire one. I insist that you take the time to consider the matter closely. It is an important decision for you, Elizabeth. Perhaps more important than you realize."

Miss Shaw rose from her chair and walked slowly over to the window. The window looked out over a small, grim urban garden—a well-worn gravel path bordered perfunctorily with rose bushes and ending abruptly at a long expanse of brick wall. The wall screened the area from the road, but it occasionally revealed, along its upper periphery, tantalizing glimpses of the luggage rack of a coach or carriage or the topmost casks on a brewer's cart— fragmentary reminders of the busy, mobile world that stretched forever beyond the confines of the school.

Something about Miss Shaw's bearing as she stood gazing out the window made it clear to Elizabeth that the headmistress had not concluded her talk, but had merely suspended it while she assembled her thoughts, and indeed, after a brief pause, her back still turned to the girl, she began speaking again, but in an altered, somewhat hesitant tone of voice, as if she were not wholly certain where her words would lead her.

"I feel that I ought to tell you, Elizabeth, make it quite clear to you, that a schoolmistress's job is not an easy or always agreeable one and that it often demands great sacrifices . . . in regard to one's personal development and aspirations. . ."

She turned around and looked directly at the girl. Elizabeth noticed something new and unfamiliar in Miss Shaw's eyes—a searching and almost plead-ing look, as if she were striving desperately to elicit Elizabeth's understanding.

"It is only natural," she continued, "that a young woman of your age should begin to give some thought to the prospect of marriage and estab-lishing a household. Indeed, such thoughts are not easily to be avoided, nor should they be. Of course, daydreaming about dashing young bucks and ro-mantic entanglements is worse than foolish, and not the sort of thing I would expect from you. Yet there comes a stage in one's life—and you are at it now, Elizabeth—when it is wise to look into one's heart and try to read what is there. The text may be confusing and obscure, but that in itself should tell one something of value; that is, it obliges one to acknowledge one's own indecision, to recognize the fact that one has not yet determined the sort of life one wishes to lead.

"What I am saying, Elizabeth, is, quite baldly, that it is difficult to com-bine school teaching and marriage. Not impossible, but difficult. Some women, such as Mme Berthelot or our own Mrs. Tucker, do succeed in doing so, but they are the rare exceptions. As you must realize, when you give the matter thought, the circumstances are not very favorable for such a combination.

"A schoolmistress must, quite literally, be a model of decorum. Her be-havior both within the school and outside of it must be free of reproach, not only in regard to her own good conscience, but in regard to the world's per-ceptions. Yes, Caesar's wife comes to mind, though the allusion is not wholly appropriate. Indeed, the opportunities for meeting marriageable gentlemen or for forming sentimental attachments of a wholly legitimate nature are at best negligible and fraught with unusual peril. You must keep all of this in mind when thinking about your future.

"I know you well enough, Elizabeth, to know that the prospect of teach-ing appeals to you, and that you are ready and eager to embrace the proposi-tion in spite of any and all of my warnings. The look on your face proclaims as much. But permit me to remind you—not warn you, but simply remind you—that you are still very young and inexperienced, and that your lack of self-knowledge might present a problem for others besides yourself. Should you accept the offer, both Pasteur Mignard and I will expect you to take your responsibilities very seriously; we will both have built our plans around you—he for the coming year, I for perhaps somewhat longer—and it is important that your commitment be firm and complete.

"Of course, Elizabeth, it is not like taking the veil. No one can expect you to anticipate how you will feel about teaching, about the school, about yourself, five or ten years hence. All I am asking is that you try to look beyond your immediate impulses and inclinations, look deeply into yourself, and explore those aspects of your being that you may perhaps have tended to avoid or to ignore. It is a bit like preparing for Confirmation, requiring the same sort of rigor and scrupulosity of judgment.

"You see, Elizabeth, I feel a special sort of responsibility toward you, not only because I am by this offer intervening in your future life, but because I am aware that you have no mother or close female relative to whom you can turn for advice. Your father is, I know, a devoted and conscientious parent, whose wisdom and moral integrity will always be a great support to you. But there are certain aspects of a woman's life that remain, perforce, outside the province of masculine experience, and in dealing with these questions it is natural that we should seek counsel from members of our own sex. I trust that this will suffice to explain to you my particular concern for your well-being and why I am anxious that we do not act in haste.

"And another word of warning, Elizabeth—a final word, I promise. Although I admire your modesty of manner and expression, as well as the rigorous self-discipline you display in regard to both your schoolwork and your personal relationships, I detect in you a tendency to prudishness. Be careful. A prude is someone who misreads the emotional needs of others, as well as of herself, and a schoolmistress cannot afford to be illiterate in such matters. It is one thing to disapprove, another to misunderstand. And although you have every right to disapprove of a person's conduct, you have no right to condemn the person himself unless you can fully appreciate the causes for his conduct and the reasons that prompted it. I am not accusing you of self-righteousness; I have never heard you speak depreciatingly or mean-spiritedly of any of your fellow students. But in the classroom I have often seen on your face a condemnatory expression, a turning away of the head, an averting of the eyes, prompted by some offensive remark on the part of a classmate. If you are to become a teacher, Elizabeth, you must learn to confront the failings of others with more forbearance. I am not, of course, suggesting that you relax your own personal standards. Quite the contrary. But I urge you to broaden and refine those standards, and you can do that only by looking about you boldly and openly. You cannot shut yourself off from the wickedness of the world, nor, as a teacher, will you be able to help your students if you habitually avert your gaze from their weaknesses and faults, from all that is not lovely and lovable in them. Remember, a teacher is not called upon to condemn a pupil's failings, but to help the pupil overcome them. In short, Elizabeth, you must learn to be a little more forgiving of others and of yourself."

As Elizabeth closed the door behind her, she noticed that her hand was trembling. The hallway was deserted, so she leaned her back against the wall, shut her eyes, and strove to subdue the wild pounding of her heart. In a sense, some of the girls had guessed correctly: the headmistress had used the occasion to paint her portrait, warts and all. But rather than leaving her naked and humiliated, the ordeal had strangely elated her. No one had ever spoken to her in such deeply personal terms. And though the criticisms caused her pain, the fact that they were addressed to her by someone she vastly admired and who seemed to take a sincere interest in her brought pleasure as well. She felt that a new intimacy had been established between herself and Miss Shaw.

Yes, she would try to be more forgiving of others, try to be more understanding—and she would start with Sarah Barnes. Yet suppose she was incapable of the effort? Suppose any sort of profound personal change was impossible, that the sinfulness within her was persistent and indelible, was an integral part of her personality? That would be truly horrible! But there *was* hope—she knew it, she *felt* it. Besides, to despair was wicked and savored, she thought, of Calvinism (though she was not quite sure of that). With Miss Shaw's help she would put aside her childish ways and become a better, stronger person. If Miss Shaw stood by her, had confidence in her, she could do anything!

She returned, as agreed, on the next Thursday. Graduation ceremonies had been held on the previous weekend, culminating in tearful, tumultuous leave-takings by the students, who were hurried into waiting vehicles by impatient parents; followed, after a brief interval, by the discreet and decorous withdrawal of the resident faculty, off to spend their holidays with aged aunts in small country villas or on their own in modest seaside lodgings; and finally, by the boisterous departure of the cooks, scullery maids, and other domestic servants—who were by now deep in the wilds of Devon, Yorkshire, or County Clare, regaling credulous relatives or doting sweethearts with fabulous tales of life in London.

Elizabeth paused outside the front gate and peered through the grille. Though overwhelmingly familiar, the place seemed strangely transformed. It were as if her memory had somehow played her false, or as if her acquaintance with this building and its setting came solely from an engraving that had been drawn from some impossible perspective.

It is all different, Elizabeth said to herself, because I am different, because I am seeing it with different eyes. Before, I was a student and belonged to the school in a way that a child belongs to a parent. Today I view it with the detached gaze of an adult. A great sadness welled up within her. If this is what it meant to be grown up—to lose one's intimacy with the things of her past—she was not sure that she was ready to relinquish her childhood. Yet as she pushed open the gate and entered the carriageway, she was overcome by a wholly new sensation in which longing mingled with melancholy, and added to her deep sense of loss an ineffable sweetness.

An uncanny stillness pervaded the courtyard. She glanced instinctively in the direction of the kitchens, which, in the course of the school year, were a constant source of activity. But the kitchen windows were closed, and the curtains drawn. She could detect no clatter of pans or clink of crockery, no muffled slamming of doors, no murmur of uncouth voices, no outbursts of laughter. She scanned the whole of the imposing facade; all the shutters of the main wing were tightly shut, except for a single window on the third floor—one of the rooms where the smaller girls slept—from which a feather bed had been hung out for airing. The building seemed in a state of suspended animation.

The front door was opened by the headmistress herself. Miss Shaw was wearing over her dress a threadbare and rather rumpled blue smock. A few strands of greying hair had dislodged themselves from her tightly drawn chignon. As Elizabeth looked up at her from the base of the short flight of front steps, she thought that she detected a trace of puzzlement in Miss Shaw's eyes. But only for an instant. The woman's whole bearing quickly assumed its habitual air of authority and control.

"You are very punctual," she said in a matter-of-fact voice. "Please come in, Elizabeth."

Miss Shaw led the way to her office, their footfalls echoing through the empty hallway. As they entered the office, Elizabeth noticed a teacup and saucer on the center of the headmistress's desk and an intricately patterned cashmere shawl, draped casually over the back of a chair. With a single sweeping gesture Miss Shaw gathered up these objects and, murmuring "Excuse me," bore them off into the adjacent room. When she reappeared a few moments later, she was no longer wearing her smock, and her hair revealed no trace of disarray.

The interview was brief. In fact, it was over before the girl had time to confront her emotions. Elizabeth announced her intention to accept the teaching assignment in Lausanne, and Miss Shaw said that she was pleased and would write to Pasteur Mignard immediately. She added a few specific details about the travel arrangements, a few generalizations about the rewards of such an experience; she shuffled a few papers on her desk, as if searching for something, then rose from her chair to accompany her former student back through the cavernous hallway to the front door.

Thus it was that Elizabeth found herself initiated into the adult world— the world of wage earners and threadbare smocks and unexpressed emotions. Standing alone outside the school grille, with the world's traffic rushing by her, she felt awestruck and exposed, but excited as well. "What now?" she said aloud to the empty sidewalk. And she began to walk briskly home with what she took for a determined tread.

During the first few weeks of the summer holiday Elizabeth refrained from discussing the details of the forthcoming trip with her father. Though Dr. Gow had voiced no objection to the plan when she had initially mentioned it to him, she could read easily enough in his face that the prospect pained him. Of course he acquiesced, acknowledged that it was "a fine opportunity," and had immediately given her a draft for twelve pounds to buy necessary items for the voyage. But the following day, when she launched into an account of the purchases, her voice bright with excitement, he cut her short with the announcement that he had some errands of his own to attend to and, taking up his hat and stick, strode purposefully out of the room.

She was hurt and disappointed by his reaction. Since her mother's death more than ten years ago, father and daughter had grown very close. Neither of them had any intimate friends, nor sought any; they had instead turned toward each other, striving to compensate as best they could for the missing wife and mother. Elizabeth had expected her father to view her yearlong absence with regret; she herself found it hard to contemplate without flutterings of the heart. However, she had also expected him to share some of her excitement in the venture. What she had not expected was that he would look on her departure as an act of desertion—which was certainly the impression that his every gesture seemed to convey. He was never one to admonish, argue, or explain. Whenever she said or did something that met with his disapproval, his eyes, even his voice, became strangely remote, and he either diverted his attention to other matters or terminated the discussion with a few distant remarks.

His indifference, not to say thinly veiled opposition, undermined her pleasure in the trip. She was sure that her decision was justified from a practical point of view, and she knew perfectly well that her father could survive her absence without undue hardship, yet she grieved at the prospect of his loneliness and could not help asking herself whether she had the right to inflict such pain on him simply to gratify certain selfish desires. It was with a lingering sense of guilt and foreboding that she rode the omnibus down to Bond Street to complete the purchase of her new wardrobe.

It was mid-July—barely a month before her scheduled departure—and London was in the midst of a heat wave. She had been trying to read, but the words floated away before her eyes. She sat down at the piano, but the notes sounded as if they were drifting upward from some underwater depth. She descended to the kitchen in search of a glass of cool water, finding relief in the shadowy dankness of the back corridor. On pushing open the kitchen door, she saw the milkman, leaning forward over the kitchen table, in earnest conversation with Hannah, the cook. He straightened up abruptly at her entrance and gave her a great gap-toothed leer of a greeting, accompanied by a tug at the visor of his greasy cap. She noticed the dark stain of sweat at the armpits and that his jet black beard and side-whiskers glistened with moisture. He seemed to her, in his burley, hirsute dampness, like a proletarianized Triton, newly arisen from some urban canal. Elizabeth was overcome with confusion. The kitchen seemed oppressively close. Without uttering a word, she backed out of the room and closed the door.

It was, she realized, an undignified and totally irrational performance that filled her with shame. To flee like that from a perfectly innocent encounter, as if she had caught the two of them in *flagrant délit!* She could not imagine what Cook would think of her. Much less that man. Undoubtedly they would think it funny, throw back their heads and have a good laugh at her expense. She retreated to the darkest corner of the sitting room and sank down into an armchair to compose herself. Her heart was fluttering wildly, and to her surprise and mortification she found herself fighting back tears.

She was angry at herself, angry at having succumbed to this outburst of feminine emotionalism. I am my father's daughter, she told herself; I am not a schoolgirl flibbertigibbet. It was a question of thinking things out, of finding a rational basis for her momentary confusion. There was, she conjectured, the unnatural heat, combined with her usual premenstrual nervosity; her pleasurable excitement at the prospect of departure, mingled with her painful guilt at the thought of abandoning her father. . . . The mere process of enumeration allowed her to regain her calm. She frowned defiance at her fleeting panic and rose abruptly from the chair. "I *will* take control of myself," she said aloud and gave a sharp look at the hallway mirror as she passed. "I will shape my own life."

That evening at dinner her father unfolded his napkin with ceremonial deliberation and announced that he was leaving for America in September.

"You remember the Philadelphian gentleman who visited us last winter, a Mr. Throneberry? He wrote me some time back proposing that I deliver a series of lectures at the Philadelphia Society for Natural Philosophy, of which he is the presiding officer, the president in fact. Of course, at the time it had seemed quite out of the question; I was still, after all, waiting to hear from Edinburgh; so naturally enough I declined. I did not even bother to mention it to you. Just imagine: America! The United States of America! Quite impossible.

"And then last week I received another letter from him renewing the offer and mentioning the possibility of my securing a permanent position on the faculty of the University of Pennsylvania, which is evidently located nearby. It is not wholly clear about the permanent position. Evidently the university is striving to enlarge its teaching facilities in the natural sciences. . . . Anyway, the prospect is decidedly interesting, and I gather that Mr. Throneberry is a man of very real influence in those parts. As we have learned, my dear, influence is the decisive factor in these affairs.

"I have just written to him agreeing to come. I am to give a series of twenty-two lectures over the course of the year. The pay is generous, more than enough to cover expenses, and then there is the chance of finding another position as well. There is even, if I understand his letter correctly, some question of my staying on at the Society on a permanent basis. Though, naturally, I would prefer the university.

"I can see that this comes as something of a surprise to you. Who would have thought, just a few days ago, that we would be thinking about America? But then, my dear Bess, who would have thought a few weeks ago that we would consider your going to Lausanne? But I have done much hard, very hard, thinking of late about my situation here at home and what the future holds in store for me—for both of us. You were much in my mind, Bess, when I decided to accept Mr. Throneberry's offer. I did not want to do something that, in the long run, might prove hurtful to you."

"But father . . ." Her thoughts came tumbling in upon her, bringing her protestations to a halt. If her father went abroad, wouldn't she be expected to accompany him? And then, what about Lausanne? And the job at her old school? How could she ever give up those precious opportunities? And whatever would she tell Miss Shaw? No, she could never bring herself to turn back now, to renounce her own dreams for the future.

And yet . . . and yet . . . She had always told herself that the whole idea behind the job was to be of help to her father, to make herself less of a financial burden to him, and to arrange things so that she could eventually be near him. Though she had never formally renounced the idea of living apart from him, of marrying, of having a separate household of her own, her imagination and all her schemes had revolved about the two of them together, in domestic unity. She knew him well, knew all his little ways, and she could not see how he could possibly get along without her. She was all he had. It was all horribly confusing. She found herself blushing with dismay.

Dr. Gow noticed his daughter's troubled state, and her distress was reflected in his own eyes. For a moment it seemed that he, her father, might succumb to their mutual emotion, that he might reach across the table to take her hand reassuringly in his. But the moment passed. His gaze cleared. It was himself that he took hold of. He spoke slowly, framing his words carefully. His voice was calm, reasonable, but underneath the argument one sensed a note of special pleading.

"I have been forced to face reality, Bess. My immediate prospects here in England are not good. My work is, I do believe, generally respected, and its usefulness recognized by, well, at least a few colleagues in whose judgment I have some faith. But I lack friends in high places, people who can help me to find an academic position, a niche where I can carry on my research secure and undisturbed. While your mother was alive, there was her annuity, which, given our modest mode of living, pretty well freed us from any financial anxieties. But at her death the income passed, as you know, to your aunt Catherine, who, God knows, needs the money, what with her four daughters and Uncle George's very peculiar ways. . . . The trouble is that the kind of work that I am engaged in is not likely to produce spectacular results or the sort of prodigious scientific discoveries that attract the dumb admiration of the public and the attention of possible patrons. I plod along, day by day, filling up my notebooks, line by line, page by page. It is careful, painstaking work, tedious, laborious work; but it is *my* sort of work, Bess, and I do it well. And I take pleasure and deep satisfaction in doing it. And it does, I believe, all add up to something in the long run.

"Basically I am, I suppose, what can be best described as a laboratory technician. A very highly skilled one, I like to think, and at times, perhaps, even an inspired one. But I realize that I am lacking —How shall I put it without sounding too self-depreciating, too dismissive?—I am lacking in a grandiose creative vision. I have no startling new theories to fling at the world. The universe I inhabit is the same dreary old universe we all shuffle about in, day in, day out. I am no innovator, no founder of a new school of scientific thought. Rather, I am a follower, a faithful disciple of a long line of thinkers, whose work I revere and respect. Mind you, Bess, I say all this without apology or regret."

He had never spoken to his daughter in this way, discussed with her his personal anxieties about his work or voiced any doubts about the limitations of his professional abilities. He saw her distress at what she did indeed take to be self-denigrating remarks and her eagerness to rush to his defense. He realized with a sense of shock that she had always regarded him as above criticism, as a man who, though yet to receive his just due from the world, remained untainted by failure. Though he had not deliberately done anything to foster in her this image of himself, he had, he knew, profited from it for years and unhesitatingly accepted her homage. Yet what else could he do? As a father he had felt it his duty to shield his daughter from the onslaughts of the world, at least until she was old enough and experienced enough and strong enough to deal with them on her own. And beyond this sense of duty lay his simple and direct protective instincts. Since her mother's death, he had done what he could to prevent her exposure to problems and concerns that were beyond her ability to resolve. As a scientist he was not likely to confuse innocence with ignorance; to a scientist, the concept of innocence hardly existed. Yet he viewed his daughter as a tender plant that needed shelter from the elements until it had reached maturity. He knew that there were dangers in such an approach to child-rearing, but in his daughter's case he felt that the risks were less than in submitting her to the sort of toughening process he had undergone in his own childhood. Besides, he was tempermentally unsuited for such a task. He was naturally indulgent as a parent, just as he was naturally inattentive and frequently absorbed in his own work. Until now he had every reason to be satisfied with the results. He admired his daughter's lofty idealism, her conscientiousness, her strong sense of duty; he took pride in her freedom from snobbery and pleasure in her lack of cynicism; and he attributed these traits in part to the fact that she had been carefully protected from a premature exposure to that "other side" of life.

Even as he was now speaking, he realized that he was not protecting her as diligently as he might, that he had allowed his own emotionalism to distract him from his responsibilities, and he hastened to mend the breach in the defenses—to reassure her about himself and about the simple sensibleness of his decision.

"The fact, Bess, that I am being courted by our American cousins is certainly a hopeful sign, an indication that my labors have not gone unrecognized. America is a new world, with new opportunities for both of us. I would like to feel that I am not so old and dull and respectable as to shun all possibility for adventure. I feel that I might perhaps make a great name for myself over there and provide you with the sort of comfort and security that seems to elude us here in England. Except for your aunt we have no close relations here. We shall be leaving nothing behind other than a few fond memories. I, for one, will be only too pleased to be translated to a society where birth and connections are less important than character and achievements, and where your virtues, my dear Bess, will not be obscured for want of Paris finery or coronets."

And so she gave it all up: the year in Lausanne, the position at the school, and Miss Shaw. Looking back, years later, she saw the decision as a watershed in her life, yet at the time it seemed to her that in following her father she was simply drifting with the natural flow of circumstances. Her father needed her, and this need was something precious, a gift that must not be refused. To sacrifice personal ambition to filial duty seemed wholly right and desirable, and the thought filled her with melancholy joy.

The headmistress took the news calmly. "I will have to write immediately to the *pasteur*. Of course, he will understand. Your place is with your father under the circumstances. It will be a great adventure for you, Elizabeth—you will find America far more exotic than Switzerland. And," she added quickly, "it will be a great opportunity for you as well. You will be free to take hold of your life over there. That is something of inestimable value."

Miss Shaw looked hard at the girl, as if she were seeing her for the first time. Elizabeth felt the force of her scrutiny and succeeded, for an instant, in meeting her eyes, but she read nothing there except intense curiosity. "Goodbye, Elizabeth. I do hope that you will be happy in your new life. And I trust that you will not entirely forget us. Though I do not doubt that we will come to seem like a dream!"

Mid-Atlantic, 1 8 5 1

ELIZABETH PROVED TO BE A BETTER SAILOR than her father. Soon after
the ship set sail from Southampton, Dr. Gow retired to his cabin and remained there in scholarly seclusion for the next three days. This left his
daughter largely to her own devices. She spent much of the time in the
Ladies' Salon and on deck gazing out at the sea.

The sea held her in thrall. The morning after their departure she had
awoken early and, fleeing the stuffiness of the cabin and the pervasive cooking smells from the nearby galley, ascended to the promenade deck. She used
her shoulder to push open the heavy plank door and was rudely greeted by a
blast of wet breeze that almost tore off her bonnet and by a loud chorus of
unfamiliar sounds: the screaming of gulls, the creaking of the rigging, the
flapping of sails, the slapping of water against the side of the ship, and a hollow rumbling of waves. She paused for a moment in the portal; then, clasping her hand firmly on her bonnet, she made her way across the gently
heaving deck to the railing. On lifting her head, the spectacle that met her
eyes drew from her a gasp of astonishment. All sign of human habitation, of
life itself, had been swept away by the shimmering flood. The world had
been reduced to but two elements, pale sky and dark, glittering water, presenting a panoramic image of apocalyptic grandeur. She stood there for a
while, transfixed, until released from the spell by a raucous flock of gulls that
suddenly swirled into view and hovered nearby like a rowdy, half-menacing
gang of Cheapside street urchins.

When the weather was fair, Elizabeth spent hours at a stretch, her travel
cloak wrapped tightly about her, gazing out over the water. The passengers
who took their regular exercise parading the promenade deck sized her up as
a "deep one" and wondered what she could be thinking about with such rapt

attention. The less imaginative of them assumed that she had been crossed in love.

She herself could hardly explain what passed through her head as she lost herself in contemplation of those empty expanses of sea and sky. It went against her nature, this attitude of complete idleness. At home, at school, if not engaged in some domestic or scholastic chore, she would be reading an instructive book or working at needlepoint or patiently perfecting some exercise at the piano. She had always seemed immune from those fits of "mooniness" that afflicted many girls her age, yet here she was at the ship's railing, allowing herself to be lulled into a vague pensiveness while she listened dreamily to the murmuring voices of the sea. What these voices said or meant to say remained unclear; perhaps the words themselves did not really matter. They were like the refrain of an old, familiar song, so very familiar that their meaning had been worn away by time, and only the mood remained. She sensed, however, that the burden of the song had something to do with the mysterious force that lay below the undulating surface of the sea and that drew its irresistible strength from the very bottom of the deep. If she was very still, very attentive, she could make out the music's underlying rhythm and feel within her a quiet contentment with the implosion of each swelling wave.

More prosaic was the awareness that the ship's forward plunge was taking her ever farther from England, from home. There was something pleasurable about being borne away in this manner, about submitting herself to the ministrations of Fate—yet there was something alarming as well. Try as she might, she could not share her father's enthusiasm for the American adventure, nor was she wholly convinced that his professed belief in its essential reasonableness was not to some degree prompted by an inner sense of discouragement. Yet she could see that there was much to be said for the move from a purely practical point of view. And it was truly admirable and heroic of her father to be willing to turn his back on the Old World and seek to prove himself in the New. Moreover, as a schoolgirl back in England she had always proclaimed her deep sympathies for republican principles, earning herself the sobriquet of "Marianne" from Mlle Desrosiers (and "sansculotte" from the impossible Sarah Barnes). And she had to admit that there was a certain attraction in the fact that her own future was once again wondrously unclear. *"Ainsi, toujours poussés, vers de nouveaux rivages. . . . "* She chanted the verses to herself, trying to recapture some of her schoolgirl enthusiasm. Yet as the gap between herself and England grew, so too did her sense of loss.

It would be easier for her father. For him, leaving England would be one more stage in the evolutionary progress of his career. His grandfathers on both sides had been north country farmers, his father a provincial apothecary. Thanks to his own industry and intelligence, and the patronage of the local rector, he had acquired a good basic education, won a scholarship to Cambridge, and, in short, moved into another realm of activity. On his arrival at the university he had felt himself a foreigner: neither his clothes nor his speech nor his unconcealed hunger for knowledge had seemed appropriate to the surroundings. Faced with the choice of mimicking the manners and attitudes of his classmates or going his own way, he had chosen the latter, not out of boldness or defiance, but out of a stubborn, innate diffidence and a shrewd understanding of his physical and intellectual resources. In time, his hard work and unobtrusive independence had awoken the curiosity of his teachers; and though he had never stooped to flattery, his sincere interest in what they had to say had proved flattery enough to win their public recognition of his accomplishments and their private commendation for his lack of pushiness. He got on. He entered into correspondence with most of the noted researchers in his field, and when he had occasion to meet these individuals at professional functions, they had things to talk about: the conversations grew animated, notebooks were extracted from pockets, and points of interest jotted down. Later, when his name came up in scientific circles he was generally referred to as a "good man" and his work described as "solid." Yet he never found himself absorbed into the professional establishment or associated with one or another group or faction. His irrepressible earnestness, his irreproachable fastidiousness—manifested in his attire and in his high moral standards—seemed to discourage even the minimal sort of personal intimacies required among colleagues.

The death of his wife seven years after the birth of their only child served to increase his sense of isolation and rootlessness. He often said to Elizabeth that his true home was his laboratory, his country the scientific community at large, and he strove to instill in his daughter a broader view of society and a higher regard for the intellect than those proffered by an English middle-class education. Indeed, Elizabeth was proud of her father's independence and considered herself "different" from her schoolmates in that she shared his enlightened outlook. Yet there remained an important distinction in their respective formations: whereas her father had fought to free himself from a background that was both socially and intellectually constrictive, Elizabeth cherished her middle-class inheritance. While regarding herself as a free spirit, she found deep comfort in the well-ordered society prescribed by her boarding school, with its respect for conventional morality and its concern for justice. The restrained, unenthusiastic piety of the Broad Church Sunday service sometimes brought her close to tears. Certain hymns, such as Watt's "God Our Help in Ages Past," opened her eyes to great vistas of metaphysical sentiment. In spite of her best resolutions, she clung tightly to her Englishness.

The majority of the passengers seemed to be Americans (except, of course, in steerage, where, with the occasional oaths and outbursts of song and the incessant whine of the fiddle they identified themselves as exclusively Irish, taken aboard in the dead of night at Queenstown). The American men, in their well-cut broadcloth suits newly acquired at the smartest Bond Street shops, always seemed to Elizabeth slightly larger than life as they sauntered across the deck, leaving in their wake a thin trail of bluish smoke and the rich aroma of good Virginia tobacco. Their wives and daughters clearly held sway in the Ladies' Salon, if only because they readily mingled with their compatriots—greeting one another across the room with the flick of a raised fan or the flash of a white-gloved hand—whereas the English invariably set up defensive positions in isolated family groups, barricaded behind their own tea things and studiously avoiding each others' eyes.

This was Elizabeth's first contact with Americans, and she watched them avidly. Although she had as yet hardly come to terms with the fact, she reminded herself that America was to be her new home and that she would in time come to think of herself as an American. She was determined to be well disposed toward them. Back in London, when the shipper had come to carry off the piano, she had called her father in from his study and pounded out an extravagantly florid rendition of "Yankee Doodle" especially worked up for the occasion. "Bravo, my Bess! A perfect overture to our adventure!" he had exclaimed and leaped from his chair to kiss her flushed cheeks.

The Addison family took it upon itself to usher her into the American enclave. Elizabeth had been standing in a corner of the salon idly turning the pages of an illustrated magazine when she was approached by a girl her own age.

"I'm so glad to see that there are other young people on board," the girl said quite simply and extended her hand. "My name is Hester Addison. You must let me introduce you to Mama and the others. You're English, aren't you? I can tell from your dress." And then she added hastily, as if she feared that she might have said something indiscreet, given the fact that her own dress was clearly made for her in Paris, "It's really wonderfully nice."

She linked arms with Elizabeth as if she were an old acquaintance and conducted her across the room. "Mama says that I am very forward, but that is really not true. It is just that I have a good eye for people, unlike my brother Titus, who comes home with some of the most unlikely specimens and causes untold embarrassment. I can always tell at a glance who is going to be interesting to know and who is going to be a bore. It's a gift, I suppose, like clairvoyance, though it seems quite natural to me, merely a matter of looking into a person's face and reading what is written there. Isn't it amazing how much one can tell from a face? I mean, the fact that a person's moral and spiritual qualities can assume a corporal form is surely one of the great unfathomable mysteries of life—don't you agree? Anyway, I'm sure that we will all get along just fine. Mama, I want you to meet . . . But heavens, I haven't yet asked you your name!"

Mrs. Addison accepted her daughter's confusion with amused forbearance, then turned on Elizabeth her bright, benevolent, and slightly ironical gaze. She was a tall, placid-looking woman, as quiet and restrained in manner as her daughter was voluble and demonstrative. Elizabeth introduced herself, and Mrs. Addison proceeded to ask the sort of sensible, undemanding questions that instantly put one at ease while giving the impression that conversational progress is being made. Elizabeth was then introduced to the two young ladies standing beside Mrs. Addison, Hester's sister Harriet and her cousin Naomi Butterfield. Both girls appeared to be a year or so younger than Hester and seemed to follow the older girl's every word and gesture with breathless wonder and suspense.

From the beginning Elizabeth found herself uncertain of the precise makeup and contours of the Addison entourage. Here in the Ladies' Salon only the feminine element was represented, but even that segment presented problems. The Addisons were traveling together as a family, accompanied by relatives and friends, yet the relationships seemed to Elizabeth strangely fluid and ill-defined. For example, while she was talking to Mrs. Addison, another personage appeared at the fringe of their group, a stout, ruddy-faced old lady of cheerful countenance whom Hester immediately took in hand and presented to Elizabeth quite baldly as "our Louise," adding, "She spoiled us all dreadfully as children, let us do all sorts of terribly naughty things, so of course we insisted that she come along as our chaperone." Our Louise laughed heartily at the introduction, bobbed her head up and down several times, and managed to say between chuckles that she was "awfully pleased to meet the young miss." The next day on the promenade, Elizabeth and Hester came upon a rather sullen boy, some fourteen or fifteen years old, with a tasseled cap pulled down defiantly over one eye. "This," Hester explained enthusiastically, "is Tad. Tad is really very clever at fixing things, all sorts of things. I'm sure I don't know how we could along without him"—at which the boy scowled darkly, remembering to give a sharp tug to his cap by way of a token salutation. "That's all right, Tad, I'm not going to kiss you," Hester said airily, and they left the boy gaping beside the rail.

Now it seemed to Elizabeth that Tad and Our Louise belonged to the category of personal servants or family retainers rather than that of relatives or friends, but she could not be sure. In well-ordered English households no such ambiguity was possible, and people's positions could be readily recognized by the degree of deference in their manner, by the way they occupied their space in a room or wore their clothes. In England, people, all sorts of people, did not mingle in such a promiscuous fashion. Yet in the Addison party everyone seemed to be thrown together hugger-mugger with total disregard for the niceties of social conventions. Elizabeth wondered whether this blurring of distinctions was peculiar to the Addisons or typically American. If the latter, American society was proving to be a deeper, more complex study than she had anticipated.

She was drawn irresistibly into the Addison orbit. Whenever any of the family members caught sight of her, there were welcoming waves and complicitous smiles. If within earshot, she was invariably included in their conversations. Talk was the family's primary mode of engagement. Whereas some of the people in the salon played cards (silently, ferociously, for hours on end) or read books or leafed through magazines or knit or busied themselves with tea things, the Addisons talked. They were all of them incessant, indefatigable talkers, constantly challenging, admonishing, quizzing, and cajoling one another or, by way of relaxation, when the conversation had reached too great an intensity, exchanging banter and harmless repartee. Their individual styles differed: Hester, for example, tended to be deliberately provocative, whereas Mrs. Addison seemed to favor the conciliatory approach, keeping an attentive ear on the general conversation and interjecting a few quiet but forceful phrases calculated to bank, if not quite extinguish, the rising flames of controversy. The younger girls occasionally introduced a tentative, sometimes almost fearful interrogatory note to the discussions and generally contributed a background of bubbly chatter. Elizabeth found the sheer volume of verbiage overwhelming. At home, even at school, she had been surrounded by people who placed each of their words with deliberation and caution. For her, language was meant to be suggestive rather than assertive; and the practice of polite conversation consisted of carefully, discreetly laying down a number of phrases until a suitable response had been elicited. It was a style of talk that thrived on hints and allusions, and on the emphatic articulation of a particular vowel sound or consonant, whose intensity could be gauged by a lack of specific references, and which often reached its highest levels of eloquence in intervals of silence during which glances were exchanged or a spoon turned meaningfully in a cup. Among the Americans there were moments when Elizabeth felt the urge to clap her hands over her ears simply to shut out the noise. It was not only the volume and profusion of the talk that bothered her, but the need to be constantly on guard against an unexpected sally or verbal assault. People like the Addisons, she realized, had no skill in the English art of the commonplace—that strategic retreat to the neutral ground of conversational banalities where both parties could regroup their forces and reevaluate the social situation. For the Addisons, a conversation was all pickets, skirmishes, and headlong charges. No truces were called, no quarter asked or given—especially among the younger set.

The leader of the younger set was clearly Hester. Harriet and Naomi, willingly or not, took their cues from her, and though they sometimes protested loudly—Harriet stamping her foot and Naomi tossing her ringlets—they inevitably deferred to Hester's judgment. As Harriet once explained, "Well, Hester just knows *everything!*" Elizabeth thought the claim excessive, but she had to admit that Hester did at times convey that impression. It wasn't that she was arrogant or even overly assertive; it was just that there was a boldness and exuberance that lent to all her actions and arguments an air, however spurious, of absolute authority. And even when she was just plain wrong, she would take hold of the proffered correction with such passionate interest that she almost seemed to triumph in being caught out. All in all, one felt that Hester mistaken was perhaps closer to the truth than the rest of us, right or wrong.

Elizabeth, too, fell under Hester's spell, but she was never at ease with her. Though almost the same age, she felt herself many years the elder; there were moments, as she stood among the "young set" listening to their animated conversation, when she was suddenly overcome by a sense of shame. She felt like a big child caught playing with the smaller children's toys.

Yet the fact that she saw herself as older and more serious-minded than her companions did not make her feel superior to them. It was different from school, where her disinclination to join in the schoolgirl prattle had caused her to adopt an attitude of aloofness that bordered on genuine disdain. She had on the whole regarded most of her schoolmates as frivolous creatures who tended to trivialize the very things she held most dear about the school: the lessons themselves and the high moral aspirations of the instruction. She knew that some of them looked on her as a prig, but she couldn't help it. For her, the great and wondrous beauty of life reposed in its solemnity and fundamental seriousness. People accused her of having no sense of humor; they told her that she never seemed to enjoy herself. What they failed to understand was the deep pleasure she derived from the cultivation of her intellect, from the painstaking acquisition of knowledge, and from the joy that she found in the simple contemplation of lofty sentiment and noble actions. She drew no delight from taking things lightly, nor did she ever court favor by professing to enjoy pastimes that she found vulgar and depressing. Her schoolmates could call her prig but never hypocrite, and on the whole they had respected her honesty; a few of the younger ones had even looked up to her with an awe that, tempered by adolescent emotionalism, came close to affection. Therefore, though at school she had felt apart from the crowd, she had never felt excluded from it; the separation had been voluntary on her part and reflected her self-assurance. In an environment where devotion to studies and high-mindedness were, after all, prescribed virtues laid down by the most elevated members of the community, her stand placed her in a clearly recognized position, alongside the grown-ups. Although she seemed a trifle young to have transferred her allegiance so completely from girlhood to womanhood, precocity of that sort was not unusual in such settings, and though it hardly increased her popularity, it wasn't really held against her. The girls had come to look upon her as belonging in some mysterious way more to the teachers than to themselves. And although she knew that she was a part of neither group, she did sense that she was living under the protective wing of the adult community and functioning as a sort of lay member of the teaching order.

Outside the school, however, the rules changed. Among the Americans she was frequently beset by doubts. Though she found Hester's conversation often flighty and sometimes lacking in good taste, there was no denying the quickness of the girl's mind or the passionate sincerity of her intellectual curiosity. To these qualities were added a "worldly wisdom" that made it difficult for Elizabeth to rest secure in her role of elder sister. Certainly there were times when Hester's high spirits and girlish enthusiasms made Elizabeth feel not only older, but positively middle-aged! Yet at other times the young American's informed commentary and daring flights of fancy left her feeling awkward and wholly inadequate to the situation, like a small child in a new party frock standing on the threshold of a brightly lit ballroom crowded with gracefully swirling dancers.

Elizabeth discovered that the Ladies' Salon was usually deserted during the hour before morning service, and she had taken to rising early to make use of the piano. One morning while she was intent on her practice, Hester crept into the room and carefully closed the door behind her.

"Oh, please don't stop. I was listening outside and couldn't resist seeing who was playing so beautifully. It's that lovely Schubert impromptu. Oh, do go on, Elizabeth." She sat down on the nearest chair and primly folded her hands on her lap. Her face glowed with expectation.

Elizabeth turned back to the piano and resumed playing where she had left off. She played the piece through to its conclusion. The playing was correct, but in comparison to the image of her listener's radiant expression, wholly inadequate. She sat there for a moment, her head bowed over the keyboard, then closed the cover with a decisive gesture.

"You're wonderfully skillful, Elizabeth. I do admire you so! I've been working on that piece for years and years, and it's still all a jumble of wrong notes. No one would ever believe that I've taken lessons since I was six. Have you heard of Mme Delmas? Well, I don't suppose that there is any reason why you should. She had some sort of a concertizing career in Europe before coming to America. She played in Paris and in Prague, and in St. Petersburg before the czar—just fancy that! Can you imagine playing before the czar of all the Russias, with his great whiskers, just sitting there, staring glumly at you? She's old and fat now and speaks the most incredible English—I wish that I could imitate it for you; Titus has got her down perfectly, *c'est tordant!* Anyway, Mme Delmas has been my teacher for years and years, and though I do make fun of her sometimes, it is really very wicked of me because she is a truly wonderful person, kind and forgiving and infinitely patient, and she still plays beautifully at times, in spite of her poor, fat, arthritic fingers. Yet after all those years of lessons I often feel that I've gotten nowhere. I'd give anything, Elizabeth, to be able to work through the music with the sureness and precision that you do. Of course, I never really practice enough, I just sit there mooning over the scores. Yet the truly wretched thing is that I know that even if I practiced faithfully every day, I would never get it right. I love music, I really do, Elizabeth. It means a lot to me. I've had the best teachers, been taken to hear the best performers—and oh, Elizabeth, I heard Franz Liszt this summer in Basle; Papa took me. But it makes no difference. I'm simply lacking in any real talent. For *anything*. And especially for the things that mean the most to me, like music and watercolors . . . and friendship. The truth is that I am spoiled rotten. I tell Papa and Mama that it's *their* fault, but Papa only laughs, and Mama looks . . . well, heaven only knows what she means when she looks like that. But Elizabeth, I do so admire the way you set about things and master them. I admire your seriousness—yes, I really do—and your gravity, and the way you seem to have your feet planted so firmly on the ground. I admire your ability to confront the world with such clear-sightedness, and determination, and *dignity*. I'd give anything for that."

Elizabeth didn't know how to respond to this effusion. She was overcome by conflicting thoughts and emotions that left her speechless and bemused. She was pleased, or rather relieved, to have her seriousness acknowledged as a desirable quality by a young person whose sincerity and goodwill could not be doubted. Yet Hester's praise troubled her because it served to awaken within her certain apprehensions about the nature of her own artistic sensibilities in contrast to those of the American girl. She knew, for example, that the deep satisfaction she found in music came in large part from the discipline required to achieve a competent performance. Without the work, she would have derived little pleasure from the piano; it was the sense of mastery, or of self-mastery, that compelled her commitment to the instrument. Hester's outburst had reminded her that there were those who desired to be mastered by the music and who only wished to give themselves to it with abandon. And though she considered such a response impossibly romantic, she could not suppress the feeling that it contained a fragment of truth lacking in her own approach to things. She knew that she could never hope to argue against that flash of emotion in Hester's eyes. She could only lower her own and murmur something about the girl speaking "nonsense," knowing full well that her own terseness would be mistaken for modesty. On the whole, Hester's compliments left her with a lingering sense of shame.

The younger set were gathered tightly together in a corner of the salon, and the conversation had reverted inevitably to the Eternal Topic.

"I must say," Hester propounded, "the only even remotely possible young man on board is Macready Junior."

"Oh, but those dreadful steel eyeglasses!" protested Naomi. "And he always looks so awfully solemn."

"Melancholy," corrected Hester. "I read a deep strain of melancholy in his features. Quite different from solemnity. And too, he is shy. *Farouche,* as the French say."

"Unlike his father, who isn't the least bit *farouche,*" said Naomi. "What a personage *he* is! Did you hear him reciting Macaulay yesterday? I didn't know where to look! And did you see the expression on your mama's face? Speaking of solemnity—your poor dear mama looked as if she were about to burst with solemnity. If the dinner gong hadn't sounded just then, we all would have come apart at the seams."

Hester stuck her thumbs in her armpits, thrust out her chest, threw back her head, and intoned in a would-be basso profundo:

> "O, Tiber! father Tiber!
> To whom the Romans pray,
> A Roman's life, a Roman's arms,
> Take thou in charge this day!'
>
> So he spake, and speaking sheathed
> The good sword by his side,
> And with his harness on his back,
> PLUNGED HEADLONG IN THE TIDE."

"Oh Hester, that is just too perfect!" exclaimed Naomi, clasping her hands together in a paroxysm of delight.

At this point Harriet couldn't resist joining in the fun. "And do you remember what he said when Papa asked him about a Mrs. Macready?"

Hester placed her hand with ceremonial deliberation over her heart and said in lugubrious tones: "I am, Mr. Addison, a widower. My wife, Sir, expired in childbirth while barely more than a child herself, leaving a grieving husband and a greeting bairn."

"Yes, yes, that's it exactly!" cried Naomi.

"And his snuff-colored waistcoat, with gold buttons!" shouted Naomi. "And the diamond stickpin!"

"Now look here," interjected Elizabeth, "I do think that you are all a bit hard on the old man. It's true that he dresses in too conspicuous a fashion, and he does have a bit of an accent . . ."

"Accent!" protested Hester, "I'd say it's a bit of a *brogue*."

"We certainly won't argue that point, Hester. Though he and his son do attend C. of E. services every morning, so he isn't one of *those*. . . . Anyway, my father has spoken with him on several occasions and says that the old gentleman is full of interesting observations. And we must not forget that he has gone through some trying times. Oh, I admit that his style is somewhat . . . flamboyant, and it's hard not to smile, but ganging up on him like this makes me uncomfortable. It somehow seems horribly unfair."

"And makes us sound like a bunch of giggling schoolgirls," said Hester earnestly. "Oh, you're right, Elizabeth. It was silly and rude of me to make fun of him like that. And, I suppose, snobbish as well, though I hate to admit *that*. Our papa too says that Mr. Macready is really an amusing conversationalist, and he is at this very moment, I think, smoking a cigar with him on the promenade deck. Besides, it was Macready *fils* we were talking about. And goodness knows I didn't intend to mock *him*. It was the contrast between the two of them that I found so odd. Though I suppose it is only natural that the son should attempt to right the balance; we all see that in different families. Certainly young Macready is as somber as his father is—well, I won't say colorful or picturesque for that will sound as if I'm making fun of him again!—as his father is *superb*. Yes, that's the right word, I think, with his great main of white hair, like the old lion in the Aesop fable. And somber as young Macready is, I still declare him to be quite categorically the only attractive man on this ship—our papas excluded of course."

"Oh Hester, what about that young baron from Saxony?" said Naomi, visibly warming to the subject. "You know, Baron Something und Something, I can never get those German names right. What about him, Hester?"

"Out of the question! With that sickly, insipid smile of his and those pink, flabby little hands. Poo! A dreadful creature! Overboard with him! Fit only for the fishes!"

"Well, at least he does smile from time to time," replied Naomi hotly. "At least he sometimes makes an effort to be polite and agreeable, which is more than you can say for that young Macready of yours."

"Oh, I suspect that young Macready can be polite and agreeable enough when he chooses to be," Hester replied. "If his father is a lion, he is no bear. Besides, it's his total lack of charm that intrigues me. It's intimidating, rather thrilling in fact. And his frowns are positively Byronic. I'd rather be scowled at by young Macready than smiled upon by a whole boatload of minor German nobility."

"How can you talk so?!" protested her sister, whose face had suddenly grown dark with indignation. "How *can* you talk like that when you are engaged to marry Tommy Codman? It isn't right, Hester, it's shameful, downright shameful. And terribly unkind to poor Tommy." Harriet sounded close to tears. "What must Elizabeth think, hearing you talk like that? What would anyone think?"

"Goodness, Etty, you make me sound like the Woman Taken in Adultery!" Hester exclaimed with a note of exasperation in her voice. Then, realizing how distressed her sister was, she continued in a more soothing and conciliatory tone: "It was only talk, Etty, and nothing more, just silly schoolgirl talk. I know how you feel about Tommy, and I am glad you are rushing to his defense. But it's quite unnecessary, I assure you. Tommy has nothing to worry about. And I am sure that Elizabeth thinks no worse of me than she did before. She knows that I am a foolish, thoughtless creature. Now isn't that true, Elizabeth?"

"I know nothing of the sort," replied Elizabeth. But the truth was that she did not know what she thought, except that Hester fascinated her, and she wished that she understood her better.

"The trouble with you, Elizabeth, is that you always try to think the best of people."

The two girls were seated together on deck, a single plaid traveling blanket draped over their shoulders, enfolding them.

"But that's not true, Hester. I mean, I don't think that I do. And if I did, I can't see what harm it does. Oh dear, I'm afraid that's rather a muddle, isn't it?"

Her companion laughed and snuggled closer. "Well, I'll tell you what harm it does, at least to me. It makes me want to take the contrary view, to kick over the traces."

"Oh Hester, what nonsense!"

"You see, you're doing it now! You refuse to believe that I am a mischievous, immature little creature."

"I do rather think that you are fishing for compliments. Which is certainly mischievous and immature of you, if that makes you feel any better."

"Oh it does, it does. Except of course that it's all wrong. About fishing for compliments, I mean. I used to think of myself as terribly mature and in control of things; that was when I got engaged to Tommy, just before we left for the Grand Tour. But now there is so much that I am just beginning to understand. Oh Elizabeth, I have learned so much in the past few months and feel ever so much wiser, but at the same time more ignorant that ever before—like a schoolgirl who has been sent from the very front row all the way to back of the class. Isn't that odd? How do you explain it? Speaking of muddles, there's one for you!"

"I suppose it is simply part of growing up. Suddenly one discovers that the world is larger, stranger, infinitely more complex than one ever imagined. It's the old 'when I was a child, I spoke like a child' refrain that we heard yesterday at morning service—the putting aside of childish ways. And then suddenly nothing is ever quite what it seemed to be."

"But that is precisely what I find so queer: that the process of growing up should make me feel like a helpless child. And you are right about nothing seeming quite what it used to seem. Tommy, for example, and my feelings about him. I've known Tommy—well, just about forever. Our parents have summer homes nearby, and we used to play together every day as children. He's almost like a brother to me. Whenever he opens his mouth, I can pretty well guess what he is going to say. I know all his tastes, all his prejudices, all his opinions. I knew exactly what he was going to give me for my birthday and for Christmas too, though he made a great point of swearing everybody to secrecy and crept about the house with a silly little smile on his face. It's not that anyone gave the secret away; it's just that I *knew*. He's so predictable! Mind you, I'm not blaming him for that; it's rather comforting in a way.

"The truth is, Elizabeth, that we have so little to say to one another. Oh, we chatter on easily enough. After all, we know the same people more or less, have been to the same places more or less, and there is always the odd scrap of news or gossip to exchange. But it's not what you call *real* talk, Elizabeth, we just make friendly sounds. We don't really—How can I say it?—touch each other with our words. And sometimes I even take to taunting him a bit—oh, it's too awful of me, but I just can't help myself!—just to provoke him into saying something interesting, even something rude. But of course Tommy—predictably enough—never does. He just goes red in the face and looks hurt and bewildered, and begins to stutter. And of course I feel rotten, for he really is a dear boy, and I spend the rest of day trying to make it up to him. The fact is he is a good deal livelier with Papa or Uncle Ben, with whom he can talk about horses or local politics. I hear him holding forth in the billiard room, and there is such manly vigor, such sureness, such animation in his voice that he almost sounds like another person!

"Last spring we went together to a series of conferences at the Boston Atheneum, on Dante. The dear boy did it to please me, and I did it of course to please myself. And I did it too, Elizabeth, because I thought that the lectures and the readings might give us something real to talk about. Tommy's got a good mind, far quicker and better than mine—he's studying law now, and I know that he'll make an excellent lawyer—but all during the lectures he kept fidgeting in his chair and tugging at his collar, like a small boy kept after school on a fine spring day. And while walking me home he would dutifully try to get all the right people into all the right circles of hell and would make such a hopeless muddle of it, become so overwrought with embarrassment and distress—as if he had inadvertently condemned his dear maiden-aunt Cory to eternal hellfire and damnation—that I just wanted to stop right there on Beacon Street and give him a hug.

"Then we got formally engaged, and it was as if we became total strangers. We could hardly look one another in the face. Isn't that odd, Elizabeth? I mean, on the one hand, there he was so frightfully familiar, so completely predictable—good old dependable Tommy—and on the other, he had become a mystery, a locked drawer. Anyway, it was a relief to get away to Europe, to get the ocean between us until the marriage.

"And once we were abroad, well naturally enough everything there seemed so very strange and different that I hardly knew what I thought about anything. Not only the buildings and the surroundings, but the people, especially the people: the way they responded to you, the way they treated each other . . . and the things that went on, or seemed to go on, in full public view, in the streets, in the shops in the squares. At first I averted my eyes from certain sights—the poverty, the squalor, the shamelessness. London was bad, but on the continent! In Italy! You know what I mean, Elizabeth, one need only glance out of a cab window. . . . Anyway, I said to myself, these are sights I should not look at, things not meant for my eyes. But one can't help seeing some of what is happening around one, and as time went on it began to occur to me that perhaps I was making a mistake in trying not to see things. As Papa's vulgar associate Mr. Thurman Potter is always saying, 'In for a shilling, in for a pound.' And after all, what is the point of coming all this way simply to avert one's eyes? Then, too, I told myself: if all these things are on display, they are somehow or other meant to be seen, and it is wretchedly provincial of me to assume otherwise. And suddenly I was eager to take in as much as I could, to see *everything!* On the grand boulevards, in the piazzas, in the museums! Harriet was always tugging at my sleeves and hissing in my ear, 'Come along, Hester, whatever are you staring at like that? It's not proper, it's not decent. What will people think?' But I knew that it was a chance, my chance to look and learn, and I refused to turn away from life—for whatever one may say, *that* too is life, Elizabeth, and I wanted to see life as it really is and to try, at least to try, to understand something. . . .

"Oh, I don't claim for a moment to be much the wiser for all of this. Perhaps, if anything, I am more confused than ever. But these past few months of forcing myself to look at things boldly, without averting my eyes or turning away, have changed me. For one thing, I feel much kinder toward Tommy. Goodness knows, I no longer feel inclined to speak mockingly of him—though of course I will from time to time. It is hard to explain, Elizabeth, but Europe has made me aware that there is more to men and women than the sort of maneuvering and musical chairs that go on in a New England drawing room, or the whispers and giggles that go on below stairs. Suddenly life has become much more complicated than I ever imagined, and though it is all a bit frightening, it is a bit exciting, too. I'd like to think the whole experience has made me less stiff-necked and intolerant than I used to be. I still make wicked fun of people, such as dear old Mr. Macready, but I really feel deep within me a great tenderness, a great pity for him, for everyone! Can you believe that, Elizabeth? I mean, suddenly I realize that life is such a ridiculous mess!" And she concluded her little speech with a toss of the head and a laugh.

Elizabeth drew the blanket more snugly about them as a sign of silent assent. The slightly tremulous undertone in Hester's voice had moved her greatly, but at the moment she had nothing to say. She tried to think what words Miss Shaw would have employed to console, encourage, and warn the young American and realized to her dismay that she had no idea. Hester, for all her childish, undisciplined ways, had gone to places, seen sights that Elizabeth had yet to visit and see, and the older girl needed time to go over the speech carefully in the privacy of her own thoughts.

It was Elizabeth who first captured the attention of the Byronic Mr. Macready.

She was at her usual place on deck, gazing out over the ocean, when she became aware of a dark, masculine presence leaning on the rail beside her. Rather than turning her head to confront it and thereby being obliged to frame an invitation of sorts, she simply drew her shawl more tightly about her by way of acknowledgment. At that gesture, the presence began to talk in a soft baritone voice, commenting unenthusiastically on the vastness of the sea.

He was indeed a solemn young man, but his solemnity helped to put her at her ease. She had never been able to deal effectively with the quips and bright comments with which most young men chose to initiate a conversation; all too often they propelled her into a terse reply followed by a sullen silence. But Macready presented no challenges; there was nothing equivocal about his address. The very banality of his remarks made it clear that he was talking to her because he wanted to share his thoughts with someone and because he had identified her as a person who might listen and respond sympathetically to what he had to say. The truth was that they had much to talk about. Both young people were now cut adrift from their native lands; both were accompanying a parent who was seeking to find new opportunities, a new home in unfamiliar terrain. She was not displeased that he had felt himself drawn to her among all the other shipboard prospects, that he found her attractive, or at least not unattractive. And though she did not admit it to herself, the fact that this particular young man had found favor in Hester's eyes bestowed on him a certain social avoirdupois.

Like all young men, he talked mainly about himself, assuming the essential viability of the topic, the words spilling out with increasing rapidity as he caught sight of the glitter of interested concern in her eyes. He wanted, she saw, to tell her everything about himself: to explain, to excuse, to tentatively explore his past actions and future prospects. His was a story whose plot was uncertain and in which the storyteller himself sometimes seemed to challenge the details. There was, she noticed, a note of bitterness underlying the narrative. His father had recruited him, virtually commandeered him, for the American adventure, and since his own affairs were not prospering at home, he could at the time find no solid reasons to prevent his signing on. Yet, he insisted, he had done so under duress. And, as Elizabeth quickly surmised, he chafed at working under paternal patronage.

Macready Senior, his son explained, had enjoyed a modest but respectable career in Ireland as a civil engineer when—out of the blue, so it seemed—he landed an important commission to build a bridge in Scotland over the Tweed. The job had come about through a chance encounter at the annual Governor General's Ball in Dublin Castle, where over the punch bowl he had struck up an acquaintance with an expansive Scottish gentleman who was involved in several major construction projects throughout the British Isles. The evening had been a congenial one; the two men had exchanged songs, toasts, and, toward the dawn, vows of undying friendship. A couple of weeks later, an engineer in charge of the Tweed project suddenly dropped dead, and a letter had been dispatched to Dublin requesting Macready's assistance. Under his supervision the work had gone well. The public applauded the elegant, neoclassical design of the structure, the company commended him for its relatively low cost, and a peer of the realm presided over its formal opening, during which many toasts were drunk, some to the young queen, some to Progress, and some to Macready himself. Other commissions followed, all in Scotland, and each of them going progressively less well. Macready's limitations as an engineer became increasingly apparent. Although his overall schemes were both inventive and appealing, he had little grasp of technical matters or, as he termed them, "petty details," and was ultimately dependent on his assistants for the successful execution of his projects. His Scottish career culminated in the collapse of a newly constructed railway viaduct on the outskirts of Dundee in which several lives were lost. And although a court of inquiry cleared him of any criminal charges (it seems the new and innovative materials he had chosen for the viaduct were inadequate to hold the weight, and the manufacturer had failed to alert him to the fact), he returned to Dublin in disgrace.

Back in his native city, he worked at small, intermittent jobs, until one evening, in the foyer of the Theatre Royal, between the second and third acts of *Richard III,* he fell into conversation with a man who was looking for someone to scout out the prospects for land investments in the midwestern territories of America! So once again, out of the blue, a deal was struck, and Macready crossed the water to try his luck in a new land.

He returned from America brimming over with enthusiasm and grandiose schemes. He had made, so he announced, important contacts, had happened by good chance to encounter a number of men of great influence and vision, and secured the near promise (only a few contractual details were to be worked out) of being put in charge of the elaboration of a plan to construct a vast network of canals connecting Lake Michigan with the interiors of the neighboring territories; such waterways, as he was fond of explaining, were a far more practical means of exploiting the potentialities of the region than the faddish and obviously ill-fated recourse to railways. (Since the fatal collapse of the Dundee viaduct, the elder Macready, as his son explained, had developed a fierce antipathy to all aspects of rail transportation.) As a sign of his confidence, Macready *père* had invested virtually all of his slender savings in various undeveloped building sites in the city of Milwaukee. Between real estate investments and engineering assignments he had no doubt whatsoever that he—and his son—would make their fortunes. "America," he proclaimed, "is a place for new concepts and large ideas." Yet, as young Macready said tersely, though his father was a grand fellow for large thinking, smaller things tended to trip him up badly. At least he now seemed to recognize that fact. Which was why he had determined to enlist his son's assistance.

Young Macready had taken a degree in engineering at Trinity College, where he had been second in his class. Shortly after graduation he had found employment with the Dublin Harbour Commission, but the recent economic crisis in Ireland had brought work to a standstill, and since he was paid on a job basis, he was obliged to take on small subsidiary assignments laying out roads and irrigation canals. These jobs took him ever farther afield, putting his Dublin post in jeopardy while hardly repaying the cost of travel and living expenses. He was, he said unapologetically, a good engineer with a solid grasp of basics and the additional asset of being an excellent draftsman, so that he was sometimes asked by distinguished older colleagues to draw up their plans for them. But unlike his father, he had never acquired the knack of striking up conversations with influential strangers. When he went to a ball, he danced a few dances, drank a few drinks, and returned home to his lodgings; when he attended the theater, he was totally absorbed—or if not, took up his hat and left. He was not a man who made friends easily, and that was, he acknowledged, a handicap in a profession where most jobs were awarded on the basis of personal contacts. He would gladly have relinquished his command of calculus for the ability to carry a tune! Such an exchange would have benefited his career. But he knew that he would never be an ornament to society, and he had to adjust his life accordingly. As for the American enterprise, he was less sanguine about its outcome than was his father. Nonetheless, he had, professionally speaking, little to lose by leaving Ireland; and as far as his sentimental attachments were concerned (here Elizabeth could not help stealing a quick glance at his grim, set features), he no longer had anything to hold him.

"Now, there's no use in pretending that I am off to America in a spirit of high adventure, or, as my father is fond of putting it, 'to give greater scope to my talents.' I go because, frankly, there is nothing left for me at home, because I was suffocating to death in Ireland."

"Yet surely you must look on America with a sense of hope? If, as you admit, you were escaping from an untenable situation . . ."

"Escaping!" He flung himself at the word. "I am no more 'escaping' than those Paddies howling below deck are escaping. It is more like being driven out I am!" Then seeing how distressed she was by this outburst, he unclenched his fist, softened his expression, and resumed speaking in a quieter, more measured voice.

"Well now, of course there is something to be said for the chance to start anew. I mean, I certainly don't feel defeated or downcast by the prospect, not at all. . . . But you see, Miss Gow, it has been a bit of a pull to get to where I am—oh yes, as far as that, Lord preserve us! And now to be on my way to America. . . . As a boy, and all through my youth, I studied hard, and when I wasn't studying, I was earning money to pay for my studies. Oh, my father helped me out. It's not that he isn't generous—quite the contrary. It's just that he isn't always what you might call *dependable*. And then he was traveling about much of the time and often short of money himself. But he did what he could for me, to the best of his ability, which is why I couldn't reject the offer to help him out now.

"When I finally received my certificate and then landed the job with the Harbour Commission, I thought to myself that I would be able to—no, not relax, for I didn't want to do that—I thought that I would be able at last to catch my breath, so to speak, that I would be able to settle into some sort of productive routine and be like those people I passed in the street, striding off purposefully every morning to their offices or counting houses and returning home every evening at the same hour, with their hats pushed down securely on their heads and their walking sticks tucked complacently under their arms. . . . Oh you can't imagine how I envied the sheer ordinariness of their commonplace lives, the stupid placidity of their expressions! After years of struggle and uncertainty, the idea of some sort of basic stability and routine assumed for me an aura of high romance! . . . Yet it seemed that the pressure never did subside for me, and I found myself rushing here and there just to keep things from falling apart. So yes, Miss Gow, I do nurture some fond hopes about America. But I'm a bit tired, too, tired and bruised from all those years of fruitless labor. So you mustn't expect a great outpouring of enthusiasm, at least not yet."

The self-pitying note that she detected in his tone prompted her to assume a firm line. She felt once again a grown-up, or at least on the side of the grown-ups, and she spoke out with the conviction of borrowed authority.

"You are still a young man, Mr. Macready, with almost your whole life before you. As you yourself state, you are well trained in your profession and thus undoubtedly will be much sought after in America. You have every reason to be hopeful. And just look at your father: old as he is, he is the very picture of energy and optimism."

"Oh, he is that, Miss Gow, he is certainly that, and there is no gainsaying it." The young man gave a rather grim sort of laugh. "And he'd be the same if we were heading for Borneo or New Guinea instead of to America."

The tone of his response disconcerted Elizabeth, but she plodded on. "You have to admit that there is much to be said for such manly self-confidence. It's a necessary quality for success—provided of course that it isn't based on falsehoods or delusions."

"Oh, I suppose you're right. I guess I have acquired my habitual gloom as a counterpoise to my father's indomitable good spirits. His attitude has much to be said for it. His enthusiasm is contagious in a way my gloom is not. It has won him many friends, wherever he goes. When he was younger, he could charm a fox from its lair. Nowadays, the eloquence is perhaps a bit out at the elbows, but when I was a child . . . why, when I was child, so terrible was that charm that he could even win over his own flesh and blood. I remember how angry I used to be with him for his dereliction and neglect. It was my aunt who brought me up, and she had trials enough of her own, poor woman—and my father hardly putting in an appearance from one month to the next. And then he would suddenly hail into view, like a conquering hero home from the wars, and scoop me up and set me on his lap, and bestow his fine gold watch on me to play with, and oh, how I would adore the man!"

Elizabeth had assumed that he, like most young men, would do almost all the talking and that she would only have to listen and commiserate and silently judge. Yet there came a time when he turned to her—almost one might say on her—and began to ask about her prospects and plans with such interest and intensity that, in her haste to frame responses, she found herself elaborating projects that until now had barely entered her mind.

She explained that her principal responsibility was to be of use to her father. She would keep house for him in America, help him with his correspondence, and whenever possible assist him in his research work. The week before they left, she and her father had visited several bookshops and assembled a small collection of elementary texts on chemistry, botany, and biology that was now stored away in a big traveling trunk in the ship's hold. It was to be her personal scientific library, and she planned to set aside two hours, perhaps three, every day for study. She had learned virtually nothing about the natural sciences at school, except for the Latin names of common English wildflowers, and she looked forward immensely to setting out on this new intellectual pursuit.

She had also bought in the Strand, with her own pocket money, a handsome clothbound sketchbook—too handsome by far, she now felt—that she was determined to fill with drawing of native American flora. It would allow her to exercise her drawing skills and develop her powers of observation.

"I do think that it is important to learn to *look*," she said earnestly, and then, catching a distant and distorted echo of Hester's voice in the statement, was momentarily overcome by confusion. . . .

If things went well, and her father could spare her, she might even start a school of her own—something on a modest scale, no more than a dozen or so young ladies, whose instruction she could supervise personally. Of course, she added hastily, this was still just a daydream, she had thought out none of the details, yet it seemed to her that she might be a good teacher, certainly teaching was something she did so want to try, and if she could somehow manage to convey to her students the deep satisfaction and sense of accomplishment that she had derived from her studies, she knew that she would be doing something worthwhile. So many of her schoolmates had viewed their classwork as dry-as-dust, meaningless drudgery—simple brute labor!—and had failed to appreciate the joys of exercising their intellects in a healthy, disciplined manner. Learning was work, but it shouldn't be dull or seemingly senseless. She wanted her students to feel alive in her classes,

aware of their capacities for growth and development. Of course, she would
have to adjust her pedagogical style to meet American standards, but she assumed that American girls were essentially the same as English girls; anyway,
it would be interesting to find out the differences. And, too, it certainly was
a bit premature to talk about adjusting her style when she hadn't had time to
acquire one as yet!

*In her mind's eye she saw a plain, nobly proportioned room, with high ceilings and
tall windows hung with diaphanous white curtains aglow with the morning sunlight.
Two rows of simple wooden desks stood modestly in attendance on uncarpeted oak
floors, and bent over the desks in attitudes of profound concentration were the young
ladies who filled the atmosphere with their studious presence. The room was wrapped
in silence, and the only visible movement was the steady, stately progress of the students' pens across their notebook pages, the gentle, intermittent sloping of their ruffled
shoulders, and the glimmers of light across their well-groomed hair. It was a vision that
infused Elizabeth with a deep sense of well-being, and that she made no effort to
translate into words.*

She went on to tell him that she might start off by giving piano lessons—
to beginners, of course, or to very young children, perhaps two or three students a week, just to earn a little pocket money. And she had thought about
trying her hand at translations from the French. The wife of one of her
father's friends in London had done that, translating stories from French re-
vues and even novels. When she was properly settled, she would look out for
a good local library with current French publications. She might even sub-
scribe to the *Revue des Deux Mondes* if it weren't too dear. . . .

Together, over the next few days, they gave free rein to their dreams of
the future, remembering to intersperse their more ambitious fantasies with
sober references to "practicality" and "contingencies" and "common sense."
Both were guiltily aware that this mutual exchange of confidences savored of
self-indulgence, but the knowledge that their relationship was necessarily a
fleeting one and that in a couple of weeks' time they would be going their
separate ways emboldened them and allowed them to overcome their mutual reserve. For Elizabeth, the opportunity to discuss her private concerns,
to share such intimacies with someone who wasn't her father, was some-

thing new and exciting. At school, among her closest friends, she had learned to keep her own counsel; even at that most languid of intervals, while they were together brushing out their tresses in preparation for bed, a note of rivalry seemed to hover on the periphery of their discussions, and she sensed that her schemes for the future were being judged and found wanting in "tone" or "taste." With her father, she had to be careful about saying anything that might possibly cast the least doubt on his ability to "take care" of her. For although he reviled domestic extravagance of any kind and made a great play of his daughter's achieving independence of both body and spirit, he tended to turn a deaf ear to any of her money-making proposals. With young Macready, however, she could let herself go. His every look and comment encouraged her to spin out her dreams—and he asked only for the chance to do the same. Their youthful voices rose and fell, soaring together into the starry night, intoning a prayerful little hymn to the inscrutable future.

One evening, while she was enthusiastically elaborating some plan for her dream school, he carelessly interjected: "That's all very well, but the truth is that you will probably be married within a couple of years to a prosperous Philadelphian and will find your time fully engaged in looking after a large domestic establishment, with servants above and below stairs and a riotous clamor in the nursery." The remark, uttered in a light voice and half in jest, brought her rhapsodic musings to an end. After a stony silence, Elizabeth coldly explained that though she had nothing against marriage, she felt that her immediate responsibilities lay elsewhere. Besides, she found it impossible to think of marriage in purely hypothetical terms and therefore refused to include it in her plans for the future. There wasn't any point in doing so, was there?

He realized the damage his words had done and regretted them. Though he never referred to the subject again, an element of strain had entered their relationship, and its lyrical nature was irretrievably lost.

The evening before the ship was due to drop anchor at Baltimore, Elizabeth and her father encountered the Macreadys on deck and stopped to exchange formal farewells.

Dr. Gow and Macready Senior, in spite of their differences in disposition and approach, or perhaps because of them, had in the course of the voyage become close companions. Like many men of science, Dr. Gow possessed a somewhat wistful respect for the cultural attainments of others, and he recognized in the stately Hibernian's outpourings of quotations and frequent literary references a genuine sensitivity of response. Whereas the young people might mock what they considered to be old Macready's histrionic posturing, the scientist half-envied his companion's intimate and emotional involvement with the mysteries of art. If Macready's enthusiasms sometimes seemed excessive, well, enthusiasm was a quality that the doctor seldom dared indulge, and at this moment of his life he found its presence, in the figure of a benevolent and unchallenging shipboard acquaintance, uplifting and relaxing—as was the old man's seemingly indomitable optimism.

As for Macready, he sensed that the mere physical proximity of Dr. Gow lent ballast and gravity to his own personality—in engineering terms, it provided solid structural support. He recognized that the Englishman's staid manner and verbal sobriety imposed a certain restraint on his own conversational habits. In Dublin drawing rooms and other convivial settings where Macready was wont to hold forth, he frequently found himself toward the end of the evening brought to bay by the pack of rival conversationalists and vehemently defending causes for which he possessed little sympathy and less knowledge—the trade policies of the Grand Porte, vegetarianism, the breech-loading rifle, Meyerbeer's operas—and he came away from such encounters with the distinct impression that though he had perhaps given off sparks, he had not shone. With Dr. Gow, however, he never felt the urge to indulge in rhetorical extravagance. The man, in short, never encouraged him to show himself in an unfavorable light, and for that reason alone Macready's friendship for the Englishman was assured.

Most evenings, after dinner, the two men could be seen together strolling the deck at a leisurely pace conducive to digestion—Macready almost military in his bearing, head held high, his leonine mane a wash of pure white in the near darkness; Gow, bent into the wind, seeming the smaller and frailer of the two, though he was in reality some two inches taller and ten years younger than his companion and still boyishly slim in figure. When the weather was exceptionally inclement, they could be found in the Gentlemen's Salon, seated in neighboring leather armchairs, earnestly engaged in talk, Macready rounding out a point by saluting his friend with a glass of ruby-colored port held delicately aloft while Gow tugged thoughtfully at his side-whiskers and meditated a reply.

Whereas their offspring were absorbed in dreams of the future, they preferred exploring the spacious domains of times gone by. The past was something they discussed with authority, as monarchs of their own memories: though one often encountered there sadness and pain, these encounters had by the passage of time been bleached of terror and fear. To talk freely of the future would be to expose their uncertainties and to approach a level of intimacy that neither of them desired. They talked about America in general terms, extolling republican virtues and condemning those class-structured societies of the Old World, where a man was dependent on the vagaries of private patronage. Macready would wax eloquent on the sheer expansiveness of the country, its physical grandeur and abundant resources, on the rich diversity of its cultural heritage and peoples . . . which often led him, by one path or another, to the compelling subject of waterways and their vast superiority to railways as a means of spreading well-being throughout the land. Speaking from personal knowledge and professional experience, he could assure his friend that with the availability of new power-driven equipment for the digging of canals and the latest advances in the design of cast-iron locks and valves, and with a sophisticated scientific approach to the efficient use of existing water resources, canal systems could be built that would prove in the long run considerably cheaper to operate and maintain than railways and that would promote a happier, healthier mode of life for the general population.

"Have you not noticed, my dear Gow, that people who live along rivers or canals are, largely speaking, a cheerful, sociable, and industrious people? Daily contact with the outside world brightens their existence, enlivens their intellects, and inspires a sense of pride that encourages friendly rivalry and hard work. And, my friend, I trust that you will not think me inclined to metaphysical tomfoolery if I venture to confess that it is my belief that the flow of water traffic, responding as it does to the rhythms of nature herself, exerts on the participants a deep and beneficial influence. Water is, after all, the primal substance. It flows in our veins. It sustains life. It promotes cleanliness and hygiene. Is it any wonder that the residents of the Pays Bas, as the region is so aptly called, are renowned for their enterprise, their conviviality and the extreme cleanliness of their domestic establishments? Not at all! Now think of the filth, noise, and stink that follows the iniquitous route of the railways. The populace cannot help being demoralized by the proximity of those vile machines. Why, you need only look at the squalid little towns that line the tracks, blighting and degrading the landscape. Oh, I don't deny that the carriages go fast and haul great quantities of goods. But at what a cost! I profess to be a modern man, Dr. Gow. I am after all, by my profession—as are you—committed to the modern age and to progress. But all that is new does not inevitably lead to the advancement of mankind. And there can be no true progress when the spirit of man is violated by the pernicious instruments of folly and greed. . ."

Most of the talk, however, revolved around evocations of their childhood and youth. They had reached the age when they were free to wander at will up and down a wide expanse of memory and to see themselves as participants in the great process of history. Macready spoke of watching the construction of the Martello towers outside of Dublin, and how he and his boyhood companions excitedly discussed the prospect of French troopships disgorging their glittering human cargoes along the shingle. Gow recalled the visit of a distant relative, white-haired and in knee breeches, who had taken part in the siege of Pondichery and was said to have contracted the "sleeping sickness" in India, describing how he and his older brother had kept a close watch on the old pensioner for any tell-tale signs of drowsiness. In retelling these stories of their early years, both men were striving to impose some semblance of meaning and coherence on the miscellaneous clutter that crowded their memories. The passion of reminiscence lay not in the uncovering of long-lost truths, but in the opportunity to reshape the past— to re-create, in effect, their own beginnings.

Now, as the two men discussed landing arrangements, the wellsprings of memory seemed to run dry. A sudden shyness overcame them, and the nascent intimacy of the past few days gave way to polite formalities. In anticipation, as it were, of their imminent parting and separation, they sensed a growing distance between themselves. With businesslike gestures they extracted notebooks from their pockets to record mutual forwarding addresses.

And as they paused there, pencils poised, and looked into each other's face, the poignancy of the moment overcame them, their expressions softened, and their respective eyeglasses seemed to give off a sudden glitter.

"My good Dr. Gow! Though America is a vast domain and our paths lead different ways, I cannot believe that we shall not meet again. In any case, I am sure that I shall hear news of your scholarly achievements, no matter where I might happen to be."

"Well, Macready, I doubt that my work will ever receive much notoriety. Certainly it will never attain the monumental proportions of your own future endeavors. But I shall think of you often, as a kindred adventurer in the New World. I am grateful that chance brought us together. Do let us try to keep in touch."

"Your hand, Dr. Gow!"

"Gladly, Mr. Macready."

Meanwhile, the young people had drawn apart for their own farewells. Macready Junior leaned against the rail and gazed out at the faint, flickering lights on the distant shore.

"God knows what will become of us. Look at that great dark mass out there; beyond it lies a vast continent of teeming cities and windswept plains, of limitless expanses of untamed woodlands and barren deserts. And all of it waiting to swallow us up, the whole boatload of us, without so much as a 'thank you' or a 'fare you well'!

"I can't help wondering at times whether America really wants or needs what we have to offer, Miss Gow. An interesting question, that! As for my compatriots below deck, who already seem to be celebrating their successes—well, I suppose that America will find a good use for their strong arms and their ferocious willingness to earn the price of another drink. But for the likes of us, with our attenuated refinements, our vague, inchoate dreams, our tattered remnants of Old World culture, and our accursed sense of self-righteousness, what use will the republic possibly find for us? Already I feel like a mountebank, about to step on shore with a sackful of trumpery wares."

Elizabeth rushed to respond, and her voice grew increasingly firm and emphatic as she spoke.

"I don't pretend to know the causes of your discouragement or doubts, Mr. Macready, but it seems to me to me that what you are saying is quite beside the point. We have lives to lead in America just as we did at home. And I like to think that when we leave this ship, we will leave behind our past weaknesses and discouragements and start life anew, not with nothing, not with just those 'trumpery wares' you refer to, but with a valuable cargo of working tools—with our ideals, our talents, our knowledge, and our hard-earned experience. I am sure that America has not a surfeit of such commodities. I am sure that a man of your professional attainments has much to offer. We *will* succeed, I know we will. And why shouldn't we? After all, didn't we come to America with the explicit intention of breaking free from our past existences? I know I shall miss my old home. I miss it now, dreadfully. But I don't feel that I am running away or being driven away. The choice is mine, and I have made it. I *am* escaping, if you will, and in the nick of time. I feel that there is the opportunity for a new and better life are out there, somewhere, just within our reach. And that surely is a good thing, a thing of bright promise, if one doesn't lose heart, lose courage at the start."

"Oh, you mustn't mind me, Miss Gow. I am afraid that the good doctors at Trinity College never succeeded in purging me of the taint of Celtic fatalism that runs in my veins. Yet if there is any trait in the Irish that I despise more than that fatalism, it is our propensity for mindless optimism, our insufferable cheerfulness in the face of unmitigated catastrophe, our idiotic insistence on seeing the bright side of utter desolation. All I am really saying here is that things won't be easy. It's a wicked world we live in—or a flawed world if you prefer, depending on your sensibilities—and there is no reason to think that we can knock it into shape with our fine phrases and good intentions. But you are right, of course; without courage nothing is possible, except sure defeat.

"I wish you well, Miss Gow. I hope sincerely that we will meet again one day. And when we do—what adventures we will have to tell!"

Philadelphia, 1 8 5 1

SHE WAS STANDING AT THE BACK of the lecture hall, waiting for her father to disengage himself from a small cluster of admirers, when a tall woman of middle years approached her and extended a finely gloved hand.

"You are Dr. Gow's daughter, aren't you? I did so want to meet you. I am Catherine Moorehouse, Mrs. Charles Moorehouse."

Elizabeth knew the name. It came up frequently in conversations with Mr. Throneberry. Charles Moorehouse had recently agreed to serve on the governing board of the Philadelphia Society for Natural Philosophy; he was a noted patron of local music events and a long-time business associate of the Biddles. Elizabeth had noticed the peculiar tone of voice in which Mr. Throneberry had announced, apropos of nothing particular, that he was "obliged" to attend a dinner at the Moorehouses' Thursday next. He had emitted a nervous laugh, which was immediately suppressed by a weak cough into a clenched fist. His eyes were gleaming, and Elizabeth surmised that the Moorehouses were people of some importance.

". . . You must be very proud of your father," Mrs. Moorehouse was saying. "He's such a splendid lecturer! Such a wonderfully knowledgeable man and so clearly dedicated to his subject. I only wish that I weren't so shamefully ignorant. I am sure that I would have understood things better if I weren't. But I suppose that is why we are here in the first place—or at least, why people like me are here. We do so crave enlightenment!

"Anyway, it's easy to see that *you* don't share our miserable ignorance. I hope that you won't be offended, Miss Gow, if I say that one can tell at a glance what a very intelligent young person you are. But of course, being an intelligent young person, you won't be! People say that beauty is only skin deep, but that is utter foolishness. I have never seen a beautiful face that was not suffused with intelligence. The vapid beauty, as far as I am concerned, simply doesn't exist. But there, there, my dear. I am not trying to flatter you. Forgive an older woman's foolish banter." And she smiled down serenely at the girl.

"Really, Mrs. Moorehouse, I have no pretensions to scientific learning. Of course, my father's studies seem less foreign to me than to many other lay people. He's very patient in explaining things. And as you can see, he has a gift for making very complex matters seem quite straightforward and accessible. Though I'm afraid that that is sometimes merely a delusion for nonscientific intellects like mine."

Mrs. Moorehouse's smile seemed to take on a deeper glow of serenity. "What a lovely voice you have, Miss Gow. Your soft English accents are balm to our ears. I suppose you noticed that we Philadelphians tend to croak when we speak, like frogs on the edge of a lily pond. Now there's no use in denying it, it is all too true! But it is *our* pond, and we grow quite used to the racket. I trust that you will resist our baleful influences. But that does *not* mean that you should avoid us. Thursday is my own special day, from ten until noon. You will promise to come by, won't you, my dear?"

The warmer, the more pressing the woman's blandishments, the colder and the more distant Elizabeth felt herself becoming. But she had no proper defense against such an onslaught of apparent goodwill. Surely she means well, Elizabeth said to herself, yet I don't really know what she is saying or how she expects me to understand her words.

"Of course I will, Mrs. Moorehouse. Thank you."

"That would be very nice of you, my dear." Mrs. Moorehouse took Elizabeth's hand in both of hers and gave it a little squeeze. "Very nice indeed!"

Elizabeth watched, mesmerized, the woman's stately progress through the crowded room, the tall, elegant form bent slightly forward like a full-blown flower drooping gently on its stem. She marveled at the vision of total self-possession, of sheer willfulness, unimpeded by assertion or desire. As Mrs. Charles Moorehouse passed through the far doorway, the room suddenly seemed deflated.

She glanced back anxiously at her father. The group around him was relaxing its hold, though a small stout woman with a red parasol tucked under her arm continued to harangue him tenaciously, while the other ladies hovered nearby. There was a thin smile etched on his lips, but Elizabeth detected the beginnings of a frown in the arch of his eyebrows, and she started off to his rescue. He spotted her approach and, lifting aloft a rolled sheaf of lecture notes, he began edging his way clear of the company. "You must excuse me, ladies, my family awaits me. Most interesting, Madam, most interesting, thank you for your comments. . ." He clutched his daughter's arm like a drowning seaman reaching for a rope, and together the two of them made their way to the door.

"I wasn't too awful, was I?" His voice was thick with fatigue.

"It was a very impressive talk, Papa. They hung on your every word."

"Did they, Bess, did they?" He was silent for a few moments. Then he said: "I'm not sure that I want to be impressive. I mean, my Bess, do you think that they had any idea of what I was talking about? Sometimes I do believe that they are merely entertained by the foreign accent, the strange cut of my jib, and my traveling exhibit of old bones and fossils."

"Oh Papa, it was a truly fascinating lecture, it really was! And so carefully thought out. Just think of the applause, and the way people gathered around you afterwards. They were so obviously excited and stimulated by what you had to say. . ."

"But their questions, Bess, oh their *questions!*" And he shook his head sadly.

Outside the building it had already grown dark, and the streets were bathed in the cold, lunar glow of the gaslights. They had been in America almost six months now and were not yet familiar with the progress of the seasons. Winter had come upon them unawares.

In fact, nothing had been quite as they had expected. True, their picture of American life had never been very clear, but they had never anticipated any great changes in their daily livings. Things in America, they told themselves, would of course be slightly different, but basically the same: just like the language. Obviously adjustments would have to be made, but it was understood that they would seek to reestablish in Philadelphia a domestic setting and routine similar to those they had in London. Elizabeth would devote herself to that particular task: it was, after all, her primary reason for accompanying her father to America. She would do what she could to create for him a home, and together they would draw the strength to deal with the demands of his new public life from the calm and security of their shared privacy.

They were prepared to spend the first few days after their arrival in Philadelphia looking for suitable living quarters, and while on shipboard they frequently reverted to the subject of their housing requirements. They had in mind a modest floor-through flat in some respectable neighborhood, not too far from the downtown, where the Society's building was located. They needed two bedrooms, a sitting room, and of course a separate, amply sized study to house Dr. Gow's books and display cases. Elizabeth was hoping that the sitting room would be spacious enough for her to stage recitals for her piano students, but because she could not bring herself to discuss with her father the subject of her giving lessons, this requirement did not figure in their speculations. They reasoned that they could afford one domestic servant, an adolescent girl or Irish woman, who would probably sleep somewhere in the attics. Elizabeth dreaded the interval they would have to spend in some rooming house or hotel while searching for their new home, but she assured her father, "Once we finally move in and get our things in place—your books and cases, and my piano, and put up Aunt Emma's portrait over the mantelpiece—it will be quite snug and quite our own!" This was the first time she would be assuming responsibility for setting up house, and she found herself quite looking forward to the prospect of selecting drapes and arranging furniture. The whole operation, she told herself, would provide one more opportunity to take charge of her life.

Mr. Throneberry met them in Philadelphia with the news that he had found them a home. Without more ado, their luggage was loaded onto the top of his carriage, and they were borne in triumph to a small but elegantly proportioned townhouse near Rittenhouse Square. On the front steps Mr. Throneberry ceremoniously placed the keys in Dr. Gow's hand. Their search for lodgings, he assured them, was over, and their domestic arrangements all but fully arranged.

The house was one of the several city properties owned by Mr. Throneberry and had been leased to a Southern gentleman named Levert, an official of the New Orleans Cotton Exchange who, for "personal reasons," regularly spent a few months of the year up North. Owing to ill health Mr. Levert was confined to his plantation for an indefinite time and on Mr. Throneberry's suggestion had agreed to sublet the house.

"It's a great bargain; you couldn't hope to do better for the price," Mr. Throneberry said with enthusiasm. "Fully furnished too, just wait 'til you see! And strictly *entre nous,*" he added in a melodramatic undertone, "I don't think he'll be coming back here for a good long while—poor fellow!"

The decoration reflected the opulently austere tastes of a well-to-do, middle-aged clubman. The furniture was plain but massive and conspicuously new. The downstairs sitting rooms gave off the warm, dark glow of well-polished mahogany. In the library they found a small glass-doored bookcase filled with volumes of the classic authors, in English, French, and Latin, uniformly bound in red leather, and the dark wood paneling was crowded with prints of celebrated English and Irish racehorses in gilt frames. From the library Mr. Throneberry ceremoniously ushered them into the dining room, where cut-glass decanters on the heavy mahogany sideboard echoed the overhead glitter of the crystal chandelier, and the broad expanse of table top, flanked by an heraldic array of tall, straight-backed chairs, spoke of lengthy after-dinner conversations over goblets of port. A faint aroma of cigars clung to the draperies.

When Elizabeth entered the front sitting room, her eye had been immediately drawn to the piano, an imposing, no-nonsense affair, with the legend "Chickering: Boston" inscribed above the keyboard. As she passed beside it, she could not resist pausing to touch the keys and was startled by the rich sonority of sound, which seemed to conform to the masculine tones of the decor; it made her own beloved Pleyel seem frail and ladylike. She was tempted to linger a moment longer to try the opening bars of a Beethoven sonata, but this was clearly not the appropriate time, so she closed the keyboard cover with a decisive gesture and hurried after her father and Mr. Throneberry, the fading notes still reverberating deeply within her.

The second floor contained two bedrooms and an alcove at the top of the landing with a love seat and a small table. Mr. Throneberry threw open the door of the master bedroom and stood aside for them to enter. In contrast to the other rooms of the house, which were decorated in somber hues of brown, mauve, and gray, the master bedroom was awash in color. The floor was covered by an Aubusson carpet with bold floral patterns in pale rose, pale blue, and pearl gray; the walls were watered silk matching in tone the rose of the carpet. A large gilt-framed mirror, featuring on its corners floating putti withdrawing golden carved drapes, was suspended directly across from the monumental bed. The walls were devoid of decoration, though one could see outlined on the silk surface shaded spaces where a half-dozen or so pictures of uniform size had once hung; Elizabeth speculated that they were family portraits that Mr. Levert had chosen to take with him. Beside the bed stood a small night table, whose pink marble top was held aloft by a grinning blackamoor in a turban. On the table were a small brass candlestick, brightly polished and with a fresh white candle in it, together with a leather-bound copy of the Book of Common Prayer in near mint condition.

"Well now, isn't this a cheery room!" exclaimed Mr. Throneberry.

Dr. Gow looked about him with a vaguely quizzical expression and after some hesitation owned, "It is, I think, a bit too . . . grand for me."

"Yes, yes, I suppose that colors are more appropriate for the young lady," Mr. Throneberry complacently conceded, and after allowing them to peer into another sleeping chamber across the way, which was small, dark, and furnished with unimpeachable sobriety (the wallpaper seemed to feature sepia-colored scenes of Old Philadelphia, with various dim patriotic manifestations presided over at regular intervals by the American Eagle with banners in his beak), he invited them to follow him up a narrow stairway to the attics.

One of the attic rooms was inhabited by the maidservant-cum-cook, Edith, who was, Mr. Throneberry informed them, visiting relatives in Allentown and would return next week. Edith was in Mr. Levert's employ and, like his furnishings, went with the house. Mr. Levert, he assured them, would take charge of her salary. "All you have to do, Dr. Gow, is remember her at Christmas—whatever you think appropriate. She is of German extraction and completely trustworthy. I can also speak well for her dumplings." From a glance into her tiny room, with everything aligned, well ordered, and squarely in place, it was clear that she was a no-nonsense sort of housekeeper.

The place was, as Mr. Throneberry repeated more than once, a tremendous, unhoped-for bargain. Though perhaps somewhat larger and grander than their needs demanded, it would certainly cost them no more than the sort of lodging they would have chosen on their own. They could tell from his voice that he assumed they would accept the arrangement, and indeed they could think of no reasonable excuse, then and there, for turning it down.

It was of course a great relief not to have had to trudge across town in search of lodgings. They were able to settle in right away, with little fuss or bother. Elizabeth was intrigued by her new surroundings and on occasion felt a flush of pleasure at the luxury and comfort of the accommodations, at the solidity and unabashed newness of the furniture, at the profusion of dinnerware, cooking utensils, and household items. Yet living in someone else's house, amidst someone else's belongings, was not what she had had in mind, and it only served to prolong her feeling of foreignness and disorientation. She had been looking forward to setting up a real home in America, and here they were, as her father said cheerfully, living as if they were in a "tip-top hotel in the Strand!" He really did not mind at all. After initial irritation at finding no suitable place for his research material and laboratory apparatuses, he managed to secure space for them in the basement of the Society's building, just four blocks away, and spent much of his day contentedly there.

Elizabeth missed the reassuring presence of their familiar household things, which remained sealed in wooden crates in the shadowy recesses of a waterfront warehouse. She found it hard to put down roots in these arid surroundings and was frequently overcome by fits of restlessness and by a strange inability to bring her mind to bear on her reading, her music, even her domestic chores. The condition was aggravated by Edith's firm resistance to Elizabeth's participation in the daily shopping expeditions for food and household supplies. "Oh, you needn't trouble yourself, Miss. I always take care of such matters around here." And something about the young woman's cool manner, the steely glint in her eyes, admitted no contradiction. Every morning Elizabeth and Edith made up a list of purchases, and every afternoon she inspected the goods, laid out for display on the kitchen table. There was no denying the servant's practical knowledge of the local shops and tradespeople, and she seemed to derive a ferocious satisfaction in procuring things at the lowest possible price—even, on occasion, denying Dr. Gow's request for a nice joint or gigot if the butcher seemed to be getting a bit above himself. But Elizabeth envied her expeditions to market and would have greatly welcomed the opportunity to exchange small talk with the greengrocer, the pharmacist, or the apparently impulsive butcher and to join the daily rounds of American life as an active participant. The excuses for leaving the house were few, and though she made a point of taking a lengthy walk through the neighborhood every afternoon, she found it vaguely demeaning to be going nowhere in particular, to have to pretend, by her brisk air and intent demeanor, that she was embarked on an errand or paying a call.

The nature of her father's professional activities turned out to be somewhat different than anticipated. Dr. Gow had gotten the impression from Mr. Throneberry that the Philadelphia Society for Natural Philosophy was a well-established institution made up, like its European counterparts, of a select mixture of distinguished scholars and well-informed amateurs who came together on a regular basis to exchange news and commentary on the latest scientific findings and ideas. His role, as he had understood it, was to serve as the Society's sole resident scholar and, if things went smoothly—as it was anticipated they would—to assume a new position, as yet unnamed, in the direction of its expanding program of public education. His immediate assignment was to deliver, over the course of the next eight months, a series of biweekly lectures to the Society's members.

The Society's letterhead stated that it was founded in 1793 and that its honorary chairman had been the first president of the United States. That was quite true. What neither the letterhead nor Mr. Throneberry troubled to explain was that the Society had been dissolved in 1811 and rechartered only two years ago by Mr. Throneberry himself. Thus, for all practical purposes, it was a new institution in the process of developing its membership and defining its mission.

At present the overwhelming majority of Society members seemed to be connected with commerce or trade, and their interests appeared to be less specifically scientific than generally cultural—and social. The members were usually accompanied to the lectures by their wives (for Mr. Throneberry had wisely waived the traditional male-only attendance rule and trusted to the women to sustain their husbands' appearance). Because the lectures took place on a weekday evening, after the gentlemen had been subjected to a full day of presumably profitable transactions, the wives tended to be the livelier and more attentive segment of the audience.

Dr. Gow found himself for the first time cast in the role of a "popularizer." In England his lectures had been devoted to the finer points of theoretical exposition and experimental techniques. In Philadelphia, however, it was immediately apparent that something else was required. He could assume on the part of his present public a general belief in the beneficent influence of culture, a profound respect for the triumphs of technology, and an initial impulse of goodwill toward the speaker of the evening; he could count on very little indeed in the way of scientific knowledge or training. In preparing his talks, he would have to, as he remarked to Elizabeth, "begin with Genesis, book one, verse one."

To his surprise, to Elizabeth's surprise and admiration, he developed into a successful public performer. His total ignorance of the mannerisms and ploys of the popular platform virtuosi of the day, along with his innate reserve and shyness, ultimately worked in his favor. People found his presentations "original" and "intense," and they appreciated and even took pride in the fact that he never seemed to court or cajole them. Their ignorance was such that they failed to perceive his talks as in any way condescending. What they did perceive was that he was striving hard to make himself understood, to make the material clear to them; they felt flattered by his attention and touched by the obvious effort he was expending on their behalf. Even when they could not quite grasp what he was saying, it was apparent that he was no humbug and "knew what he was talking about." At the conclusion of each lecture they vigorously applauded his high seriousness, his fine diction, the solid Latinate structure of his sentences, and they took pleasure in the ease and fluidity with which he handled arcane scientific phrases and terms—like an acrobat flipping effortlessly through the air. His very lack of charm won their confidence and enlisted their loyalty. Among themselves, the members—and the members' wives—spoke of "our" Dr. Gow in self-congratulatory tones tinged with something very like affection.

Although her father derived satisfaction from his ability to attract a decent number of people to his lectures, his ambitions lay elsewhere, and unfulfilled. Increasingly his thoughts turned to the university as a place where he could do real work and find a proving ground for his professional aspirations. He was, however, at a loss as to how to approach the authorities there. No representatives of the science faculty at the university had seen fit to become a member of the Society; nor, given the nature of his present mission, was he anxious to secure their attendance at his talks. Mr. Throneberry had presented him on his arrival with a letter of introduction to Professor Gotthelf, the head of the university's science faculty, but Dr. Gow had hesitated in using it. Whatever Mr. Throneberry's position in the city, it was clear that it could carry little weight among scholars. After long reflection, Dr. Gow thought it better to present himself directly, under his own signature.

Professor Gotthelf replied immediately. He had recognized Dr. Gow's name, mentioned with praise an early article on cell structure that had appeared in the *Annals of the Royal Botanical Society,* and was eager to meet him. Within a few minutes of their first encounter the two men were engaged in an animated discussion, happily citing sources in a number of European languages.

Professor Gotthelf was a small, trim, pink-cheeked man in his early sixties. He had come from his native Prussia almost thirty years ago but still retained a thick accent that tended to grow thicker as his enthusiasm mounted. The colorful flavor of his speech and certain idiosyncratic movements of his head and hands were a constant source of merriment to his younger colleagues, who frequently mimicked them among themselves, though more out of clannishness than mockery. As a department head, he was kindly to the point of slackness, would hear no evil of anyone, and was utterly free of malice or envy. Though his own scientific researches seemed to have culminated in an endless series of inconclusive experiments conducted in an increasingly desultory fashion (his famous remark, "I sometimes tink, my friends, dat I am barking up der vrong tree," was a favorite set piece for impersonators), he nonetheless retained a lively interest in the field at large and kept up with all the scientific journals in English, German, Dutch, Italian, and French that overflowed the shelves and tables, and even the chairs of his spacious office and lent to it a rather jolly air of cosmopolitan disorder. He was generally liked by all, and even the more ambitious of the faculty members, who affected to despise his lack of scholarly achievement, relaxed and grew expansive in his company precisely because he presented no professional challenge. When at the end of the day he made his way across the campus, he was invariably accompanied by a cluster of students or colleagues, so that the brief walk to the waiting carriage took on the air of a Lilliputian royal progress.

A couple of months after their first meeting, Dr. Gow was invited to dinner at the Gotthelf home. Elizabeth's name was included in the invitation.

A fiacre took them to a part of the city they had never seen before, with substantial houses, built largely of stone and set back on large expanses of lawn or half-hidden among ancestral groves, between which one caught now and then a fleeting glimpse of the river. Their conveyance entered a semicircular carriageway, sheltered from the road by a high brick wall, and came to a stop in front of a brightly lit entrance porch. It was all much grander than they had expected, and Elizabeth and her father exchanged a quick interrogatory glance before descending from the vehicle. The door was opened by a manservant who helped them off with their cloaks, then led them to the front parlor where their hosts and a handful of other guests were assembled.

Professor Gotthelf was a widower who had remarried late in life a very wealthy Philadelphian in her middle years. Although it was her first excursion into marriage, she had meditated long and deeply on the peculiarities of the matrimonial state and had critically examined the domestic establishments of friends and relatives (in particular those of her three younger sisters), which, she concluded, afforded much room for improvement. Her family had long been connected with the university as trustees and patrons, and she had met the professor at the Biddles' reception for the new chancellor. She was beguiled by his quaint charm and by the respectful attention that he had received from a number of the city's cultural leaders. It subsequently occurred to her that the somewhat exotic facets of his personality would perhaps provide an interesting complement to the more conventional aspects of her own. Moreover, it was clear to her that he was someone who would benefit greatly from being taken in hand by a sympathetic and knowledgeable woman. She had been distressed by the general shabbiness of his clothes and by his lack of social finesse: at one point he had all but turned his back on the wife of the chairman of the university's Board of Governors in order to exchange greetings with a ridiculously attired woman with a horrible laugh who was newly married to an insignificant member of the faculty. With patience, good humor, and tactful admonition, such errors could, she felt, be corrected. It was a cause worthy of her effort, and she was fully prepared to devote all her energy and hard-won experience to the care, training, and promotion of her husband. She would withdraw into the background, the better to bring him into relief. Whatever sacrifices this withdrawal would entail, she could in time come to look upon them as her personal contribution to the world of scholarship and learning—in effect, constituting another link in her family's long and honorable association with the university.

As for the professor, having spent his childhood in poverty, his student days in bohemian frugality, and subsequent years in decidedly pinched circumstances (the appointment to the university following the birth of his sixth child and the onset of his first wife's invalidism), this sudden cohabitation with wealth left him momentarily bemused. But being of a naturally compliant temperament as far as superficial matters were concerned, he quickly adjusted to his new style of living without relinquishing any of the simple, outgoing mannerisms of his previous life. He moved amidst the fine china and glittering silver, the overstuffed sofas and monumental sideboards with an air of complete detachment, as if his association with these objects, though undeniable, was entirely coincidental. His wife, who had counted on these new surroundings to inspire in him a sense of dignified reserve, was sorely disappointed. In fact, she discovered that the flexibility of his character resembled that of finely tempered steel. Though he never contradicted her and accepted her suggestions and criticisms with cheerful appreciation, even professions of gratitude, he invariably went his own way, which was much the same way as before. True, she had managed to spruce him up a bit: his suits were made by the best tailors, his coat was always well brushed, and his boots polished to high sheen, but he wore the clothes as if they were a gift from some good fairy to cover his nakedness—which was not far from the truth, but it hardly created the impression his wife had desired. It was very trying to her. But in time she began to look on her husband's disregard for conventions as a telltale sign of his tainted lineage, and to her most intimate friends she confided that he carried in his veins the blood of a debased and superannuated European nobility. And she took it upon herself to compensate for his failings by her own rigid adherence to accepted norms.

On the Gows' appearance in the doorway all conversation was suspended. The ladies were in possession of the sofas and armchair, while the men assumed various postures around the mantelpiece. There was a fire in the grate, and the flames lapped hungrily at a fresh log, while the highly polished brass knobs on the andirons gave off a hard glow.

The silence was broken by the professor, who called out, "Goot, goot, now der party is complete!" and hastened across the room to greet them. He took Dr. Gow's hand in both of his and held it long, as if it were a delectable object he was reluctant to relinquish. Then, turning to Elizabeth, he peered intently into her face and, seeming to find what he sought there, bestowed on her an affectionate smile. "Velcome, Miss Gow. It is delightful to have you vid us. Come, I must present you to my lady," and he led her by the hand to his wife, who was enthroned near the fireplace in a high-backed armchair.

Elizabeth felt herself underdressed for the occasion. Her next-to-best gown suddenly seemed shabby and hopelessly out of fashion. But Mrs. Gotthelf, as if reading her thoughts, proclaimed in a cheerily offhand manner, calculated to set everyone at ease, "Tonight is a very informal sort of affair. After all, most of the gentlemen are distinguished associates of my husband, and with such *interesting* company there is surely no point in insisting on ceremony." This pronouncement was greeted by murmurs of "Hear! Hear!" from the proximity of the mantelpiece and by a tentative clapping of hands from one of the sofas.

Elizabeth was taken in charge by the only young man in attendance, who was introduced to her as Professor Gotthelf's son. The physical resemblance was striking: the same high coloring—pink cheeks, pale blue eyes, blond hair. But whereas the father's hair was almost pure white, the son's was flaxen; and whereas the father's smile spread instantaneously from lips to eyes, enveloping and illuminating the whole of his face, the son's smile was restricted to the corners of his mouth. The young man displayed none of the old man's effusiveness and spoke without any trace of a foreign accent. He was courtly, serious, and self-assured, and like most young men whom Elizabeth encountered on social occasions, he assumed a vast interest on her part in his biography and beliefs.

She learned that he was completing a dissertation at Harvard in the field of natural sciences, under the supervision of a new professor from Neufchatel named Agassiz: a first-rate man. At the moment he was torn between botany and zoology. The trouble was that the most advanced work was really being done abroad, and he now felt that he could greatly profit from a couple of years at a German university. . . . But how to find the time? Most of the scientists of his father's generation were too given to abstract theorizing, to broad generalizations, and didn't pay enough attention to fieldwork and to the newest techniques of laboratory experimentation. In his opinion, most of the elder generation of scientists really aspired to be philosophers or theologians. This was particularly true at Harvard, where many of them seemed to ape the mannerisms of Unitarian ministers. So while his fellow students sat around discussing the meaning of Nature and the origin of the universe, he would slip away to the dissecting room, where the real work was being done. He hated the pretentiousness of most students and teachers alike (Agassiz was an exception!). It was his belief that the role of science was to contribute to the well-being of society, pure and simple. "I am not ashamed of placing my faith in Progress, Miss Gow, and in the human spirit's ability to rid itself of the follies of the past. Don't you feel the same?" And without waiting for her reply, he reached out for her empty punch glass and hurried off to refill it.

Dinner was announced. The professor made a great fuss about taking Elizabeth in, though his son was already at her side and had extended an arm. "No, no, unhand her, you young villain. She is mine by right. I am the oldest, and she is the *newest*. You vill allow me, Miss Gow?"

At table she once again found herself next to the professor's son. As they took their places, one of the ladies near Mrs. Gotthelf exclaimed in a loud, sugary voice: "What a handsome couple the young people make!" Their hostess smiled upon them benignly, then, wagging a finger at her stepson, called out across the table, "I trust, dear Rupert, that you won't forget that you happen to be committed elsewhere." And Mrs. Gotthelf went on to explain to the company at large that the young man had recently become engaged to the daughter of Senator Drew, though the official announcement was not to be made until the Drews returned from Europe next month. A polite murmur of applause greeted this interesting item of news, followed by a faint, resonant clatter as the guests addressed themselves to the turtle soup.

Elizabeth felt her cheeks burning. This is ridiculous! she said to herself as she turned to smile her congratulations upon her neighbor. The fact was that she was not now obliged to go through the tiresome courting-dance routines—those carefully choreographed twirls and turns that unattached young couples were expected to perform at social occasions of precisely this sort. It was a particular relief because she happened to find Rupert physically unattractive. There was something washed-out and insipid about his appearance; and the businesslike precision with which he dealt with the food before him, as if turtles had been slaughtered and soup made to provide his personal nourishment, repelled her. Nonetheless, she could not help feeling vaguely humiliated, for it almost seemed as if Mrs. Gotthelf's remarks had been addressed not to her stepson, but to Elizabeth—as if she were being publicly warned to keep hands off the young man.

Elizabeth was young enough not to feel defensive about her single state. Still, it was galling to be reminded that she was generally considered to be "on the market," especially by someone like Mrs. Gotthelf. She told herself that people could not know how deeply committed she was to looking after her father—that she was neither on display nor on the lookout; she told herself, too, that Mrs. Gotthelf had certainly not intended to hurt her, and that in all probability she had simply meant to save her any possible embarrassment by making Rupert's situation perfectly clear. Elizabeth was indeed relieved that he was "committed elsewhere," and as the evening wore on and he continued to regale her with detailed plans of his future career, she felt downright *merry* that he was. And yet . . . and yet, at the very back of her mind the knowledge that this eminently undesirable young man was forever beyond her reach disturbed her. She thought: how hateful it is being young!

She glanced down the table at her father. The doctor was a man of moods and capable of lapsing unexpectedly into a sullen silence, even in the midst of a dinner party. Tonight, however, he seemed in his very best form. At such times his stern, darkly handsome cast of features was burnished by enthusiasm, and he spoke with a vigor and fluidity that made up for his almost total lack of humor. He was extolling the new techniques in plant cross-fertilization as practiced on the Continent and explaining the implications they held for the future of worldwide food supplies. Elizabeth was pleased to see that some of the people at her end of the table were neglecting their partners and straining to catch his words.

Over the fruit and nuts the gentleman across from him asked what he thought Throneberry's plans were for the Society. At that question Mrs. Gotthelf suspended her own conversation to interject: "Well, Dr. Gow, if I were you, I wouldn't count too much on good Mr. Throneberry. I don't doubt that his intentions are all very fine, but people like him tend to lose interest after a while. After all, he is a newcomer here and hardly acquainted with the scene. And I'm afraid that we Philadelphians are a stodgy lot . . ."

"*Ach ja,* dot ve are!" muttered the professor.

". . . And with the exception of my husband, much set in our ways. We tend to be suspicious of newcomers and slow to take them into our confidence."

"Forgive me, Mrs. Gotthelf, but I must object to that statement. Here we sit at your table, my daughter and I, surrounded by friendly faces, and we were first set ashore barely six months ago."

"Oh Dr. Gow, of course your case is entirely different. As a distinguished scholar, you are definitely a known factor. And we need only glance at your daughter to want to claim her as one of our own. Mr. Throneberry, however, still remains something of a stranger to us. His background is obscure, and his wife's is, if anything, even more mysterious. Clearly he is rich. Very rich, perhaps. But I would like to think that money alone counts for little among us. More to the point is the *use* that one makes of money. I understand that Mr. Throneberry has made large contributions to the Widows and Orphans Mission, and of course he has spent a sizable sum in reactivating the Society. We can only applaud such generosity—especially since it brought you and your daughter to us. Such gifts imply a noble and civic-minded spirit. And yet, Dr. Gow, it is difficult to understand what his motives really are."

"Surely, Mrs. Gotthelf, his motives are perfectly clear. He simply wants to be accepted. Accepted by you, accepted by those people in the community who share his aims and interests. It may perhaps be presumptuous of him, but it surely is not difficult to understand. Nor does it seem to me that such ambition deserves reproof."

"Of course it doesn't, Dr. Gow. And I assure you that no reproof was intended. We should of course be flattered that a man of such philanthropic inclinations seeks our acceptance, whatever his background might be. My heart indeed goes out to him, Dr. Gow. The trouble is, if I understand things correctly . . . the trouble seems to be that he has attempted to combine an essentially scholarly activity with a social one. You gentlemen at the table can address the subject better than I, but even as an ignorant female, I think that I can see where the confusion lies. People here *are* impressed by the fact that he is willing to put a good part of his personal fortune into sponsoring a scholarly institution, and I am sure that we would gladly lend him our wholehearted support, that we would willingly, yea gratefully and humbly, accept his generous gift to the community at large if it did not entail accepting as well his personal society. Mind you, Dr. Gow, I have nothing, absolutely nothing, against the man and am only too happy to assume that his intentions are the best in the world. It is simply that I do not *know* him. As I said, it takes a while for people around here to get to know someone, and until we do, we tend to remain horribly, hopelessly parochial in our dealings. I trust in time we will come around to him. It is all a question of time, Dr. Gow, just time."

"My relationship with Mr. Throneberry has been wholly professional in nature, but I can assure you, Mrs. Gotthelf, that in all my dealings with him he has shown himself thoughtful, considerate, and generous to a fault."

"Your testimony carries great weight, Dr. Gow. And from what you say I don't doubt that he will indeed succeed in winning our hearts. I can only pray that he doesn't give up on us too soon. That is what I really meant to say."

On the way home that evening they settled back in their respective corners of the carriage and gave themselves up to their thoughts. Finally Elizabeth said in the darkness, "What do you suppose Mrs. Gotthelf meant about Mr. Throneberry?"

"Oh, that she doesn't like him, I suppose, or rather, doesn't approve of him. That he won't, for whatever reason, get their support."

"But what does *that* mean?"

"For him, disappointment; he loses the chance to make a place for himself in local society—anyway, among the Gotthelf set. For us, the eventual dissolution of the Society."

"Oh Papa! Do you really think so? What would we do then?"

"I've never seen the Society as anything permanent, Bess. It is now very clear to me that I couldn't go on forever there, even if that were possible. And I am hopeful that something will turn up at the university. That is where I really belong."

"They seemed very cordial, Papa. They hung on your every word."

"I liked them, Bess. Unless I am mistaken, they are a decent, straightforward lot. The men, I mean. The women I can't fathom."

"And Mrs. Gotthelf? Is she really so hard to fathom?"

In the darkness she could not see his face, but she heard the smile in his voice:"I hope so, my dear. At least I'll give her the benefit of the doubt."

They rode on in silence for a while, rocked in their private cogitations.

Again it was Elizabeth who broke the silence. "Then there *is* hope?"

"They need someone like me at the university. Professor Gotthelf said as much, in pretty plain language." His voice came out firm and clear over the clatter of the wheels and the wheezing of the tired springs. He seemed positively cheered by the outing, which did much to dissipate the vague sense of depression that she herself had brought away from it. She realized for the first time how very much her father disliked his present obligations at the Society and how much he yearned for a position on the faculty of a reputable university. She was eager now to get home and to get into bed, where she could gather her thoughts around her in absolute silence and calm.

She resolved to make an effort to go out into the world. The following Thursday she went to one of Mrs. Moorehouse's "at homes." The room was crowded. The company was exclusively female, except for a couple of elderly uncles and the schoolboy brother of one of the ladies who was pressed into service to pass around the cakes. Elizabeth had thought it all out beforehand. She would not worry about her dress, which, however dowdy and unfashionable, was decently cut and perfectly respectable. Nor would she allow herself to be intimidated by the self-assurance of the other guests, who, after all, were in their native element. Instead of letting her foreignness inhibit her, she would use it as a support. She reminded herself that she was better educated and more accomplished than most of the girls assembled there, and though lacking in their smartness and social ease, was probably more interesting, if not because of her intellect, then because of her exoticism.

Rather than withdrawing immediately to the background, as was her wont on such occasions, Elizabeth adopted on trial an air of calm aloofness and stood her ground. The new manner seemed to work. Whereas in the past she had tended to be overlooked by her better-dressed, more vivacious contemporaries and had spent most of her time on the periphery, exchanging banalities with elderly ladies in mobcaps, today she was approached by several stellar representatives of the younger set, who asked her earnestly about her impressions of their city and pressed her for comparisons with London. At one point she was quite surrounded by a cluster of bright young faces, drinking in avidly the familiar place names of fashion and romance: Windsor Castle, Kensington Palace, Mayfair, the Strand. . . . For the first time in her life Elizabeth was pleased to recall her only visit to Mme. Tussaud's and managed to conceal convincingly her horror and revulsion. She felt exhilarated by her listeners' attentiveness—though perhaps a trifle fraudulent.

Her hostess beckoned her from across the room. Mrs. Moorehouse was seated on a large, velvet-covered sofa. A cashmere shawl, aswirl in colors, encircled her shoulders. Though as imposing as ever, she somehow seemed more approachable; perhaps it was simply because she was seated and not towering over one, perhaps because she was at home here and domesticated by the setting.

"Come, my dear. Sit down beside me. Let us talk together a while. I do so want to get to know you better."

She asked after Dr. Gow, hoped that he "wasn't feeling restless among us." Then she quizzed Elizabeth at length about her schooling in England:

"As a parent with four daughters of my own, I am naturally curious about such matters." Her questions were intelligent and to the point, her manner earnest and unaffected. Elizabeth quickly warmed to the subject: it was the sort of conversation she liked best, in which she could be most frankly and fully herself, and in which she had something very definite to say. Mrs. Moorehouse was particularly concerned about the instruction of foreign languages. Elizabeth had given much thought to the matter, and carefully, quietly outlined her ideas on the teaching of both German and French. Mrs. Moorehouse was all attention; she folded her hands on her lap, sat up very straight, looked intently into the speaker's face, and on occasion nodded her head in affirmation. Finally, taking notice of the people hovering around her, she sighed, and gave Elizabeth's hand a gentle squeeze. "We must talk more about this later. So very interesting! Thank you, my dear, you have given me much to think about."

Elizabeth left the Moorehouse home with a feeling of accomplishment. She had forced herself to enter the social lists and had come away—decidedly not triumphant—but unvanquished and unbruised. The strain of having to sustain a new public persona for herself had left her exhausted, but it *could* be done. And it seemed to her that in Mrs. Moorehouse she had found a real friend. She even began to entertain certain half-formed daydreams in which she saw herself floating at ease through the higher realms of Philadelphia society—apart from it, completely free, but accepted and sought after; this daydream was occasionally diverted into a little fantasy about marrying a well-to-do suitor who would help support her father's work and invite him to share their household—a vulgar little fantasy, indeed, that she shamefully cast from her whenever she caught it taking hold on her imagination. She had never in her past had the least social ambitions, had always viewed them with contempt; nor did she now wish to assume any sort of rank in the hierarchy. What intrigued her was the sudden intimation that perhaps for her, here in America, the hierarchy did not exist and that she could live in a world of her own making. In that case, was it really such a vulgar thing to be successful? Was it utterly selfish to contemplate the possibility of personal happiness? She felt within her the stirrings of new longings, new hopes.

A couple of weeks later, at one of her Thursdays, Mrs. Moorehouse drew her aside.

"I have a very special request to make of you, Miss Gow. Please don't feel obliged to reply at once." She wanted to know whether Elizabeth would consider taking in charge the instruction of her two youngest daughters, ages six and eight, until such time, of course, when the girls could be sent to a proper school. "I'd leave the program of instruction entirely up to you, though I assume that it would include geography, elocution, penmanship, and, if you could manage it, a touch of solfeggio—enough so that they could read music, or at least recognize the notes."

Seeing Elizabeth's mounting confusion, she paused a moment, then hurried headlong on.

"They are really good girls, but obviously lacking in inspiration as far as their studies are concerned. I have done what I can, but, you know, a mother does not have the right sort of authority when it comes to getting lessons done as they should be done; at least, *I* don't! As for their present governess, well, she was quite adequate for the nursery, but now that the girls are a bit older. . . . I won't say a word against her; she means well, it's just that she has certain personal problems, too, and when I had that nice little chat with you the other day, it occurred to me that you were just what the girls needed. I'm sure you would do them a world of good, Miss Gow, and that they would take to you immediately. And you needn't live in if you don't wish to; we wouldn't require that at all. You could stay with your father, and I would have the carriage sent around for you in the morning, and it would take you back in the evening, just after the girls' tea. But you mustn't answer me now. Take your time to consider the matter, and let me know sometime next week, if you can. We can talk fees then; I'm sure that you will find us appreciative of your services."

The woman's manner was so effusive, her desire so nakedly sincere, that Elizabeth could not bring herself to pronounce her reply. The most she could manage to say was that she would have to discuss the matter with her father.

It was only as she descended the Moorehouse front steps that the full implications of the offer struck home, and she clutched at the handrail to steady herself, to catch her breath.

When she reached home, she was so distraught that her hands trembled as she untied her bonnet.

"You're not looking quite yourself, Miss," Edith remarked as she took charge of her outer garments. "If you wish, I could bring up your supper on a tray."

"I won't have it," her father said firmly. "We have not yet reached the stage where I have to send my daughter out as a governess. We did not come all this way for *that*."

"She said that I could live at home. Still . . ." Her voice faltered.

"Still, it amounts to the same thing. I won't have it." Then, seeing that his daughter was close to tears, he added in a calmer voice, "I am sorry, Bess. Sorry for the confusion and blindness of the woman. Sorry for my having exposed you to it. I simply do not know what is going on in people's minds over here; it is so hard to read their intentions. It is another country, Bess, and I suppose neither of us has quite worked out how things are done."

She went into the front hallway and took down her cloak and bonnet from the clothes stand where Edith had put them. She wanted some fresh air, to take a walk. The alternative was to shut herself in her room.

So much, she thought, for her efforts at "going out in the world." So much for her vulgar little daydreams. The people at Mrs. Moorehouse's accepted her easily enough; they enjoyed listening to her accent, savored her exotic references. But since she wasn't well to do or well born or even particularly striking in appearance, they basically regarded her as some sort of high-level servant. Wasn't that what Mrs. Moorehouse had in mind all the time: engaging her to take care of her youngest girls? Elizabeth herself had fantasized about starting a school of her own, about giving piano lessons in her own home, but hiring herself out as a governess was a very different sort of proposition. Once she was caught up on that circuit, it would be hard to break free. She would be expected to take her meals in the nursery. And later, if she stayed on, in the kitchen, with the rest of the staff. Yes, she would have to refuse. And since those were the terms on which Mrs. Moorehouse had received her, she would have to give up the acquaintance.

The snow was almost gone. A few soiled patches remained, on the shaded side of the street, under the evergreens. One more March rain would wash them away. She would have to think things out again, try to get a grip on her future. The crocuses were out along the riverbank, but the wind was still cold. She drew her cloak more tightly about her. She had been right to seek out people, to resist withdrawing into herself. Yet these were not her people; she felt terribly the lack of someone in whom she could confide. She could not bear putting more burdens upon her father, having him worry about her; he had worries enough of his own, and her job, after all, was to try her best to make things easier for him. She increased her pace to a quick, businesslike tread. I can at least pretend I am going somewhere, she said to herself.

"Well, Bess, things are moving along faster than I expected. It seems Mrs. Gotthelf was right." Mr. Throneberry had dropped by Dr. Gow's basement laboratory that afternoon to explain that he was transferring his business operations to Cincinnati.

"Country's changing," he had explained. "The future lies to the West. I'm dead sorry to leave Philadelphia. Have made many good friends here. Put down roots. So has Mrs. Throneberry. But the business would stagnate if I stayed, and I'm not yet ready to give it up and put myself out to pasture. Too many plans for the future. Too many big ideas. And there are too many people counting on me to follow through. Too many people dependent on my savoir faire."

Mr. Throneberry had talked over his departure with the Society's Board of Governors that afternoon at lunch. They had discussed various ways of keeping the Society afloat in his absence. It was a noble institution and had proved a great boon to the community. "A beacon of intellect, shining its light o'er the city," one of the luncheoneers had said. But the long and the short of it was that its activities would have to be drastically curtailed with Mr. Throneberry's departure, and, that being the case, it was pretty well agreed that there wasn't much point in continuing on a reduced basis.

Wouldn't do justice to the institution's noble concept and past history. Better to go out in glory. Thus, the way matters stood now, the Society would be formally dissolved at the end of the year and the building either sold or leased.

"I guess that leaves you, Dr. Gow, high and dry. That's the worst part of it for me. But a man of your standing is sure to find a solid position soon. And I think that I made it clear at the outset that I couldn't offer you a guarantee of permanence. . . . Anyway, I hope you will stay on in this house until something turns up. There is no sign of Levert returning, at least not for another year or so. And, of course, you can count on me to pay your regular stipend until then, until matters are settled for you." Mr. Throneberry paused a moment, smiled, then looked grave, then added in voice weighted by emotion, "I'm very grateful to you, Dr. Gow. You've been a real brick."

". . . So you see, Bess, things are moving along."

"Oh Papa, I won't be unhappy to leave this house. I have never felt at home here. But where ever will we go?"

"That's to be seen, Bess. It so happens that the university is looking for someone in the natural sciences, and I was just about to drop a gentle hint to Professor Gotthelf. I'll be a bit more forceful in my expression now. The truth is that I am relieved that my connection with the Society is coming to end. I've felt a certain obligation to Mr. Throneberry. I certainly did not want to leave him in the lurch, but the situation has never seemed—What shall I say?—quite *real* to me."

They lived the next two months in patient anticipation of news from the university. Elizabeth had never seen her father more cheerful and relaxed. His final lectures, though sparsely attended (news of the Society's imminent demise had traveled fast), were conscientiously prepared, carefully delivered, and appreciatively received. The faces looking up at him from isolated segments of the hall were alert and attentive and followed, so it seemed, his painstakingly elaborated arguments. He felt that he was leaving the field with full honors.

The evenings he spent in his library, making notes for future projects, and, most particularly, drawing up an outline for a series of lectures designed for advanced students at the university. Levert had unaccountably neglected to put any sort of desk in the library, so Dr. Gow did his writing seated in a large wing-backed armchair with his notebook spread open on his lap. At ten o'clock Elizabeth would fetch him for their prebedtime cup of hot milk, which they took together in the kitchen. Sometimes he would carry his notebook with him, as if he were reluctant to give it up for the day. And sometimes he would attempt to explain to Elizabeth what he had been working at when she had tapped at the library door. At such times she would give him her rapt attention, taking deep pleasure in the play of his seemingly rejuvenated features and in the tone of self-assurance that she heard in his voice. Those late-evening sessions in the soft glow of the oil lamp, at the great knife-scarred kitchen table, with the great dark expanse of soapstone sinks looming in the background, were among her very happiest memories of Philadelphia.

Professor Gotthelf came in person to bring the news.

"Vot am I to say, Dr. Gow? As a papa, I am naturally pleased dot Rupert got der appointment and relieved to have him settled nicely. But as a man of science, I am frankly appalled. Der boy is, as dey say, only half-cooked. I tremble to tink of him on der loose in my laboratories. . . . Vot is more, between der two of us, he does not need the money. Like me, he has got a wife who can pay for all of der groceries and such. But vot vill you? Der decision vasn't mine. It vas out of my hands. Ven I heard that der boy vanted to put forvard his name, I told dem all, I abstain from der voting! Vot else could I do? If dey had any sense, dey vould have chosen you. But let me tell you, Dr. Gow, vot dey had in mind vas dat his future fodder-in-law is der *ricchissimo* Senator Edvin E. Drew. Und to be honest vid you, I tink dat dey don't vant any more foreign accents. Foreign accents make dem nervous. Vun ting you can say for my boy Rupert is dot he speaks good Philadelphian. Like a native! Unlike his papa . . ."

At first, it seemed to Elizabeth that her father had taken the news remarkably well. He reminded her on a number of occasions that America was a large country and that people with his training and background were in short supply; it was simply a question of sitting tight. But as the weeks went by and no offers of employment turned up, he became increasingly moody and remote.

He spent much of the day closeted in the library, emerging only to eat his meals or to take long, purposeless walks on his own. At table he was silent, pushing the food around on his plate in a listless manner and generally avoiding her eyes. When she caught sight of him from the parlor window returning from one of his walks, his figure seemed somehow shrunken and reduced, and his usual elasticity of gait had been replaced by a slight dragging of his left foot. She noticed, too, that he had acquired an apologetic little cough, which further curtailed his conversation and increased her sense of isolation from him.

The dread moment of their day was the arrival of the mail. Each delivery took the form of a brief dramatic skit, repeated daily, with only barely perceptible variations in the actors' individual performances. The play would begin with the postboy's three sharp raps on the front door and his cracked-soprano voice calling out "Poh-host!" A long moment of silence would follow. Then Edith could be heard clumping upstairs from the kitchen and making her way with unhurried tread down the front hallway. Next came the sound of the front door being unbolted: first the top bolt, then the lower one. A murmur of voices could be heard, sometimes punctuated by a coarse boyish laugh, then the dull reverberation of the heavy door being pushed shut. The bolts were more quietly slid back, and another long silence would ensue while Edith presumably turned the letters over in her hands before placing them in the silver salver on the hallway table. Then her receding steps would announce her return to her quarters below. The whole house now assumed an air of suspended animation. Elizabeth would lean forward in her chair, her open book abandoned on her lap while she listened and waited—waited for the sound of the library door opening and of her father's footsteps as he moved slowly, almost reluctantly it seemed, to the hallway table. Then the deep silence as he gathered up the letters, a silence broken only by a single, half-suppressed cough and the retreat, at a somewhat more hasty pace, to his sanctum. The drama ended with the closing of the library door. Only then could Elizabeth manage to regain hold of the words scattered across the page of the open book.

Mr. Throneberry sent out his monthly bank drafts from Cincinnati. The last one arrived two weeks late, accompanied by a letter in which he apologized profusely and explained that he had been away and his new office manager had misunderstood his instructions. The delay added another dimension to their anxieties.

One by one the replies from the colleges and universities drifted in. They were generally respectful (even when they misspelled his name), often complimentary, and invariably negative. A few held out vague hope for an indeterminate future. The president of Princeton University spoke of his desire to increase the size of the faculty over the next few years and would be gratified if he could in time acquire Dr. Gow's services. There was one offer of employment, unsolicited by her father, from a seminary for young ladies somewhere in western Massachusetts—they had gotten his name from a former student now living in Philadelphia. The pay was very modest, and they could not provide him with housing on the grounds, though they were willing to offer an extra fifty dollars per annum toward living expenses. He kept the letter on his dressing-room bureau for almost a week before declining.

Elizabeth was increasingly oppressed by a sense of her own helplessness. What with Mr. Throneberry's monthly stipends and their own as yet untouched savings, they were not suffering from any immediate shortage of funds. Yet Elizabeth half-regretted now that she had not accepted Mrs. Moorehouse's offer. It might have served as a bulwark against the future and, more urgently perhaps, given her something to do. But for her to take on a job now would only increase her father's distress; besides, who knew where she would be living in a few weeks' time? She would have to wait on him to secure an appointment before she could launch out on her own.

"What do you make of this, Bess?" He held aloft a letter.

"Who is it from?"

"Remember Macready? On the boat?"

Her heart skipped a beat. Then she said, "You mean the flowery old gentleman?"

He nodded assent and handed her the letter.

She turned the paper over and glanced at the signature: *Wm. Macready,* written out across the bottom of the page in a big, bold hand, with a decorative flourish underneath.

The letterhead bore the legend "The United States Hotel, Milwaukee, Wisconsin," and beside that was a small engraving of an imposing four-story structure topped off by a cupola. The letter read:

Dear Dr. Gow—

I have just returned from a private dinner at the Governor's mansion in Madison, where I had the pleasure of evoking your name in the company of some of Wisconsin's most distinguished educators and illuminati. More particularly, I had a lengthy conversation with John H. Lathrop, president of the newly established University of Wisconsin, who was familiar with your reputation and expressed great interest in the possibility of your joining the faculty. He and Eleazer Root, Chairman of the Board of Regents, are men of integrity, foresight, and lofty ambition, and are determined to make the fledgling institution into one of the nation's foremost Citadels of Learning. Since I was uncertain of your present professional commitments, I agreed, on their suggestion, to ascertain whether you would consider entertaining a formal communication of interest on their part. Though I am writing now from Madison, please address your reply to me per above.

I trust that all is going well with you. As for myself, after some initial disappointments, owing largely to the recent monetary crisis, I am now embarked on a monumental undertaking that promises to have salubrious effects on the regional economy, and beyond. But we shall, I hope, have occasion to talk of this and other matters anon.

I write in great haste. It is three in the morning, and I leave for Chicago at the break of dawn.

My respectful regards to your daughter.

Faithfully yours. . . .

"Well?"

"How strange it all is, Papa. And coming from Mr. Macready."

"This is a large country, full of strangeness and surprises."

"But Wisconsin! It's almost in Canada, isn't it? What do you think, Papa?"

"I don't know. Besides, it all remains very unclear as yet. Macready is, I think, something of . . . an enthusiast."

"But you will reply, won't you?"

"Of course, Bess. I have to reply."

"And you will tell him. . . ?"

Dr. Gow shrugged his shoulders. "I'll have to wait and see what the Wisconsin people have to say. The illuminati, I think he called them."

"Oh Papa! What about the Indians?"

"Indians? I really don't believe that Indians are much of a question, my dear. Besides, if they are, they should prove a boon for the university. The native population is, I understand, in dire need of decent formal instruction." And he smiled grimly.

Madison, 1852

THEY ARRIVED LATE AT NIGHT. Elizabeth, who had been dozing, was not aware of having entered the town until the coach jolted to a stop and the coachman called down to them through the trap, "Well, good people, here we be!"

He had brought them directly to their lodging house. Leaning out the coach window, Elizabeth saw delineated in the moonlight a plain, no-nonsense, two-story frame building, the entrance lost in shadows beneath a broad expanse of porch. There was a faint glow of light behind a downstairs corner window. Except for that dim solitary beacon, the place seemed submerged in slumber.

Yet as the coachmen began unstrapping their luggage from the roof of the coach, the front door opened, and light flickered across the porch, all the way to the stairs. A woman stood framed in the doorway. She was wearing a dressing gown and a large, shapeless mobcap and held a lantern in her hand. As she moved toward them, her figure cast a monstrous shadow against the side of the house, like a figure in a children's Christmas pantomime.

The woman hastened down the steps and flung out a greeting to the coachman, calling him by name and cheerfully chiding him for being "even more behind time than usual." She then turned her attention to her guests, lifting high her lantern to light their ascent from the vehicle. She was, Elizabeth could now see, well past her prime, but still vigorous in body and spirit—the sort of woman, one could tell at a glance, who was used to doing things for herself.

Elizabeth alighted first, handed down by the coachman; then came her father, who moved with deliberation, taking a firm grip on the handrail before tentatively positioning his foot on the carriage step. In the flickering lamplight he appeared frail and travel worn, and the landlady lunged forward instinctively to relieve him of his hand luggage. He declined her assistance with a shake of the head.

"You'll be bone weary after that trip," she said to him. "Unless you and the young lady would be wanting a cup of tea or anything, I'll take you directly to your rooms. Mind the steps now. Here, let me lead the way."

The rooms were, like their proprietor, neat, cheerful, and straightforward. "I've closed the shutters against the mosquitoes. They're fierce here in summer. Breakfast is at half-seven. It's served below in the front parlor; you'll hear the bell. I'll bring up the gentleman's shaving water at seven. There are only two other guests at present, both legislature gentlemen. One of them snores something terrible, but I put him at the back, by the landing, and he shouldn't bother you much. And Miss, if you do hear a snufflinglike sound outside your door, don't be afeared. It's only the dog. I'd have him out in the yard, but he's old and lame and gets chewed up by the neighbor's hound. He came all the way with us from Harrisburg, Pennsylvania, following the wagon on foot, and is the only member of my family still around the place, so, you see, I sort of spoil him. I figure he hasn't very much further to go."

On arising from bed the next morning, Elizabeth threw open the shutters and looked out on her new homeland. The sky was a wash of pale blue and already shimmering faintly in the heat. She had been told that the lodging house was on the town's principal thoroughfare; in that case, the street remained as yet a conduit for the city fathers' unfulfilled aspirations. A scattered array of primly modest frame buildings shyly confronted one another from opposite sides of the street, while between lay naked plots of land, still raw from recent clearing. Through the gaps one perceived fragmentary views of distant hills.

Leaning out the window, Elizabeth could see at the end of the street the handsome facade of the new State House, with its obligatory porticos and cupola. Though it was a workday morning, few people seemed to be about. Several buildings down a man was loading lumber onto a cart, another was taking down the shutters on the front of a dry goods store, and directly across the way a woman had just this moment come out onto the porch with a broom in her hands and was standing there, gazing pensively into the sky. A couple of hawks, slowly turning in the air high above the rooftops, served to emphasize the stillness of the scene. The place seemed almost preternaturally quiet, and Elizabeth found herself holding her breath to catch the underlying layer of sounds—the crow of a cock from a distant backyard, the faint clatter of a board being loaded into a cart, the dull hum of a fly alighting on her windowsill. . . . An aura of unreality pervaded the scene, bleached of its color by the glare of the summer sun. It was almost as if she were looking at a picture or engraving of the town, rather than at the town itself, and for a fleeting moment she wondered whether she might not be still asleep. But the dreamlike illusion was suddenly shattered by her father's dry cough in the neighboring room.

They had just sat down to breakfast when there appeared in the doorway a lanky youth of sixteen or seventeen, decked out in his Sunday finery. He stood there indecisively, twisting his cap in his hands; then, gathering courage, he plunged into the room and made his way self-consciously to their table. There he paused again, cleared his throat, and addressing the jam jar announced that he was Professor Becker's son, who had been sent to fetch them. "I'm early. No need for you to hurry any. I'll just go and sit on the front porch 'til you're ready."

The landlady, who had observed the scene with amused concern, nodded her approval. "Yes, you go along, Jake, and let the people eat their breakfast in peace. And while you're waiting out there, you might just as well take a couple of biscuits with you."

"Very kind of you, Ma'am, don't mind if I do." And then, as if sensing that this response was somewhat lacking in polish, he added, "Thank you very much, Mrs. Winterhoven."

"He's a good boy," she confided to them when he had left the room. "And a clever boy, too. Built a clock he did, built it all by himself, when he was maybe twelve or thirteen years old. Mostly out of wood, works and all. Keeps pretty good time, too. I've seen it myself."

The carriage was little more than a domesticated farm cart. Jake handed Elizabeth a light blanket to wrap around herself. "It's too hot for this, but the roads are mighty dry and dusty, and some ladies like something to cover their clothing with."

The boy sat bolt upright on his seat and cracked the whip smartly over the horse's head. They started off down the street at a brisk trot.

Dr. Gow leaned forward to inquire whether they would be passing by the university.

"Yes sir, we will. In fact," young Becker pointed with his whip, "that's it right over yonder."

"Where? I don't see anything."

"Well, there isn't all that much to see. Not *yet* there isn't. Except that clearing over there. And if you look sharp now, you can make out the foundation of the new student lodging house, over by the big elm. And there's going to be a whole group of buildings round about. The architect brought his drawings over to our house the other day and spread them out on the dining-room table. It's going to be right impressive when it's all properly built and finished."

"But where are the classes held now?"

"Oh, they'll be mostly at the Ladies' Seminary building in town and at various places hereabouts."

"I see." The doctor sat back on the bench. He looked pensive.

They turned off the main street and almost immediately entered the countryside.

Elizabeth wondered: What was it about this New World landscape that filled her with anguish? The vegetation was not so very different from that of her native England; nor was it simply a matter of scale—though the horizons were oppressively vast, and the sense of a limitless expanse of landscape beyond those horizons did at times seem a little uncanny. But it was the primitive power that she felt enfolded just below the surface of the earth that marked the true difference, and the awareness that mankind was here only on tolerance. In England, no matter how savage or desolate the natural scene, one knew that it was a part of the human environment. There was no place in England that the human eye had not penetrated, where the imagination had not ventured; there was no corner of the island, no matter how remote, that had not been absorbed into the human consciousness and endowed with layers upon layers of age-old memories. On encountering the barren, wind-swept deserts of this new land, one felt the primacy of the soil, the ineffable strangeness of man's presence, and the fragility of his hold. Gazing out at the great line of trees that stood just beyond the freshly cleared fields along the road, one could not help feeling that nature was simply waiting, patiently poised to reclaim all.

Here, in a scenery that yielded no traces of Roman roads or feudal strongholds, Elizabeth was overcome by a chilling sense of antiquity—an antiquity that reached well before and beyond mankind's fugitive efforts at civilization. That great flock of crows, sleek and efficient among the corn, suddenly appeared to her eyes as survivors of that earlier age, before the intrusion of wandering bands of Indians, before the arrival of settlers, and she saw in them the sure and rightful inheritors of the land.

The intervals between the houses grew progressively longer, and the acres of young corn gradually predominated over the rows of brassicas and potatoes. The dwellings, frank faced and unpretentious, edged as close as possible to the road. One sensed that their inhabitants dreaded isolation more than they cherished privacy. As the carriage passed, children and dogs came racing out of nowhere, window curtains parted ever so slightly, and in one instance a woman boldly stepped out onto her front porch and, shielding her eyes from the sun, took them in with a long, hungry stare. Elizabeth shrank back instinctively from the public scrutiny; the boy responded with a gay flourish of his whip, and Dr. Gow stared straight ahead, seemingly lost in thought.

Some half-dozen people were gathered on the Becker porch to greet their arrival. As the cart drew up, a man disengaged himself from the group and hurriedly descended the steps. He was tall and massively built, and his russet-colored hair, clear blue eyes, and beaklike nose bespoke his relationship to the young driver. Except for the rugged work boots obtruding from the bottom of his trouser legs, he was formally attired in dark broadcloth.

Franz Becker, professor of German and French, welcomed them to Wisconsin, to the university, and to his home. "It being vacation time, we thought we'd have an informal gathering here at my place, just to get acquainted. Everyone managed to come except for Professor Conover, our ancient languages man, who sends you greetings and regrets. He's having a well dug at his farm, been at it for more than a month, and, as he puts it, expects to cross the Rubicon sometime this morning. The rest of the faculty are all with us on the porch and eager to meet you. Let me give you a hand down, Miss; mind the step, it's rather narrow."

Elizabeth took them all in at a glance. Only one dark-suited gentleman was young, almost a boy in appearance; the other men were all about her father's age, except for a white-haired figure, clearly older than the rest, who was standing a little apart from the others and who looked on through glittering, gold-framed pince-nez, a benevolent smile on his lips.

They stepped forward one by one to introduce themselves and to shake hands with her father and give a little bow of the head to her: Orestes Mac-Donald, professor of philosophy and rhetoric; William Smith (the boyish-looking one, who on closer inspection appeared to be in his midtwenties), mathematics; David Reid, physiology and hygiene; and Ezra Carmichael, chemistry and natural history. Carmichael was leaving for California in a week's time, and it was his position that Dr. Gow would be assuming. The group now stood aside to make way for the older gentleman, whose smile had grown to illuminate his whole face.

"And I, Miss Gow, Dr. Gow, am John Lathrop, chancellor of the university, professor of civil politics and ethics, sometime instructor in political economy, drillmaster in sophomore Latin, assistant architect, assistant to the head gardener's assistant, and general factotum. We have exchanged much correspondence, Dr. Gow. I am delighted at last to make your acquaintance."

The chancellor was a small man, a head shorter than the other men present, shorter than Elizabeth herself, yet so confident, so dapper, so self-contained that he wore with ease the mantle of authority. Elizabeth thought him the daintiest man she had ever met. From his finely spun white hair brushed back neatly from a lofty brow to the soft sheen of his black leather pumps, he presented a picture of immaculate grooming. His eyes, of a pale celestial blue, shone out from beneath two snowy billows of eyebrows. She was particularly fascinated by his hands, which were as pink, smooth skinned, and delicately articulated as those of a late-Renaissance Madonna.

He reached out to each of them in turn and clasped their hands in both of his, murmuring in a warm, resonant voice, "Welcome, welcome." Then, stepping back a couple of paces, he lifted one hand aloft in what Elizabeth momentarily mistook for a gesture of benediction, but which the little congregation understood as simple request for silence, and after clearing his throat with a discreet little cough, he launched into an oration.

It was a meticulously prepared little speech, much used and long since committed to memory, though gracefully amended for the present occasion.

The chancellor greeted Dr. Gow on behalf of the Wisconsin Board of Regents, the faculty of the university, and those good citizens of the state, including the governor and the legislators, who helped bring about the establishment of the university and supported its ideals. Since the university was a new institution, these ideals retained their purity of intention, unsullied by compromise and unfettered by tradition. As someone recently arrived from Europe and steeped in the rich heritage of Old World scholarship and learning, Dr. Gow would appreciate to the full the peculiar responsibility that this pristine quality bestowed on all those actively involved in setting the future course for the university. They were founders, not followers, and it was their weighty charge to define by their teachings the values by which the university was to function and to justify these values by their personal example.

"The university is the depository and almoner of the intellectual treasures of the ages—not only of the ages past, but of the present age as well. As such, it is the foremost agent of progress. There are, in our glittering new republic, those among us who fear progress, tremble at the thought of change, who proclaim that the advances of man and science are impious deviations from the Divine Plan. Yet to deny the concept of human progress or to assign arbitrary limits to this progress would surely be to allege the imperfection of this Plan—to assert the Supreme Being's deliberate withdrawal from the governance of His world. God created Heaven and Earth and saw that it was good; and He placed man in the center of this, His creation. And man, working through Nature, and in concord with its innermost harmonies and functions, has forged civilization and asserted the primacy of progress. Indeed, it is the natural sciences"—here the speaker inclined his noble head toward Dr. Gow—"that provide the foundation on which all great civilizations are built. An understanding of the natural sciences—that is, an understanding of the manner and means by which the Divine Scheme of things is revealed to man—is essential to an understanding of mankind. Without reference to this knowledge and a reverent respect for nature's laws, all efforts in moral philosophy, literature, and the arts become mere travesties of life, gothic extravagances, fit subjects for ridicule and scorn."

He spoke of the fusion of the Old World with the New and of how the traditions of the past would be subjected to "a refining fire that would purify them of all corruption and imperfections." He dared to hope that the faculty, dedicated to the instruction of idealistic and impressionable youths, would "cleave to its own highest aspirations and ambitions, and bring into being, here on the shores of Lake Mendota, a temple of learning, consecrated by the love of truth and a reverence for knowledge."

As the chancellor spoke, his voice steadily increased in resonance and volume until it seemed to Elizabeth that the Becker porch had become a podium from which the speaker was addressing a great gathering somewhere beyond. Instinctively, she turned her head to take a quick glimpse at the neighboring field, where she spied a brown and white heifer, peacefully grazing; and nearer at hand, between the house and the road, two geese were staring up at them with rapt attention. She then shot a look at her father to see how he was responding to the scene. His features were fixed in an expression of profound solemnity, but she thought that she detected in his eyes a sharp glint of amusement.

When the chancellor had finished speaking, there was a moment of appreciative silence, in service for applause, and then Dr. Gow responded with a few words of thanks delivered in what now seemed almost like an undertone.

The last words were hardly out of his mouth when, as if on cue, the porch door swung open, and a woman appeared bearing a large tray on which reposed an earthenware pitcher and an assortment of glasses. "Lemonade!" she sang out and smiled serenely on the general assembly. She was an outsize figure of a woman, tall, sturdily built, with streaks of gray in her tightly drawn-back hair, which framed her massive head like a helmet. Her eyes sparkled with avid curiosity. Professor Becker greeted her with, "Martha, well met!" and turning to the Gows said simply, by way of introduction, "My wife."

Behind her hovered three other wives, somewhat diminished by Martha's formidable presence. They were introduced in turn as Mrs. Carmichael, Mrs. Reid, and Mrs. Smith. They intoned their greetings in sweet, cheerful voices, gave in turn a little bob of the head (which Elizabeth was coming to recognize as the democratic, New World form of the Old World curtsey), and swiftly withdrew into the background, where they could watch the proceedings undisturbed. Mrs. Smith, the wife of the boyish-looking mathematician was the shyer, more self-conscious of the three. She blushed visibly on being introduced and cast at Elizabeth an eager, penetrating look. From the ripeness of her form and the faint shadows under her eyes, Elizabeth surmised that the young woman was enceinte.

Martha deposited her tray with a clatter and a triumphant cry of "There now!" Then she went over to Elizabeth and to the young woman's consternation gave her a long, tight hug.

"My, it's good to have another young one amongst us. We need more youth here." And laughing at the girl's confusion, she continued, "Don't you mind my forwardness, Miss Gow. We are all in this together, so to speak, and there's no use in standing on ceremony. I know that we shall be great friends—unless, of course, we quarrel! Anyway, until we do—and I trust that we never shall—you might just as well call me Martha, and I'll call you Elizabeth, or Beth, or Bess."

The bold frontal attack had caught Elizabeth completely off guard. She felt awkward and stiff in the older woman's embrace and was sure that Martha had sensed her resistance. Yet she had almost succumbed! For a moment, with her head pressed against Martha's ample bosom, she had felt a pang of anguish, akin to pleasure; she had been completely disoriented by the warmth and givingness of the woman's body, and by the exoticism of her personal smell: a mixture of freshly laundered cotton, perspiration, carbolic soap, and a faint but pungent medley of various barnyard scents. Something within Elizabeth wanted to linger a while in the mysterious haven of this stranger's embrace, but like a swimmer suddenly overcome by a wave, she instinctively fought her way clear. Her conventional English upbringing with its dislike of unexpected intimacies reasserted itself. So too did her fear of being dominated.

As Elizabeth was to learn, Martha made no effort to moderate her massive physical presence. Her gestures were expansive, her pronouncements emphatic, her laughter loud. She despised pettiness in all forms, whether it had to do with luncheon fare or schemes for the future. Her opinions were

presented as passionate convictions, and she looked on careful reasoning—
"hairsplitting," she called it—as moral cowardice. Perhaps the vehemence of
her opinions was owing to the fact that she did not fully trust them and felt
that they had to be cuffed about like naughty children. She would often exchange one passionate conviction for another, and when the contradiction
was pointed out, laugh heartily and proclaim that such inconsistency was
sure proof of her ability to listen to good advice. She was, she insisted, never
afraid to change her mind. In her heart of hearts Martha did not place much
faith in book knowledge and regarded most academic people as lacking in
that most important of intellectual qualities, Common Sense. This was one
conviction that she kept pretty much to herself, not, as she once explained to
Elizabeth, out of fear of offending—for as she often said, she was never afraid
of ruffling a few feathers—but out of tenderheartedness. She knew from
long experience that bookish menfolk were ill-equipped to deal with the
hard realities of daily living, and as she saw it, it was her role, the role of all
good wives, to help restore balance in this tipsy community of teachers and
scholars by providing a solid ballast of practical knowledge and sensible, loving care. Though she never claimed to be an intellectual and admitted that
she often lost the thread of an argument in the heat of a debate, she never
doubted the sureness of her instincts or questioned the purity of her intentions. She liked people, meant well by them, and trusted that they would
perceive that she was basically on their side. Her utter frankness was, as she
saw it, a pledge of goodwill.

"The ladies are preparing lunch inside," Martha said to Elizabeth, "Won't
you lend us a hand?" She opened the door wide and led the way. "We'll leave
the gentlemen to their academical gossip." Then added sotto voce, "It will
give us a chance to talk about the things that really matter around here."

Elizabeth felt out of her element in the large, cluttered kitchen; she stared
about in confusion at the pots, pans, and utensils that mingled promiscuously on the tables and tops of cabinets or hung down aggressively from wall
racks and rafters. Martha took in her disorientation at a glance and did not
press her into service. Her own hands moved with masterful assurance over
the surfaces, meting out quick culinary justice to the assembled materials,
while she managed to keep an eye on her helpmates and to quiz Elizabeth on
her plans and prospects. Mrs. Carmichael and Mrs. Reid had been put in

charge of the baking; they hovered about the stove, peering into the oven every now and then and issuing, with flushed countenances, excited little reports on the progress of the pies. The youthful Mrs. Smith was meticulously arranging food on platters, a faraway look in her eyes. Elizabeth stood beside her hostess and watched with unfeigned admiration as Martha rapidly made order out of chaos.

"Are you much of a gardener?" Martha asked. "I don't mean ornamentals, I mean kitchen gardening—cabbages and the like. It's essential to have a garden around here. Buying vegetables at the market is absolutely ruinous. Besides, marketing would take up all your day. Most people hereabouts grow their own, and any surplus goes for barter. . . . Well, don't worry, I'll give you a few pointers, and it will all become second nature to you in no time. Truth is, I love rooting about in gardens, anybody's garden. And I love giving advice. . . .

"The important thing is to find a house with a nice piece of land. It needn't be a big plot, but you'll want it well drained and with lots of direct sunlight, of course. Now you be sure to keep that in mind. Don't go and get a place without a good garden plot, no matter how nice the house or how inexpensive it may be. Believe me, without a good garden plot it's *too* expensive, whatever the asking price.

"You still unattached? Well, that's only natural considering how young you are and that you've been traveling around in foreign parts. No matter what they say, traveling is no way to find a husband. You've got to be settled in a place for a while in order to choose properly. Unfortunately, there don't seem to be many marriageable men about here of late. It seems to run in cycles. Just a few years back most of the men were single and looking for wives. Nowadays, however, they come out here fully equipped, all ready to settle down and start a family. Or else they are just passing through, and it really isn't possible to give them a good look-over. No point in grabbing someone on the run, like picking a pig in a poke. Of the faculty, only Conover is unmarried. He's under thirty-five and has a nice piece of property, but I'm afraid he's a dead loss as a marriage prospect. A confirmed bachelor if ever I saw one and fixed in his ways. Then there's the new Lutheran minister. He's young and from what I hear very much on the market, but—well, you'll have to see him for yourself to get the picture."

She questioned Elizabeth about her father's health. The young woman was disconcerted by the directness and intensity of the questioning. Besides, she did not know what to say. She was aware that her father had been sickly of late, but she had never thought of him as being really *sick*. True, his cough had been with him for several months now—so long that she had come to accept it as part of his personality, like a nervous tic. They had told each other that he was simply run down, in need of a bit of rest, and once the two of them had settled into their new home and his professional anxieties for the future had been more or less laid aside, his former vigor would return. She was alarmed that Martha should regard him as a semi-invalid, or even as someone in frail health. It occurred to her that the older woman might possess a particularly morbid cast of mind: she had known such people at school. But as she thought back on the solicitous manner with which people had been treating her father of late, she began to have terrible doubts. In her confusion she heard herself protesting that her father was, in fact, getting considerably stronger by the day. Yet, as she said the words, their untruthfulness came home to her, and she suddenly felt faint with anguish.

"Well, I trust that you're right," Martha replied. "But in any case, remember that you now have friends in these parts, and if you need any help, we're here to give it. Don't try to take too much on yourself, young woman. That's only common sense."

On the way home, Elizabeth watched her father closely. The visit to the Beckers seemed to have aroused him from his lethargy, and though he appeared troubled and frowned to himself a number of times, she preferred these signs of turbulence and agitation to the terrible "absences" of the past few weeks.

"Well, Bess," he exclaimed on their return to the lodging house, "it seems that the university has a present enrollment of fourteen students, men and boys, and has no fixed classrooms or laboratories. We are, as our chancellor might put it, at the very dawn of discovery."

"It *is* a beginning, Papa. And you will have a hand in shaping things. At least the people here respect you. They know your work, and they appreciate your presence."

He gave a hollow little laugh. It was a strange sound. "How far do I have to go to find respect, to be appreciated? Eh, Bess? To the ends of the earth, it seems. I might just as well be a charlatan in a good suit of clothes."

"That's not fair, Father!" She was genuinely indignant.

He realized that he had spoken carelessly, pettishly, and sought to make amends. "You are right, Bess. They are certainly good men, upright men, and I do believe that they mean well by me. And in spite of their rough edges, they are by no means ignorant. Carmichael has done some very competent work, really quite interesting, and I am told that Conover has written a Latin grammar that is used in the best schools throughout the country. Moreover, they are full of high ideals, which is no small thing. But it is *their* country, Bess, not mine—at least not yet mine—and you must forgive me if I occasionally express how out of place I sometimes feel in it. It is, I suppose, a question of old dogs and new tricks. And speaking of new tricks, did you hear that I am expected to teach a course in *agriculture?* I cannot quite get used to frontier living."

"You can, Papa, and you will. In time. And you will help to make something of the place. People will come because *you* are here. You'll see! It's all very rough and raw right now because it is all so very new, but in a few years it will grow and expand and become a distinguished seat of learning. Just think, Papa, of the University of Padua in the thirteenth century, and how rough and raw it must have seemed back then!"

"The University of Padua?" He laughed lightly now, without irony or constraint. "The University of *Padua!* Now there's a delicious comparison for you! Wherever did you come up with that one, Bess? Or was I dozing during a part of our chancellor's oration? Ah, my dearest Bess, I am glad to have you with me; I don't know how I would get by without you. You certainly have the right attitude for this adventure of ours, and I shall do my best to learn from you. Yet," his merriment suddenly subsided, "yet I sometimes feel that I have gone as far as I can go and can't go a step farther."

They found a house on the outskirts of town. It had been built two years before by a young Bavarian couple. He was a master carpenter by trade and intended to do a bit of dairy farming on the side. She died in childbirth the year after the house was finished. He had never learned English properly and decided to go to Minnesota, where he had relatives. The barn and pasture had been immediately sold to the neighboring farmer. Now only the house was left. Because the owner was impatient to move on, Dr. Gow was able to buy it for four hundred dollars.

It was a small, solidly built house. From the road it resembled any number of plain, clapboard-covered farmhouses in the vicinity, but once they stepped inside the front door, its individuality was revealed in numerous little touches that immediately won Elizabeth's gratitude and affection. A generously proportioned oak staircase in the hallway had a decorative newel post, entwined by a carved vine leaf motif that was repeated over the mantelpiece in the front parlor. Downstairs there were two corner cabinets with glass doors, and generous window seats in the parlor overlooking the road. The upstairs had never been completely finished off, except for one small room, paneled in pine and painted white, with a leaf and acorn pattern stenciled in green at the ceiling. The room had been intended as the nursery. Elizabeth immediately requisitioned it for her sewing area. There were two other bedrooms upstairs. Dr. Gow insisted on dividing his in two with a partition, to make a small study—though the space subsequently proved too hot for much use in summer, when he did most of his reading and correspondence in the room downstairs newly designated as the library.

A month after they moved in, their furniture arrived from the warehouse in Philadelphia. The mahogany sideboard was somewhat overbearing in the low-ceilinged dining room, yet there it inevitably came to rest. As for the larger and more imposing of the two chaise longues, it was trundled from room to room before being retired to the attic storage space. But Elizabeth managed to find a place for all the knickknacks. Glass paperweights, Devonshire figurines, potpourri jars, framed cameos and silhouettes, inlaid boxes for various shapes and sizes—objects that in England had meant little or noting to her, that she had regarded as clutter from abandoned memories, now emerged from their wrappings strangely transformed, appearing to the young woman's astonished gaze both utterly new and poignantly familiar, like childhood playmates encountered by chance in the street many years later. She reclaimed each of them with a pounding heart and distributed them strategically about the house, where they became not so much me-

mentos of the past as bulwarks against the future. For the first time since ar-
riving in America—indeed, for the first time in her life—Elizabeth found
herself preparing a home.

Her father seemed disappointingly indifferent to these preparations. He
would on request help her push about a sofa or hang a mirror, and occasionally he would volunteer a comment, "It's pleasant to see your grandmother's
teapot again," or "Don't you think the rug is too close to the fireplace?" But
most of the time he would respond to her suggestions with "Do whatever
you think best, my dear. I have complete faith in your judgment." He did,
however, get involved with the installation of the new cookstove and spent
almost the whole afternoon discussing flues and drafts with the two burly
Irishmen who had brought it all the way from Milwaukee. Yet on the whole
he remained aloof from the proceedings, leaving Elizabeth with the feeling
that she was playing a solitary game, like furnishing a dollhouse.

She was at long last settling in. It gave her a sense of satisfaction to refer
to people as "neighbors," to be able to follow the thread of local gossip, and,
on one occasion, to put a wagon load of bedraggled strangers on the right
route for Lake Waubesa.

Tuesday was her shopping day. She would hang a basket over her arm and
walk into town to do those little errands that did not require the use of the
trap. At the dry goods store, Mr. Murray now greeted her by name, and
when they had discussed her needs and assembled her purchases before
them, he would draw out his great black ledger from beneath the counter,
spread it open with a solemn, ritualistic gesture, and, murmuring beneath
his breath "Now let's see," begin to record each of the items under her very
own name written in large copperplate letters on the top of the page. She
liked to know that her transactions were being inscribed in Mr. Murray's
book, along with those of other respectable citizens of the town. To be in
Mr. Murray's book, safely tucked away under his counter, was to her truly
belonging.

From there she usually proceeded directly to Mr. Shaw at the Overland
Stage office for letters and parcels; to Mr. Bertollucci for special cooking
needs, such as herbs and spices; to Lewis's Emporium for pencils and letter

paper and drawing material. En route there were the usual faces, perceived in passing: the white-bearded "messenger boy" seated on a barrel outside the print shop of the *Madison Gazette*; the Negro porter, dressed in a threadbare blue tunic, in the doorway of Mason's Hotel; the woman selling posies on the corner near the barber shop ("One for your sweetie, two for a dime!"); the local drunk wedged into the bricked-up window recess of the Farmer's Bank of Wisconsin, his bleary gaze fixed with mournful avidity on the trembling swing doors of O'Hare's Saloon directly across the street. These and other familiar faces contributed to the texture of her Tuesday expeditions, to her sense of place, and to the perception of a discernible pattern in her existence. They reminded her, by their very repetition, that she was part of a community.

And then there were the people who came to her. There was Mr. Levi, the Hebrew peddler, who would appear at her back door during the last week of every month, bearing a full supply of mercery goods—needles, threads, buttons, and clasps—along with detailed reports of the climactic conditions as far away as central Iowa, delivered in a softly caressing tone of voice and with an occasionally peculiar turn of phrase that hinted at translation from another, more ornamental language and that infused the remainder of her day with a faint fragrance of exoticism. And there was the scissors-and-knife man, a taciturn and slightly sinister figure, his head as bare as the round grinding stone on his cart. His arrival was always unexpected; he seemed to come from nowhere and departed hellbent for oblivion. The iceman and his boy came from the other side of town, and by the time their wagon reached the Gow house, it contained more straw than ice; during the summer months it left a thin trail of water on the dusty road. And there was a steady stream of miscellaneous itinerants—Bible salesmen and religious pamphleteers, pot menders and odd-job men, and just plain beggars with nothing to offer but tales of hard luck and phantom hopes—each of them simply passing through and never to be seen again, but all of them representative of their types and conditions and providing a sort of continuum. Their comings and goings set the house in motion while bestowing on it an air of permanence. And as she stood in the doorway, watching the latest of these traveling people disappear around the bend in the road, Elizabeth felt that she was at last putting down roots.

And then there was the garden. The roots there, tentative as they might be, testified to a commitment to the future. Although the pasture had been sold to the farmer across the road, the house lot retained a half-acre of land, part of which had already been established as a small kitchen garden. As a gesture of welcome, the neighbor brought over his team to turn the soil and to lay down a full load of manure.

That first spring Martha came as promised to help with the planting and threw herself into the task with her characteristic vigor, tucking up her skirts and trudging about intrepidly in the freshly turned soil. She marked out rows with a hoe and went down on her knees to make sure the seeds were properly in place. Peas were pressed into the ground with a firm finger, and carrots poured from a beneficent palm were then covered with handfuls of soil and patted down. "It's dirty work," Martha proclaimed enthusiastically.

Elizabeth found herself fetching and carrying—seeds, tools, sticks to mark the rows, and pail after pail of water—or hovering above Martha's kneeling form and nodding assent to a steady outpouring of earnest advice and buoyant predictions of disaster.

"Mostly you'll be feeding the rabbits. A fence will help, but not much. You could use a dog, maybe two, one to keep the other up to mark. It is late for the peas; they will probably burn away unless we get a really good rainfall in the next few days, which isn't very likely. Now don't you forget to put those little paper collars around the peppers, or the cutworms will get them for sure." Crouching there in the dirt, she suddenly threw back her head and laughed. "Now isn't it all a misery! But don't worry, Bess, you'll survive just fine. Somehow one always does, unless you just quit in disgust—and I can see that you're not a quitter."

Elizabeth was grateful for Martha's help, especially since her father had not as yet regained his full strength and tended to tire quickly working in the sun. She was grateful, too, for the older woman's companionship. Over the past few months she had increasingly felt the lack of female friends, people in whom she could confide. Of course, she could discuss things with her father; he was always interested in anything she had to say. But she was reluctant to reveal to him any of her anxieties for fear that he would worry excessively over them. He had a tendency of late to become particularly upset if he felt unable to answer any of her needs—even on occasions losing his temper and accusing her of being inept or overdemanding. She understood his frustration and sympathized with him, but it meant that she had to be always on her guard in their conversations together, making sure that she let nothing slip out that could in any way be taken as a challenge or a reproof. For example, she had been careful not to tell him about her intention to do the garden that morning in case he should insist on returning early from the university to assist in the work. He would undoubtedly be cross when he came back to find the planting done; he would quiz her sharply about the individual plantings and scold her for laying out the beds all wrong. But he would be too weary at day's end to take her dereliction to heart. And secretly, unacknowledged even to himself, he would be relieved to be spared the labor.

With Martha she felt no such conversational constraints. Elizabeth could give voice to her minor anxieties and complaints without fear of unleashing unwonted emotions. Admittedly, Martha's physical size could be intimidating at times; the way she towered over one was not conducive to the exchange of intimacies. Yet despite her size and the twenty-year difference in their ages—as well as the older woman's intermittent efforts to assume a motherly posture in regard to her young friend—Elizabeth found herself replicating the same sort of casual relationship that she had formed with some of the girls at school. In Martha's company she fell back into that freedom of expression that is usually the prerogative of youth, when one is all too willing to test the boundaries of friendship and one's capacities for understanding. It was, Elizabeth knew, a relationship different from real friendship—the sort of friendship she had yet to experience and could only infer. But if it was not real friendship, it was at least a semblance of the real thing and as such brought her some small quotient of emotional relief.

Here in Elizabeth's kitchen garden the relationship between the two women revealed all its perilous nervosity. Martha strode through the freshly turned soil with the air of a barbarian chieftain making his triumphant way through the smoldering ruins of a subjugated town. In her hand she brandished Elizabeth's new hoe; she stopped here and there to indicate a good place to lay out a seed bed, vigorously scoring the ground to mark the spot, and for the sheer pleasure of running the gleaming blade through the yielding earth. She seemed wholly in her element, whereas Elizabeth, trudging behind and clutching her skirts to keep them from trailing in the dirt, felt clumsy and inadequate, miserably distracted by the thought that her shoes would need a thorough cleaning at day's end. The young woman noted with chagrin that the hoe she had purchased last week and that had struck her at the time as a particularly graceful example of its kind, with its smoothly turned oak handle tapering nicely toward the snugly fitted ferule, had in Martha's masterful grip somehow shrunk in size and changed, as if by magic, from a noble lance to a plebeian broadsword.

"If I were you," Martha sang out, "I'd forget about planting more peas. It's already too late in the season; you'll be lucky if you get much sweet corn. . . . Squash will do you fine. And it keeps well through the winter, better than carrots. You might put the squash along the edge here and among the corn. . . . And Bess, don't forget to ask that man across the way—Beasley, isn't it?—for more manure. The soil's poor. No, not really poor, but you can't ever get enough good fresh manure into it, especially when it's just starting out." And she smiled knowingly at Elizabeth as if to say, "Well, that's the way the world is, and we just have to recognize the fact, don't we?"

Elizabeth instinctively averted her gaze. She was irritated by Martha's smile and its implied complicity, by her authoritative tone of voice, and by the way in which she placed herself squarely in the middle of the garden, almost seeming to straddle it with her personality. She was irritated, too, by her own irritation, by having to fight back an impulse to say something unkind or cutting to her friend, to perversely resist her advice, to insist on doing things her own way, however wrong or inappropriate that way might be. Martha's efforts at being motherly reduced Elizabeth to a rebellious and obstinate child. When she lifted her eyes again, the dark look of petulance had given way to a soft blush of shame, and she heard herself murmuring eager words of assent, mingled with half-formed phrases of gratitude.

"Mercy, Bess, there's no need to thank me. After all, we're friends, aren't we? And I know how strange and foreign all this must seem to you. Why, when I first came out here, I felt the same as you do. Had to learn everything anew. I was brought up in Salem, Massachusetts. Not a city perhaps, like London or Boston, but nonetheless a settled and civilized place, very different I assure you from the wilds of Wisconsin. Franz's folks were peasants back in the Old Country, and though he was born in Connecticut and went to the seminary in New Haven, he has good peasant blood running strong in his veins. For me, however, the change to rural life wasn't easy, and I had to learn to cope with things—how to keep a house going without regular servants or dependable help of most any sort, and how to get along without the little comforts and benefits of town living. And how to grow a garden! Oh, you learn all sorts of new things out here. And you learn to get along with all sorts of people. The fact that you, like me, come from a genteel background and are the wife—or rather the daughter—of a professor at the university is all very well, but it doesn't mean that you can hold yourself aloof from your neighbors. No matter who they are, you've got to keep on civil terms with them. You may not like them, you may not approve of their ways of doing things, you may not even understand their language, or they yours, but somehow you have got to deal with them because they *are* your neighbors. That's the big difference about living out here on the edge of the world and living in a civilized town. On the whole, Bess, you'll find they are decent enough people (with some notable exceptions, of course!) who really do appreciate your efforts to be friendly and helpful to them; and goodness knows they have a lot to offer in return, not only in the way of hard practical matters, but in a sort of frontier wisdom that comes only from experience. Oh, it takes some getting used to before you learn to strike the right notes with them, but you'll do just fine, Bess, if you give yourself the chance. You're naturally shy, just like me. But you don't put on airs. And if you could only learn to take things a bit easier and show people that they can't get at you, they'll accept you right enough for what you are. And you've got me on your side, Bess, if ever you need help or advice. Or simply a shoulder to cry on."

So Elizabeth let her friend have her own way without opposition and struggled mightily to conceal any signs of her own ignoble rebelliousness. She knew instinctively that for all Martha's tactlessness and brazen self-assurance, the woman was wondrously sensitive to any slights, real or imagined, and that she would have to be as careful with her friend as with her father.

Noticing the abstracted expression on the young woman's face, Martha smiled sympathetically.

"Yes, it all takes a bit of getting used to. But just think, Bess, in a couple of months you'll be filling your apron with green beans, stepping daintily over cucumbers, young melons, and winter squash. . . . And once you've worked the soil with own hands and tasted the fruits thereof, you'll truly feel right at home here. You'll feel yourself quite the native!"

Martha seemed to be shimmering in the early summer sunlight; only her shadow before her on the upturned soil seemed solid and substantial. It was to the shadow that Elizabeth addressed her reply: "Yes, I suppose so. . . . But of course you are right!"

Madison, 1853

WITH MARTHA'S HELP and her own dutiful attentions Elizabeth's garden did indeed prosper, and by early September she was busy putting aside in the cellar provisions against the coming winter. The process brought her satisfaction, but little enjoyment. As a naturalist's daughter, she took a certain academic interest in the growth and generation of plant life, but she missed in the garden the pleasing symmetry of the delicate drawings in her father's botany books. Stripped of their exotic nomenclature, the entangling plants lost some of their magic.

She did not enjoy kneeling on the ground, working the soil with her hands. She did not share Martha's delight in digging her fingers into the moist earth; she took no pride in a dirt-streaked face or mud-spattered clothing. Things grew for her, not through any complicity between herself and Nature, but by the sweat of her brow. In her heart of hearts she found the work demeaning. And though her reason rebelled against this instinctive revulsion, though she told herself again and again that laboring in the garden was a quasi-sacramental activity, a celebration of God's merciful bounty, though she reminded herself that gardening was a favored pastime of poets and philosophers, she still could not rid herself of the feeling that the whole process of wresting nourishment from the soil belonged to a lower sphere of human endeavor, associated with procreation and the bodily functions. It was silly and stupid of her, she knew, but out in the middle of the garden she felt defenseless and exposed and was sometimes overcome with embarrassment when suddenly accosted there by visitors or passers-by.

The arrival of the piano in early September brought her great joy. She greeted it in the roadway like an old friend and trusted confidante, hovered about it with solicitude as it descended from the dray, and eagerly made a place for it in the parlor—exiling the étagère, with her mother's display china, to an obscure corner of the dining room. As soon as the instrument was eased into position and its protective coverings removed, as soon as the wagoners had made their clumsy exit, amidst much hitching of trousers and tugging of caps and sly sidelong looks at the young mistress of the house, leaving behind them muddy boot prints in the hall and the rank smells of sweat and cheap whiskey, Elizabeth ceremoniously installed herself at the instrument and proceeded to fill the room with the notes of a Hummel sonatina. Her fingers were stiff, her touch uncertain, and the piano decidedly out of tune, but she played with an energy and passion wholly new to her. She wanted the music to penetrate the farthest corners of the room, to saturate the furniture and walls, to exorcize the surroundings of everything alien to her. She wanted to bring into the house a remnant of the Old World culture, which had become dearer, more precious to her in recent months.

Even in Madison, with its state capitol and silk-waistcoated legislators, with its university and its academical aspirations, the cultural roots of the community did not run deep. The occasional Indian who wandered into town, ragged, dirty, and sodden with drink, seemed to have a firmer, surer relationship with the surroundings than did the people who passed him by with averted eyes. He belonged to the place—its lake, its hills, and the vast tracks of wilderness that lay behind—in a way they did not. She associated the reeling native son with the drunken English farm laborer whom one encountered at the close of market day in a small rural town, or the grimy, wizen-faced industrial worker, groping his way along the wall of a public house in London or Manchester. Elizabeth had always felt that these lowly individuals, though outside the orbit of normal social intercourse, were an integral part of the local scene. As the Bible says, "The poor are always with us," and these indigenous types had a just claim to antiquity. However primitive their appearance or degenerate their behavior, they were deeply rooted in the English soil—"as common as dirt" people scornfully said, yet, too, as basic, as elemental, as dirt. And yet another phrase sprang to mind, this one reverentially intoned: "From ashes we come, to ashes we will return," and she knew that the dread she felt at these encounters came from a sense of her commonality with these social dregs, an awareness that though class and up-bringing set her and them apart, the elemental man dwelt somewhere within her, and it was only sheer willpower that kept her in the ascendancy. Here, on the frontiers of civilization, where class distinctions were blurred and even democratic principles gave way to naked necessity, she saw herself threatened by something worse than oblivion—by the annihilation of her past. That was why she clung so tenaciously to her cultural attainments, such as they were, and to her slim learning. Though resigned to exchanging her citizenship and eager to adapt to her new homeland, she was resolved not to give up her heritage. Like her father, she believed that it was the divine gift of intelligence that made man foremost among God's creatures; she believed that science and the arts were embodiments of this intelligence; she believed that learned people like her father were the torchbearers of culture to the New World and that people like herself were the humble keepers of the flame. She told herself that there were obligations involved, both social and personal. These thoughts were all very sketchy. But within her stirred a dark fear of "letting go."

There came to mind Barbara Cutter, the wife of a young Madison lawyer. Though barely twenty-seven she seemed ageless, stripped of her youth. Mrs. Cutter had been raised in the city of Hartford, Connecticut, where her father was a prominent magistrate. She had spent two years at school in Switzerland, where she learned to speak fluent German and French. When Elizabeth met her for the first time, while shopping in town with Martha, Barbara was wearing a rumpled gray dress whose hem was hanging loose in the back, and there was a faint smudge of soot on the right side of her nose. Her voice was pleasant, her diction pure; she spoke at length about the virtues of carbolic soap for laundry (they were in Lewis's Empo-rium) while her eyes gazed vacantly about the store. On subsequent en-counters she displayed a listlessness and paucity of conversation that bewildered Elizabeth, who had made an unusual effort to draw her out. Once, in the company of her husband, she had reached out a hand to caress his cheek, seemingly oblivious of the fact that the room was full of people.

Elizabeth had been shocked by the gesture, by the public display of physical intimacy, by the absent little smile that played about the woman's lips. There was an air of self-abandonment about the young wife that Elizabeth found alarming.

And so, if the garden received Elizabeth's dutiful attentions every day, so too did her piano; and every day she spent some time perfecting her watercolor technique and frowning over her battered French grammar. "Our little scholar," her father was wont to call her in affectionate tones during her schoolgirl days. He had used the phrase again in recent weeks, but with a slightly cutting edge to his voice and a vaguely puzzled expression on his face. He could not understand why she threw herself into these activities with such ferocious determination. Of course, he appreciated her need to cultivate her mind: he was after all a modern man, with strong convictions on the right of women to develop their intellects to their utmost capacities, which for the sake of argument he assumed to be the same as men's. Moreover, he regarded her accomplishments with genuine satisfaction. They gave firm proof of her discipline and industry, provided a wholesome pastime, and served as a social enhancement. Yet there was no denying the fact that by masculine standards she was neither a scholar nor an artist—nor did he expect her to be. Whether he *desired* her to be one or the other he never asked himself and therefore remained loyal to his egalitarian faith. The truth was, however, that at this moment he would have preferred that she devote more time to genteel idleness, to growing gently into the full flower of her womanhood. There was a new hardness about her that disturbed him. She had always been a rather solemn little girl: he had come to accept that as one of the sad legacies of her mother's death. He did not want to see this solemnity grow into primness and self-absorption. After all, he looked to her for youth, vigor, and a certain buoyant optimism. Besides, he loved her and wanted her to be happy, whatever that might mean. He wanted her to marry, have children, reintroduce into both their lives an element of family life, with its comforting bustle and propinquity. He was aware that he himself could not supply the warmth and attentions necessary to bring her into full being as a woman, and he trusted in her ability to venture out to the encounter of these qualities. She was not unattractive; she was even, he thought, quite pretty, if she would only allow herself to smile a little more.

. . . And then, she tended to dress in a style that, though always proper, was perhaps a trifle severe for a person of her age. Of course, he knew next to nothing of such matters, had no more idea of what young ladies wore in London or Paris than in Shanghai, yet it did seem to him that Elizabeth could introduce something into her attire—perhaps an interestingly patterned shawl or even a few pastel-colored ribbons—to relieve the matronly aspect of her wardrobe. He remembered the bright blue silk sash that her mother had worn the first evening that he met her. . . . Ah, but styles were far different then, and women, perhaps, more forward in their manner. Besides, he would hardly know how to broach the subject. It was too much for him. She clearly needed a mother's attentions to bring her out. He was too involved with his own work, too cut off from society, too tired of late to be of help to her. He loved her dearly, he worried about her, but he had absolutely no idea what was going on in her mind. What was more, he knew no way of finding out.

Winter came. Snow fell. The landscape assumed a soft, lustrous grandeur, then, as the cold set in, a brittle brilliance. It was a cold such as Elizabeth had never experienced before: sharp, penetrating, insistent. She found it invigorating after the insidious chill of an English winter. She noticed that one took elaborate, ritualistic precautions against the onslaught of a Wisconsin winter, that each household adopted its own stratagems. She perceived a thin, high note of danger in the air that quickened her senses.

Her weekly excursions into town acquired a slightly altered interest. The horse's hoofs rang out loud and clear on the frozen road, and jets of vapor streamed from his nostrils. The snow-covered fields stood out solid and pristine, with a sort of shimmering emphasis in the harsh winter sunlight. As she moved through the landscape, the young woman was acutely aware of her own physical reality, in sharp distinction from the vibrant reality around her. "I am Elizabeth Gow," she said to herself, "twenty-two years of age, an Englishwoman now living in America, neither English nor American, my own being, moving between two worlds at this very moment, in the winter sunshine, moving across the snow-covered wastes of Wisconsin, a thousand miles from the sea. . ." She was overcome by a sense of her remoteness in space, her isolation from "civilized" society, by which she meant a visible presence of a living tradition reaching back in time as far as the imagination could penetrate, and by a sense of her own individuality. Where formerly she had felt anxiety and trepidation at being on her own, now, aloft on the front seat of the trap, racing through the windswept countryside, she felt a flush of exaltation. She saw herself momentarily as a heroic figure out of some Nordic romance, and the landscape suddenly seemed suffused by a silent melody from one of the Mendelssohn piano pieces she had so labored to master and that now flowed effortlessly through her being.

As she entered the town, the buildings closed around her, the exaltation subsided, yet there lingered within her a heightened sense of her own existence that caused her to look about her with eager eyes. The people she passed in the street, their heads bowed respectfully against the wind, their hands clasping coat collars or clapped firmly onto bonnets or hats, each bearing their own personal bundles and preoccupations, seemed to her figures in a pageant, whose significance was almost within her grasp. As she took up her basket and descended from the trap, she was aware that she too had a role to play in this mysterious pantomime, and she smiled a faint, complicitous smile.

"I've been told, Miss Gow, that you play the piano beautifully, and I could not help wondering whether you might consent to assist us at our Sunday services. It's a bold request, I know, but there we are, with a perfectly good piano and no one to do it justice. I might add that there is a small honorarium. Wretchedly small, I'm afraid, a mere pittance. I mention it only to show our goodwill and appreciation."

He was a tall, ungainly man, with lank black hair and a pallid complexion highlighted by angry eruptions of pimples. The eyes, as it were, did special pleading for the face: they were bright blue and glowed with childlike eagerness. He had accosted her in Lewis's Emporium among the corsets and ladies' undergarments, and though he was plainly oblivious of the surroundings, she was anxious that he might suddenly perceive the awkwardness of the site for their conversation.

"That is very kind of you, Reverend Hoffmeister, but I am afraid that my talents have been much exaggerated. Besides, as you know, we attend the Presbyterian services on Sunday."

"Oh, I do know that, of course I do, Miss Gow, but our services are at eight, so there really should not be any problem. As you have undoubtedly discovered, the Protestant communities in Madison strive to be cooperative. Reverend Pierce is a good friend of mine, and members of our little choral group participated at last year's Christmas oratorio at your church. Please believe that I would not have ventured to have bring up the matter if I were not sure that it was wholly normal and proper to do so."

As he spoke, Elizabeth noticed that his fingers plucked nervously at a button on his jacket. He caught her glance and plunged the offensive hand into a trouser pocket.

"Well, let me speak to my father about it. Of course, I am flattered to be asked, one *does* like to be asked. . ." She was moving slowly along the aisle, toward the crockery, drawing him with her.

"Of course, Miss Gow, do please speak with your father. I understand entirely. It is only natural and proper. May I hope to hear from you soon? My little congregation will await your word with impatience." His mixture of obsequiousness and brashness disconcerted her.

"Yes, certainly, Reverend Hoffmeister. I'll let you know as soon as I can."

"It would certainly be a great boon to us, Miss Gow, if you could see your way to helping us out. With your permission, I could come to your home sometime next week to receive your response. What day would be convenient for you?"

"Well, I really don't know. . . . Oh, Tuesday I suppose. In the afternoon."

"Tuesday would be fine. Perfect! Shall we say at three? 'Til then, Miss Gow!" (She wished he would not assume that triumphant air; it was entirely uncalled for.) "And my respectful regards to Dr. Gow!"

Elizabeth fled from the store without making her purchases.

That Sunday afternoon she had come across her father in the parlor. He was seated in an armchair, by the window. The light streamed onto his face, which was uplifted to the sun—eyes closed, mouth slightly open, a look of intense concentration on his features. The uniform pallor of the complexion, combined with the fixity of his expression, gave to the face the appearance of a mask, a mask designed to represent, perhaps, supplication. She had never felt him so remote, so utterly removed from her and their surroundings, and for a fleeting moment of panic she thought him dead. But the gentle rise and fall of his faded red waistcoat and the way his hands grasped the armrests, so firmly that the knuckles gleamed with whiteness, reassured her of his presence and stilled the wild beating of her heart.

Reason told her to withdraw and leave him to his sleep, or to whatever quest engaged his spirit, but a residue of panic still fluttered within her, and she could not resist the urge to pull him back to her, to ensnare him in the mechanism of life.

"Father," she called out softly, then more pressingly, "Father, are you asleep?"

His fingers grasped the armrests yet more tightly, as if he were striving to pull himself up from a great depth; then the grip relaxed.

"Bess?" The voice was almost plaintive.

"Oh, I'm sorry, Papa, I didn't realize that you were resting." Then she added in what she hoped was a cheerful, offhand manner, "It's so seldom that I ever catch you napping like that."

"The sunlight. The sunlight was so unusual for this time of year that I could not resist giving myself up to it for a few moments."

"Are you quite well, Papa?"

"Yes, yes." There was an edge of impatience in his response, which he struggled to subdue. "Well, I'm not quite back to normal as yet. Still a bit fragile, as the ladies say. But yes, I am getting better, Bess."

She knew that it was not the moment, that she was moving too fast, but her anxiety simply overflowed.

"Papa, you are a doctor, you're knowledgeable in these matters. As you say, you are not quite yourself as yet. . . . I mean, whatever you have, whatever you *did* have, was certainly something serious. . . . What is your professional diagnosis?"

In the past such appeals had always provoked a lengthy, measured reply. As a man of science, he was committed to rational explanations and seemed to relish the careful elaboration of cause and effect. Moreover, he had made it part of his pedagogic practice to seize on such homely instances for use in his daughter's general instruction. When, for example, he had broken a rib in a carriage accident several years ago, he had her take down from the shelf a large volume on human anatomy, and the two of them had spent the better portion of the afternoon reviewing together the sublime framework of the human form. Therefore, though she knew that he was still half-drugged by sleep, she was shocked by the vehemence of his response.

"There is *nothing* seriously the matter with me. I have the remnants of a catarrh, brought on in Philadelphia. Otherwise, I am in excellent health—or rather, in the process of regaining my normal excellent health. I do my work at the university, more than my share there. Naturally, I am tired at the end of the week. I won't be treated like an invalid, Bess."

"I assure you, Father, that I do not mean to treat you like an invalid. I am sure that I never treat you like an invalid. It is just that I can't help worrying sometimes. . ."

He saw that she was close to tears and attempted to soften his tone.

"There, there, Bess, no need to take on so. I appreciate your concern. It is just that I am tired at times and hate to be bothered by needless questions about my health. People do not understand how wearisome such questions are! Anyway, I am the doctor, Bess, and you can trust me to look after myself. Enough said on that matter!"

She was neither consoled nor reassured by his reply.

The reverend Hoffmeister sat bolt upright on the very edge of the chair, his new stovepipe hat held firmly on his lap, as if it were a very young and very untrustworthy child.

"I am disappointed, Miss Gow, that you are unable to help us out, though of course I do understand . . . the inconvenience for you. But you surely cannot blame us for attempting to enlist your able assistance. And I trust that you don't consider us forward in doing so."

"Of course not, Reverend Hoffmeister, of course not. I am only sorry that I couldn't be more obliging."

He shifted slightly on his chair; he cleared his throat; he gave no sign of terminating his visit, though it seemed to Elizabeth that their conversation had ended several phrases back. She was beginning to find him obstinate as well as tedious, and if he were not so very unattractive, she would be down-right angry with him. As it was, she hesitated to make any gesture, to express any emotion, that might possibly reveal to him the physical repulsion he inspired in her. So she sat patiently, her hands folded on her lap, waiting for him to bring things to a conclusion.

"I realize," he stumbled on, "that the position is not a particularly interesting one for you. Of course, if it could be combined with directing the choir, you would surely find it much more rewarding, more worthy of your time and your talents. There is in fact a possibility, a *decided* possibility I might add—though this is strictly confidential, Miss Gow, and I must ask you not to breathe a word of it to anyone)—that our present choir director will be relinquishing the post in the not-distant future." And he beamed at her a conspiratorial smile.

"Really, Reverend Hoffmeister, I know nothing whatsoever about choral music. I have no experience whatsoever in choral music. I can hardly sing a note myself. Therefore, I assure you . . ."

"Oh, it would not be difficult for someone with your musical abilities to acquire the requisite skills, it really wouldn't, Miss Gow. Why, our present director could hardly read music when he took charge of the choir." The clergyman then proceeded to describe at length the various duties and functions of the position and to indicate the ways in which the musical activities at the church might be expanded and improved if the proper person were placed in charge.

Though her patience was fading, she heard him out. It was preposterous! She had no intention of taking the job, under any circumstances. And she strongly suspected that he realized this all too clearly and was brazenly holding her captive with his talk. But she was determined not to struggle, to show no sign of her discomfiture, not to allow him the satisfaction of seeing that he had aroused her emotions.

Finally his words came to a halt. She made no response but looked straight at him with what she trusted was a polite but distant stare. A wall of silence rose up between them. He coughed discreetly into his fist. Essayed a smile. Then he suddenly stood up—and in the process, somehow managed to lose hold of his hat, which tumbled to the floor at his feet, spilling out of its interior a pair of white gloves. The gloves were slightly soiled, and one of them had become unstitched around the thumb. Instinctively she averted her gaze while he lunged to retrieve the articles, reaching first for the torn glove. When he arose—his face flushed, his eyes swimming with confusion—a pang of pity seized her, and, on reaching the door, she extended her hand and wished him a sincere good day. Goodness knows, she bore him no ill will, did not want to hurt him, to hurt anyone. Yet as she closed the door behind him and stood there, the doorknob still in her grasp, she realized that the gesture had been a mistake, an act of weakness on her part. He would undoubtedly and perversely misconstrue her attempt at kindness. Oh, the greediness with which he had snapped up that little scrap of cordiality! She shook her head. It was pathetic! A bit alarming, too. The man was incorrigible!

The winter wore on. There was a strange, unexpected thaw in late February. Pussy willows came out by the creek, and a boisterous flock of crows appeared in the neighboring field. Then the cold returned, more biting than ever, to be followed by a swirling avalanche of snow that left them encased in white silence. Slowly, imperceptibly the roads were cleared again, and the flow of traffic resumed, tentatively at first and not without a touch of bravado—such as Mr. Levi's arrival one morning on snowshoes! Then the routines reasserted themselves, and people went about their business with an air of quiet resignation.

The murmur of voices in the downstairs hallway brought her to her feet. Though she could not make out the words, she caught the note of urgency, along with the odd sound of scuffling boots. She hurried to the landing with a pounding heart and leaned over the railing.

The Beckers, father and son, had her father between them. His face was ashen and wore an expression of intense concentration as he shuffled slowly through the hallway. He was clearly determined to walk on his own, and it was obvious that he couldn't. The Beckers supported him on either side, keeping a firm grip on his arms and emitting hearty phrases of encouragement: "That's the way, Dr. Gow!" "Steady as she goes!" "Not far now."

The pathetic little parade halted momentarily on Elizabeth's appearance in the hallway. The Beckers extended to her a silent but profoundly eloquent greeting, their eyes wide with pity and distress. Her father simply murmured "Oh" in a flat, noncommittal voice and turned away his gaze, as if he had been caught out in some shameful act. Then the procession resumed.

They stretched him out on the chaise in the parlor. He was so weak that Franz had to lift his feet onto the piece. Elizabeth hovered behind them, nervously rubbing her hands on her skirts, and feeling helpless, useless, almost undone. As they loosened his cravat, he cursed vehemently under his breath.

"I'll fetch a blanket," she said and rushed upstairs, returning with the old quilt made by her grandmother that she had snatched from her own bed. She spread it with trembling hands over her father's prostrate form. His eyes were closed, and he was breathing heavily, but he managed to mutter something that sounded like an expression of thanks. Elizabeth bent down and kissed his forehead, which was slightly moist and startlingly cool.

Franz Becker drew Elizabeth aside to a far corner of the room and in hushed tones narrated the course of events. Dr. Gow had been in his laboratory, helping several students set up an experiment. It had been a question of moving some heavy equipment—a task he should certainly have left entirely to the boys. Anyway, he had suddenly been convulsed by a coughing fit. According to one of the students, his feet had simply given way beneath him, and he had collapsed on the floor.

"The students of course were struck dumb and stood about wringing their hands. Absolutely helpless. Finally one of them ran off in search of water, and another bestirred himself to come after me—as you know, I have an office at the end of the corridor. I was just getting ready to leave for home, just locking the door. When I arrived on the scene, your father was seated on the floor, his back against one of the laboratory sinks, with his eyes closed, just as they are now. He was horribly pale. I sent one of the boys off for Dr. Johns. Your father then began to protest that he was quite all right. Of course he wasn't. He couldn't even get to his feet without help. Jake had come by with the carriage to take me home, and it seemed to me that the best thing would be to get your father back here, where he could get some rest. He made a terrible fuss, said that he wanted to stay on and work—imagine that!—but we finally managed to persuade him to come with us. It's odd, but he seems to have no idea that there is anything much wrong, even though he can hardly lift his arm. I left a message for Dr. Johns to follow us here. He should be along any time now." And then he added in a whisper, his eyes bright with concern, "He fainted twice in the carriage."

Dr. Johns was a large, pink-cheeked man, with kindly eyes and an ungainly manner. Wisps of white hair stuck out from under his stovepipe hat, which, when removed, revealed a gleaming bald pate. His steel-rimmed glasses were slightly askew, his clothes rumpled, and he looked like a man who had been suddenly awakened from a nap. Dr. Johns's office was in the center of town, and he lived directly behind it in a single bedroom-cum-kitchen with a collection of assorted cats, all of them called "Kitty." He had come to Madison many years ago, but no one seemed to remember him when he was other than balding, elderly, and unkempt. Like a number of old-time doctors, he was known on occasion to treat animals, and he extended to them the same deferential concern that he gave to his other patients. Though his hands were extraordinarily large and callused and trembled a bit of late, his touch was gentle and sure. He belonged to none of the local churches and was generally believed to be a "free thinker," but strangely enough nobody held that against him, regarding it as simply another sign of his naïveté and "forgetfulness," like his frequent failure to present any bill. He was never judgmental and was always available at any hour of day or night. On the whole he was regarded with affection rather than with respect, though most people agreed that he displayed more "good common horse sense" than Dr. Hartly, the only other physician in town, who had a tendency to take matters into his own hands regardless of the afflicted parties' wishes or sensibilities.

As Elizabeth helped the doctor off with his coat, Professor Becker narrated once again the circumstances of the patient's collapse.

"Oh dear, oh dear," Dr. Johns murmured at the conclusion of the narrative and cast a sympathetic smile at Elizabeth. He asked permission to examine the patient in private; taking up his battered leather bag, he entered the front parlor and delicately closed the door behind him.

Elizabeth and the Beckers retired to the kitchen, where the doctor found them half an hour later.

"Ah well, he's a very sick man, Miss Gow." It seemed to her that the words were coming from a great distance away, and she was dimly aware of the homely Welsh intonation in his voice. "Very sick indeed. I see no immediate danger, but he will need careful looking after."

"Is he dying, Doctor?" The words sprang from her.

The old man winced at the forthrightness of the question.

"It isn't for me to say, Miss Gow. I have seen too many untoward things in my day to answer that. I'll tell you, though, that his lungs seem to be giving out, both of them, and a man can't go on living without a bit of help from his lungs. All we can do now is watch over him, keep him still, and hope for things to mend, somehow or other. If you are inclined to prayers . . . well, there be people who do say that prayers are the best medicine in cases like this. Unfortunately, I don't carry any with me in this bag of mine. I'll give you, though, this bottle of laudanum, which will help him to rest and relieve the pain. The proper dosage is written on the bottle. You might start with half of that at first, and see how it does for him. Considering the state he is in, it is amazing that he has kept on his feet as long as he has. Amazing. Your father has a remarkably strong constitution, Miss Gow, and we can only hope that it will somehow carry him through."

He was installed in the upstairs bedroom, and the long vigil began. The house seemed to close in around the two of them. Elizabeth went out only to do essential errands; the rest of the time she spent within hearing range of her father's weakened voice, often in her own bedroom, adjacent to his. In spite of the sense of profound solitude enfolding her during her father's illness, however, Elizabeth was not without company. At the outset of his confinement, a steady stream of visitors had descended upon the house. As was the custom of the country, neighbors, friends, and colleagues took it upon themselves to minister to the dying man and to accompany him, step by step, on his final journey.

These visits were initially announced by discreet tappings on the front door, heralding for the most part neighboring ladies and faculty wives bearing offerings of cooked food. As the weeks went by, they began to slip unannounced into the house by the back door so as not to "bother" Elizabeth. They would deposit their offerings on the kitchen table—freshly baked breads, meat pies, even from time to time a roast fowl—or set about some

needful domestic chore on their own initiative. Elizabeth would unexpectedly encounter a neighbor at the kitchen sink washing the dishes or on her
hands and knees in the front hallway cleaning up the traces of mud tracked
in by the other visitors. As her father's illness progressed, all sense of privacy
melted away, and their home was opened to the world. The act of dying, the
most profoundly personal of all undertakings, became, she discovered, a
public occasion.

Dr. Johns came every day to "look in on his patient," though his visits
were increasingly brief and ceremonial. After he had gone through the mo-
tions of extracting the daily dosage of laudanum from his battered leather
bag and done what little he could to make his patient "more comfortable,"
his large, weather-beaten hands hung heavy at his sides.

Chancellor Lathrop paid several calls. On his first visit Elizabeth's father
was in one of his black moods and all but refused to acknowledge the chancellor's presence, keeping his eyes closed during most of the interview and
replying to the well-meaning inquiries with monosyllabic retorts that were
little more than angry grunts. As Elizabeth accompanied the guest to the
door, she stammered an apology on her father's behalf, which was gently
rejected with a slow shake of the head. "My dear, your father clearly has
other things on his mind than entertaining visitors. I shall come again
when, I hope, my presence shall be less intrusive. I am anxious to let him
know how grateful I am for his choosing to come to us and how much his
being here has benefitted us all. Another time, then! And courage, my
dear."

Of all the regular callers, Martha was the most assiduous. She soon grad-
uated from the kitchen, where for a time she held absolute sway, to the sick-
room. In spite of Elizabeth's protests, she insisted on changing the patient's
bed linen herself and carrying it off, virtually by force, to her own home,
where it was promptly laundered, ironed, and then returned. She also took
to emptying Dr. Gow's chamber pot whenever she had the opportunity to
do so. Elizabeth would occasionally see her bearing the vessel in triumph
down the stairs or through the back hallway, and it was all she could do to
keep from crying out in anguish. She was powerless to curtail her friend's re-
lentless activities. "Now don't you bother yourself, Bess, you have more important things to do. Just sit there and keep your father company, and leave

the chores to me. He needs you beside him. I'll take care of the running about." Her father at this stage seemed to have lost all sense of personal modesty, and no longer cared who was prying under his bedclothes. Elizabeth was left to blush inwardly on his behalf.

She felt that her father preferred to be alone, that even her presence at his bedside required of him a degree of receptivity that was beyond his power. He seemed to be totally absorbed by his thoughts and kept his eyes firmly closed, responding to questions in only the most cursory manner. At times he lashed out at her for apparently no reason at all, refusing her ministrations, telling her to leave him alone, to go away—though of course he was completely dependent on her for everything. She was hurt by his hostility, but more bewildered than hurt, for all her senses seemed numbed by sorrow; she came to accept his irritable remarks as a sort of ventriloquistic intervention on the part of Death itself.

Toward the end his manner softened. There were moments when he squeezed her hand and looked beseechingly into her face as he wept quietly—but that was only during the last few days, when he was well dosed with laudanum. During the span of his confinement, which lasted just under a month, she felt herself hardening, not toward him, but toward life. When he died, almost imperceptibly at dawn, with a faint sigh, it seemed to her that he had already left long ago and that the figure before her on the bed was not the man she had grown up with, but a child, a helpless, bewildered child bearing her father's features. She wept for that poor lost child, with its terrible anonymity, and for herself, now alone in a foreign land.

During the days immediately following her father's death Elizabeth had little time to herself. Her days were full, too full.

After the anguish and turmoil and confusion of the past few weeks, she felt an urgent need to come to grips with the great event, to comprehend what had actually happened. She wanted the solitude to wander at leisure through her past life, to impose some sort of order and meaning on the mass of undifferentiated memories that crowded in upon her. She needed to reconstruct a coherent and comprehensive image of her father to replace the fragmentary and distorted pictures of him left to her from his deathbed agony. She needed to see things whole. But she was not given the opportunity.

Her acquaintances seemed to be colluding in a plot to prevent her from turning her attention to those matters closest to her heart. Indeed, folk wisdom—and local custom—ordained that the community should intervene to distract her from the demoralizing influence of morbidity by immersing her in the routines of daily living ("life must go on") and by instructing her in the proper performance of the demanding role of Grieving Daughter ("it cleanses the soul and restores the spirit to mourn the departed," provided that one does so with a dignity and decorum that reflects confidence in God's judgment and an acceptance of the consolations of an afterlife).

Though the ladies of her church took full charge of the funeral preparations, they went out of their way to secure her approval of each and every detail of the ceremony, from the choice and arrangement of flowers to the precise location of the burial site.

Because the congregation was a relatively new one, the parish offered a rich choice of grave sites in its still underpopulated cemetery. Elizabeth instinctively selected a site in a remote corner of the graveyard, in the shadow of a stone retaining wall, but the next day she received a visit from Mrs. Harper, the deacon's wife, imploring her to reconsider. Mrs. Harper reminded her that the site was only a few yards from the toolshed, the proximity of which "detracted from its dignity." Moreover, it afforded no view of the hills, "which were particularly attractive in late spring, with an abundance of pink rhododendrons." Mrs. Harper told Elizabeth that she had lain awake "half the night" worrying about the matter and had come to the realization that Elizabeth, "what with being all distraught and such," had chosen in undue haste. Though the woman spoke in a hushed, reverential voice, appropriate to a house of mourning, her passionate concern rang clear. Elizabeth heard her out with awe. For a moment she hardly knew how to respond. She was tempted to say something to the effect that the deceased was probably indifferent to the view and that his involvement with the landscape was now of a wholly different order, but she managed to suppress such thoughts and to blurt out instead a few half-articulated phrases of gratitude. Yes, of course Mrs. Harper was right. She would change the site. She would talk to the rector today. Yet the next afternoon, when a delegation called to ask her to state her preference for the placement of the service programs—Should they be laid out individually on the pews or put in a neat stack at the entrance to the church?—Elizabeth burst into tears. Her collapse met, of course, with an outpouring of sympathy: the ladies crowded about her, almost suffocating her in a profusion of bodices, while the rector stood by, tugging manfully at his side-whiskers. She felt like a fool, but she gained for the rest of the afternoon a respite from their nagging attentions.

The widows and orphans of the parish dropped by, singly or in pairs, and it seemed to Elizabeth that she was being drawn into some Masonic sorority, gently and against her will. She came to realize that her mourning garb constituted a uniform of sorts; widows were of the officer class, while the loss of a parent enrolled one in the ranks. On the street in town people she hardly knew nodded gravely in passing or touched the brim of their hats in a solemn salute. Reverend Hoffmeister appeared on her doorstep to convey his heartfelt condolences, as he put it, and he took the occasion to seize her hand and give it a sympathetic squeeze. Admittedly, death was the Great Leveler, but she did not see why it should promote such uncalled-for intimacies.

Only when she retired to her bedroom for the night could Elizabeth be alone with her thoughts. Seated at the dressing table, she loosened her hair and let it fall in glistening cascades over her shoulders; then she set to brushing it, first one side, then the other, first slowly, drawing the brush with long measured strokes through the tresses, then deeper, more quickly, with an increased sense of purpose. As she brushed, she peered into the mirror, trying to read the thoughts in the face that gazed back at her. But the calm, expressionless features remained indecipherable. Only the eyes, with their look of vague puzzlement and yearning, hinted at some inner disharmony and distress.

She lay in the dark trying to rethink her life. Until now she had lived on the periphery of it, the center being fixed on her father, his work and his wishes and his expectations. Even at boarding school it seemed (at least in retrospect) that she had lived for if not actually through him. She had been planet to his sun, moon to his earth. With his death, all changed. She was thrown out of orbit and sent plummeting through a great void. She closed her eyes tight to stop the vertiginous fall.

She would reclaim her own life and fix it firmly in time and space. She would seek out a new center, within herself if possible, if not somewhere within the world. She really did not know much about the world. She had never allowed herself to look directly at it; a sense of prudery or simple timidity had always prompted her to avert her gaze. Not that she had ever knowingly rejected it; rather, she had always felt ill-prepared to meet it on its own terms and had preferred to live apart from it or to engage it on a personally restricted basis. But the time had clearly arrived when she must venture out to its encounter.

The first thing was to make plans for the future. If the present was confusing and obscure, she could perhaps impose some sort of coherent shape on it by projecting it against the future. Making plans had now become a wholly different process. Before, making plans had meant spinning out elaborate daydreams; now it meant coming to grips with practical matters, confronting reality.

Money matters were clearly a primary concern. The story of her immediate future was outlined in the large black ledger that still reposed in the upper lefthand drawer of her father's bureau. A couple of days after his death she had turned over the pages and had been deeply touched, and grateful, for the meticulous attention he had lavished on his bookkeeping. The last entry was made with a scratchy, ill-cut nib, one month and four days before his death: a deposit of $53.43 in his Madison bank. Because he had obliged Elizabeth to keep her own accounts of household expenses, she was able to have some idea of the dollar-and-cents cost of daily living.

The house was paid for and therefore provided her with rent-free lodging, exclusive of the annual eight-dollar property tax. The money in her father's bank account should, she figured, be enough for her live on without any supplemental income for another year and a half, perhaps two full years if she disposed of the horse and carriage promptly for a reasonable sum. Beyond that, she had nothing except the household belongings, whose value was, she assumed, largely sentimental. There was nothing that she could bring herself even to think of selling at the present moment. As for economies: food was the major expense, but it would hardly be worthwhile for her to invest in a cow, or even a goat or pig, just to feed herself. Poultry was another matter, though she regarded chickens with distaste. They were dirty, stupid, greedy little creatures, and she would certainly derive no pleasure from looking after them.

Her scheme of starting a school was, she now realized, too raw and unformed to be put into execution. A grandiose dream that belonged to a former life! As to giving piano lessons, that remained a definite possibility, though none of the calculations she had worked out added up to a livable income.

Martha suggested that she take in a boarder, maybe two—respectable working ladies or widows, with good solid recommendations of course. Elizabeth found the idea repugnant. An older woman, she saw clearly, would attempt to take her in hand, either out of misplaced maternal instinct or the simple desire to dominate; and a person of her own age would interfere with her privacy. She had been the only woman of the house too long to accommodate herself to a domestic rival. Nonetheless, in the face of Martha's mounting enthusiasm, she refrained from voicing her objections. "I've got some quick-bread recipes you would find useful," Martha was saying, "And you could put your kitchen garden to good work in feeding your guests. The winter nights are dreary, Bess, and it's downright comforting for a single person to have other women in the house. Though, of course, Bess" (here her voice took on a confidential tone), "I am sure that you needn't expect to remain a single woman yourself for very long."

Marriage was indeed the ultimate solution, the deus ex machina that would render all her plans needless or obsolete. While her father was alive, she had consciously thrust the subject aside, telling herself that it was "childish" to indulge in fantasies when there was no flesh-and-blood matrimonial prospect at hand, or even in mind. Because she was still young, she had not yet begun to grow anxious about finding "someone suitable," and because she regarded marriage as a more or less certain eventuality, she had continued to cling to the last vestiges of her girlhood and "independence." Now, however, that she was on her own, she understood the need for a protective presence that would help to assure her freedom from the pressures of society. She was beginning to see marriage from a new perspective. Unmarried, she was hemmed in by restrictions, besieged by would-be suitors, exposed to the critical gaze of the community—her every public action scrutinized and discussed, and all her private behavior open to speculation. Married, she would have a chance to reestablish her private life amidst a domestic setting. Marriage, she told herself, was—could be—a partnership of two different auras and identities. Yet to her ill-informed imagination the differences between men and women remained both formidable and indistinct. She told herself that before entering into such an all-embracing relationship she needed to have a clearer understanding of her own feelings (which were far from clear now) and of what would be expected of her emotionally—and physically. Equally unclear was how to go about finding out what she needed to know. For want of any clear responses to these questions she fell back on a phrase: she would be enlightened by love!

He was leaning forward on the chair, his hands clasped together on his knees. She could see from the look of intense concentration on his face and from the way his thin, moist lips framed every word that he was striving manfully to express himself with the utmost clarity and control, to impose upon her the heavy import of his message. Yet the words seem to wash lightly over her like stream water rushing over a rock. Froth and foam: she couldn't absorb them. She was vaguely alarmed at her inattentiveness. She knew her attitude was inappropriate, perhaps even rude. When she was sixteen, an elderly, well-meaning relative had taken her to a Christmas pantomime clearly intended for very young children, and it had been all she could do to manifest a sign of polite interest. Now, once again, she was acutely aware of the inadequacy of her response. She could see that her abstracted manner was only making things harder for the poor man. On sitting down, he had taken a deep breath and launched into a what was obviously a carefully prepared and well-rehearsed speech, which now for want of a duly attentive audience was beginning to flounder and take on water. A high-pitched whine of desperation had entered his voice.

" . . . I realize, Miss Gow, that you are still in mourning and that I am broaching this subject at what is perhaps a most inopportune time. My only excuse is that my feelings for you are such that I can no longer keep them to myself without either playing the hypocrite or depriving myself of your company, which quite simply I find myself unable to do. And let me add, Miss Gow, that seeing you as you now are, alone and in distress, only undermines my resolve to hold myself aloof from you. I long to spring to your side, to share with you as best I can the heavy burden of your grief, to help console you for your inestimable loss.

"As a clergyman, Miss Gow, I am often called upon to visit the afflicted, the heavy in heart, to offer them the consolation of the sacraments and the Holy Word. It is my duty and my privilege to do so, and I can assure you that I take the task much to heart. But with you I find—oh, how shall I express myself?—with you I find that I come not only as a man of God, but, quite simply, as a *man*; and what I have to offer is not only the consolations of my calling but something else as well. Oh, a poor thing, Miss Gow, certainly a poor thing compared to those other, all-sufficient gifts, but . . . you see . . ."

He had jettisoned his ballast and was now bailing frantically to keep afloat.

"The point is, Miss Gow, ever since I first saw you that afternoon at the Ecumenical Fete, I knew that you were someone very special to me, and as time went by, I found that you had become—oh, certainly unbeknownst to yourself!—a precious part of my life.

"I think of you night and day. I know that I have no right to do so, but I do. I know, too, that I shouldn't be talking to you like this. I should in all decency exercise more restraint. But I can't. Even with the discipline of my calling and the assurance of my faith, I can't. Believe me, Miss Gow, I have prayed for strength, for guidance, and to be honest, wholly honest, I have prayed that you might look with kindness on me. . . . I know that I hardly deserve kindness from you, yet you can surely find it in your heart to forgive me for praying for it, for praying for a miracle. You do forgive me, don't you?"

The question seemed to her grossly unfair.

"Really, Reverend Hoffmeister . . ." she protested, but not knowing how to frame her response in terms that would neither offend nor foster false hopes, she left it suspended.

He saw that he had at last awakened a spark of life within her. His eyes flashed. He braced himself for a final desperate effort.

"I realize that I do not cut a dashing figure." (He paused here to smile wanly at her, displaying a mouthful of yellow teeth.) "I know that I am hardly the answer to a fair maiden's dream. Yet the heart that beats within me is as true, as valiant, and, yes, as virile as that of many a more nobly formed man. Oh, I don't mean to imply that this unprepossessing exterior conceals within it a knight in shining armor! Alas, that is not true. I am all too aware, too painfully aware, of my inner failings and imperfections. I have my weaknesses and passions—like other men. Like other men, I am a sinner. But though imperfect, I am not a bad man, Miss Gow. And with you beside me I would be a much, much better man. Your presence would transform my weaknesses into strength, my passions into virtue. I need you, Miss Gow, I need you desperately, and that need is, as I see so clearly, a God-given sign that we are meant one for the other.

"No, please, Miss Gow! Please! I don't want you to give me any sort of answer just now. I understand that all this must seem quite sudden to you— though hardly to me! I'm afraid that I have let my feelings for you carry me away. I hadn't meant . . . I should have waited until you were recovered from your great, your very great loss, until your emotions, your thoughts, were less troubled and overstrained. Until you have had the time and opportunity to get to know me better—as a neighbor and friend. Forgive me. Just look at my hands! They are trembling. Appalling, isn't it? But it's a sign of my own emotions, of my deep feelings for you. But I shall leave now."

He rose somewhat unsteadily from the chair. His chest was heaving, his features distorted through the effort to regain his composure.

Elizabeth, too, was standing.

"Reverend Hoffmeister, please understand that I do appreciate the honor you do me in making this . . . this proposal, but I feel that I must in all frankness . . ."

"Please, Miss Gow"—his voice had suddenly regained its firmness, he was almost shouting her down—"I don't want you to commit yourself to anything just now. I have been hasty. There is no need for you to be hasty as well. We shall see each other again, not too *un*often I hope and trust, and things will be undoubtedly clearer for you in time. For the present, I ask only that you not think too unkindly of me. Nothing more."

"Reverend Hoffmeister!" Now it was Elizabeth who was trembling, not with passion but with indignation. "I think that we can spare ourselves needless anguish if you will permit me to say that much as I respect and . . . admire you, I cannot be your wife."

"*Cannot,* Miss Gow? Is there someone else then?"

"No one!"

"Then it is *will not,* not *cannot.* Perhaps as we come to know one another better, you may relent. I shall continue to hope."

"I do wish that you wouldn't, I really do." She brushed by him, leading the way to the hallway and the front door.

Gradually, the rhythm of the days changed. The flow of people through the house subsided, replaced by a hushed silence. As the winter wore on, lingering well into March, Elizabeth became increasingly restless. She wandered about the house, ostensibly taking stock, putting things in order. Sometimes she found herself standing in the center of a room, gazing about with bemusement. Instinctively she found herself drawn to her writing desk. Pulling out the top drawer, she withdrew the small crimson leather case. As she opened the case, she held her breath. The image before her gaze was flickering and insubstantial in the lamplight, as if reluctant to meet her hungry gaze. She had to tilt the portrait this way and that until the outline of her father's features could be called forth from beneath the surface of the metal plate, until by holding it just so she could evoke and entrap the elusive face. It seemed to her that the expression on that face had somehow undergone a change from one of intense concentration to vague bewilderment and discomfiture; the air of assertive intelligence that had marked the original image was now replaced by a pathetic note of interrogation. She tilted the portrait again until the lines receded back into shadows, and then she gently closed the case. It was no use. Her father wasn't to be found there, at least not in the form she wanted to remember him. The case had become a casket, and she hastened to entomb it in the deep recesses of the desk.

After her father's death the old familiar objects seemed to have been drained of their associative qualities, become pallid mementos of a forgotten past. Though nothing as yet had been moved—her father's clothes still hung in the wardrobe, his slippers still stood beside his bed—the whole house had to Elizabeth a strangely empty air. She moved amidst the furnishings like a guest in the home of an absent friend or relative.

To quell a deepening sense of homelessness, she sought refuge in books, in a program of "self-improvement," but no sooner had she settled into a chair and begun to engage with the text than the question "improvement for what?" insidiously intervened, and the page before her became a jumble of senseless phrases. Novels, taken up for sheer distraction, seemed impossibly remote and artificial, and lay abandoned on end tables and chairs with book-marks protruding from the opening chapters. There were long sessions at the piano when she simply let her hands roam at random over the keyboard. She had never played with more freedom or, as she was dimly aware, with more musicality, but when totally enveloped by the music, she would sud-denly be pierced by a yearning for escape, a terrible longing to be some-where, anywhere else, and the music would come to a faltering halt. At such times she envisioned herself springing from the piano bench and rushing out, hatless, coatless, into the snow-covered fields—and she would clasp her hands in her lap and struggle to keep back the tears.

She was appalled by these onslaughts of sensitivity, ashamed by her grow-ing sense of loneliness and isolation. She had always prided herself on being an independent sort of person, incapable of self-pity. She now understood that this image was based on aspirations rather than experience. It seemed that she wasn't who she thought herself to be. That being the case, who ex-actly was she? And how could she expect herself to respond to all the situa-tions now confronting her? It was terrible to sit alone in a room and feel oneself bereft of a personality.

She had always regarded introspection as vaguely self-indulgent, akin to daydreaming and conducive to brooding. When she was downhearted, the best remedy she knew was work: "taking oneself in hand," as she put it. Work included such cultural activities as practicing the piano or improving her watercolor techniques or reading a beneficial book. Of course, there were the household chores as well. Careful attention to domestic duties, including menial drudgery, was essential to building and maintaining a strong character; yet it was culture that lent merit and meaning to that strength and put it to good use. Culture, as Elizabeth saw it, gave physical form to the spirit. It refined and elevated the intellect. Above all, it took one out of one's self and liberated one's mind from the idle distractions and demeaning desires that given half a chance would enslave the spirit. To confront culture face on was, she believed, to turn one's back on human frailty, on the dark side of existence, and to draw life-giving force from the pure effulgence of mankind's noblest sentiments. The tragic plight of the poor was that they passed their life mostly in the shadows, cut off from the sources of spiritual illumination; the only light that reached them was filtered through chapel windows or reflected in acts of charitable kindness. Thus, her every impulse was to look out and up and not within. To keep herself turned to the light.

Of course a certain amount of introspection was necessary; that she knew. Wasn't the act of consulting one's conscience a form of self-examination? And she did try when saying her evening prayers to look into her heart and honestly weigh her thoughts and actions against her aspirations and ideals. But she was beginning to wonder about the accuracy of her scale! As the room faded from view in the waning light of early evening and each object gradually relinquished its form to the encroaching shadows, so too did her very being seem to dissolve gently within her and dissipate itself in a great, overwhelming nothingness.

She made up her mind to move. The house itself meant next to nothing to her now. She no longer regarded it as a home. Nor did she feel held to the community by bonds of friendship. Rather, her acquaintances seemed to hem her in. She needed air. She needed room for change. She needed a new setting in which she could reinvent her life.

A close companion, a friend she could freely confide in, would at this moment have made all the difference. If there had been someone with whom she could have discussed her anxieties and fears, someone with whom she could talk away her fantasies and dreams and who could have helped her to better understand herself, she would have certainly been tempted to stay. But there was no one.

The only individual among her acquaintances for whom she felt a strong attraction was Anne Smith, the wife of the professor of mathematics. Sensitive, soft-spoken, with a milky white complexion reminiscent of an English tea rose, she was barely a year older than Elizabeth. In company, Anne held herself slightly apart, contributing next to nothing to the little exclamations and eager affirmations that bulked out the body of the talk. When she spoke, it was to make some sensible, conciliatory remark or to clarify a point that had somehow got mangled or misinterpreted in the careless exchange of banter. In spite of her apartness, there was nothing standoffish about her. She was pleased to be included in the company and interested in what went on. She followed the conversation with a calm, attentive gaze, smiling softly to herself when something pleasant was said, or very slightly pursing her lips when something struck her as sad or regrettable. Elizabeth was fascinated by her. The young woman's face seemed to radiate a mysterious assurance and inner calm, and Elizabeth found herself furtively scanning Anne's features in the hope of catching a glimpse of the secret source of this mystery. Sometimes, in the flash of her eyes or in the gradual, breathtaking evolution of her smile or in the curve of her arm draped with languid grace over the back of a chair, Elizabeth felt that she had actually understood; but when she tried to convert her perceptions into thought, the meaning vanished. She longed to know Anne better, to pass beyond that facade of polite cordiality that the young woman presented with such discouraging impartiality to the world. She longed to somehow, in some slight way, disrupt her equanimity. She longed to make her blush.

Anne had received Elizabeth's overtures of friendship with her kindly smile, but it was soon apparent to Elizabeth that they would never be intimate. She recognized those sudden bouts of preoccupation that she had encountered in other young wives and understood that Anne's real life, at least for the present, was elsewhere, beyond her reach.

Martha, on the other hand, made a point of being accessible. From the outset she had wanted nothing more than to serve as Elizabeth's counselor, confidante, and friend, and now that the motherless girl had become an orphan, Martha looked forward to absorbing her into her own family. But Elizabeth did not want to be absorbed. Though she had come to accept and even to a certain extent count on the older woman's intervention in her life, she had no desire to be drawn into Martha's domestic orbit. Indeed, she found the atmosphere of the Becker household vaguely oppressive and (though she scarcely admitted it to herself) physically repellent.

During the long, drawn-out winter season, virtually all the social gatherings at the Beckers' gravitated to the kitchen. It was their style. Although greetings were exchanged formally enough on the front porch, and visitors lingered briefly in the frigid, underfurnished parlor, it was understood that one didn't stand on ceremony at the Beckers, and that once preliminaries were dispensed with, one simply made oneself "at home." Which meant, so Elizabeth learned, that one abandoned drawing-room conventions for kitchen comforts.

The kitchen was large, incredibly cluttered, and invariably overheated. Martha always seemed engaged in the preparation of Gargantuan repasts—chopping vast piles of foodstuff, stirring steaming pots, lifting trays of bread or pies into and out of the oven—and the cooking odors mingled promiscuously with the smells of wet woolens, aged dogs (two or three of which could usually be found passing their declining years in close proximity to the stove), candle wax, and humankind. Though normally shy and soft-spoken outside the home, the male Beckers, father and son, were boisterous and voluble on their own turf, hurling bantering remarks at each other and at Martha, who dodged them adroitly among her battery of pots and counterattacked with verbal volleys of her own, marking each hit with the triumphant wave of a ladle or the bang of a lid. Such jocund scenes were calculated to put guests at their ease and allow them to partake of the superfluity of familial affections. Elizabeth appreciated these performances and found them commendable insofar as they reflected the broad-mindedness and generosity of spirit that she regarded as refreshingly and characteristically American. Yet after a few minutes her impulse was to flee. The cheerful din made it difficult for her to think, much less to talk, and the stifling atmosphere obliged her to contemplate the possibility that she might very shortly be sick to her stomach. Though one side of her wanted intensely to adapt itself to the surroundings, the other, more instinctive side rebelled against them. The graft would not take. She found the Becker household regrettably but essentially alien to her nature.

In leaving Madison she would be leaving nothing more than a small, worn-out fragment of her past. True, her father's grave was there: a permanent landmark, conclusive evidence that her memories of the place did not belong wholly to the realm of dreams. Yet if she stayed, the dreamlike quality of the experience might grow and eventually subsume all; she would sink into a state of passivity. She saw Madison as a false start, an endeavor that had lost its purpose with her father's death. In leaving, she would start anew, on her own terms. She would no longer be Dr. Gow's daughter, orphaned or otherwise, but whoever she set out to be. She would be free from the suffocating ministrations of the local widows and wives—and from Reverend Hoffmeister's obsequious bullying.

There were practical considerations as well. A larger town would offer more opportunity for her to earn a living wage. She could, she felt sure, make her way as a piano teacher if there were a large enough body of students from which to draw. In Madison she already knew virtually all the girls and young women who were studying piano or were ever likely to study piano, and they were hardly a sufficient number to keep the already established piano teacher, the redoubtable Frau Schmidt, in dress money over the next few years. Moreover, the sale or rental of the Madison house would help defray expenses while she was building up a dependable clientele elsewhere.

She crossed the room to the small desk that her father had bought her for a birthday gift shortly after their move to Madison and extracted from one of the pigeonholes a bundle of letters bound with a black ribbon. The envelope she was looking for was of a bluish tint with a large black seal. On receiving the letter, she had read it hastily, hardly taking in the words. Now she brought it over to the window and unfolded it with deliberation. The letterhead, printed in gothic letters, read: "Macready & Sloan, Civil Engineers, Surveyors, Land Agents, Rooms 2 & 3 Phoenix Building, Cor. East Water & Michigan Sts., Milwaukee, Wisconsin." The handwriting was bold and free flowing.

Dear Miss Gow—

I was greatly saddened to read of your father's passing in this morning's *Sentinel*. It is difficult to believe that he is gone—taken from us in the very prime of life! The loss is a calamity, not only to those fortunate enough to have known him personally, but to the world at large, which is henceforth deprived of the fruits of his great learning. True, he leaves behind him notable achievements in the realm of Science, and all those scholars and seekers after truth who came in contact with him will carry his inspiration with them throughout the remainder of their days. Yet one cannot but lament the loss of that bright intellect and the great achievements that were yet to come!—even though one realizes that in the larger scheme of things nothing of his spirit has been wasted or lost.

Your father was a bright, perhaps the brightest, ornament of the university, and I confess that I took some pride in being instrumental in bringing him to that noble institution. Alas, that pride is now drowned in tears of regret at not having profited personally from his proximity. It was a comfort to know that he was so near, and I had looked forward eagerly to renewing our friendship as soon as my own affairs had become somewhat more settled, and the weather more propitious for travel. But Time waits for no man, and I carelessly squandered those golden hours of his tragically brief stay amongst us. It is a lesson learned too late!

For you of course the loss is greatest. To lose a parent is always a cause for profound mourning, and to lose an only remaining parent and to lose him so suddenly and in a foreign land must, if possible, add to the anguish. Please accept, Miss Gow, my most sincere condolences. If I can be of any possible service to you, great or small, I hope that you will not hesitate to avail yourself of my ardent desire to assist you. I can be reached by post at the above address, and if I am away on business, which I frequently am, the mail will be promptly sent on to me by my associate.

Your faithful servant—

William Macready

Once again she was struck by the letter's poverty of expression, its failure to enlighten or console. She lifted her gaze to stare blankly at the empty road and across the road to the barren landscape beyond, still awaiting the first stirring of spring. Oh, she didn't blame the old man for his inability to refresh her spirits; all the letters were like that, only serving to increase her sense of desolation, emphasizing by their sheer inadequacy the magnitude of her loss. No, she was grateful for the sincere if awkward gesture of goodwill. He did mean well, and, after all, what could he say under the circumstances? What could anyone say? She looked again at the paper in her hand and reminded herself that she had not sought it out for consolation but for purely practical considerations. Yes, Mr. Macready had plainly offered his help, and it occurred to her that she might be able to use it.

Milwaukee seemed a likely place for her purposes. It was larger than Madison and growing rapidly; at the same time it was small enough so that her talents and attainments, however modest, would not go wholly unappreciated. She hoped to cull a profitable harvest of piano students from among the burgeoning population. Moreover, it was close enough to Madison to make the process of relocation relatively simple and inexpensive. And she found the name of the town—*Milwaukee*—strangely appealing. *Madison* had always had a cold, impersonal sound to her ears, whereas there was a pleasing note of exoticism—even, let it be said, an intriguing note of barbarism—about the name that evoked faint, sweetly rapturous memories of reading *Lalla Rookh* in the upstairs window seat at school, with the late afternoon light silvering the pages. . . . But of course, the practical considerations were all that mattered.

She would write Mr. Macready to help her find lodgings there. Surely he would be able to do that. She was not quite certain, but it seemed to her that his letterhead indicated that he had something to do with real estate. The prospect of traipsing about the city on her own seeking accommodations filled her with dread. She would hardly know how to begin. It would surely be doing her a great service on his part to spare her the strain and indignity of climbing strange stairways and knocking on strange doors. She would write him this very afternoon. Now!

She returned to the desk, the letter still in her hands, but instead of putting it back with the others, she spread it out on the writing ledge and pulled out the chair. How odd it was the way the white-maned old man had intervened in her life! Such people were like supernumeraries in a stage play— outside the general action, but necessary to keep the plot flowing. . . . She drew a fresh sheet of letter paper from the drawer, dipped her pen lightly in the well, and began to write: *Dear Mr. Macready* . . .

Milwaukee, 1854

THE NOTES STUMBLED TO A STOP, tentatively, haltingly repeated themselves, and stopped again. The little girl withdrew her hands from the keyboard and dropped them into her lap. "Oh dear!" she exclaimed and looked up at her teacher with a pout of annoyance. "My fingers simply *won't* behave nicely this afternoon. Naughty fingers!" Her little voice was bright and perky. There was a cunning gleam in her blue eyes.

"Do try it once more, Celia," Elizabeth said. "Beginning with the opening measure. And keep in mind the beat. It is dum-dum, dum-dum-*dum*."

Mrs. Hermann stifled a nervous cough. Out of the corner of an eye Elizabeth could see her sitting bolt upright, clutching her parasol in her lap; she could feel the waves of hostility emitting from the woman.

"I do think that my hands are too tiny for so *many* notes," the little girl said brightly, "but I shall try again."

"It seems to me," Mrs. Hermann interjected, "that the child is perhaps a bit bored with the piece. You have kept her on it for three weeks running. She's played it until she can hardly hear it anymore. Perhaps it is time to move on to something else."

Elizabeth felt very weary, very calm. The woman is simply responding instinctively, she told herself, to protect her young. Nothing is more natural. I must not take it personally.

"I realize how tedious the piece must seem by now, but I would like Celia to be able to work through it with a bit more assurance and control before taking on the next piece I have in mind. I regard the fingering here as useful and fundamental. I am sure that she can master it with a little more concentrated practice."

"Are you saying that Celia does not practice, Miss Gow?" The voice was cold with anger. "I can assure you that she practices faithfully every day."

"I am not saying that she doesn't practice, Mrs. Hermann. My point is that it would be very useful for her to get this piece down properly before moving on."

"Well, Miss Gow, it seems to me that the job of the teacher is to teach students so that they *can* move on. With her last teacher she always progressed very nicely, had a new piece every week, and performed part of a lovely Handel sonata at the year-end recital. She was among the best of Mrs. Schneider's pupils—among the younger ones, that is. Of course, it is not for me to say, but it may well be that the piece is not wholly appropriate for someone at her stage. Her hands are, it is true, still very small."

"That should not be a problem, Mrs. Hermann," and she was about to add that it was a standard exercise for beginning students, but held her tongue. Instead, she said to herself: the trouble is that your daughter has no interest whatsoever in music; she simply enjoys being perched up there on the piano stool, displaying her velvet frock and her bright ringlets of golden hair.

"Problem or not, I do not see how you can expect the child to 'get down' the piece, as you put it, if you can't show her how. We are all quite sick of it at home. I am sure that she would like to try her hand at something else, wouldn't you, Celia?"

"It *is* a tiresome old piece, Mummy. But if Miss Gow really wants me to stay with it, I will try to play it better. I'll try as hard as ever I can, Miss Gow." She bestowed on her teacher her most winning smile and nodded her head so vigorously that her curls leaped up and down in joyous affirmation.

"I am sure that you will," Elizabeth responded. "Let us give the piece one more week. I know that it can be wearisome to work so long over a single exercise, but wearisome work leads to mastery. There really are some important things to be acquired here."

While the little girl was gathering up her music and cramming it away with cheerful finality into a handsome red-leather folder, embossed in gold with the letters C. H., her mother had drawn Elizabeth aside and was speaking to her in an earnest undertone.

"Frankly, I am somewhat disappointed in you, Miss Gow. When Mrs.

Schneider departed, I really did not know where to turn. Then I saw your notice and had a chance to talk with you, and well, I did feel that you would be quite suitable for Celia. I don't mind mentioning that I was favorably impressed by the reasonableness of your fee—that is, in comparison with those of Miss Bowers. Of course, she has an excellent reputation, but she really charges a great deal. Besides, I felt that Celia was not quite ready for Miss Bowers as yet—and I am sure that you would agree that there is no point in spending a fortune just to give a child a background in fundamentals. Be that as it may, it seems to me that Celia is not making the sort of progress that I had hoped for. To some extent the fault is mine. I admit that I have not been able to supervise her practice as closely as I ought; social commitments make that very difficult. Then too, as you know, Celia has been rather poorly this winter. She has always been a delicate child and must not be overstrained. And as a mother, Miss Gow, I see *that* as my main responsibility: to make sure that the child does not exert herself beyond her limited capacities. She is naturally gifted and eager to succeed, but prudence requires me to keep her from overdoing. At the same time, she needs encouragement. We all do, don't we, Miss Gow? She needs to feel that she is making headway, getting somewhere with her work. After all, she is only a child, Miss Gow, and a remarkably sensitive one at that. Frankly, I think that more public recitals would be a great help. Celia always does her best when required to perform. She knows how to rise to an occasion, to meet a challenge of that sort. Mrs. Schneider had four recitals a year, not just two. You might consider that as well." The woman managed to produce a parting smile and extended her hand graciously. "Good afternoon, Miss Gow. Come along, Celia!"

"Good afternoon, Miss Gow," the little girl sang out and dropped a near perfect curtsey. Then, with a final toss of her curls, she danced out the door just behind her mother.

Elizabeth heard them descending the stairway, the sharp staccato of the mother's boots accompanied by the soft patter of the child's pumps. She stood there in the center of the room, her hands clasped before her, lost in thoughtless reverie. Then, with a shake of the head, she broke free of her invisible bonds and crossed over to the window, where she drew aside the curtain and gazed down at the street. Mrs. Hermann and Celia were just emerging from the front doorstep. She watched them making their way up the street, the child skipping lightly at her mother's side. At one point they halted in their progress for the mother to say something to her daughter, the woman bending forward, earnestly seeking out the child's face, and driving home her remarks with a wag of a finger. Then they resumed their way, setting out with quicker, more determined strides, until they disappeared around the corner at the junction of Broadway.

At that moment a large cart, laden with barrels and drawn by two stalwart dray horses, rounded the corner and rumbled down the street at a smart pace in the direction of the house. Perched high on the driver's seat was a burly young man with a greasy black cap pulled down over one eye. He glanced up at Elizabeth's window as he passed and, seeing her there, saluted her with a broad smile and an extravagant flourish of his whip. Elizabeth jumped back from the window as if struck. She leaned against the wall, her heart pounding. The suddenness of the apparition had caught her completely off-guard. She had not had time to register the fact of his presence before he was upon her, flashing up at her that bold, triumphant look of recognition. It was as if he had fully expected to find her there, watching out for him, exposing herself to his greetings. The effrontery of the man! She felt thoroughly flustered and humiliated, and, in a sense, violated—as if he had, if only for the instant, forced his way into her room, penetrated her private space.

She struggled to regain her calm. She was behaving, she thought, like an hysteric. He passed this way in the cart every day at this same time: she knew that, and he certainly knew that as well. The rumble and rattle of the vehicle filled the street and shook the window panes. But just because he had accidentally caught sight of her now, he had no right to assume, as his expression seemed to proclaim, that she was there expressly on his account. The salute was uncalled for. It was provocative and annoying. And her distress was compounded by the realization that she had handled the situation badly. She should have held her ground and simply let his greeting go unnoticed on her part. Or better yet, since she had no cause to be rude to the man, she could have acknowledged it with a dignified and impersonal nod of the head. Her disorderly retreat from the window would have appeared for all the world as if she had been caught out in some shameful act! Yes, she herself was to blame for her discomfiture. She would know better in the future. . . . But oh, he should not have smiled at her like that, with his mouth twisted into a silent laugh and his lips open slightly to reveal the red, moist flash of his tongue! He had no right to look at her like that! A civil tug of his cap would have sufficed. After all, she knew him only as a tradesman: Tommy Haynes, who delivered coal in winter, ice in summer; a hanger-on in her landlady's kitchen, and an occasional handyman about the house. On one occasion he had entered her lodgings: when the pipe on the new stove had collapsed, and she had offered him a few formal words of thanks. He was nothing to her. Less than nothing. Even in a democratic society like America, certain social proprieties had to be maintained, and a woman was obliged to protect herself against unlicensed familiarities.

Since her father's death, she had become increasingly aware of her vulnerability to the outside world. As a single female, unattached to any household, she felt herself constantly exposed to public scrutiny. The situation was wearisome and demeaning, and full of unexpected happenings that demanded her constant vigilance. For example, her relationship with Mr. Macready had given rise to some bizarre complications.

The old gentleman had responded immediately and effectively to her letter. It was he who had found her present lodgings for her, signing her on with the landlady before Elizabeth had even set eyes upon the place. She had been annoyed at the peremptory way in which he had taken charge of things, yet when she saw the rooms for the first time, she found them more comfortable and commodious than she could ever have imagined and at a monthly rate that was only very slightly higher than she had anticipated paying. He had by his account spent many hours in the search, visited many places before settling on this one, and though she would have much preferred being included in the final decision, rather than confronted with a fait accompli, her sense of relief was accompanied by a sudden rush of gratitude.

The landlady, Mrs. Lancaster, accompanied them on the tour of the rooms, but it was all she could do to get in a word of her own. Macready had informed himself of the rules and customs of the house and undertook to impart them to Elizabeth on the landlady's behalf, as if poor, flustered Mrs. Lancaster's command of English was somehow deficient and he had kindly volunteered to translate for her. The grand manner with which he flung open doors and ushered the ladies over thresholds conveyed the impression that he was leading them through spacious, marble-floored apartments in some venerable Roman palazzo, rather than through the two and one-half rooms of a modest, if respectable, Milwaukee lodging house. In spite of his high-handedness it was hard to resist the old gentleman's enthusiasm or to take umbrage at the sincere pleasure he displayed in presenting Elizabeth with the new home he had found for her. Even Mrs. Lancaster's tongue-tied irritation melted away during the course of the tour. She gazed about the premises with wondering eyes, as if the place were wholly new to her; and when Macready grew lyrical on the peculiar charms of the establishment, Elizabeth noticed a blush of pleasure suffusing the woman's well-rouged cheeks.

Yet in the very midst of the proceedings Elizabeth was overcome by a momentary thought that literally brought her to a standstill. Macready's sheer exuberance put him at fault: his manner seemed less that of an aged cicerone than that of a young man about town installing his new mistress in a *hotel meublé*.

The vision lasted but a moment and was dispelled with a toss of the head. After all, Macready was old enough to be her father, her grandfather perhaps! And clearly any outsider—Mrs. Lancaster, for example—would have no difficulty reading the scene correctly. Yet Elizabeth came away with the nagging feeling that affairs were not being conducted in the very best, most decorous way.

The old gentleman became a regular visitor. They met once a week, generally on Tuesdays, in the downstairs sitting room, where Mrs. Lancaster would lay on a substantial afternoon tea at Mr. Macready's expense. Again, Elizabeth felt vaguely uncomfortable at being paid for in this manner, but her initial protests were brushed aside with a wave of the hand. "My dear young lady, the expense is a small matter to me and sheer extravagance for you. It's only reasonable that I should pay. Moreover, I don't know where we could hope to find a more decent and convenient setting for our little *conversazioni.*" Elizabeth did not see how she could protest more vehemently without implying more than she meant to imply. Indeed, the setting was quite proper. The downstairs sitting room was a quasi-public area, where the half-dozen lady lodgers habitually received visitors or simply dropped by to use the writing desk or to peruse the random selection of magazines that Mrs. Lancaster deposited there, neatly stacked on a small side table. As often as not, their conversation was overheard by one of the ladies of the house, firmly established in a nearby armchair, seemingly absorbed in her reading or crochet work.

Macready felt, as he explained, "an obligation to keep an eye on her." The obligation grew, she gathered, from his shipboard acquaintance with her father, which he easily expanded into something more binding. Soon he had cast himself in the role of an "old friend of the family," and though she knew that this assumption of familiarity was based on false premises, she accepted it as one of his "peculiarities" and as a harmless if somewhat aberrant manifestation of his goodwill.

As a family friend, he naturally took great interest in her efforts to establish herself as a music teacher. He advised her on appropriate places to advertise her services and displayed particular concern about the precise phrasing of the notices, scribbling innumerable drafts in a pocket notebook and weighing each word on his tongue, to assure that the description conveyed, as he put it, the "quality and refinement" of her instruction as well as its "technical polish." She found the results a trifle verbose but bowed to his greater awareness of the native sensibility. He quizzed her closely on each of her pupils and ruminated deeply on their family names, repeating them over to himself in a whisper, trying to evoke from them some echo of recollection in his memory. Sometimes, when a name struck him as particularly puzzling, he would extract from his frock-coat pocket a small volume, much battered by use: the Milwaukee City Directory. Removing his steel-rimmed glasses, he would bring the volume close to his nose and peruse the pages with a brisk businesslike air until he found what he was searching for; then he would tap the page once with his glasses and read the entry aloud: head of household's full name, occupation, and street address. On the basis of this sparse information he was then prepared to offer a judicious speculation on the pupil's origins, fortune, and respectability. When Elizabeth pronounced a name that he recognized, his eyes would flash, and his ruddy cheeks would glow with satisfaction.

The roster of people he knew by name was enormous and seemed to encompass virtually every aspect of city life. Yet it was no broader in its scope than his sense of fellowship and his tolerance. Elizabeth came to understand that he rarely spoke ill of any acquaintance. The worst he ever said of someone he knew personally was that "the chap was erratic" or "not always reliable." In general he was lavish with his praise, and Elizabeth had on occasion been surprised to discover that people described by him as "paragons of learning" or "born leaders of men" turned out on chance meetings to be quite ordinary creatures, bearing to her eyes all the usual marks of mortality. She regarded his steadfast loyalty to each and every one of his friends, his refusal—his constitutional inability—to say an ungracious word about any man he had shaken hands with or stood drinks for or exchanged cigars with as yet another sign of his strange boyishness—like his blushing whenever he was pleased or bounding up the front steps two at a time when he came to call. On the whole, she found his generous outlook an engaging trait, though it left her somewhat uncertain about the true nature of his personal associations.

She had managed at one of their first Tuesday teas to inquire about his son and had been told that the young man had married "and gone off to Charleston." She was taken back by the bald finality of the remark. In posing the question, she had fully expected a vague generality along the lines of "Oh, the boy is doing famously . . ."—some such thing. A silence ensued while she busied herself with the teapot, and he methodically, vigorously polished the lens of his glasses with a none-too-clean handkerchief. She felt his deep distress at his son's desertion and his stubborn refusal to cast blame. He clearly had no inclination to pursue the subject further. She filled their cups, and they moved briskly to another topic of conversation.

After he had left, a feeling of vague depression settled over her. She found it difficult to concentrate on her book. Finally she laid it aside and went over to the piano, but after fussing impatiently with the piano stool, which had been adjusted for one of her students, she got up and went into the bedroom. She stood for a moment in the doorway, looking about her blankly; then, galvanized into action, she set about sorting her clothing, removing all the summer things from the wardrobe. The garments to be put away for the winter she laid out on the bed; those to be brought to Mrs. Shea for laundering were tossed unceremoniously onto the floor. When the wardrobe was empty, she dusted it with a cloth, getting down on her knees and reaching far into the corners. In the process she came across a long-lost button from her winter coat. She gazed down at the object now safely nestled in the palm of her hand, and there came back to her all the foolish anguish the loss had occasioned her—the futile search for a replacement in all the shops in town and, finally, the purchase of a whole new set and her sitting up late one night sewing them on. She closed her fingers around the button, closed them so tightly that her knuckles were white. Then she rose from her knees and brought the button over to the mantelpiece, where she deposited it in a small silver box that held several such objects of indeterminate value—a cameo brooch with a broken clasp, a single pearl earring, her father's old watch fob—and closed the lid on it with a sigh. From beneath the bed she pulled out a large cardboard box, extracted from it folded sheets of tissue paper, and started to wrap the clothing on the bed. Her depression persisted. Her fingers grew clumsy; the tissue paper tore at her slightest touch. It was all futile. Turning her back on the clothes-strewn bed, she threw a cloak over her shoulders, tied on a bonnet, and went out for a walk.

It was a mild autumn afternoon, with a scent of burning leaves in the air. Across the street, in an empty lot between two buildings, several boys were playing a game of rounders with quiet intensity. She saw them out of the corner of her eye as she hurried past: the running, leaping bodies, the flash of golden hair, a red calico shirt criss-crossed by black braces. She heard the crack of the bat, the sound of running feet, and above the muffled grunts a hoarse, childish voice crying out "Atta boy, Charleee!" repeated at intervals and gradually growing fainter, until at one point the cry seemed to hang suspended among the treetops, only to be carried off by a light breeze of early evening. As she walked, her depression gave way to a gentle melancholy. The late afternoon sun raked the neighboring buildings with its rays, giving a rosy glow to their red brick facades and setting their upper-story windows

ablaze. Suddenly it seemed to her that the whole street had become transfixed, caught up in a ceremonial act of immolation, and she found herself
murmuring aloud, "How lovely, how lovely!"

She returned home half an hour later, calmer, almost happy. Her bedroom presented a shocking scene of disorder: drawers gaping open, the
wardrobe door ajar, clothes seemingly strewn everywhere. She stood on the
threshold and gazed about her with amazement. Throwing up her hands in
mock horror, she exclaimed aloud, "How terrible!" and set about putting
things in order with the tender resignation of a mother straightening up the
room of an absent child. She finished wrapping the summer things; then
from a large cedar chest at the foot of the bed she extracted her winter
dresses and hung them in the wardrobe, pulling them straight on the hang-
ers and smoothing out the creases as best she could. They would all need a
touch of the iron before wearing. Her winter coat, which had been dyed
black after her father's death, looked shabby and declassé among the other
garments. She would order a new coat, something smarter, of the new
length, with a bit of a nip to the waist. She had seen some handsome pearl-
gray worsted cloth at Mason's. At the time she had thought it was rather too
expensive; besides, she had told herself that it was not really a very practical
color. But now she felt that she sorely needed a new coat—a nice coat.
Surely she should be able to afford herself that one luxury. She did not see
why she always had to go around in blacks and browns and navy blues, as if
she were trying to melt into the shadows. One could be ladylike without
being downright drab! Yes, she would buy the cloth tomorrow, first thing.

When she had emptied the chest of the winter clothes, she refilled it
with the summer garments, laying them out neatly in the wrappings. She
closed the lid of the chest with a little exclamation, half-whispered, half-
sighed: "There!" She would not open the chest again until the spring, at
which time they would reemerge from their wrappings pristine and unchanged. But she. . . ? Would she be the same then as now? But it was useless trying to foresee the future, just as it was futile thinking about the past.
When she had been a little girl, in England, past and future had seemed to
flow one into the other, forming a lifelong continuum, and it had all seemed
so simple then, a question of making resolutions and sticking to them. Now
it was a question of dealing with contingencies, most of them wholly unex-

pected. Here, in America, only the present mattered. She must try to remember that.

Yet as she lay in bed that night, with the moonlight filtering in through the lace curtains, she could not keep her mind from drifting back to the past, to those nights at sea, those few fragile nights, when she and young Macready had stood together at the ship railing, had gazed together out over the dark, glistening expanse of sea, and had talked in challengingly confident voices of the future. No, she had felt no consuming passion for him; he had stirred in her no tumult of desire; and had he attempted then to take her in his arms, she would surely have pushed him away firmly, unhesitatingly. And yet . . . and yet, she had felt in his company a calm, a comfort, a physical ease that she had experienced with no other young man. If she had not looked on him then as a lover, she had come to look back on him with a growing sense of affection and gratitude; and she realized now that she had always clung to the belief that he was somewhere out there, available to her in case of need. Of course, that had been sheer folly on her part! The fact that he had remained fixed in her memory, against a background of moonlit nights, did not mean that he was actually entrapped there, like a fly in amber. He had quite naturally walked away, into real life, leaving behind only the shadow of a memory. When she tried to visualize his face, the features seemed dim and indistinct in the darkness. Only his voice came to her clearly out of the night—not the words, for she remembered little of what he said, but the pleasantly abrasive timbre of the voice and the earnestness, the urgency, of the intonation. It was as if he had been trying to mold the future with his voice, to shape it to some desired form. And she had shared in the effort, lifting her voice to join his in a solemn duet.

She learned to put young Robert Macready from her thoughts, to efface him from her memory until he was merely a shadow of a shadow. Oddly enough, perhaps, her weekly encounters with Macready *père* facilitated the process. The real if much attenuated resemblances between father and son were quite simply absorbed by the father, until the young man was all but obliterated, and Elizabeth began to see the two as one, to look back on the young man as a youthful version of the old, as if she were capable of ranging in memory over a span of several generations. In a few weeks, young Macready had ceased to exist for her as a person, being replaced by the old man, his father.

Therefore it was all the more bewildering and disturbing to her, a sudden and wholly unexpected excursion into the high grotesque, when one afternoon over tea the old man proposed marriage. She was so astounded by the proposal that she thought she had misheard him, and with her teacup still poised in midair, calmly asked him to repeat what he had said. He did, and the look of disbelief that still lingered on her face was so terrible to him that he lost his bearings, and instead of resorting to the loving sentiments he had tenderly laid aside for the occasion, he found himself stumbling into phrases of plaintive self-defense.

"I understand, Miss Gow, that this may come as something of a surprise to you, given perhaps the very real discrepancy in our ages and the fact that I may have assumed in your eyes a somewhat paternal posture. Yet I would like to think that we have known each other long enough for a degree of intimacy to have grown between us, and in spite of the differences in our ages, it does seem to me that our temperaments and outlook on life are not dissimilar. I do believe, my dear Miss Gow, that we would get along quite famously as husband and wife. And surely you will agree that mutual compatibility—and esteem—are more important to a marriage than a mere similarity in age. Though I am, I suppose, old enough to be your father, my feelings toward you are those of a suitor, a youthful suitor I dare say, in the full flush of ardor and admiration, who happens, to his embarrassment and chagrin, to be wearing the features of a man of advanced years. Yet hearts do not age, any more than do hopes, and I assure you that I am a vigorous man, sound in mind and body, and more youthful in spirit than many a man half my age. Though some people might well look on it as an unconventional sort of match, it would not, I am convinced, prove to be an unwise or unhappy one. I would look after you, Miss Gow, cherish and protect you, and to the deep regard and affection that I already feel for you today would be added the humble gratitude that a man my age must invariably have toward a woman *your* age who consents to be his bride."

Once again she felt assaulted. First Reverend Hoffmeister, now old Mr. Macready. It seemed unjust that men could impinge upon her in this way, simply because she was single and unattached. Yet her indignation abated somewhat in viewing his embarrassment. Clearly, he had read the glint of anger in her eyes and the set of her jaw. No, she could not really be cross with him. His romantic impulse was just another of his extravagances. Fortunately the sitting room had no witnesses to the scene, and she hastened to bring it to a close before one of the other lodgers entered or Mrs. Lancaster put in an appearance to see if the teapot needed "refreshing."

"Please, Mr. Macready. It is all very unexpected. I mean, I never suspected that such thoughts were ever on your mind; and really, I do think that I have never given you any cause to entertain them. If I have, it was wholly unintentional on my part, and I ask your forgiveness."

"My dear Miss Gow, your conduct has always been irreproachable. There is no question of such a thing . . ."

"Then I would be very grateful, Mr. Macready, if you would agree that we both put this conversation from our minds, forget it entirely. I appeal to you as a *friend* and would like to continue to think of you as one."

"I cannot, Miss Gow, erase the sentiments. That is beyond my power. They are etched—indelibly—on my heart. But I hereby retract the words. Consider them now unsaid. We will sit here together as we did a few moments backs, sipping our tea—sit together as old acquaintances and, yes, as good and trusted *friends*. . . . Ah, is that our landlady I see peering around the door? Undoubtedly she is coveting our china, impatient to carry it off to the sink. I suppose that I have once again overstayed my time."

He rose from his chair, gathered up his hat and cane. "Good day, Miss Gow. A charming visit. Let us meet again soon." He bowed in her direction, a slight bow, hardly more than a nod of the head, slow and ceremonious— and from beneath his bushy white eyebrows shot her a quick, conspiratorial glance. He placed the hat on his head, gave it a light tap with his hand, and turned to leave; but in the doorway he looked back and, lifting his cane aloft so the silver pommel gleamed, gave her a final gallant salute before leaving the room.

The experience left her shaken, if only because it was so totally unexpected. She was disturbed by her inability to anticipate events, by her failure to see in advance where Mr. Macready's conduct was leading. It was clear that he had been as surprised by her reaction as she had been by his proposal. He had been carrying on in what he had considered a perfectly normal and honorable way, and suddenly she had lashed out at him. It was she who had been perverse and unconventional in ignoring the clearly posted signs. Was she really so hopelessly naïve, so completely lacking in discernment? If so, she had every reason to be alarmed; if so, she was a menace not only to herself but to others. In order to survive, she had to be less passive, learn to impose her will on circumstances—otherwise she would be constantly forced on the defensive, even by people who, for the most part, wished her no ill. Certainly Macready was no villain. He had been genuinely helpful to her from the very outset, before there had been any question of his having "designs" on her. And he had never treated her with anything but respect—unlike, for example, that wretched Reverend Hoffmeister, who had tried to bully her into submission. That Macready was not quite a gentleman could hardly be held against him. Nor even, on consideration, could the fact that he was a lecherous old man. Though she might be naïve, she was not so very naïve as to think that relations between the sexes could be sustained without any reference to physical differences. After all, she was the daughter of a scientist, brought up to believe in the moral integrity of the natural order. That men should desire women and women be attracted to men was, she felt, "reasonable" and even "good," provided that such desire was suitably directed and properly controlled. She had been careless with Macready because she had failed to consider him as a potential lover. She had more or less assumed that a man of his age and demeanor would have resigned himself to a single state, though she realized now that such an assumption had nothing to do with the nature of things.

Moreover, she had always been ill at ease with the concept of celibacy, had even found it, in some obscure, unreasoned way, morally repugnant. She recalled the brother of a classmate of hers at school who had fallen under baleful influences at Oxford, converted to Roman Catholicism, and entered the seminary at Maynooth to study for the priesthood. She had last seen him at the annual school fete. To her surprise he had displayed the same ruddy cheeks, the same boisterous high spirits as always, running races with his younger brothers and taking great interest in the meat pies and meringues.

Yet the sight of Sam Nichols-Leigh in a seminarian's robes had filled her with embarrassment. It was as if he were flaunting his chastity, and by extension his sexuality, so that she had felt compelled to avert her eyes.

Of course, at the time she had not thought the scene through in those terms; she had only been aware of a vague sense of discomfort and confusion. But now, as she strove to resolve the question of old Macready's sexuality, the memory of the young seminarian came to mind, and she felt obliged to examine her views on the subject in the same forthright manner that she examined her conscience in moments of contrition, before her evening prayers. Yet how hard it was!

If one wanted to explore the darker regions of the spirit, assistance was sure and near at hand. The bookstores and lending libraries offered many experienced and deeply knowledgeable guides; her own shelves would supply material to inspire and enlighten her if she applied herself with diligence and devotion; moreover, spirituality was a subject she could discuss in depth with even the most casual of acquaintances. She was amazed and impressed by the subtlety and thoroughness that Americans applied to the matter of spiritual well-being. They brought to religious concerns a philosophical and psychological frame of mind that she found intriguing—quite different from the pietistic influences of her childhood, though terribly difficult to comprehend. She had recently read several essays by Mr. Emerson that had brought her close to tears, both from the nobility of the expression and from her inability to grasp the essence of the argument. Yet she knew that she could without shame openly discuss her confusion regarding Transcendentalism during the Sunday evening meetings at the parish house; she could lay bare her soul. But exploring the darker regions of human sexuality was another matter! The guides were few and sibylline, the oracles difficult to interpret. In this matter she would have to rely on her common sense and her powers of observation. She would have to be careful and alert. After all, she told herself, sexuality belonged primarily to the realm of natural phenomena. . . . Unless, of course, it was touched by love. When love intervened . . . well, she would face that aspect of the subject later! Meanwhile, she would have to train herself to be more diligent in detecting signs of danger.

"We don't see much of Mr. Macready these days." Mrs. Lancaster's words, like most of her pronouncements, were rich with innuendo.

"He appears to be much concerned with his affairs. He travels a great deal. Upstate, I believe."

"He's a fine gentleman," Mrs. Lancaster asserted. "And a lovely speaker, so I've been told. My nephew Philip, the dark one with the nice mustaches, heard him give a eulogy on Paddy McLaughlin, the fire chief that was, at the Lodge a couple of nights ago. He said it was the finest public discourse he had ever heard in his entire life. People were moaning aloud. It was that affecting."

"Yes, he is a well-spoken man."

"But it is not just the words, if you know what I mean, Miss Gow."

"Yes, of course I do, Mrs. Lancaster."

"It's the *feelings*."

"Quite. Yes."

"It does seem like a while since he has been around here."

"He was here but Tuesday last. For tea."

"So he was. There were the oat cakes; he quite liked those, didn't he? But still, he isn't as regular as he used to be."

"I suppose it is the work. He said he was very busy with a surveying job upstate."

"I suppose that's it. Though it isn't like him to be so irregular in his ways. He's a fine gentleman though. And he did most particularly relish those oat cakes if I recall."

"He did indeed, Mrs. Lancaster. They were a great success all around."

"Still, it's been a while. I suspect that we'll be seeing him again soon."

"I suspect that we will."

"Busy, you say?"

"Very. That's what he gave me to understand."

"Ah, well." Mrs. Lancaster went away clearly unappeased.

Although Mr. Macready and she had agreed to banish the proposal of marriage from their minds, its exiled presence cast a shadow between them. When he did visit again, the conversation flowed on much as before, their gestures and mutual attentions seemed much the same, and even as astute an observer as Mrs. Lancaster had trouble detecting any differences in their demeanor, yet as she bore away the tea things to the kitchen, she sensed, as a sort of aftertaste to the encounter, that something had changed. Mr. Macready's manner had become a trifle heartier, his laugh a little more strident, and Miss Gow's responses had assumed an added precision and deliberateness. Most apparent, however, were the simple facts that he lingered a little less over his tea and that the intervals between the visits became longer. Formerly he had come around once, sometimes twice a week. Now he appeared once a fortnight. Mrs. Lancaster had the impression that he was passing out of the young lady's life. And the impression confirmed her belief that something "very deep" had passed between them. As she said to her good friend Mrs. Ryan, "A man don't leave a woman unless they have been together first. And a gentleman always leaves the lady in a gentleman-like manner—he don't just scurry away." The more she thought about it, the greater her admiration for the couple grew. Though she found Miss Gow a bit standoffish and Mr. Macready not quite as generous with his tips as his expansive manner seemed to promise, she deeply approved of the refined and decorous way in which they went about breaking off their relationship. As she told Mrs. Ryan, "It was a rare sight to behold, and one that did honor to the establishment."

Elizabeth was both saddened and relieved by the estrangement. The old man represented her last link to her past life, to a time when she was still little more than a schoolgirl and not yet an American. In spite of his rather ramshackle air, she had always thought of him as someone to whom she could turn in moments of need. On the other hand (his recent indiscretion aside), he could be a time waster and a bore, and it was perhaps inevitable that she simply let him drift away from her and out of her life. He had helped her, and she was grateful. Perhaps some day she would have it in her power to repay him. But given the awkwardness that had now come between them, it would be kinder and easier all around for them to go their separate ways.

Mrs. Hermann and her Celia soon dropped away, to be replaced by Mrs. Meyer and her Hilda. Indeed, throughout the winter there was an ever-increasing flurry of activity in the downstairs hallway, a hushed murmur of female voices, followed by the sedate patter of footsteps on the stairs and the hesitant tap on the door. By the end of the year Elizabeth was able to discern a distinct pattern in the flow of students and was beginning to form a general idea of her own strengths and peculiarities as a teacher.

Her hopeful assumption that there was room in the budding metropolis for another piano teacher of "refined talents" had proved correct. Milwaukee seemed to have temporarily outgrown its resident musical faculty, and the cultural aspirations of the newer settlers seemed ever higher. Several of her pupils' parents spoke with heavy Germanic accents, punctured with strange expletives and unaccountable emissions of dry laughter. Their daughters tended to be docile, somewhat morose, but on the whole quick to learn. At first it had been the advertisements in the newspapers that had brought them around; within a few months, however, most of her pupils came to her by word of mouth.

Elizabeth noticed, however, that although she had little trouble obtaining students, they were mostly beginners who stayed with her until they had mastered the basics and then moved on. She was puzzled and hurt by these desertions, which she initially attributed to her demanding standards and the general austerity of her manner. Certainly she had nothing to offer a Celia Hermann, who wanted nothing but praise and constant encouragement. But what about the others, the most musical and diligent of her students? How to explain their seemingly inevitable departures? Surely she could not blame these departures on the rigor of her instruction or on her lack of easy charm. No, that would be begging the issue. She regretted that she had no one with whom she could discuss the problem, no one to whom she could turn for advice. Well, she would have to find the answer on her own. She believed strongly in facing up to the truth. It was an essential part of making one's own way—every bit as important as working hard and doing one's work conscientiously. Most women, she felt, lived on illusions: it was their way of preserving their purity and resisting cynicism. Purity was important to her, too; she feared contagion by the world. Yet she felt that truth was a surer defense against infection than illusion. Be honest with oneself: that was the sum and substance of her philosophy. A simple creed, a solid creed—but one strangely lacking in specific guidelines. The mere will to be honest was somehow not enough; one needed the means or the ability to penetrate layer upon layer of received opinion and wishful thinking; and once that was done, one needed the courage to look boldly on what now lay exposed. The only way that she knew to test the validity of one's quest was by the resultant pain: the more honest one was with oneself, the more hurtful the revelations. And what then was one to do with all that pain? How was one to dispose of it? That she did not know. All that she knew was that she had to keep it for herself and not attempt to pass it off on others.

After much thought she concluded that the reason why most of her better students left her was precisely that they were able to do so. After a few months of work with her they were sufficiently skilled to move on to more "advanced" instructors such as Miss Bowers or Miss Chisholm, both of whom had received degrees from proper conservatories. When the desertion occurred, the usual parental explanation, after a rambling introduction full of vague, gratuitous compliments, was that little Sophie or Cora or Gertrude was perhaps "ready for a change," often followed by the comment, intended to soften the blow, that the child had grown "a bit stale of late" and would probably benefit from the challenge of a new setting.

Yes, it was all very just and reasonable, she told herself. She was, after all, only a lowly amateur who had nothing to offer the young pianist beyond the initial stage of instruction; in a sense, their moving on was a sign that she had done her work well. And yet . . . and yet, she would dearly have liked to establish a long-term relationship with at least some of her better students, to have had the satisfaction of guiding their progress beyond the most elementary exercises, and to have watched over them as they grew and developed. She would have liked to know them better as individuals and to have inspired their personal loyalty as well as their respect. But clearly that was not to be. Honesty compelled her to face the fact that she must content herself with a position at the very bottom of the instructional ladder. After all, someone had to be there; and if she did her job skillfully, conscientiously, she would have the satisfaction of knowing that she was fulfilling an essential role in the whole process, that she had established a place for herself in the community.

It is never easy to come to grips for the first time with the bold fact of one's mediocrity—especially when one is twenty-three! And oh, the continual desertions did so get her down! In spite of herself, she found that she was growing ever more distant and aloof from her students in anticipation of their seemingly inevitable departures. And she was gradually coming to think of herself as an essentially cold and unemotional person, a person unlikely to, perhaps incapable of sustaining an intimate relationship with anyone. Because she refused to play the hypocrite, she found herself assuming the persona of the woman she thought herself to be. Her greetings at the door were ever more brisk and businesslike; her smiles were reserved as tokens of approval for a piece well learned, a passage correctly played; she neither flattered nor cajoled her pupils, and she delivered her criticisms in an even, dispassionate tone of voice that allowed no appeal or excuse. The severity of her manner intimidated some of her students, though the better ones and their parents took pride in it, felt reassured by it, and confidently assumed that it concealed the proverbial heart of gold. Whether or not that was the case, it increasingly came to conceal a sense of barrenness, a desolation, and a lack of belief in much of anything, most especially in herself.

Life was taking on for Elizabeth a disconcerting dreamlike quality, so that she hardly dared to confront any of her fondest convictions for fear that they would simply melt away before her eyes. There were times when even the Milwaukee street scene would assume an aura of unreality. She would find herself, market basket on her arm, staring into the sanguinary window display of Zuckmeyer's butcher shop as if she were a childish spectator at a magic lantern show. She would now have to pretend that she was a grown person in order to buy two lean lamb chops for her dinner and force herself to play the role in a calm, firm voice, accompanied by suitably grown-up gestures. . . .

During the ensuing weeks she made an effort to go out into the world. The effort consisted for the most part in attending more church functions and helping out in the domestic arrangements connected with the various church festivals and benefit events. The role of lady volunteer did not come easily to her. She had no small talk whatsoever; and where others bustled, she delved. Moreover, she found herself to be miserably inept. She had no idea how to go about arranging flowers in a bowl: her bouquets stood stiffly at the altar like grenadiers at attention. And the pudding she brought to the charity supper sat neglected on the sideboard, passed over by all the greedy-eyed feasters, except for the dreadful Mr. Robinson, who declared in a loud, challenging voice that it was "Very tasty indeed!"

The single men in the congregation seemed to find her intimidating, or else, like Mr. Robinson, with his constant leer and wheedling ways, were totally unattractive to her. There was a pallid young man who for a period of several weeks took to hovering near her and whom she occasionally caught casting soulful glances in her direction from his pale blue, myopic eyes. His name was Josiah Chapman; he was nineteen and the junior member of Chapman & Son, Haberdashers, of East Water Street. By all accounts he was a nice boy, with pure morals and secure prospects, but the way he glided about on the toes of his highly burnished black shoes made her flesh creep. In any case, he never quite managed to address her directly; she certainly offered him no encouragement to do so, and he eventually disengaged himself to drift away toward more hospitable prospects.

To the extent that she formed any friendships, it was chiefly among the widows and spinsters, who graciously went out of their way to claim her as one of their own. An elderly couple, a magistrate and his wife, took her under their wings and invited her from time to time to share a frugal repast in the intimacy of their dimly lit and underheated home, during which they yielded up to her the accumulated wisdom of almost a half century of combined living. As for the young couples, they seemed wholly preoccupied with one another; and the young unattached women of Elizabeth's age clung jealously to the security of their own tightly knit circles of acquaintance. Still, the church gatherings provided her with a social context of sorts; the very familiarity of the faces was in itself congenial.

Spring turned suddenly into summer. The first stirrings of release from winter were brutally subsumed by mugginess and heat. Though this was Elizabeth's fifth summer in America she was still not prepared for the onslaught of the season. When she arose in the morning, she methodically enclosed her body in the petticoats and undergarments habitual to her girlhood and appropriate for an English clime. She had laid them out the night before, as she had laid them out for many years, and each seemed to play its part in the ritual of her awakening as she repeated the familiar gestures in front of the full-length looking glass in the bedroom. Yet as the day progressed, she felt increasingly weighted down, increasingly clumsy and unkempt; at midday she would often withdraw to the bedroom and hastily, almost guiltily remove some article of underclothing, reminding herself that this was after all Wisconsin, not Devon or Kent. Yet on emerging from the room, she invariably felt vaguely indecent and exposed, in spite of the fact that others still found her overdressed for the weather. "Oh Miss Gow, how *can* you wear a woolen dress on a day like this? I'm sure that I would simply *die!*" She realized that her students half-admired her for the eccentricity of her attire and took a certain pride in it. It helped to compensate for her lack of charm.

That fifth summer in America was a season of particular ferocity. Once the sun had risen over the rooftops, the Milwaukee streets were all but deserted of pedestrians, and those people who were abroad clung to the shady side, moving slowly, warily, like figures in a magic lantern show. Most of Elizabeth's students had left town with their parents, retreating to lakeside chalets or grandparents' farms. Elizabeth stayed on, ostensibly to administer to the two students who had requested summer tuition, but mainly because she lacked the incentive to leave the city and find somewhere to go. Time hung heavy on her hands. It was too hot to venture out on needless errands. She made an effort to reawaken her interest in embroidery, but the initial results seemed shockingly juvenile and banal; after an afternoon's labor, she stuffed the unfinished pattern back into the sewing basket and pushed it out of the way behind the armchair. There were moments of sheer restlessness when she wandered about the rooms, distractedly swiping at the furniture with a cloth, mechanically going through the little gestures of domestic industry. Most of the time, however, she spent stretched out on the chaise, a book abandoned on her lap, her mind drifting back and forth between the things perceived dimly about her and half-formed memories. Though the shutters were closed, the room was vibrant with daylight, which pierced through the slats and crevices, making flickering bright slashes across the ceiling and wallpaper, and throwing off sharp reflections from the glass globe of the oil lamp overhead. There were moments when the whole room seemed splintered and fragmented, the interplay of light so violent and frenetic that she was forced to close her eyes against the blinding confusion.

Then she would just listen. The noises from the street suffused the room—muted, distant, yet preternaturally distinct; the rumble and creaking of passing vehicles, the clippety-clop of a solitary rider, often accompanied by the faint jingle of his accouterments; the snort of a horse; the sudden outburst of barking dogs, cut short by a sharp curse and frightened yelp; a child's long, drawn-out call, followed by the echo of another child's faraway reply. . . . Nearby, within the confines of the house, were the muffled sound of laughter and the clatter of pots from the kitchen below; hovering at hand, the insistent buzz of a fly.

Just before noon Tommy Haynes's wagon would thunder by, piled high with barrels from the brewery. The house trembled ominously at its approach, was shaken violently as it passed, and then subsided in a series of tremors as the wagon made its barbaric progress into town. Sometimes its coming would take her by surprise, and she would clutch at the furniture and close her eyes tight against the onslaught. Usually, however, as the noon hour approached, she found herself preparing for the event. This perhaps was even worse, for she would lie on the chaise, rigid with tension, her book clasped tightly against her bosom, listening intently for the very first faint rumble. And as the sound increased, she would lie there desperately still like someone overtaken by a speeding locomotive and pressing herself prone between the tracks, praying for the train to pass harmlessly over her. . . .

Tommy Haynes was a great favorite of Mrs. Lancaster. There was always a pitcher of ale awaiting him whenever he dropped by with the coal or ice, and his entrances below stairs were often accompanied by shrieks of laughter from the landlady and a scuffling of feet as he went through his comic routine of pursuing the portly widow around her kitchen. Elizabeth had witnessed the scene on a couple of occasions when delivering her breakfast dishes to the kitchen. She found the spectacle vulgar and demeaning, both to the landlady and herself, but since the play was obviously innocent in intent, she did her best to suppress her disapproval and even managed to adumbrate a wan smile—the sort of smile one reserved for very small children who had committed, all unbeknownst to themselves, an act of impropriety.

"Oh, he's the very devil!" Mrs. Lancaster had proclaimed with relish one day after his departure. "Married at sixteen he was, and he's now the father of five. Why, I don't know what we would do without him here. I simply couldn't manage by myself. And he's as handy and as helpful as can be."

Elizabeth could hardly bring herself to look at the young man. It was not that she found him repulsive, like young Chapman or that dreadful Mr. Robinson, but there was an assertiveness in his manner, a sort of physical arrogance, that made her uneasy. When she encountered him in the hallway or on the back stairs, she sensed that he was somehow challenging her, and she did not know how to respond except by averting her gaze. She felt clumsy and stupid at these encounters, as well as angry at herself for behaving like a flustered schoolgirl. There was no reason whatsoever why she should allow herself to be intimidated by the man. The heat and her solitary habits were clearly getting to her. If she did not take care, she risked becoming an hysteric! She would have to get a hold on herself. Next time she met him she would greet him openly and politely, as she would any other tradesman, menial, or passing acquaintance. Goodness knows what the man must think of her with her wild, furtive ways! She was letting the situation get thoroughly out of hand.

And indeed, during their next few chance encounters she was in complete control of herself. She looked him calmly in the eye, greeted him by name in a sprightly voice, and passed him by. It did seem to her that she had actually managed to quell his arrogance, or at least to keep the man safely at bay. He was as boisterous and mocking as ever, but a new, quizzical look had entered his gaze. Behind the swagger and the grin she noticed for the first time a note of uncertainty.

Yet these little victories were won at a cost. In his presence she was fine:

polite, cordial, distant. But alone in her room she was put to rout. He would suddenly barge into her thoughts unannounced, and there was no way to evict him. He would linger about her, swelling in pride and insolence, filling the room with his being. So real did he become, so pressing and overbearing, that she could smell the sweetly acrid odor of his sweat. At such moments she would hurl herself at the piano, pounding out a progression of senseless chords, or pace the floor shouting snatches of verse remembered from school, or, as a final resort, grab her parasol and hurry downstairs for a feverish walk under the summer sun. And every weekday, just before noon, he would ride with wild abandon through her room.

Mrs. Lancaster mounted the stairs expressly to announce—breathless with the climb and the joyful burden of her message—that she had decided after all to replace the wallpaper in Elizabeth's bedroom.

"You're such a good tenant, Miss Gow, and indeed I feel myself dreadful remiss in letting the paper get to such a state. It's the roof leak of a couple of years back that started the trouble. I should have had it redone then, but what with one thing and another, and you so eager to come in right away as you recall. . . . Well anyway, I've made up my mind to have it done right and proper, and I've spoken to Tommy Haynes about the job, and he can get to it at the beginning of next month. They'll be cleaning the vats at the brewery then, and he'll have his mornings free for two weeks running. Oh, he's the very devil he is, and you'll have to keep an eye on him, you will! But all jesting aside, Miss Gow, the man is a good worker and will do a decent job for you. He did the whole of Mrs. Ryan's house, parlor to attic, and the paper is as nice and neat and tight as a body could wish for. As I said to Mrs. Ryan, it's like a seamless garment—those are my very words."

The first thing next morning Elizabeth went downstairs to tell Mrs. Lancaster that, on second thought, she really could not have the papering done next month; it would interfere too much with her teaching schedule, it really wasn't possible. Mrs. Lancaster gaped with astonishment, then flushed with irritation. She protested that the job would not be a noisy one—why, Miss Gow need only tell Tommy Haynes not to whistle while he was working! And she could close the bedroom door while the students were there.

Or, if she preferred, Tommy Haynes could absent himself from the premises while she was giving lessons. Yes, that might be the best of all, "if only for appearance's sake, if you know what I mean." But Elizabeth was so insistent, so grimly determined to have her own way, that the old lady, who had made her own way in life by practicing a certain amount of compliance, gave up the fight with a shrug of the shoulders and a slow, disbelieving shake of the head.

As she said to Mrs. Ryan that same evening, over a cooling pitcher of ale in the kitchen, "There's simply no telling about some people. Wasn't it she herself who brought up the matter of the wallpaper the very first time she set eyes on the place? And now that I've gone and arranged to get the job done, at no cost whatsoever to herself, she comes to tell me that she can't abide with the bother of it all! Now, can you fancy that? Why, you'd think that she was afraid that Tommy Haynes would drop his paste pot and make a grab for *her!* Oh, there's no telling about some people, Mrs. Ryan, none at all. If I have learned one thing in life, it's *that.*"

A week later Elizabeth sat down at her table and wrote a brief letter to William Macready accepting his offer of marriage.

Milwaukee, 1857

THEY MOVED INTO A NEW HOUSE three months before the birth of their first child. It was a narrow, three-story building, faced in red sandstone, one of a dozen similar row houses destined to fill out the north side of a city block, a short walk from Macready's office. When they arrived, the plaster was still wet in the downstairs hallway.

The Macready house stood second from the corner on the "finished" end of the block. Five doors down from them the building lacked windows and was little more than a sandstone shell, swarming inside with carpenters and plasterers; contingent to the shell was the timber frame of the neighboring dwelling; and the end lots were nothing more than a large muddy ditch filled with rubble. Across the street, extending the whole of the block, stood a tall wooden fence that screened from sight the back of a livery stable and several temporary warehouses. The fence was papered over with advertisements and public notices, most of which had lost their urgency and grown faded and inarticulate with age. From time to time a ragged team of paper-hangers would straggle by with their buckets and brushes and hastily throw up a bright new announcement, which for a day or so seemed to alter the whole configuration of the fence and drew people to their parlor windows for a brief, incurious look.

During the day the street was full of noise and animation, reaching a near crescendo shortly before noon: the ceaseless coming and going of vehicles of all sorts and sizes, bringing in building materials and carting away debris; the shouts and laughter of the work crews, along with intermittent bursts of song; the cries of caterers and vendors, selling refreshments to the laborers and casting cunning glances at the newcomers to the block, making calculations against the future. And above the clatter of vehicles and the hubbub of voices came the banging of hammers, the creaking of cranes, and the sharp, incisive clang of chisels and picks.

Elizabeth found the constant din wearying. But to Macready's ears it was, as he put it, the "cheering sound of progress," and he left the house each morning, on his way to the office, with a light step. He seemed thoroughly at his ease amidst the tumult, like a much-decorated old campaigner out on maneuvers. Toward the end of the block he would pause to cast a professional eye over the construction site, to acknowledge greetings, and to call out a few words of encouragement to members of the work crews. He appeared to know everyone by name, from the dark-browed Irish laborers with "hardly a bit of the English on them" to the pot-bellied foremen with their seemingly inexhaustible flow of Anglo-Saxon expletives.

When the chief man himself, J. T. Shirley, was on the site, Macready lingered a little longer than usual. Though Shirley was some thirty years his junior, Macready felt a deep affinity for this dapper little man who played the part of developer, architect, chief engineer, and real estate broker for the whole project, and who was generally referred to in absentia as "Big John"—some said because of the grandiose nature of his undertakings, others said because of his diminutive stature. He had arrived in the city with nothing in his pocket but a gold cigar case engraved with his initials, and in less than a half-dozen years he had made a name for himself in the financial community as a man "who got things done." He was in fact a man after Macready's heart, displaying as he did a spirit of high adventure in his business transactions, along with certain cultural refinements that showed him to be something other than a vulgar entrepreneur. There was about him a touch of mystery, a dash of romance, that spoke directly to Macready's temperament.

It was said that he came originally from Massachusetts; that he was the son of a prominent minister; that he had a degree from, or perhaps had merely attended, Bowdoin College; that he had won and lost a fortune in the California gold fields; that while in California he had lived with a Russian duchess, or more probably a Russian countess, by whom he had had a daughter; that he knew the whole of Book 4 of the *Aeneid* by heart, so that you need only give him the beginning of a line and off he'd go, straight to the end, with an ease and fluidity that would make you think he had learned Latin at his mater's knee; that in the past couple of years, through adroit reinvestment of the bank mortgages on his Milwaukee property, he had made more than five thousand dollars on the Charleston Cotton Exchange. Because none of these rumors, or numerous other ones concerning him, had been positively verified or even traced back to their primary sources, they lent to his presence an aura of Fable that was somehow, to Macready's eyes, more imposing than the mere collaboration of Fact. Whereas the men of substance in the city, weighing their words with caution, would refer to J. T. Shirley as a "a possible comer" and "someone to watch," Macready would proclaim to all and sundry that his friend was "a true visionary" who would take his place among the "makers and shapers" of Wisconsin. When, four years later, Shirley was declared bankrupt and left town for parts unknown, Macready was dumbfounded, but his faith in his friend remained essentially unshaken. Though it was not the sort of belief he could hope to articulate in public, it seemed to him that J. T. Shirley had simply stepped off the street and into the realm of Ideals—that he had for the time being crossed over from Fact to Fable. And several years later, he felt a flush of emotion when Shirley's name resurfaced, once again engulfed in the luminous mist of hearsay. It was now reported that the man had returned to California and had become the proprietor of a large and terrifically smart hotel in San Francisco, frequented by millionaires and English lords. Whether this person was the same John Shirley was not wholly certain, but something about the man's style made it more than likely; nor was it certain that the John T. Shirley who later served with such dash and distinction as a cavalry officer in the Confederate army and met a hero's end in the Battle of Kennesaw Mountain was the same man. Yet true or not, Macready somehow felt that the rumors befitted his old friend and vindicated his own deeply held loyalty.

At the moment, however, J. T. Shirley was still a figure bright with promise, and the project taking shape before them, outside Macready's spanking new home, was an imposing monument to the future. After a ritualistic exchange of cigars the two men stood together, shoulder to shoulder, surveying the scene, each of them drawing, in his own way, deep satisfaction from the hectic activity going on around them and from their splendid isolation at the front of the stage. As always on such occasions Macready sought to encapsulate his soaring sentiments in some ennobling quotation. He closed his eyes and waited expectantly for the words to emerge from behind his memory. "Blest and thrice blest the Roman"—he had the good sense to suppress the sudden outflow of grandiloquence, but he could not resist, his eyes still closed, reciting the words to himself:

> " . . . Who sees Rome's brightest day,
> Who sees that long victorious pomp
> Wind down the Sacred Way,
> And through the bellowing Forum,
> And round the Suppliant's Grove,
> Up to the everlasting gates
> Of Capitolian Jove."

"Virginia?" Shirley held the cigar aloft, eyeing it thoughtfully.

"Havana. It's an imported leaf. I ordered a crate of them through Ahearn's."

"First-rate smoke, that. Ahearn's eh?" And he replaced it in his mouth with a grand gesture of finality. A halo of cigar smoke encircled both their heads.

Although the rooms were dark and their proportions ungenerous, and although a faint aura of dampness crept up from the cellars to pervade the whole of the downstairs (it was almost six months before the plaster in the front hallway completely dried), Elizabeth took to the house at once. Perhaps because it reminded her, in its very faults, of her childhood home in London. Perhaps, too, carrying a child disposed her to like any place where she could set about, unrestricted, to building a nest. That the house was utterly new, untouched by history or a past, was strange to her. If one stripped off the wall coverings or pried up the floorboards or crept about the attic crawl spaces, one would find no trace of previous habitation, no signs of life, except perhaps a truant trowel or plastering pan or an empty whiskey bottle—recent construction crew relics that conveyed little emotional resonance. She had never dreamed of permanently settling herself in such a house, a house where she had not felt herself to be a tenant in time, a passer-through. She realized now that European concepts of permanence were peculiar in an American setting. Even the London house, the one place she had ever really thought of as her home, had possessed a forceful personality of its own, beyond the reach of her affections or influence—a personality based on unknown past as well as unknown future generations of inhabitants. This house, pristine and virginal, was different, though no less imposing in its way. As a tabula rasa it presented unfamiliar challenges. Well, she was ready for them. Hadn't she made up her mind on marrying that she would start afresh, that she would make a go of it?

It was agreed that she would give up teaching. "After all, my dear, there is no point in your working. I trust that I shall be able to provide for my wife—and family." He took her hand in his and gave it an affectionate pat. The decision seemed proper to Elizabeth. She was preoccupied with the prospect of motherhood, and her days were full enough with looking after the house, doing the shopping, keeping accounts. Besides, she knew that giving lessons was not wholly suitable for a married woman. It was one thing to earn money as Miss Gow, quite another as Mrs. Macready; the former was acceptable in polite circles, the latter, unless she was a widow, regarded with vague misgivings. Yet in relinquishing the teaching, she realized how much she had come to depend on it, not just for the income, but for the little gratification it had afforded her, and for the lift it had given her self-esteem. She had always felt herself awkward and constrained in the presence of those bouncy, pampered, bright-faced young ladies. Her clothes were never quite right, her responses were always lacking in spontaneity; her pupils had made her feel prim, dour, prematurely old. Yet she now appreciated the fact that however ill at ease she might have been, she did possess the ability to pass on to others, or at least to some others, a useful body of knowledge, and that this ability, by no means universal or wholly insignificant, helped to define her as a person. She had been learning to see herself as a teacher. It was a role in which she was beginning to acquire a certain authority. Now she would have to present herself to the world as a wife and mother. Having lost her own mother at an early age, she had no clear model to follow. She had only the most general idea of how the part was to be played. All the particulars, the interesting and essential particulars, were lacking. She looked to William to guide her.

"It's as you wish, my dear. I have complete confidence in your judgment." He lowered his newspaper and smiled across at her. There was in his gaze an expression of pride and frank pleasure that made her blush and look away. "Just keep track of the bills. And give them to me to pay. Since old Fergusson is an acquaintance of mine and likes to drop by the office now and then, I might just as well settle with him personally."

"But don't you think, William, that it might be terribly extravagant on my part? I could probably do without them. Or find something similar at Hemsley's for half the price; oh, I am sure that I could. Really, William, I was quite taken aback by the cost."

"You need them, my dear, and you ought to have them. And since you say that they are indeed the nicest you have seen, you might just as well take pleasure in buying them. Just send Fergusson the measurements or whatever is required. No, not another word. I insist on it, Elizabeth."

And that's the way it was. She learned quickly to deny herself since he would deny her nothing.

It was, all of it, far different from what she had expected. William was gentle, considerate, kind to a fault, but there were moments when they were together in the same room, even side by side in bed, when she was hardly aware of him. When she had been living with her father, his presence had pervaded the whole house, even when he was shut away in his study. Over the years she had learned to anticipate his moods, to read the meaning in his least gesture, in his most furtive glance, in the slightest modulation of his voice. She had learned to interpret his silences. Such, she understood, was the nature of intimacy: a sensitivity to the feelings of others that transcends all conscious efforts at attentiveness. Yet attentiveness had been there, kept alive by the sheer force of her father's personality, whose aura hung in the air, even in his absence, like incense in an empty cathedral. After his death the aura inevitably faded, for that, after all, was what death was about: the depersonalization of space. Released from that aura's influence, Elizabeth had grown slack and self-indulgent, had allowed herself to wander unprotected into the treacherous realm of reveries, until suddenly she had looked about her and taken fright. As a married woman, she anticipated a revitalization of her attention, a reawakening. Marriage, as she saw it, would require a constant watchfulness and a loss of total independence. She welcomed the change, even the loss, as a means of acquiring a firmer grip on her life. William's presence would restore to her that needful tension of domestic intimacy, would redirect her wayward emotions to an acceptable abode. It would help to protect her not only from the constant badgering and petty interference of the outside world, but from herself.

Yet that presence, though real enough, was strangely elusive. As was to be expected in a man of his age, William was set in some of his ways. He arose from the connubial bed at 5:30 in summer, 6:15 in winter. His morning toilette was an elaborate affair, lasting a full three-quarters of an hour and performed in strictest privacy behind a large screen in a corner of the bedroom. As it progressed, the room was gradually infused with the scent of shaving soap and eau de cologne. When he emerged, stepping brightly into the morning light of the bedroom window, his thick mane of snow-white hair flowed back in waves from his lofty brow, his cheeks glowed from the vigor of his ablutions, and his pale blue eyes looked out with myopic wonder through glinting, steel-framed glasses. He wore invariably his faded, blue velvet dressing gown and slippers; otherwise he was fully dressed, down to the tiny diamond stickpin that winked from the folds of a white neckcloth.

At night he came to her in the dark, after undressing behind the screen. She never saw him naked—never for that matter saw him in any more casual attire than his dressing gown and slippers, except for fleeting glimpses of him in his long white nightshirt and cap before he extinguished the lamp and slipped discreetly into bed. She was touched by his modesty, understood his reluctance to expose his old man's body to her gaze, and was grateful for it. Far better to leave their love-making to the dark. That way one could, if one wished, think of it in terms of the visitation of a god. There was no point in playing at poets or princes. . . .

His origins, like those of a god, seemed hidden in the mists of time. She had no idea of his early life—what his childhood had been like or who his parents were. The long expanse of years between his youth and their marriage was hardly less nebulous, and represented by a handful of stock anecdotes whose significance seemed less certain to her with each retelling. Once, when she attempted to draw him out on the subject of his first wife, he had said, quite simply, "Her name was Mary"—and nothing more. On other occasions he had protested that he had no interest in the past, that there was no point in looking backward. "Think of Orpheus, my dear! Besides, I feel that I have started life afresh in marrying you. Everything that came before was just a dream." Which was all very well for him, but it was devilishly hard for her to be wed to a man whose personality was purportedly based on dreams!

And like a god, too, he had a tendency to fade away, to remove himself to other spheres. His days were spent mainly at work. Though his office was only a short walk from home, he chose to take his noon meal at the City Hotel or at the more colorful Baltic House, an establishment much favored by commercial travelers, where he could keep abreast of the goings-on about town. The business week ended at noon on Saturdays, when Billy the office boy would, with a bustling air of importance, put up the shutters, and William would ceremoniously lock the door. Yet he would often return to the office on Sundays to feed the cats and to deal with any leftover paperwork. At home he was almost invariably cheerful, courteous, even courtly in manner, though he would sometimes lapse into abstracted moods, so that she would have to repeat things. It was possible that he might be a bit hard of hearing; at his age that was only to be expected. Yet in spite of Elizabeth's subtle efforts to determine that fact, the evidence remained inconclusive. He heard well enough, it seemed, when his interest was engaged; and he referred to the deafness of several of his elderly acquaintances in a tone of shocked bemusement. He never spoke sharply to her or raised his voice. He hated domestic arguments or unpleasant confrontations of any sort, and if he could not ward them off with good-humored banter or conciliatory generalities, he would lapse into smiling mutism. Later, when she began to quiz him closely about financial matters, a deeply aggrieved look would come into his eyes, and he would begin to back slowly toward the door, his right hand groping in empty air for the cane that hung suspended from the coat rack—seeming for all the world like a somnambulant enmeshed in a nightmare, so that the sight of him suddenly sickened her and made her desist. He seemed congenitally unable to engage in a personal dispute or even to bear a grudge. In those respects he was decidedly *un*godlike, more like a small child or faithful dog. In any case, she had no way of getting to him. He either dissolved in soft phrases or simply slipped away.

The first months of her marriage had passed peaceably, uneventfully, in a sort of lethargic stupor that resembled contentment. Then had come the move, and she had busied herself at setting up the new household and watching over the servant girl, Molly, who was eager and sweet-tempered but still very raw, and whose concept of cleanliness remained rudimentary and rustic. The time was largely taken up with establishing new routines and, later on, with preparing for the arrival of the baby. But these activities were less occupations than preoccupations, and the hidden strain in Elizabeth's life came from a sense that she was still waiting for things to begin.

Then the baby came, but it seemed more a process than an event—exhilarating at first, then debilitating. She kept telling herself that her life had changed, that she had changed, that her whole relationship to the cosmos had, through this birth, changed drastically. Yet a sense of flatness persisted, and the infant lying beside her in the bed, his naked, blue-veined head nestled against her bosom, seemed little more than another useless appendage of her weary body. Then finally one morning she felt his groping hand upon her, and she clasped him to her, overflowing with love. In the touch of his flesh and the abandonment of her kisses, she found a new pleasure as well as a new sweet pang of anxiety.

One day, not long after Willy was born, she called on William at his office. She had never visited him there during working hours, though he had once shown her around the premises on a Sunday afternoon and introduced her to Boadicea and her tumbling litter of kittens. She had been surprised by the tenderness he displayed toward the cats, by the sentimental look that had come into his eyes, and by the cracked, cooing voice in which he had referred to the "darling little brutes." She had been struck, too, by the easeful pride with which he moved about his modest little domain, running his hand in affectionate greeting over the solid, well-worn furniture. She had felt then a twinge of jealousy toward the place, sensing instinctively a rival to their home, but she recognized at once that it was the same sort of irrational resentment she felt toward all those friends and acquaintances of his previous life, before their marriage, and she had endeavored to thrust it from her, making a great fuss over the kittens and admiring the "efficient" arrangement of the furniture, which she found oppressively massive and shabby.

Today's excursion was the result of a sudden impulse, prompted partially by the first really warm weather of spring. After three days of sullenly overcast skies and intermittent downpours, the sun had finally broken through and now reigned in splendor overhead. The baby was sleeping soundly after a restless night. Elizabeth called downstairs to Molly that she was going for a walk and hurried out of the house like a child released from school.

William's office was a fifteen-minute walk from home, in a district of the town given over to warehouses, import-export businesses, and various enterprises, large and small, having to do with lake and river traffic. There were seldom many pedestrians about, but the neighborhood emitted an air of solid industry; behind these grimy, no-nonsense facades, businessmen at large desks quietly elaborated their schemes, while all around them clerks scratched away in ledgers, recording orders and receipts in clear, bold hands. There was little here to attract the attention of passersby. The only shops in the immediate neighborhood were a tobacconist and a small, trim pawnbroker's establishment, featuring today in its window a display of gentlemen's watches forming a sort of garland around a highly polished french horn. There were two saloons on the block, well-run, businesslike places frequented by thickset Teutonic drinkers, whose worst excesses were outbursts of maudlin sentimentality. Laborers, especially those of a Hibernian cast, were not welcome, and the least sign of hilarity was promptly suppressed. The overall atmosphere of the street was decidedly masculine; parasols were an incongruous sight here, and Elizabeth felt slightly self-conscious as she hurried on her way.

On reaching William's building, she paused outside to compose herself and to peer into the premises through the front window. William's office had previously been a snuff and tobacco shop, and the window had for several years been filled with brightly colored boxes and tins, stacked one on top of the other, along with, in one corner, a painted wooden sculpture, half life size, of an Indian chieftain in full regalia holding aloft a sheath of tobacco leaves; on the base of the sculpture was the inscription "Best Virginia." Over time the display had acquired a thick layer of dust, and several of the tins and boxes had tumbled from place, to lie in corners or to press against the dirty pane, until one day it was all swept away, transposed to some dim little window of the memory, and in its place had been placed a large wooden sign bearing the announcement: TO LET. Now the brightly polished glass displayed across its surface the legend "William Macready, Civil Engineer, Surveyor, & Land Agent" in gilt lettering, and in one corner of the window case stood a plaster bust of George Washington that Macready had installed half in facetious homage to the departed redskin and half out of a surge of patriotic sentiment for his adopted land. The eye, however, no longer lingered on the window ledge but was drawn directly within. During working hours, the office itself was on display. Peering through the glass, Elizabeth saw in the foreground Billy the office boy, propped on a stool in front of a small desk, laboriously copying out invoices, his brow creased with concentration, his tongue protruding slightly. In the background, against the wall, was William's monolithic bureau, its top revealing a vast array of pigeonholes overflowing with papers. His back was to her, and she was stuck by its vulnerability: though he was tall and upright, something about the way his coat bunched at the neck proclaimed the wearer to be an old man. He was engaged in conversation with a visitor seated, or rather sprawled, in a chair beside the bureau, his features illumined with animation. Elizabeth, suddenly fearful that she would be caught in the act, drew herself up and, after a quick, parting glance at her own reflection in the glass, proceeded to make her formal entrance through the front door.

As she swung open the door, Billy tottered momentarily on his stool, and the gentleman visitor hastily retracted his long legs, which were stretched out before him, and snatched off his hat.

"Well, what a delightful surprise!" William called out. "Welcome, my dear." There was real pleasure in his voice. "Let me introduce you to my good friend Sidney Bodecker. You've heard me speak of him. A distinguished local attorney and an eloquent spokesman for justice in the state." Elizabeth noticed, out of the corner of her eye, a half-full bottle of whiskey on the desk and two empty tumblers. "Bodecker, Mrs. Macready!"

"It is a real pleasure, Ma'am, a very real pleasure." When he stood up, he was a tower of man, with a great mass of reddish side-whiskers that trembled when he spoke. "I am just on my way now, but I am right glad that I had this opportunity to make your acquaintance. 'Bye, Macready, we'll be talking again soon." He bobbed his head at Elizabeth, clapped his hat on his head, and strode to the door, which Billy flung open for him with a deferential air.

"I did not mean to interrupt your meeting, William." She was genuinely apologetic; she shouldn't have come. "It was just that I felt like taking a walk, the weather was so agreeable of a sudden. And I did want to ask your opinion on a certain matter."

"But it is a delight to see you here, my dear. You quite brighten up the old place. Do sit down; let me look at you."

The chair was still warm. She perched on its edge. He saw her gazing at the bottle and removed it briskly from sight, slapping back the cork and replacing it in a lower drawer of the desk with a businesslike air. "Here, Billy, be a good lad and rinse out these glasses, will you now?"

The place smelled of tobacco, whiskey, eau de cologne, and ink. William was indeed very much at ease here, quite in command of his surroundings. She, however, felt decidedly out of place. The very effusiveness of his welcome served to underline the oddness of her presence. Billy was gaping at her with all his might and main.

"It's Fraenkel the butcher, William. When Molly went for the meat this morning, he told her that he hadn't been paid and wouldn't give her anything until he had. He finally relented, but the poor girl was quite upset—you know how Molly is. And I must say that I was cross and a little puzzled by his behavior." She had not meant to bring this up, not here, not now, but she felt the need to excuse her presence, so she stumbled forward with her explanation. "I was under the impression that you were taking care of those bills in person. I did, if you recall, turn over the whole lot of them to you a couple of weeks ago." She did not mean to sound judgmental. She did not even care very much about the matter, it wasn't of any importance. She tried to sound as casual and unconcerned as possible, but because she was ill at ease, a note of tension crept into her voice.

"You did, my dear, you did indeed. Mea culpa. I'll see Fraenkel about them this very afternoon. I am sorry, Elizabeth, what with one thing and another the matter quite slipped my mind. It certainly would not do to antagonize the butcher. Why, where would I be without my chops?"

No, she should not have brought the matter up here, in the office, with the boy looking on. It lowered herself. It was humiliating for William. How could she be so awkward? She was thoroughly ashamed of herself. She rose hastily to go.

William escorted her to the door and on the threshold took her hand in his. "Thank you for coming by, my dear. I am sorry for the little mishap with the butcher, but happy that it brought you to me. You enter like the sunshine."

"Please, William . . ."

He laughed lightly, then assumed an expression of formidable sternness. "I will address myself to that wretched butcher. See him this very afternoon." Then, smiling again: "Good-bye, my dear." And before closing the door he called after her: "And a kiss for little Willy!"

He saw the butcher. But several weeks later it was the draper who, after a multitude of polite little preludes, requested payment. "But I thought," she stammered in confusion, "that Mr. Macready had seen to that!"

Although she received the household bills and kept accounts, it was Macready who paid them. She would have preferred it otherwise; it meant that she had no way of balancing her account books and made her feel that her clerical labors were a sham, mere playacting. Yet Macready insisted that he liked dealing in person with the merchants, which, given his nature, she believed and understood. So she let the issue pass. Besides, money never appeared to be a problem with him. He gave her an adequate personal allowance; and whenever she asked for some extra sum to meet an unexpected expense, he never refused and usually tried to press upon her whatever he had in his wallet. He always received the latest bills with equanimity, never examined them in her presence, and never subsequently questioned her concerning them; his only response was to ask her if she found them "quite correct" before stuffing them into his frock-coat pocket.

Money! She would never have dreamed that such a thing as money could ever play a prominent role in their intimate relationship, could ever play a role so intimately destructive. During her father's lifetime, money, or rather the lack of it, had been a troubling specter. Though they had never been destitute, at times her father's professional future had been far from certain, and the matter of money had loomed large. But these impending financial crises had only served to draw the two of them closer together. And because one was ultimately dependent on the outside world for money—for the shillings and pounds, the dollars and cents, the jingling clatter of small change—money could never, Elizabeth firmly believed, seriously affect one's inner being. If you worked hard, if your conscience was clear, the visitation of poverty was a misfortune that you must learn to endure like sickness or war. Surely money had no power to pollute the secret sources of marriage. The very text of the wedding vows made that clear: "rich or poor, in sickness or in health." No, it was not poverty or the prospect of poverty—the constant need to economize, to cut corners—that served to undermine her faith in William; rather, it was the sudden and terrible realization of his fecklessness and unreliability. She had known from the start that he was something of a romantic and a dreamer; she doubted whether he would ever be in the world's eye a "success." Yet she had told herself that his advanced years and long experience with life, along with his even temper and unrelenting kindness, were a guarantee of wisdom and of his basic solidity. She had assumed in marrying him that he would provide her with the sort of benevolent patriarchal support that she had lost with her father's death. But the money problem now brought home to her a childlike side to her husband's character that she had not suspected, and she found herself—at first with reluctance, then in desperation—taking on the parental role in their little talks about finances.

The first major crisis arose when she learned, quite by accident, that he was planning to take out a mortgage on the Madison house. The house, it is true, had formed the bulk of her marriage dowry, but she had always looked on it basically as her personal property—the rent from the place was paid directly to her and constituted her sole private income—and she had never imagined that William would ever interfere in the management of the property without consulting her.

"But my dear, I fully intended to tell you all about it. It is just that the whole situation arose quite suddenly, and I simply decided to make certain inquiries at the bank about the possibility of raising some ready cash on a mortgage. It was only an inquiry, my dear, only an exploratory gesture. Of course, I would have let you know before any papers were signed—if, that is, the situation necessitated that."

"What situation, William? I have no idea what you are talking about."

"It is all very complicated, my dear; I won't bother you with the details. It has to do with certain land purchases that some of us have made in connection with the projected Winnebago canal. Surely you have heard me talk about the canal? It's an excellent scheme, my dear, one that will greatly facilitate the flow of trade throughout the state, and, I might say, throughout the whole of the Northwest. Old friends of mine at the State House consulted with me about the undertaking, asked my advice on technical aspects of the canal's construction, and in return for my professional services were kind enough to let me in as a quasi-partner in the affair. Subsequently, certain difficulties arose. A rather dubious railway company, owned as I understand it by a consortium of cutthroat bankers in New York, has made noises about running a railroad line through the same general region. We even suspect them of having illicitly obtained a copy of our confidential survey in order to prepare their prospectus. Anyway, it is still possible that our canal will be built, in which case the land would naturally be of very great value . . ."

"But William, will you please explain to me what your Winnebago canal has to do with the mortgage on my house?"

"You see, Elizabeth, being in such a favorable position owing to my connections in the State House and my intimate involvement with the business, I naturally joined my friends in making bids for certain tracts of land along the canal route. As I said, the details are all very complicated, but I found myself short of ready cash when payment for the purchase came due. The mortgage was simply an idea, my dear, a feasible concept among several concepts. There now, there is no point in troubling yourself about it any further."

So he was, she discovered, not to be trusted. He was basically an honest man, an upright man, a man with lofty ideals and a romantic sense of chivalry—but a man, too, who was easily duped. Before their marriage she had noted his buoyant good faith, his propensity to think the best of others, his energy, enthusiasm, and infuriatingly indomitable optimism, but now she realized that these qualities meant that he frequently found himself involved in schemes whose primary goals and advantages lay largely in his own imagination. When these plans fell through, he was not one to resort to recriminations or indulge in bitter reflections. Outright deceptions he tended to regard as simple misunderstandings. He seemed incapable of holding a grudge. Or, for that matter, of learning from experience.

Ironically, these traits were usually associated with youth, not age, and Elizabeth had married him for his ripe maturity, not for his belated youthfulness. She took no pride or pleasure in the fact that he still retained a quick light step on the stairway and a mind given to new enthusiasms and fresh adventures. To her, he was quite simply and irremediably an old man; she saw nothing wrong or disgraceful in that. But any apparent deviation from that image only displayed his inadequacies as an old man, constituting a perversion of personality and filling her with misgiving. She was still young enough to see youth as no virtue in itself. What mattered most was that things were as they seemed. Though she understood that one could not always protect oneself from mishaps and the force of circumstances, she liked to think that one could at least trust one's own perceptions not to deceive one. In her relationship with William she often felt uncertain and disoriented, in regard not only to his behavior, but to her own.

She hated their little confrontations as much as he did. Moreover, she despised herself for provoking them. She found herself playing the part of an ill-tempered shrew, heard her voice emitting shrill, harsh sounds that were utterly foreign to her ears. At such moments she seemed literally beside herself. And though she knew her outbursts to be justified, knew that William was behaving irresponsibly in his refusal to face the issues, that did not make her role any less distasteful to perform. Though initially dismissive under her attacks, insisting that nothing was wrong, that she was surely seeing things in the worst possible light, he would gradually assume a more conciliatory response, begin to display signs of alarm, and often end by appearing shamefaced and even contrite. The alarm she deemed salutary; she was not so sure about the shame. The horrible wounded look that came into his eyes—it was a hurt she did not mean to inflict. She knew instinctively that such shame was a corrosive element in any intimate relationship, and even though the cause could be removed and the pain forgotten, the damage remained. After each dispute she told herself that she would have to be more gentle with him, have to learn to keep him in line without doing irreparable harm to his pride, to his tremulously sensitive masculinity. In short, she would have to treat this aged, gregarious husband of hers like a not-quite-mature and timorous son.

Over the next few months the distance between them grew. Having come to the realization that she could not build a life on William's wisdom and experience, she strove to construct her own, centered on the home and the child. This emotional detachment from her husband brought with it less tension in the household. Her weary resignation took on the air of peaceable acceptance; she too avoided confrontations. She returned to her piano and watercolors, and enjoyed long outings with the baby in the tree-lined parks and along the sparkling lakefront. She managed to take her anxieties in hand, to subdue her temper. There was a reconciliation of sorts, and on the surface at least harmony was restored. A second child was conceived, and Elizabeth dared hope to herself that this further addition to the family might con-tribute more ballast to William's wind-tossed bark. But an old man's foibles are different from a young man's follies, and William's reactions to paternity caught Elizabeth off-guard. One Sunday afternoon, after dinner, the three of them were together in the front parlor. Baby Willy was playing happily with his blocks on a sunny patch of carpet, while Elizabeth looked on lov-ingly, and William systematically worked his way through the latest issue of the *Sentinel,* an expression of benign engagement on his face. The child, Elizabeth thought, was being particularly endearing, and she could not resist interrupting William's reading and half playfully chide him for his apparent indifference to the spectacle. He lowered his newspaper and cast a quick glance over his spectacles at the little creature disporting himself in the sun.

"A charming sight, charming indeed. But you see, my dear, I have been through it all before, many years back, and it is hard to revert to the old sentiments. Of course I adore the little creature and his little pink toes and all that, but after all, the second litter is not quite the same."

He spoke lightly, in response to Elizabeth's gently bantering tone, but she was cut to the quick.

"How can you speak like that? Really, William, it is not only unfeeling, but downright insulting—and obscene."

"Come now, my dear," the newspaper trembled in his hands, "I did not mean it like that. I only spoke in jest, Elizabeth, spoke carelessly in jest. What I really mean to say, my dear, is that at my time of life the idea of paternal dynasties has lost its grip on the imagination, and the child, dear as it is, has lost that compelling, that magic link, to the future and is merely, or rather wholly—it is a fiendishly hard concept to express, I'm afraid—is wholly and entirely the creature that one sees there, our little Willy, playing so nicely in the sunlight. It is, I assure you, an affecting spectacle, my dear, but when I look on the child, my thoughts pass directly to the mother, and my sentiments entwine themselves about her."

Elizabeth began to doubt the wisdom of having the second child, and as the pregnancy advanced, this doubt turned to something very like dread. During the last few weeks before the baby was born, she was tearful and depressed and found herself several times a day praying wildly and irrationally to God for the infant's safe delivery and good health.

James Francis Macready was born on a steamy July morning, a few hours after the first news of the Confederate victory at Manassas. He was a thin, fragile-looking baby with pale, almost translucent skin, who entered the world with a whimper rather than a cry. The midwife eyed him critically, pinched him here and there, gave him a couple of vigorous shakes, and pronounced him to be a "real clinger" (by which she meant, in her own peculiar terminology, someone with a strong grip on life), before turning him over to his mother with a smile of grim satisfaction. Elizabeth drew the infant to her protectively. "Poor little mite," she murmured, but what precisely *she* meant by that expression was not clear, even to herself.

After brief interludes as Wee Jamie, then Jamie, the baby came to be known as Frank. "It's a manly, American sort of name," William explained.

"Frank Macready has about it a ring of real *solidity*." It was almost as if the boy's father were openly acknowledging the need for more of that particular quality in the family. Certainly, in choosing "Frank" for a name, William was, for once, yielding poetry to prose.

So the house acquired in time an air of animation, full of voices and footfalls and untamed sensibilities. Yet Elizabeth's fondness for it had faded; it somehow had lost its aura of solidity. It never managed to become the haven of security and repose that she had hoped for from a home. There were too many dark corners, too many narrow stairwells, and too many things left unsaid and unaccounted for floating about the corridors like drafts from under ill-fitting doors. The handsome new drapes in the front sitting room blocked out the sunlight, and the twists and turns of the upstairs passage to the nursery always struck her as mean and forbidding at night, the candlelight dashing grotesque shadows against the wall. And in the second year of the war a ghostly presence was introduced into the structure.

She had heard him give an odd little cry from the front hallway, a sound she had never from him before, like that of a frightened small animal suddenly brought to bay.

"William? William, what is it?" The vision of her stricken father suddenly came to mind, and she rose quickly from her desk and hurried to him.

He held a letter in his hand. The shattered envelope lay at his feet. "Our Robbie has been killed." His voice was firm, if a trifle hoarse, but he was ashen pale, and his hand trembled slightly as he extended the letter to her.

For a moment she was confused. She had never heard him refer to "our Robbie" before, yet the truth rushed in upon her as she took the letter from him, and she was unable to focus her gaze clearly on the free-flowing and very feminine handwriting. The words tumbled toward her haphazardly:

> . . . though we have never met . . . very sadly. . . . inform you that your son
> . . . my dearest husband . . . killed at Shiloh last week . . . deepest
> sorrow . . .
>
> Mrs. Caroline Macready

"Oh, William!"

He had for some reason taken off his eyeglasses and was clasping them against his chest; without them his face looked naked and very vulnerable.

She took a step toward him, but he turned slowly from her, saying in a low resolute voice, "Excuse me, my dear," crossed the hallway to his study, and closed the door behind him.

When she saw him again an hour or so later, he rebuffed her efforts at condolence. "He had no right to be in that war. It was none of his business. He had a young wife and other affairs to look after. It was no business of his. All utter wastefulness and folly—wastefulness and folly."

They never spoke of him again, though Elizabeth did think of him from time to time. One winter evening several months later, when passing the study, she was overcome by a feeling that the young man was there behind the closed doors in the darkness, and she stopped to lean against the wall, her hand pressed tightly against her pounding heart, listening, listening intently for the faint sound of his breathing.

The sitting-room drapes were drawn back, and Willy and Frank were together on the carpet, sharing the patch of afternoon sun. Willy, frowning with concentration, was in the process of constructing the tallest tower in the world, while Frank looked on with bright, eager eyes, awaiting the supreme moment when he would extend his little booty-covered foot to send the whole thing tumbling down.

Here in the sunlight the children felt themselves apart, even remote from their parents, who were off in the shadows at the other end of the parlor. Such independence was exhilarating and would have been a little frightening, too, were it not for the sound of parental voices in the far background. The voices rose and fell, sometimes dropping to a near-inaudible whisper, so that Willy paused momentarily in his labor to listen attentively, his head cocked slightly to one side. Though the voices were reassuring in their familiarity—the mellifluous if somewhat threadbare baritone of his father, mingling with his mother's plangent contralto—they were not this afternoon soothing or comforting. There was an intensity, an abrasive undercurrent to the sound that informed the older boy that his parents were wholly engaged in adult affairs. There was no use, Willy decided, in calling his mother's attention to his masterpiece. She would only feign interest and offer him nothing more than a flat, dispiriting "Very nice, dear." He sighed to himself but went on doggedly with his painstaking labor.

After nearly five years of marriage Elizabeth felt that the crisis had come. She was no longer even angry at William, just despairing of ever being able to make him mend his ways or of adapting herself to them. She simply could not go on living in this atmosphere of continual uncertainty and disorder.

Two weeks ago he had informed her that the mortgage payments on the house were overdue at the bank and that they would have to live "pretty close for a while until matters righted themselves a bit." When she had pressed him, he admitted that the new sideboard and sofa they had bought together just last month were not actually paid for, but—as he had added in lieu of explanation—there was no reason for her to worry unduly because the financial situation was "tight" everywhere owing to the war, and land purchases were naturally in an uncertain state. Basically, however, the economy was sound, and he himself had some very interesting prospects, having to do with the transportation of war materials from Lake Michigan. It was just a question of waiting for things to loosen up, he assured her, for the cash to flow again. Meanwhile, one had to live, and he saw no reason why she shouldn't cheer herself up a bit with a few new household furnishings. At the time she had been so overcome by anxiety that she had not even the strength for protest, but had fled the room with a heavy heart.

Now he was telling her that the bank had "made difficulties" about their arrears in payment and that they would be obliged to move to more economical quarters—"for the time being." It was simply a question of retrenching a bit until the turnaround in the marketplace. The news was not really surprising to her. She had been living in dread of such an announcement for the past two weeks, since she had fled from him with her heavy burden of fear. Nonetheless the news took her breath away. If only, she thought, she had not run away then, but had insisted on knowing all the details! Perhaps she could have advised him. At least she could have had time to prepare herself for the event. But William never seemed to deal in hard facts, only hopes and speculations. And he seemed impervious to her advice, smiling away her suggestions as if they were idle compliments. She hated the way he seemed to stumble into events, treating them as acts of Nature over which he had absolutely no control. Disasters were visited upon him like bad weather, and like the weather he saw them as wholly impersonal, totally unavoidable—and sure to change! No, she despaired of ever influencing him. Her main concern now was to keep the family together and to protect her children, and herself, from her husband's ruinous goodwill.

"Are you aware what you are asking of me, William? And of the children?"

"I *am* sorry, my dear. Please believe me, it is not how I wanted things to be. But things will turn around again. In fact, just yesterday . . . Well, I do have some bright prospects for the future."

"Oh, *William!*"

Her exclamation startled him. He stood there, speechless, blinking back at her, his lips quivering in a strange way, so that she dared not look at him. Finally he blurted out in a husky voice:"Well, my dear, what am I to say?"

"It is just that I do wish that you wouldn't push everything off into the future. It is the present that concerns us, William. It is the present we live in—eat in, sleep in, try to get along in. Goodness knows that I am not one for living only for the moment. I need to plan ahead. But I can't make plans on airy expectations and dreams. And what are we to do *now*, today; what are we to live on, how am I to look after the children? What about *their* future, William? Their future is being forged here in the present. How are we to bring them up properly, see them raised for a profession, if we are obliged to send them out in a few years to earn their living in a shop or factory?"

"There is no reason to exaggerate, Elizabeth. It is not as if we are destitute, not at all. It is just that we'll have to live a bit closer for a while. As a matter of fact, just this morning I heard of a rather attractive suite of rooms in a house off Water Street. The building is owned by the widowed sister of a friend of mine, Bartholomew J. Tilden, of Tilden & James—you know, the furriers. She's a highly respectable person. Husband was a lawyer; died young, hardly forty; very promising career, I am told—would have been a senator one day. We could put most of our furnishings in storage. The boys would share a room—no real hardship there, in fact, Frank would be delighted. The neighborhood is not so pleasant as this, but it is not wholly unattractive and on the way up. I would still be a relatively short walk from my office."

"And what then, William, what then? Where will things end? Will we move next to a single room in Irishtown?"

"Really, Elizabeth, take a hold on yourself. I realize that this comes as a bit of shock to you and that the move will be hard, dreadfully hard on you. I do realize that, my dear, and it pains me terribly to put you through it. But when you are involved as I am in the rough and tumble of business transactions, dependent to some degree on the vagaries of high finance, you understand that setbacks of this sort do occur en route and that you have to wait them out until affairs right themselves. Why, that's the very key to success! And one day we will, I trust, be secure from such buffeting of fate. You'll see, Elizabeth!"

"Let me go back to Madison, William. With the boys. I could at least provide them with adequate shelter, decent surroundings. I could resume teaching, earn a little money. Put in a garden. And you could send for us when things, as you put it, turn around again."

The words struck him like blows. Suddenly he became a defenseless, bewildered old man.

"Are you proposing to leave me, my dear?" His voice was low but tremulous with emotion. She wished now that she had not blurted out her wishes so hastily, that she had taken the time to lead him gently to her way of thinking. She had been meditating the Madison move for some time now, though more as a daydream than as a practical alternative. She could, she knew, have presented the plan in less hurtful terms. She did not mean to hurt him; she felt no hostility toward him, only a desire, a desperate, urgent desire to take hold of events once again, to cut herself free from the entwining bonds of Celtic fatalism that were slowly paralyzing them.

"William, do be reasonable. As matters now stand, you are spending more and more time away from home, at your office or on the road, upstate. Naturally, you are increasingly preoccupied with your affairs. Meanwhile, as you now recount, our home life is disintegrating before our very eyes . . ."

"I thought that you would have more fortitude, Elizabeth, that I could count on you to stand by me."

"Please, William, let me finish. I am not abandoning you, I am not criticizing you, I am simply asking you, as your wife, for your permission to take our children back to my place in Madison, as soon as the tenants' lease expires in May. I am simply making a practical proposal to meet the crisis we are now confronting. Instead of wringing my hands helplessly, I am trying to be of some help. I *am* standing by you. Can't you see that?"

"But what about me? Where am I to live? You forget, Elizabeth, that my livelihood is here in town. I can't move to Madison without losing—everything."

"I'm not proposing that you move to Madison as well. I thought it was clear, William. You could easily find a single room here in town; it would be far more economical than taking a whole suite of rooms for your family. And you could visit us, come to us, whenever you were free. As you say, William, it would only be for the time being. So you see, I am not abandoning you, William, I am not deserting you in your trouble; I am simply proposing a workable domestic arrangement that will not utterly destroy us. I can't go on living like this, in constant fear of ruin and feeling myself unable to do anything whatsoever to bring a halt to the horrible process."

He looked aggrieved, but not so completely undone as a few moments back. He was beginning to recall the natural frailty of women, their need for security, their instinctive dislike of adventure. Given those circumstances and the irrational, irrepressible force of maternal concern, he thought that there might actually be something to be said for Elizabeth's suggestion. He launched haltingly into a formal reply, gaining in verve and fluidity as the speech progressed. He began by remarking on how much he relied on Elizabeth and the boys for moral uplift and support, on how much their absence would be a great hardship for him; yet, he continued, he could see the benefit of her taking the children to more spacious and salubrious surroundings until the situation in Milwaukee was happily resolved. Though the temporary separation would indeed be a very great hardship for him, he did agree that it would be best for all of them and relieve her and the children of the strain of his current business anxieties. . . . In short, he ended by making the move seem like a protracted holiday in the country that he was generously bestowing on his beloved family. "And once I see you settled in, Elizabeth, you and the boys, I will turn my attention to business matters and not rest from my labors until I can have my family by me once again, in comfort, peace, and security."

"Oh Mamma, Mamma!" Willy was tugging at her skirts. "Frank has knocked down my tower again, and just when I had got it *so* high. And I wanted you to see it. He's a wicked boy."

"Don't pull at my skirts like that, Willy!" And then seeing his crumpled face and his eyes filling with tears, she was overcome with contrition and gently ran her fingers through his silky brown hair. "He's naughty, Willy, not wicked. I'll talk to him, and you shall build me another tower, even higher than before. You will do that for me, won't you?"

The boy beamed assent.

Madison, 1863

THE PEAS FAILED TO GERMINATE THAT SUMMER. She had planted them in two long rows, pushing each seed deep into the soft earth with her finger, and covering them carefully to keep them out of sight of the birds who wheeled about excitedly overhead. In spite of the regular intervals of rain and the generally mild weather that prevailed to the very end of June, only a few sparse shoots emerged from the ground to cling weakly to the trellis that she had hopefully constructed for their support. On scratching the soil, she uncovered seeds withered and rotting in their little graves. She had bought them from a nearby neighbor, an elderly Scandinavian widower, whose sheer hideousness and utter decrepitude she had rashly mistaken as pledges of probity. He had scooped the seeds out of a wooden crate with tremulous, dirt-encrusted hands and poured them into her outstretched sack, with much spillage and an exclamation of "There you be, lady!" in a croaking voice that seemed to imply that he was bestowing upon her the precious heritage of his accumulated years of agricultural lore.

Yet the seeds, as she knew now, and as she should have seen then, as any experienced gardener would have noticed at a glance, were dry and long past their prime. The price he had asked for them had been surprisingly high, so that she was obliged to rummage in her purse for the additional coins, murmuring apologetically, "Oh yes, of course. . . ," while he stood there with an outstretched hand like the gnarled limb of a dead apple tree. The seeds were now shriveled and wasted like the old man himself; gazing down at them, she realized that he had not only boldly and defiantly over-charged her, challenging her openly in her ignorance, but must surely have mocked her in the privacy of his squalid little hut as he recounted the coins that evening by the glow of a smoking oil lamp.

The garden as a whole had been a disappointment that first year back in Madison, partially because she had counted on it so much. At planting time she had led the boys, in their bare feet, out to the center of the plot, and each of them had ceremoniously placed a few seeds in the earth. Frank was too young to understand what he was about and subsequently, to his confusion, had to be ordered out of the garden in peremptory tones. Both Frank and the garden proved to have strong, independent spirits.

This time Martha was not there to help her with the garden, and although Elizabeth could have profited from some advice, she preferred making her own mistakes to suffering the older woman's officious, good-natured ministrations. She enjoyed the freedom of her domain and found solace in the solitary nature of the activity, in directing her attention to each plant, in bestowing her anxious concern on each insect-ravished leaf. For her, the garden was an island, by no means enchanted, but nonetheless cut off from society and immune from its challenges and humiliations. It was there that she waged her solitary wars, and though defeats and setbacks were frequent, victories fleeting and inconclusive, she derived deep pleasure from the campaign, directed against the noblest of enemies.

Elizabeth had encountered Martha in town shortly after her arrival. Martha had aged perceptibly since their last meeting. Her hair was streaked with gray, and her bronzed face finely etched with lines around the eyes and mouth. Yet age had not diminished her. Indeed, it lent to her person a new and imposing air of authority. She seemed more formidable than ever.

The two women stood on the plank sidewalk outside Gleason's Choice Meats and read in each other's features the bold imprint of the intervening years. A certain physical awkwardness attended the encounter since Martha was laden with parcels, and Elizabeth had two small children tugging impatiently at her skirts. But when Martha put down her bundles and extracted from her pockets a couple of boiled sweets, everyone relaxed.

"Why Martha," Elizabeth exclaimed with a smile of genuine pleasure, "you *are* a wonder! Do you always keep a supply of sweeties for chance encounters of this kind?"

"Well, to be honest with you, Bess, those were my own private stock that I was hoarding for the trip home. But I think that they have been put to more satisfactory use now. My, just look at those faces! Seems to me that

children know how to enjoy sweets in a way that we grown-ups can only as-
pire to. Now tell me all about yourself, Bess. How long are you here for, and
whatever are you up to?"

Though the spark of renewed intimacy was struck at that first encounter,
and though the flame flickered momentarily during their next two or three
meetings, the fire never took hold. The two women now occupied quite
different realms. Martha, from monarch of the domestic hearth, had moved
out into the world, extending her beneficent reign over the community at
large. As she explained to Elizabeth, the new university chancellor's wife was
a frail and sickly creature, a dear, lovable little person, but virtually a recluse,
unable to bear the burden of the social duties incumbent on a chancellor's
wife. In his need, the chancellor had turned to Martha to lend a hand in arranging the university's various social functions and receptions. She had
been pressed into service, as she put it, not only by the chancellor—who was
incidentally a noble and good-hearted man—but by the academic community as a whole. It meant, of course, that she was obliged to spend much of
her time away from home, at the chancellor's house, and was saddled with a
seemingly endless round of social engagements to look after, including receptions for visiting dignitaries and legislators. But fortunately, her boy was
quite grown now—engaged to be married!—and Franz, who was still a
child at heart, was learning to get along on his own a bit and was actually
managing to feed himself when the necessity arose! In fact, it was Franz who
had persuaded her to take on the job. Basically, she insisted, she was a selfish
person and a homebody, but he had convinced her that she owed it to all of
them to do what she could for the poor man. Anyway, she was now caught
up a whirlwind of activity and could spare little time for renewing an old
friendship. Though Martha could feel sympathy and concern for the young
woman whose marriage, she inferred, had turned out to be something of a
comedown and disappointment, she had, so she told herself, enough on her
hands trying to cope with the demands of two separate households—as well
as with the ill-concealed hostility of her future daughter-in-law—to take on
yet another responsibility. Besides, she had the distinct impression that Elizabeth, always a willful young woman, had now moved definitively beyond
the range of her influence.

The members of Elizabeth's church group welcomed her back with cordial solicitude, but she felt no real warmth toward any of them, except for the very aged Mackay sisters, who seemed to her to glow with inner serenity and passionate kindness. Whether they actually remembered her, Elizabeth could not be sure; yet they greeted her and the two boys, whom of course they had never seen, with a gleam of recognition in their eyes, as if their sudden apparition was the fulfillment of a long-held wish. The blessings they bestowed on the three of them—the dry kisses they placed lightly on Elizabeth's cheeks, the frail hands they laid lovingly on the boys' tousled hair—seemed to come from beyond the grave.

She was relieved to hear that Pastor Hoffmeister had married—a rich widow with two grown daughters—and after a domestic scandal, recounted to her in hushed tones and elaborate innuendo that she never bothered to heed or understand, had moved away. Her own married status would have put her beyond his reach, but she had dreaded the inevitable chance encounters with him and submission once again to his unseemly gaze.

She was virtually friendless. Yet she was so preoccupied with the tasks of keeping up the house and garden, of making do with her limited and always uncertain resources, and, above all, of looking after the boys and sheltering them from the anxieties that constantly beset her that she had little desire for sociability. From time to time she would sense a hollowness within her, an undefinable hunger, an indistinct impression of absence, but the emptiness would almost immediately be filled with worries. She was basically too unhappy to be lonely.

William sent her money, at first toward the end of every month, then, as time went on, irregularly and at increasingly distant intervals. The money was accompanied by sprightly little notes, announcing in vague terms that he was busily employed and either expecting future payments on the job or having received a "token compensation" until the project had, as he put it, "reached fruition." Though times were hard and certain combines from the East were exerting a nefarious influence on the healthy development of local trade and industry, he looked forward to happier days when they could be reunited again under one roof. . . . Though the contents of the notes remained roughly the same, the accompanying sums varied greatly, from a couple of dollars to, on one surprising occasion during her second summer in Madison, as much as twenty. Yet as the payments tapered off, and Elizabeth became increasingly hard-pressed for cash, she could not bring herself to write him for more. Whatever William's faults, he was always generous, even lavish with his funds, and she sensed that if he failed to send more money, it was because, for good reasons or bad, he had no more to send. Being a proud man, he could not bring himself to admit his inability to provide for his family; being a childlike man, he chose to thrust the thought from him; and being an old man, he could not be nagged or cajoled into changing his ways.

So much she told herself. At heart, however, she knew that her reluctance to remonstrate with him came from her own pride, her refusal to appeal against what she judged to be his growing indifference to her, and from an understanding that the only real security for herself and her children lay in her own ability to earn a living. Though William might indeed in his old age one day strike it rich, that prospect could not be anywhere included in Elizabeth's contingency plans for the future or even be admitted among her most self-indulgent daydreams. For William, hopefulness and prosperity were virtually the same thing, and failure could come only with despair. But for Elizabeth, such concepts as prosperity—or poverty—meant next to nothing. Unlike William, she couldn't live on concepts; it was cash she needed, to keep her children adequately fed and clothed and to secure their house against the winter.

A few weeks after her arrival she had placed an advertisement in the *Madison Gazette* announcing her availability as a teacher of piano and solfège to young ladies, both beginners and students with "previously acquired skills." When several weeks had gone by without a response, she supplemented the newspaper ad with a carefully calligraphed notice that was posted on the bulletin board just outside the entrance to Lewis's Emporium—though she blushed to see herself arrayed alongside the vendors of prize sows, wooden dentures, and whale-bone corsets and always hurried by the store with lowered eyes. The weeks continued to pass, and there were still no requests for her services. The situation was both distressing and perplexing. As far as she knew, her only rivals in town, since the recent departure of the redoubtable Frau Schmidt, were a very elderly gentleman who played the organ in the

Episcopal church and who always smelled faintly of peppermints and the widow of a local pharmacist, Mrs. Brody, who was bubbly, bright, and overflowing with encouraging exclamations, but whose plump little fingers seldom managed to strut triumphantly through a simple exercise.

There was something about Elizabeth that put people off; she herself thought that it might be her English reserve, her inability to mingle freely with strangers, her unwillingness to barter confidences, whether false or true, in return for social acceptance. She surmised that people suspected that she neither wanted nor needed their flattery. She was sorry that she aroused such suspicions but knew them to be not wholly unfounded; she knew, too, that she was unable to change. Her great hope was that people would also recognize her seriousness of purpose, her eagerness to put her talents and abilities, however modest, to good use; that they would see her as a devoted and conscientious teacher who would do her best by their children, as someone who, whatever her faults and limitations, would give them good value for their money. Her musical ambitions were modest. She was content to take the beginners and the dregs.

Her assessment of the situation was in fact off the mark (something she was to perceive dimly several years later when she had grown more attuned to her surroundings). It was not the formality of her manner—that severe and slightly distant air that she naturally assumed in the presence of new acquaintances—that caused people to steer clear of her. On the contrary, her manner proved an asset with most mothers, who looked on such austerity as wholly suitable, even reassuring, in someone dedicated to the instruction of the young. Though slightly intimidated by her, they were also impressed. What troubled them was her aura of social ambiguity. Though she was decidedly married, with two small children, the relationship between husband and wife seemed perplexing to them and certainly irregular. Though her manner and deportment were those that the good people of Madison had come to associate with the privileged class, Mrs. Macready was obviously living on the verge of destitution—you had only to look at her patched, threadbare clothing to see that, and the anxious way she eyed the scale at the grocer's. Of course, the town was used to receiving newcomers who were down on their luck; why, land's sake, most people came here originally to start life afresh, came here with little more than the clothes on their backs, and you couldn't help but wonder about those who arrived with a ready-made fortune and a complete set of fine chinaware! Yet you had to prefer people you could read readily, whose story was open to all and easy to grasp. Elizabeth was something of an enigma, a circumstance that relegated her to that special class of people regarded as undefinable and by extension unreliable. In recent years notable examples of this class included the well-spoken and wondrously skilled but reclusive veterinarian from Aberdeen, Scotland, Ben Buchanan, who one Christmas morning hanged himself from a rafter of his barn dressed in a woman's petticoat; and Mrs. Berger, the banker's wife from Chicago, who except for her weekly visits to church never set foot outside her house, until she ran off to California with the nineteen-year-old son of the Methodist minister. They, of course, were spectacular, almost legendary personages, whom nobody with any sense would mention in the same breath with Elizabeth Macready. Indeed, it was hard to imagine Mrs. Macready committing any sort of impropriety, even indiscretion. Still, the accumulated experience of the community taught that people sometimes did strange and unexpected things, and the local inhabitants clung to this folk wisdom as a gauge of their sophistication.

Then there were Elizabeth's children. Though both boys were exceptionally polite and decorous in public, sitting up straight in church and never nagging their mother for sweeties in the stores or kicking out at each other when her back was turned, still, they were not popular children, even with grown-ups. Willy, the elder of the brothers, was a good-natured but lethargic child, given to daydreaming; and Frank, though lively and eager to please, was mercurial, secretive, and generally regarded as sly. Neither of them represented to the neighbors the beau ideal, or even the norm, of clean-cut, outgoing, manly mannered American boyhood. Their looks, too, failed to inspire confidence: Willy with his soft, shapeless body and pale, almost translucent complexion in which one could trace the blue veins in his brow and neck, and Frank, already in miniature the man he would become, with his stocky frame, swaggering gait, and knowing, vaguely suggestive glances. The children's "oddness" was naturally enough visited on the mother.

Elizabeth's only piano student during her first year in Madison was Angelica Bianchi, the eleven-year-old daughter of an Italian mason. The girl was intelligent, precociously mature, and wholly uninterested in learning to play the piano. She responded quickly and easily to her teacher's instructions, but did so with a bland indifference tempered by natural politeness. She never practiced, and if Elizabeth's attention were momentarily diverted—if, for example, she were compelled to leave the room to quell some noisy dispute between the boys or to attend to some unexpected caller at the door—she would return to find Angelica staring dreamily into space, a soft smile on her face, her hands folded on her lap. Her parents, who spoke little English, and that only with stammers and blushes, were anxious that their daughter, an offspring of their old age, should acquire the proper accomplishments of a young American lady. Angelica always arrived punctually, if not really wholeheartedly, with the weekly payment in coins tightly wrapped in a twist of paper, which she deposited on the letter tray just inside the front door. Elizabeth was several times on the point of terminating the lessons and saving Angelica's parents money they could ill afford to spend, but she could never quite bring herself to do so, in part out of a reluctance to hurt their feelings and undermine their confidence in a daughter whom they obviously adored, and in part because the money was needful to her own economy. There were several occasions when Angelica's weekly contribution made it possible for Elizabeth to pay for the evening's meal.

To Elizabeth, looking back from the secret chamber of old age, those first two years of her return to Madison seemed enshrouded in a mist of distress that concealed all detail of the dangers and afflictions. The period became a source of recurrent nightmares that lasted the rest of her life, though her memory of the actual events remained fragmentary and confused so that she had increasing difficulty separating real happenings from the dreams. Because she took no pleasure in reviewing that particular segment of her past, she allowed the sequences to become blurred beyond all hope of orderly retrieval.

Certainly the period was stained by the constant anxiety over money and the attendant humiliations of poverty. Then, too, Willy had come down with measles and recurrent earaches that left him whimpering helplessly with pain. And during that first or second summer Frank had broken his leg in a fall from a tree, and the leg had to be reset twice. The well had fallen in and had to be dredged, and the stonework redone. A neighbor's cow had gotten into the vegetable garden and had trampled down most of the tomato plants and some of the corn.

During that first winter an elderly, half-crazed bachelor, a former trapper turned pig farmer who lived in a tumbledown shack two miles away, had rapped at her kitchen door late one evening. Not wanting to seem rude or unneighborly, and assuming that the old man was in need of help, she let him in. He stood there before the stove, jabbering away with toothless gums, rolling his eyes, and making extravagant gestures with his hands. Elizabeth solemnly attended to him, straining to make out his message, until suddenly it became entirely clear that he was attempting to articulate obscenities of the foulest and most elemental kind. Moving quickly, she gripped him by the shoulders, turned him about, and propelled him out the door, saying in a firm but not hostile tone of voice, such as one would use to reprove a misbehaving child, "Good night, Mr. Tilson, *good night!*" and bolted the door behind him. He continued to drop by the house at irregular intervals, always late at night, and she would shout to him through the closed door, "Please Mr. Tilson, go home, the children are sleeping!" or "I am very busy now, I can't see you" or, on one occasion, "You'll awaken my husband." Usually the rapping would stop after a few minutes, and she would hear him muttering to himself as he made his way back to the road, but one evening, very late, he started pounding on the door with both his fists, as hard as he could, and kept it up for a quarter of an hour. From then on she took to keeping an ax on top of the kitchen cupboard. After the first heavy snowfall he stopped coming, and early that spring she overheard a conversation in the butcher shop, from which she learned that the man had fallen through the ice at the mill pond shortly after Christmas and had drowned.

Late in the spring of that first year William had arrived unexpectedly one cold and rainy afternoon. At the sound of a horse Elizabeth had glanced out

the kitchen window; dimly perceiving a familiar form sitting high in the saddle, she had rubbed hard at the steamed-over pane and peered again more
intensely. The boys, who had been playing on the kitchen floor, looked up
at her when she gave a little cry.

He brought the horse to a smart stop before the gate and, seeing them assembled on the front porch, doffed his hat in a jaunty salute. His mass of
snow-white hair seemed luminescent under the soft rain.

Elizabeth, who had been making bread, wiped her hands on her apron,
draped it over the porch railing, and hurried down the steps to greet him.
Willy, after a moment's hesitation, raced on ahead of her, shouting "Papa!
Papa!" and little Frank, who clearly had not recognized the old man on the
horse, instantly sized up the situation and rushed after his brother, crying
"Papa! Papa! Papa!" The boys together held his horse as he dismounted.

He was, she thought, what is commonly called a "fine figure of a man,"
with his tall, portly, still-unstooped frame, nearly six feet in height, and his
lofty brow and leonine head of hair: the very image of a Fourth of July ora-
tor. Yet how old he was! She had forgotten how old! When they had been
living together, she had not noticed the wrinkles, the pendulous dewlaps,
the discolored skin. Now, after a separation of several months, it took some
getting used to. They stood now a few feet apart, gazing at each other, taking each other in; then Elizabeth, suddenly aware of what he might be reading in her eyes, rushed forward and hid her face against his chest.

He smelled of horse sweat, eau de cologne, whiskey, and damp woolens.

"Mercy, William, you're soaked to the bone. Come along into the
house. There is a fire in the kitchen."

The smell of the whiskey vaguely upset her. She knew that men drank
whiskey; she had never seen William drunk or even in a state when the
liquor seemed to incapacitate him; nevertheless, she disapproved of his
drinking. Her father never drank, except for the obligatory glass or two of
wine in company. William's drinking somehow seemed like a slight to her
personally, an effort to distance himself from her. She resolved to say nothing about it.

It was a tense, unhappy visit.

Elizabeth found herself unable, or perhaps more simply unwilling, to respond to William's affectionate phrases, his little gestures of solicitude and

concern. She bustled about the house doing this and that, seemingly intent on attending to his needs, on making him "at home," but in reality preventing any opportunity for tender confrontations. There was a great to-do about heating up water on the stove, about airing out bedclothes. The boys were filthy and unkempt and had to be thoroughly washed and buttoned into clean clothes in honor of their father's visit. Willy was set to cleaning his father's boots, under paternal supervision, while she worked away at the butter churn. And all the while she felt a deep sense of shame. She knew that she was acting ignobly, displaying an ungenerous spirit; that her evasiveness, her refusal to meet his eye, revealed a lack of charity on her part, of forgiveness. Yet she could not help herself. Her sense of bitterness and betrayal was too profound; she was too bruised by the worries and humiliations of the past few months to suddenly make herself well and whole and to respond with dutiful abandon to William's sentimental overtures. That evening she made up a bed for him on the sofa, explaining that since Willy's recent illness she had both of the boys sharing her bed with her. William lent her a hand, cheerfully turning their joint spreading of the sheet and blanket into a courtly ritual, but she could see that he was hurt.

The next morning she heard him singing outside her window as he performed his ablutions at the pump, singing the old familiar song in his cracked but not unmelodious baritone—"The minstrel boy to the war is gone, / In the ranks of dead you'll find him." She felt a surge of sympathy for him—and of pity for them both. But when she had risen and saw him standing there in the kitchen, cheerful, clean shaven, and primed for departure, her heart hardened again, and she set about making his breakfast with a brisk, businesslike air.

On leaving, he took her head in his hands and kissed her lightly on the brow. "Take care of yourself, Elizabeth. And may we all be together again soon." Then, while Willy held his horse, he heaved himself into the saddle and sat there, that fine figure of an old man, his white hair ruffled by the spring breeze. "Bye, bye my dears!" And with a final wave of his hat, started down the road at a brisk trot.

Her memories of this dark and troubled period of her life were set in the dull light of late afternoon, under an overcast sky; the season was perpetually the end of autumn, on the eve of the first snowfall of the year. . . . It was not a part of her past that she ever willingly explored, even at the first onset of old age, when many of her most painful memories had been softened and transformed by nostalgia. Those first years in Madison after her marriage were all but expunged from the canon of her history, and when at some sudden turning of the imagination she would unexpectedly encounter them, she would thrust them aside with the excuse that she had not been quite herself back then. Certainly some of her actions had been wholly out of character and seemed no more credible or convincing than those of a personage in a trumpery three-decker novel of the sort that the girls at school had kept hidden under the bedclothes.

Indeed, the lowest moment of that darkest of times, the memory of which still filled Elizabeth with shame, could only be attributed to a temporary derangement of mind occasioned by despair. The chronology of the event was unclear, but she must have written the letter at the point of acute financial strain, probably when the well had collapsed and had to be rebuilt, and sometime after she had lost her temper with William on one of his subsequent visits and had ordered him out of the house, had told him in a tremulous voice, almost shouting, almost crying, that he was improvident and irresponsible, that he stank of whiskey and set a deplorable example for her sons. . . .

She had seen in the newspaper a passing reference to Thomas Codman, the dynamic young congressman from Massachusetts, and the image of her shipboard companion Hester Addison, Tommy's future wife, had come vividly to mind. If only, Elizabeth had thought, she could return to then and begin her life again from there! She thought with fascinated dread of young Macready and his dark closeness at the ship railing in the shimmering moonlit night. But no, she would have chosen another path entirely, a dedication to work and self-improvement, even perhaps to solitude. She would have become like Miss Shaw, a figure who held herself apart from the petty squabbles and distractions of ordinary life—a figure noble, pure, beneficent. . . .

Several nights later, when the children were safely locked away in sleep and her mind was racing with yearnings of renewal, she sat down at the kitchen table and penned a long letter to Hester—Mrs. Thomas Codman covering three full pages in her compressed, copperplate script. When writing letters, Elizabeth usually wrote several drafts; composition did not come easy to her. This time, however, it was as if she were taking dictation from a sure, firm voice within her. There were no drafts, no copies; she simply set herself to the task of putting down the words on paper without a fault or blot. Yet no sooner had she disposed of the letter, deposited it at the post office the very next morning, than its contents fled from her memory like a dream. She could recall a feeling of great urgency and the fervent effort to express this feeling in a measured manner, but what exactly she had written, what phrases she had used, what arguments or excuses she had proffered, she could not remember. For the next few days she caught herself shaking her head in disbelief, as if by doing so she could shake off the action itself or at least all memory of it.

As the days passed, she half-convinced herself that the letter had been lost in the mail or misaddressed or perhaps never actually been written. Then one morning, while she was in the process of paying for a few groceries at the general store, carefully spreading out the small change from her purse on the counter, the postmaster sang out to her from his booth across the aisle, "Oh Mrs. Macready, Ma'am, there's a letter for you from out New England way!" As she turned to stare at him, he leaned far out of his little cage and smiling broadly placed the letter in her reluctantly outstretched hand. She thrust it into her shopping bag and hurried home with a pounding heart.

Back at the house she went into her bedroom, closed the bedroom door, and sitting on the edge of the bed opened the letter with trembling hands. As she read, a deepening sense of shame took hold of her so that the words began to swim before her eyes. It was all she could do to make it to the final salutation.

Dear Mrs. Macready

It was truly wonderful to hear from you after all these years. I have thought of you often, and of that journey across the ocean which was I suppose for both of us a passage into womanhood. To think that you married William

Macready! That news did surprise me, but then, as one grows older—and I trust wiser!—one learns how very callow were the impressions of one's youth and how very little one really understood about the people about one.

Dear Elizabeth—and I hope that I may call you that, because that is how I address you in my heart—as I write these lines your image is so vividly before me that I feel that I can almost reach out and take your hand. How lovely you look, with those sparkling eyes of yours, and that delicately tinted complexion that I ardently envied and admired—along with your accomplishments as a pianist and your air of self-assurance. And above all, your modesty and good sense. If I behaved particularly badly in your presence it was because those qualities intimidated me so! The truth is that I was a frivolous young thing who was justly chastened by your example. I trust the intervening years along with the responsibilities of motherhood and married life have improved me somewhat. But whatever improvement there may be surely owes something to you as well, and for that you have my deepest thanks.

How sorry I am to hear that you are presently going through trying times! I find it difficult to believe that a person of your qualities and character will not eventually triumph over adversity, though I am not, alas! unaware that life is full of apparent injustices and that good and noble-hearted people are often subjected to severe trials before their final vindication. You speak of the possibility of finding a position as a governess here in New England. I shall certainly make inquiries among my acquaintances, but I do not think that the prospect of your finding a position through me are very hopeful. And frankly, Elizabeth, I do not understand what you would do with your two boys. It is difficult to imagine a situation where your children could be accommodated. Then too, I cannot in good conscience advise you to leave your husband, even though the separation would be, as I understand it, only temporary. He needs you by him, and such a separation would inevitably serve to widen the breach between you. But I am sure that you understand all this better than I do!

I, too, have two young sons—Samuel and John, ages six and five—and am expecting another child in May. Having lost two children in infancy, I await the new arrival with fervent hope and prayers. Each child is indeed a precious gift. I am sure that your boys are a great consolation to you in your troubles, and will be a firm support for you in the years to come.

I am enclosing, my dear Elizabeth, a small sum of money, which I hope will be of some use to you in your present difficulties. I wish that it could be more, but my household budget is already overspent, and I have had this year numerous demands on my very limited private resources. I am convinced that things WILL turn out well for you if you can manage to fight off that dreadful ogre of despair that I seem to see lurking between the lines of your letter. COURAGE, Elizabeth! I only wish that it were mine to give, for I am sure that it would serve you better than this money.

Thank you for writing to me. It was good of you to remember a little flibbertigibbet like myself. Do please write again and tell me how you are getting on—and consider me always—

Your faithful friend—

Hester Codman

Elizabeth never replied to the letter. She folded it carefully and put it away in the top drawer of her bureau along with the account books and business documents. Then, one evening several weeks later, on coming across it unexpectedly, she carried the letter to the kitchen and thrust it into the stove. The money did indeed prove useful, but she was almost relieved when it was spent. She knew that she should not have touched a penny of it without having first thanked the giver, yet she failed to perform this most basic of courtesies. Her behavior throughout had been outrageous, but so wholly unlike her that she found it hard to believe that she, Elizabeth Gow Macready, had actually participated in the chain of events. When she looked back on the Affair of the Letter, it seemed to belong more to the realm of dreams or nightmares than to real life. One could view such occurrences with horror, feel oneself soiled by them, but they seemed beyond the scope of apologies or excuses. Of all the incidents of those troubled years, it was the one that brought home to her most clearly the terrible vulnerability of human nature to the corrosive powers of unhappiness.

Gradually, almost imperceptibly, the times of acute financial anxiety passed. Through a chance encounter with the editor of the local newspaper who had known her father, Elizabeth was invited to contribute articles on "general subjects of interest to the ladies." The little pieces, seldom more than a couple of columns long, paid next to nothing and were not always accepted for publication. (A brief essay entitled "Autumn's Bounty" was judged thoughtful and edifying and taken with alacrity, whereas a more ambitious piece titled "Beethoven's Deafness" was deemed "morbid" and "too intense for family readership.") Although these occasional publications added little in the way of money, they earned her a degree of respectful attention—the next best thing to acknowledged respectability—and a place on the community's cultural scene.

In an attempt to resolve the problem of schooling for her own children she established a dame school for the neighbors' children as well. Within a couple of years she moved the classroom from her own parlor to a small converted stable a half-mile down the road. There she taught boys and girls between the ages of six and twelve their alphabet and multiplication tables and attempted to awaken their minds to the power and beauty of the English language. The fortunes of the school fluctuated from year to year depending on the nature and number of the juvenile population, and there were times of economic crisis when it seemed close to extinction. Yet it survived, providing Elizabeth with a modest income sufficient to her modest needs. Under her watchful eyes, generations of children grew to adulthood and in turn sent off their own children to fill their ghostly spaces in the old schoolhouse, where the air was perpetually thick with the smell of chalk dust, coal fumes, and imperfectly washed young bodies, and with the drone of childish recitations—monotonous, monotone hymns to learning, reverberating through time in the rafters above. . . . Over the years Elizabeth's world was filled with faces at all stages of development, from apple-cheeked infancy to gray-haired maturity, each blending into the other and forming at the back of her memory a crowded blur of humanity.

She herself aged rapidly, willingly, almost it seemed deliberately. With her steel-rimmed pince-nez firmly in place and her hair pulled tight into a knot at the back of her head, with her piercing gaze and decisive manner, she managed to assume the appearance of a prim, no-nonsense schoolmarm. The observant onlooker might yet discern in the features of the still young woman a disconcerting mixture of ages that hinted ever so slightly of play-acting. If our observer happened to be a man of the world with a keen eye for women, he might just catch a glimpse of the eager young girl behind the mask of wary experience, and with a slow shake of his head toss his cigar stub from him with a sigh of regret.

In the early years in Madison, though, Elizabeth's interest was centered largely in her two boys. It was for them that she struggled to earn a living, to provide a home, in them that she placed her hopes for the future. Her initial concern was to protect them from the coarsening influences of provincial American life. Unlike their parents, the boys were American born, and though Elizabeth took a certain satisfaction from that fact, she feared for their development in a society that favored above all else either getting ahead (that is, making money) or staying in place (that is, keeping a grip on one's holdings, however small and mean). The playmates her sons brought home with them after school were, on the whole, good-hearted, tolerably well-behaved children, but they spoke what was to Elizabeth's ears a debased language consisting largely of expletives and exclamations, and when asked to elaborate on an observation or opinion, they fell into fits of gaping wonder.

The neighboring boys, once out of petticoats, tended to be dressed in work clothes, clean but threadbare, even on visits or in church; and their hair was cropped so ruthlessly that their ears stuck out. Speech, clothing, hair—Elizabeth knew perfectly well that such things had little or nothing to do with character and virtue, that what really mattered lay elsewhere. Certainly she was no snob. She had no admiration for wealth or social standing and acknowledged in her heart the essential nobility of the Harringtons, who slaved away on a wretched five acres of stony farmland on the edge of town, whose children wore patched hand-me-downs, and who seldom had enough shoes for all of them at once, yet who never complained, were always cheerful, and promptly came to the help of others when there was hay to gather before a storm or a new barn to raise. Nonetheless, she wanted her own children to have not only decent clothes but a certain degree of refinement, to be able to respond appreciatively to a cultural heritage that stretched beyond their immediate horizons, to learn to nurture within themselves things of the intellect and the spirit. If life in Wisconsin encouraged them to develop the manly traits of independence and self-reliance, that was all for the good. Yet she feared that the rough and tumble of daily living might wear away whatever small but precious heritage her sons might have had passed on to them. On the one hand, she wanted them to assume their birthright as native-born Americans and not to suffer from the yearnings and telltale foreignness of their parents; on the other, she was personally repelled and disheartened by the rawness of the American scene. She vowed that she would instill in them from their earliest years a respect for learning and culture as an integral part of the democratic ideal. They would be strong-willed but tolerant and possess enough self-assurance to resist the pressures of the herd. The idea of producing "little gentlemen" on a modest income in semirural midwestern America was, she realized, preposterous. Yet she told herself in those early days that she could through instruction and example acquaint them with good manners and through watchful attention make them attend to their books. The only wealth she could bestow on them was a love of learning, and she trusted that this gift would set them apart and lead them on their way. Back then she assumed that the boys would one day go off to college, perhaps in the East, and walk the paths of Concord with Mr. Emerson.

Such were the young mother's dreams. As such dreams do, they faded away as she awoke to the reality of her children's existence as independent beings. It all turned out different from what she had expected, so very different that in the end she hardly knew whether she was disappointed or in some mysterious way thankful and relieved.

Willy was an obedient boy and could be counted on to behave properly if properly forewarned. As a small child, he was content to play quietly by himself in a corner of the room with blocks or a basket full of old wooden spindles. Initially, Elizabeth was thankful for the boy's placid temperament, especially after little Frank came along, a sickly, restless baby demanding much attention. But as Willy grew older, she found his passivity unnerving and would interrupt his solitary games to send him off on errands—fetching logs from the woodpile or water from the well—anything that came to mind, simply to force him into a show of vigorous activity. On such occasions he seldom manifested more than a faint sign of rebellion and would set about his task uncomplainingly, but only after first having put his playthings in order or placed his crayons carefully in their box so that everything would be just so on his return. If in the interval Frank had disturbed the placement of his things, he would burst into tears of frustration and throw himself onto the floor, where he would lie inert, sometimes for more than an hour. He was clever with his hands and, if given enough time and left alone and undistracted, could put together again almost anything that he had taken apart in a moment of curiosity. Yet Elizabeth found that teaching him to read was a slow, laborious process. In his eagerness to please her he would guess wildly at letters, at words, and she had to exercise all her patience and gentle forbearance to keep him from losing heart. After he had started school and had assignments to do in the evening, he would sit late at the kitchen table, bent over his work, a look of fierce concentration on his face. The glare of the oil lamp exaggerated the boy's pallor and the deep furrows on his brow as he attempted to absorb the information before him by dint of sheer willpower. At such times Elizabeth could hardly bear to look at him. She knew that he studied mainly, perhaps exclusively, to win her approval. Though the result of his labors drove both of them near to despair, she could not withhold her praise for fear of breaking him. There was something about Willy's mind that refused to accept abstract concepts or ideas. He lived as it were in the center of his senses, and what he understood best, what succeeded in impressing itself on his sensibilities, was what he had seen or touched and then meditated upon in privacy and quiet. The process of learning required of him a period of long gestation; if he was interrupted or hurried, a look of hurt and panic would come into his eyes, and he would stammer an utterly random response, which in the classroom would provoke an outburst of wild laughter. In the end she had to concede that she would never make a scholar of Willy. She had taken pains with him, sat up with him over his books, patiently gone over every page of his reading, reviewed every line of his exercises—but whatever he seemed to learn by bedtime had vanished by the dawn. His very willingness to learn discouraged her. It was clear that schooling was wasted on him. He was her greatest failure as a teacher.

At the age of fourteen he went to work as a "helper" at Bronson's Dry Goods Store. Though he had become a growing source of embarrassment to her in the classroom, towering over the little boys around him in the back rows, his absence brought her pain, along with a lingering sense of guilt for having given up on him and sent him off into the world. She had always thought of academic achievement as the means by which her children would advance in life and had rashly assumed that given their background and her participation, success in school would come easy to them. Though poor and without influential connections, she regarded her little family as apart from the herd—an attitude William did nothing to discourage—and during those difficult years of the boys' early childhood she had clung to the belief that by dint of personal sacrifices and hard work, by a refusal to succumb to the deadening effects of daily drudgery, she could assure her children's eventual escape into a brighter, freer, more spacious existence. This belief, or dream, helped to arm her against the onslaughts of depression and despair that marked those final years of her own youth and her gradual awakening to the essential mediocrity of her own mind and abilities. On letting Willy cross over to that other world, that workaday world in a provincial American environment, passing his days surrounded by barrels of half-penny nails and pickled cucumbers, exchanging idle banter with a motley clientele of shirt-sleeved locals, who punctuated their public asides with ejaculations of tobacco juice aimed in the general direction of the strategically placed spittoons, she had acknowledged to herself how badly she had misjudged things and how little she had understood. Yet when walking by Bronson's of a Saturday morning and catching sight of her son sweeping off the front steps, a dark blue apron tied smartly about his waist and on his face an expression of solemnity, pride, and, yes, deep contentment, she was filled with wonder and humility and troubled by a sense of doubt that was very close to hope.

By all accounts Willy was an exemplary employee. Although he had seemed to retain nothing from his nightly sessions with his schoolbooks at the kitchen table, he soon managed to memorize the precise location of every item in the store, from sewing needles to ploughshares, along with their prices. He found particular pleasure in taking inventory of the stock, reveling in the wonder of the store's riches, and moving from shelf to shelf, notebook in hand, as he recorded these treasures in his careful, childish hand. For the first two years at the store he lived at home and seemed to Elizabeth a changed boy. He was still quiet and sedentary as of old, awkward in his movements and blushing furiously when flustered. Yet he seemed less anxious, more relaxed, and at times he chattered away over the evening soup with an openness and animation that were wholly new. Much of his conversation meant nothing to her, for he talked almost exclusively of the day-by-day operations of the store, of merchandise and pricing; it was like overhearing the talk of a stranger, yet she was impressed by the youthful ardor he brought to the subject of dry goods, and by his high tone of moral indignation at the failure of a promised delivery or the production of defective items. The boy's face lit up in a way it had never done in the classroom, and he spoke with a passion and conviction that for years she had hoped to arouse in him for matters closer to her own heart. Why, she wondered, had she been unable to tap this inner source of energy within him? Was it owing to some deficiency in herself as a teacher? Were her cultural horizons too limited? Or was there something drastically remiss about her own intellectual development? These were questions she was never able to answer to her own satisfaction. The most that she could say was that she felt that her son was somehow safe—and completely foreign to her. When he was promoted from helper to clerk, he moved from home to a small attic bedroom above the store.

The case of the younger son was different but equally bewildering. Frank was as mercurial and quick-witted as his brother was placid and deliberate. He was an outgoing, high-spirited boy; though grown-ups judged his manner a bit forward and brash and were occasionally made uncomfortable by the hint of irony they detected in his broad smile and laughing eyes, he came to be much admired by the more adventurous of his juvenile peers. He was shorter than most of his classmates and slender in build, with a mass of reddish brown hair that tended to stand up straight and gave him an impish air. (In middle age he would grow stout and bald and puckish in appearance.) Too slight to be much of an athlete, he nonetheless was highly skilled at marbles and jackknife toss, had deadly aim with a slingshot, could spit through his teeth, and piss for distance. Though not a leader, he was an enthusiastic follower who often inspired older and cooler heads with a sense of reckless daring. The parents of his friends tended to regard him as a bad influence on their children.

In the early days he compensated his mother for his mischievous behavior by showing himself adept at schoolwork. He had, Elizabeth discovered, a remarkably retentive memory and acquired information swiftly and effortlessly whenever he was inclined to do so. He knew his alphabet by heart at the end of the second lesson and marched about the house triumphantly chanting the letters at the top of his lungs until shushed into silence by an indignant brother and a secretly delighted mother. He could read at five, knew his multiplication tables up to twelve at six, and when not up to some prank was an attentive and eager participant in the classroom. Such attributes gave Elizabeth real, perhaps inordinate satisfaction, and prompted her to overlook or play down his failings.

She was particularly pleased by his early enthusiasm for the piano. Willy had appeared intimidated by the instrument, had seemed (as she once described him to someone) "positively tongue-tied at the keyboard," as if his shyness extended even to inanimate objects. Frank, however, treated it as an old chum and was soon able to pound out simple exercises with vigor and precision, though every piece—lullaby, waltz, or folk melody—acquired at his hands a distinctly martial air. Indeed, his style of playing was not what she considered in her heart of hearts genuinely musical, but she told herself that it was perhaps appropriate to certain masculine temperaments and might in time evolve into a sound that was pleasing to modern, less timid ears. She was learning, at long last, to make allowances.

As Frank grew older, his tendency to get into scrapes caused Elizabeth increasing anxiety and continually scratched away at her illusions. There were the familiar boyish misdemeanors: snitching apples from a neighbor's orchard, accidentally setting fire to the hay meadow, being found dead drunk with a couple of twelve-year-old companions and a half-empty jug of malt liquor behind the barn. Elizabeth told herself that these incidents were natural by-products of her son's high spirits, part of the process of growing up. She was trying to teach herself, as a mother of boys, to be less rigid in her expectations; and since there was no father in the house to whom she could turn for advice, she did not know what to expect from her children, except that they would not conform to her antiquated image of a childhood ideal. Nonetheless, she worried about certain antisocial aspects of Frank's behavior and the reputation he was acquiring as a troublemaker and nuisance. She worried even more about his seeming inability to feel any real contrition for his misdeeds or to assume any responsibility for their consequences. She was alarmed by his habit of pleading complete innocence until confronted by incriminating evidence; his avowals of remorse were, to her knowing eyes, lacking in conviction. At such times she was overcome with panic at her inability to reach him. The two of them seemed to be speaking different dialects of a language whose apparent similarities only fostered confusion and misunderstanding. In her frustration she would find herself shouting angrily at him, plainly out of control. She knew the futility of nagging, but she continued because she could not help herself and because she was at times genuinely afraid for him. The boy's desire to please her, his innermost need to win her approval, prevented him from breaking into open rebellion, but as he grew older, he tended to lead a dual existence. At home he was generally cheerful and obedient, displaying an easy-going acquiescence to Elizabeth's ways. Increasingly, however, she felt that his real life lay elsewhere, but she had no glimpse of that life except when he got into another of his little "scrapes." He would then submit to her lectures with downcast eyes and a penitent air, accepting them as a just punishment for the crime of getting caught, and sincerely resolving to be more careful in the future.

Though Frank caused her anxiety and distress in a way that Willy never did, though he was plainly the more troublesome child, she felt a greater tenderness for him than she did for her elder son. Perhaps Willy's failure to satisfy her expectations had undermined her confidence and laid bare her own vulnerability—and that of her boys and of life itself. Resigned as she now was to inevitable disappointment, she nonetheless yearned for some encouraging portent that would save her from despair, and she managed to find in Frank's incorrigible naughtiness an exuberance, a zest for living, that perhaps boded well. She was, momentarily at least, beguiled—like his bad companions—by the sheer adventurousness of his feats, by his willingness to take risks; and though she could not condone such behavior, she could in those years of his childhood and early adolescence sometimes excuse it as a necessary part of growing up. She saw in his high spirits the influence of his Irish blood. If Willy was a throwback to the dour Welsh strain in his mother's heritage, Frank reveled in the untamed urgings of Macready's hidden ancestry. And the lingering affection that she retained, in spite of all, for her husband was reawakened by the boy's irrepressible optimism and his eagerness to take life heartily by the hand.

When Willy went off to live above the store, Elizabeth found herself increasingly preoccupied with Frank. In the evening, after dinner, they would push aside the plates and settle down to long discussions about the future, Frank's future, and to making plans. Generally it was she who made the plans, while he would listen sympathetically, encouragingly, as if the future being planned were not so much his but her own—as if she were inventing an amusingly improbable story to while away the time; and while he listened, he'd help himself to another slice of pie. Frank had displayed an early aptitude for figures, and Elizabeth contemplated his one day going to the university to study engineering. Later, it occurred to her that he might be more suited for law, and that the give-and-take of the courtroom might be a better match for his temperament than the drawing-board drudgery required of an engineer.

As he ventured deeper into adolescence, his schoolwork became increasingly erratic, so she found herself revising her narratives. At home in the evening he was unable to sit for more than a few minutes over his books, and as soon as her back was turned, he would slip out of the door, leaving the open volumes strewn across the table, the pages pale and staring under the flickering lamplight. Attempts to discipline him were futile. Her nagging only drove him into sullen silence and left her feeling humiliated and degraded. By the time the danger signs were clearly apparent to her, she knew that she was losing him. She could not change his nature; he was who he was, and she would have to live with him and try to be of help to him as best she could.

Dreams of his going to the university were gradually expunged from her imagination. At first he had deflected all references to advanced schooling by meaningless shrugs or exclamations and lunges into another topic. Finally, when he was nearly seventeen, he launched into a formal statement of protest.

"Look, Ma, where is the money to come to put me through college? You've hardly got anything as it is, and I don't want to go on living off of you like this for four more years. It just isn't right. I ought to be out in the world, earning a living of my own. Even old Willy is doing that. And heck, Ma, you deserve a break after all these years of scraping along on your own. With both Willy and myself earning our own keep, you'll be able to take it a bit easier. Maybe even fix up the place a bit, make it a bit more comfortable and up-to-date. Listen, I was talking to a couple of fellows down at the hotel, smart-looking young men and well spoken too. I'm sure that you would have been impressed by them. They said that there were lots of jobs going abegging in Chicago, good jobs for people with a bit of gumption. They are selling farm machinery, traveling about the whole region, staying at the best places and earning *heaps*. Do you realize, Ma, that they make for themselves thirty-three dollars for each of those new combines that they sell? And that doesn't include their salary from the company! And you can bet your life that nearly every farmer who is worth his salt just *has* to have one of those machines. And they said that their company is simply crying out for smart young salesmen! With that sort of money I'd really be able to help you out for a change. And wouldn't that just please me! You bet it would! Why, in no time at all you'd be able to give up school teaching and spend your time any way you wanted, reading books or playing the piano or planting more flowers out in front of the old family mansion. . ."

She started to protest that she did not need more money, that she was used to "scraping along," but she knew that he would not believe her, or want to believe her, so she said something futile like "I can manage well enough as things are" and left it at that. The thought of Frank's running off to Chicago to seek his fortune alarmed her. It was not, she told herself, that she wanted to keep a hold on him. Indeed, his restlessness now pervaded the house, and letting him go would bring her a certain sense of relief. Yet it was plain to her that he was still too much of a boy, a dangerously impressionable boy, to be trusted among the hazardous influences of the big city. His very boldness and eagerness for new experiences would put him at risk. Even Willy, with his shyness, unworldliness, and instinctive caution, would be more fit for survival in such a setting. She held her peace, knowing that any effort to dissuade him would only hurt his pride and inflame his desire to go. But she made up her mind then and there to talk to Mr. Eisley after church that Sunday about the possibility of his finding a position for Frank at the bank.

Though she barely knew Mr. Eisley outside the context of church functions—the Sunday evening Bible study sessions and the annual spring fete—
he was immediately responsive. He looked at her searchingly from beneath
his bushy white eyebrows and said that he would be happy to see Frank for
an interview anytime next week. Then he took her hand in his and gave it a
sympathetic squeeze.

A couple of days after the interview the old man spoke privately with
Elizabeth at the bank. His desk was in a corner, separated from the rest of the
room by a highly polished brass railing. From this vantage point he could at
a glance take in the whole of the operation: the cashier's counter across from
him, the bookkeeper's desk against the far wall, the ink-stained ledge near
the main entrance where clients wrote out their drafts and deposits. On entering the door people paused a moment to compose themselves: the men
removing their hats, brushing cigar ash off their waistcoats with a quick, instinctive flick of the fingers, and the women clutching their folded parasols
to their bosoms and lifting their heads high. Whether these signs of deference were prompted by the sudden vision of the dignified old banker seated
at his command post across from the entrance or by the looming presence of
the large green safe enthroned on the dais behind him would be hard to say.

Mr. Eisley spoke to her in professionally subdued tones, choosing his
words with care. The lad was, he said, clearly bright and quick-witted, but
he was still young and untried and needed perhaps a little "settling down."
Mr. Eisley was not at all sure that Frank was temperamentally suited for work
in the bank. The nature of the business required dogged, wearisome adherence to routine, and certain free-spirited individuals could find the activity
tedious and confining.

"We do try here," he said with deep solemnity, "to be as stodgy as possible, and your son's bright face and youthful exuberance would certainly add
a discordant element to the surroundings. Yet," he added after a slight pause,
"that may not be such a bad thing." Seeing Elizabeth's features suddenly
relax, he hurried on to say that he was prepared to take the boy on as a sort
of general factotum, at two dollars a week, on a strictly provisional basis.
"No promises, no commitments. We'll just have to see how things turn out.
I've raised three sons myself, Mrs. Macready. It's an unpredictable sort of
business; glad that I don't do it for a living."

He accompanied her personally to the door and held it open for her. Elizabeth was suddenly overcome with gratitude that her son would be working in such calm and gentlemanly surroundings. Before parting, she turned to Mr. Eisley and said imploringly, "Frank's really a *good* boy!"

"Of course he is, my dear, of course he is."

On leaving the bank, she stopped to stare blankly into the neighboring shop window. There was nothing to see there but a dusty display of old harnesses and riding accouterments and her own reflection staring dimly back. How strange, she thought, that she should find herself apologizing for her own children, rushing instinctively to their defense. It was not what she had imagined way back then. Experience tore away the trappings, reduced one to an animal. She was a lioness protecting her cubs, offering her own flesh to the thrusts and slashes of the world. Perhaps this was simply the true state of motherhood. Yes, each child was a precious gift, as life itself was a precious gift, and life for all its preciousness was full of anguish and suffering.

To her immense relief, Frank actually flushed with pleasure at the news. When she had first broached the subject of the job, he had muttered grimly that he "wasn't counting on spending his days shut up in a dreary mausoleum of a bank, writing in ledger books and buttering up old ladies. There's no future in this old town, anyway. Chicago's the place, or even Milwaukee." Yet the prospect of quitting school and joining the ranks of wage earners clearly appealed to him, as did the fact that the new job would require the purchase of a new suit with all the "fixings," for, as he proclaimed with grudging admiration, "they dress right smartly at the bank." Moreover, Elizabeth could see that for all his bluster and bravado he felt certain qualms about leaving home. The question of laundry still loomed large for him: ever since he could remember the path to clean clothes was by way of the hamper under the back stairs; and for all his bold talk among the boys he would miss sleeping in his own bed, in his own room, with the familiar tracery on the ceiling, the familiar shadows on the wall forming a magic enclosure against the night. And he told himself that there was something to be said for not having to spend his hard-earned wages on room and board, and for having someone at hand who was accustomed to attending to his particular habits and needs. Yes, there were solid reasons for biding a bit longer at home. Though both he and his mother knew that it was only a matter of time before he flew from the nest.

Indeed, no sooner had he taken the job than he began trying his wings. Increasingly, he took his dinner in town, so as, he explained, to help with the closing up. Increasingly, he returned home late in the evening, after the time she habitually went to bed. In spite of herself she would lie awake, pretending to read, waiting for the clatter of his boots on the front porch and listening intently to his cautious tread on the stair, her heart sinking at each hesitant step or stumble. After midnight, if he were still not home, she would abandon all pretense at reading, turn down the lamp, and stare into the darkness.

Her days were full of activity in the schoolroom, full of constantly reiterated gestures and phrases that imperceptibly assumed a note of overemphasis to compensate for their overfamiliarity, and full of faces, the faces of children before her, some eager, some sullen, all responsive in some manner or other to her attentions, their expressions constantly changing under the shifting intensity of her gaze. All these images were suffused by the distinctive odor of the schoolroom, almost suffocating at times, but never wholly unpleasant—the garden odor, as she came to know it, of youthful humanity. And her nights were dark chasms, reverberating with echoes of anxiety.

When Frank finally moved out and made his break for the big city, an unexpected calm came into her life. Somewhere within her there remained a great, unfathomable sorrow, but it was too indistinct to be either challenging or challenged, and she found that she could patch together a reasonably satisfactory sort of life out of this mixture of sorrow and calm. With Duty as her sword and Resignation as her breastplate, she could face the world without fear or confusion. Yet there were times when she caught herself listening, listening intently for the lost music.

Clarksville, Iowa, 1929

"WELL, YOU'RE NICE AND SNUG NOW, aren't you, Granny? Here, let me set those cushions right. Is that better? I said, is that better, Granny?"

"I heard you, my dear. Yes, yes, I'm just fine, thank you."

"Not too close to the stove? Would you like me to move your chair back a bit?"

"I'm fine, thank you. Just leave me as I am."

"Granny's like Red," one of the children piped up. "Likes to get her nose right up to the stove. Don't mind the heat at all."

"When you're Granny's age, the heat is a blessing, Chuckie. Granny can't race about like you and your sister. And when you're young, the blood is naturally warmer."

"Red still races about, and he sure loves that stove, Ma. Just look at him there."

"Dogs are different. Dogs are greedy, they don't have any sense. Dogs aren't *people,* Chuckie."

The boy thought a moment but could not make much of her argument. He turned back to his matchbox collection, spread out before him in grand array on the floor. I hope Uncle Teddy comes on a visit real soon, he said to himself. Uncle Teddy smoked a pipe and was always boasting. He used up lots of matches.

The voices buzzed about Elizabeth like vaguely bothersome insects. The woman means well, she thought, but is always interfering. Perhaps that is what *meaning well* means. Still, she wished she could be left alone. It took all her concentration to hold firmly to her thoughts, and when she was interrupted like that, the thoughts scattered like frightened sheep.

She peered around her cautiously, striving to regain her bearings. She was in a large farmhouse kitchen, pungent with the smells of baking, wood smoke, and boiled linen; and there was a very faint, underlying odor of cow manure, brought in from the barn by the men's boots, which now stood at their ease against the wall. Directly before her was the black cast iron stove with two large cauldrons of laundry steaming away on its surface; turning her head slightly, she saw a long soapstone sink overflowing with unwashed mixing bowls, wooden spoons and ladles sticking out from them. On the floor in front of the sink stood two gleaming metal buckets, one of them flashing at the brim with milk. She took in the long expanse of table, covered with blue and white checked oilcloth and flanked by chairs of assorted styles and sizes. The chair nearest to her had a sagging rush bottom. It was all familiar to her now, and she sighed with a mixture of resignation and relief. The ceiling was pressed tin, painted brown, with a fleur-de-lis motif marching diagonally across the surface. She wouldn't look in the far corner, where a strip of flypaper dangled overhead and twisted slowly in the mysterious currents of air. The wallpaper—tiny, tight bouquets of forget-me-nots against a cream background—was still fresh, having been put up less than a year ago. She had been kept out of the room for two whole days while the menfolk were installing it, and then she was ceremoniously led in, accompanied by the whole family, who crowded around her to savor her reactions. "Well, what do you think of it, Granny?" the woman had asked, while everyone peered greedily into her face. "It's a mockery," Elizabeth had replied, and they had all burst out laughing because she had mouthed the words with such vehemence and because it was simply impossible to know whatever Granny meant by that!

On the wall near the stove was the tasteless calendar with a colored advertisement featuring a beardless young man who was smiling fatuously at a lighted cigarette held in his hand; he reminded her of Little Jack Horner, and she turned from him with a frown of disapproval. The only other decoration was a framed needlework sampler, done, she recalled from the legend, at the age of eleven years, two months, and seven days by herself (or was it her mother?), and which read: "How excellent is thy loving kindness, O God!

therefore the children of men put their trust under the shadow of thy wings." She did not like it, she had never liked it; it made her feel sad, though she could not for the moment remember why. There was nothing else worth looking at. The place was generally offensive to the eye, yet safe, accommodating, and, she admitted, definitely familiar. Nonetheless she refused to think of it as "home." No matter what people said, it was certainly not *her* home. Her home was different. She closed her eyes to visualize it, but all she could find there in the obscurity was a dim image of heavy dark draperies—brown velvet, she thought—with slits of light shining through the tops and bottoms, and somewhere in the distance the sound of a piano. She listened intently to catch the tune but could not quite make it out. It had faded now, was gone. Everything was gone.

"Where's Willy?" she said aloud.

"Why Granny, shame on you! You know perfectly well that Daddy passed away way back in 'nineteen. You remember that. I do believe you are teasing us."

The children halted in their play to glance up at the old woman's face, then at their mother's. They had never thought of Granny as much of a teaser. They wondered if it was not their mother who was now teasing them all.

"Of course I remember," Elizabeth said firmly. "I was just thinking aloud."

"Well, for goodness sake, you gave us a bit of a turn. I mean, we all know that you can remember things like that."

"Of course I can, of course I can." Elizabeth hated having to defend herself. That young woman would never understand anyway. It was best to say nothing, to keep one's own counsel. Besides, she couldn't at the moment recall the woman's name. She knew perfectly well that she was her grandchild, one of Willy's children, but the name escaped her. Mabel? It must be Mabel. Then who was Edith? It didn't matter, didn't matter . . .

Every night when she had been put to bed, and her bedside lamp turned low, she would say her little prayer: "Dear God, please take me to Thyself this night. Amen." It was always the same prayer. She had no other boon to wish for, except perhaps the remission of her arthritic pains, and death would cure them nicely.

Oh, the pain was bearable. And she was looked after. She had pretty well given up worrying; there was nothing much left for her to worry about. Except for an occasional attack of those Nameless Terrors, which up until now she had always managed to fight off. She wasn't so helpless and senile as to allow *them* to get a hold of her! Her body might betray her and her memory be faulty, but she still had her *mind*. Nonetheless, the cost of getting through the day was hardly worth the candle. It was easy enough sitting by the stove, thinking about things, ruminating over the past, but it seemed to her that she was always going over the same ground, over and over again, and really getting nowhere. And there were the constant interruptions, being tugged and hauled about, being propped up and put down, interspersed by little alarms that rattled her nerves—when, for example, she accidentally wet herself or spilled her food. She was beyond humiliation. The truth was that she hardly felt that these things were happening to her, to the real her that dwelt within that ramshackle, malfunctioning frame. Yet she was always obliged to respond, to respond properly in a ladylike manner to ignorant questions and futile gestures, and it was all very wearying. Even sleep provided an unsatisfactory respite because sooner or later she invariably woke up.

A few mornings back, while that woman was helping her out of bed, Elizabeth had remarked aloud, but mainly to herself, "I would like to die," and that bald statement, uttered in a calm, matter-of-fact voice, had provoked an emotional debacle. "Oh Granny, you mustn't ever talk like that!" The woman's voice had been heavy with reproof, and there had been tears in her eyes. "It's wicked of you to talk like that. You *know* we love you." Elizabeth had been dumbfounded by the response. She had simply expressed a wish, a reasonable, natural wish, like asking for a drink of water or to be taken to the cabinet, and Mabel (for that was the woman's name, it came back to her now, Willy's daughter who had married Fred Schmidt, and come to live on the farm in Iowa), and Mabel had become upset and carried on in a distressing fashion; she had become wholly *undone,* as people used to say. But then you could hardly expect her to understand, you could hardly expect any young person to understand. You had to be old to realize that when you said something like that, you were not whining or complaining or casting blame. An old person would understand perfectly.

William had seemed old when she had married him, but she realized now that he had not really been old then. He had still thought that he was young, which meant that he had not yet crossed over to true old age. The truly old had no further business of importance to transact with the young. They no longer bridled at young people's snubs and inattention, no longer felt compelled to raise their voices, to rap their canes against the floor, to indulge in outrageous hyperbole to make themselves heard. Basically, they wanted nothing so much as to be left alone, to be allowed to work things out on their own as much as they were able. The secret of the old, which they cannot share with the young, is that nothing really matters all that much. There is life and there is death, and that is that.

She had got along contentedly enough in her old age until certain things had begun to happen to her. There had been that fall from the stepladder in the pantry; then that long illness when she had lain abed for days, without telling anyone, while the stain on the bedroom wall grew larger and larger from the leaking roof. Then Willy had insisted on taking her in and put her in a room upstairs in his house; then he had died, and his daughter—her granddaughter Mabel—had come to fetch her, bringing her by autocar, with that dark, quiet man Fred Schmidt driving, all the way here, to Iowa. They were kind enough and meant well, but they kept trying to drag her into their lives. She tried to be polite and conceal her irritation, but she really was not very interested in their affairs.

She wished that she had William with her. He had been a most unsatisfactory man, but at least he would have understood things better than these young people. Of course, even if she had taken him back, way back then, he would have left her again before she had even entered her fifties. Mr. Todd at the post office had handed her a letter from Milwaukee, bearing on the back of the envelope the wax seal of the Little Sisters of the Poor. She had turned the envelope over in her hands, admiring the neat, chaste handwriting and wondering about its contents, but because she had many errands to do that morning, and because she had a certain prudery about reading letters in public, she had put it in her market basket and waited until she got home to examine its contents. It was from the mother superior of the Milwaukee convent, informing her that William had died in the convent a week earlier, following a fall from a horse. She apologized for the delay in sending her the news, but since Mr. Macready had been living alone, they had mistakenly assumed that he was a widower and had only learned of her existence through a friend of his at the funeral service. His death had come quickly and without great pain, only a couple of hours after the fall, but she assured Elizabeth that her husband had received the last rites of the church in full consciousness and had gone to his rest with the peace of reconciliation upon him.

The news had come as a shock—not so much the fact of his death, for he had passed from her life several years back and had in the interim wandered in his usual feckless way into great old age, to a time when the surprise was to find him still counted among living. No, what made her catch her breath (beside the ever-stunning finality of the event) was the information that he had died in the Roman Catholic faith. It was, as she saw it, yet one more act of betrayal on his part. Bad enough that he should have been a secret drinker, a spendthrift, a waster, and a dreamer—but to be a Papist as well! Either he had been born into the religion and had kept that knowledge to himself, or he had, in his usual thoughtless, self-indulgent way, converted to the faith in his old age—again, she repeated to herself, either a final act of deception or a final act of desertion. In any case, he was now, according to the mother superior, lying at rest in St. Mary's Parish Cemetery, among his coreligionists and many of his fellow countrymen. So much for his Trinity College degree and Anglo-Irish airs! In the end, he had quietly taken up his hat and slipped out the back door to join his lowly companions. . . .

She learned later that he had left nothing behind but a few debts and a large trunk full of clothing and sundry personal effects. The horse he had fallen from had belonged to a friend. His funeral was paid for by his lodge brothers. Elizabeth eventually received in the mail a half-dozen books, presumably the remainder of his library, including the City Directory of Milwaukee, a well-worn Latin grammar with "nota bene" penciled frequently in the margins, and a nice copy of Thomas Hood's *Poems,* inscribed on the flyleaf, "To my friend William Macready, with New Year Salutations, from George MacCarthy, January 1st, 1871." Also, wrapped in a soiled bandanna was his gold pocket watch, which Frank subsequently appropriated as "a keepsake of my old daddo."

For her there now remained only shadowy memories of the man. Even back then, nearly a half-century ago, when she had withdrawn to her room, letter in hand, and sat on the edge of her bed, trying to assemble a few words of prayer for his attention, even then she could hardly remember what he had looked like. She had closed her eyes to see him better, but she had seen only the darkness; she had searched desperately amid that darkness until suddenly, a faintly luminous shadow had emerged and come toward her, as he used to come to her in the night, wrapped in his invisible nakedness, and she had opened her eyes in alarm and had gazed with wonder into the sunlit room. Later when she thought of him, it was his voice that came most readily to mind, that melodious, slightly cracked baritone reciting wordless verses in a high-flown incantatory style or relating interminable anecdotes with a narrative artistry undermined only slightly by his own irrepressible glee. She saw then in retrospect that for all his defects of character and affectations of manner, he had possessed an irreducible core of joyfulness that in death redeemed all.

Was it, she wondered, really so dreadful to desire to be liked? In her youth she had taken it for granted that the noble gesture, the heroic posture, required an aloofness from acclaim, an indifference to praise or disapproval. The truly good man, she had thought, listened only to the dictates of his conscience and turned with scorn from the dull murmur of public opinion. Yet now she was not always sure she heard what her conscience was trying to tell her, and the old slogans sometimes sounded hollow to her ears. To be liked, to bring pleasure with one into a room, sometimes seemed to her in her confusion the highest of all achievements. All works vanished, were washed away by the tides of time, but that little touch of delight somehow endured. . . .

The blanket that lay draped over her knees was slipping. She plucked at it with irritation. She had driven William from her because of his frailties, because she had been strong and had feared that his weaknesses would eventually sap her strength and drag down her and the children. She had driven him away to save herself and her boys, yet she was no longer quite sure what had been saved, what lost. The truth was that she hardly knew the man. "William, who are you?" she said softly to herself, careful not to say the words aloud here in the kitchen, with the woman hovering near her, for fear of interruption. It was less a question than an expression of wonderment at her own ignorance. And it was answered only by silence. "But he was my *husband,*" she protested, "and the father of my children."

"Are you all right, Granny?"

"Yes, yes, my dear. Just lovely."

"Here, let me fix that blanket, it seems to be slipping."

Yet, she thought, she hardly knew her children either, though she had watched over them for years, though she had fed them and washed and mended their clothes and held their naked little bodies in her hands, their little boy bodies, so foreign and yet so familiar. They were her own flesh and blood, and goodness knows they had meant the world to her—were, at least for the years they had lived with her, her vision of the world, all the rest of the universe being ordered by their place in it. Yet in the long run they remained complete enigmas to her. And that being the case, what could one ever hope to understand about anything? Or perhaps it was only those things closest to the heart that remained ultimately mysterious.

How strange it all was! As long as she had watched over the boys, cared for them, kept them bound to her, they had seemed like awkward, inept young creatures, always on the verge of being totally submerged by the world. It was only when she had abandoned them to her own disappointment that suddenly they appeared to bob to the surface of life, right themselves, and float boldly away. Had she suppressed them with her love? Or had she simply been stubbornly wrongheaded in her ambitions for them? Now, from her chair near the stove, she could hardly remember what she had wanted for them. She had wanted them to cut a figure in the world. No, that could not have been it. What was the point of that? She had wanted them to be *good* men. But whatever did that mean? When she closed her eyes, she could not visualize it, them. . . . She shook her head, shook the thought from her. She had wanted them to love beauty, share her rapture for the arts. She tried to recall that rapture, the way she had given herself up to the soaring harmonies of music, yet she could recover nothing, could not even bring to mind a single melody, a snatch of song—could feel nothing, see nothing—except, oh yes, the distant image of a very small girl in a dark velvet dress perched on the edge of a piano stool, methodically running her hands up and down the keyboard; but there was no sound, nothing, absolutely nothing. . . . She had wanted them to be happy. No, that was not it either, for surely she had never had any clear vision of happiness, could conceive of it only as something other than itself: success or power or health—complete and radiant health. Perhaps what she had really wanted for them was to be *safe,* safe from the insidious, destructive, soul-destroying pressures of the world. She had done her best to build up their defenses, but in the end she had failed. They had rushed out to meet the enemy with open arms. . . .

Could she say now, from her throne at the very pinnacle of experience, that she had been right or they mistaken in their attitudes toward life? She had loved her children, at least she had cared for them and feared dreadfully for them, but she had never taken pride in them or enjoyed that particular satisfaction of being able to boast of their exploits to other parents. Even in her own private meditations on their careers, she never had the sense that time was rounding out their lives in some meaningful, discernible manner.

And yet . . . and yet Willy at least seemed to have a certain real contentment with his lot, if not because of her, then in spite of her. He never complained, ever, of being ill-treated by others or by her or by that opposite of the Godhead sometimes called Fate. A sales clerk at sixteen, he remained a sales clerk all his life and dealt with the world pleasantly, even confidently, from that other side of the counter, making brief sorties to assist a customer or to attend to private matters. Male customers of the hardier sort would occasionally take advantage of his open, ever-eager manner to ride him a bit, exchanging among themselves sly winks and lugubrious frowns at his wide-eyed wonderment and confusion. In the give-and-take of masculine jocularity Willy was all take, but even the most boisterous of the regulars came to respect his trusting, good-humored (if humorless) response to their playful jibes, and any brash newcomer who attempted to join in the fun was sure to be promptly and brutally put down. The ladies appreciated his patience, the absence of the least trace of irony or aggression in his manner. He was helpfulness itself, without ever bringing a blush of irritation or embarrassment to a young woman's cheek, even in his halcyon days, before his hairline began to recede and he began to sport pendulous blond mustaches. Over time he became a comforting presence on the local scene. People returning to Madison after years abroad in the great world would inevitably lament the many changes and disfigurements that had occurred to the old place: the hazardous increase in traffic, the boisterous bad manners of the new generation of undergraduates, the proliferation of saloons and eating places, catering as it seemed to the lowest elements and basest instincts of the population. Then they would suddenly catch sight of that familiar form behind the storefront window, and they would momentarily suspend their complaints, smile softly to themselves, and murmur contentedly, "Well, if that isn't old Willy!" His hair was thinner and grayer and combed carefully, strand by strand, across his scalp rather than brushed back with abandon as in days of yore. He was if anything even more angular and attenuated in appearance, but his features remained wondrously unchanged, bore the same high color in the cheeks, wore the same boyish openness of expression, well beyond the middle years and into old age, so that the old customers continued to call him "Willy" to his face instead of "Mr. Macready"—though they expected their young offspring to address him as "Mr. Willy" at least and to mind their thank-yous and pleases, for he was, after all, a local institution to whom homage was due.

He remained at the store for fifty-three years, after Bronson's Dry Goods had changed to Higham's Hardware, then to Higham & Forsters' Hardware & Painting Supplies. He went, as it were, with the real estate, and subsequent owners never had any reason to consider him as other than a good asset and useful acquisition. Just to see Willy bustling about the place, his blue apron strapped about his waist, gave everyone—owners, customers, and creditors alike—a feeling that everything was all right, that business would go on as usual, that stock would somehow be replenished, credit continue to be extended, and bills paid. Elizabeth followed her son's career from a discreet distance. Though they lived only a couple of miles apart, the truth was that they had little to say to one another, and both were shy in the other's presence—the son because he felt that he had let his mother down, the mother because she sensed that she had failed to hold him up, to lend him her full support and approval.

When Willy was nearing forty, he married. The news took everyone by surprise because everyone saw him as an inveterate bachelor and impervious to change. The marriage, however, was soon absorbed by the community and was generally perceived as a slight modification of his image, nothing more. His bride was the younger daughter of Ezra Higham of Higham's Hardware and the sister of Thomas Higham of Higham & Forsters' Hardware & Painting Supplies. She had worked for many years as a cashier at the store, so people had little difficulty thinking of the two of them in the same context. Dorothy Higham was a year older than her husband and had long been considered a confirmed spinster. There were three children of the marriage, the last of which died at birth, almost taking the mother with him. The elder boy's name was John. She remembered his name. He was a solemn boy, who was clever at school and went off to college in the East. The daughter was presently stirring the cauldron full of boiled linen with a wooden ladle.

Elizabeth, who had been pretending to be asleep, stole a long look at the woman, taking in her broad hips, her raw hands, her large and coarse features rosy red and perspiring from the heat of the stove. "My granddaughter," Elizabeth said to herself, "My American granddaughter." She had never thought much about Willy's wife. For years previous to the marriage she had known her as a vague figure fluttering dimly over the cash box at the distant, business end of the counter; and when Dorothy emerged as Willy's wife, she turned out to be a plain, gray-haired woman with ink-stained fingers and watery, myopic eyes of no distinguishable color. Yet it had evidently been a good marriage. Yes, there was, she supposed, no other phrase for it. The two of them always seemed comfortable together; they never quarreled or went into sulks. From the beginning one would have taken them for an old couple who had long since come to terms with their differences and now lived together in mutual tolerance and contentment. Elizabeth wondered what had happened to Dorothy. No point in asking the woman, who would simply get upset and scold her for her forgetfulness. It seemed to her now that Dorothy had survived Willy by a short time and then simply had faded away.

Frank's wife presented quite another picture. He had announced his marriage as a fait accompli by letter—one of those appallingly childlike letters of his, written in a broad, bold hand and full of exclamation marks and underlinings. He brought his bride out to Madison by train a couple of weeks after the wedding. Elizabeth had been taken aback by her youthfulness. She looked like a child decked out in her mother's not-quite-best finery. The broad-brimmed hat—the latest style in Chicago, Elizabeth was assured—seemed too large for her, and while strolling outdoors with Elizabeth, she frequently clapped her hand to her head to keep it from blowing away, accompanying the gesture with little birdlike cries of alarm. The child was clearly in a state of near terror and constantly on the verge of tears.

Heaven knows what Frank had led her to expect, but she was obviously desperate to make a good impression on his mother and clearly despaired of doing so. In spite of the new outfit, the pink parasol, and white gloves, she had the air of a little servant girl fresh off the boat from Ireland; and indeed, when she managed to stammer out her greetings (all but dropping a curtsey in her confusion), the accent was unmistakable in its purity. Her name was Maureen, and she had met Frank while working as a chambermaid in a Chicago hotel. As the girl was preoccupied with admiring the new kittens, tenderly pressing each of them in turn to her cheek, Elizabeth had remarked to her son on his bride's extreme youthfulness, and Frank, evidently taking her comment as a criticism, had protested in an angry undertone that she was "almost nineteen." Elizabeth subsequently learned that her real age at the time had been "almost sixteen." By then the revelation mattered not at all, but during that first visit the spectacle of these two distressingly young people parading about as a grown-up married couple had been difficult for her to take in. At the first sight of them, making their way with solemn tread up the path from the front gate, she had felt a strong urge to rush to them and clasp them in a protective embrace. Yet to do so, she knew, would reduce them instantly to children, spoil their little performance, and provoke Frank's ire. The result was that she felt ill at ease throughout the visit and was afraid that her restrained manner might be seen as a sign of disapproval and hostility. In fact, her overriding sentiment at the time was one of terrible, heart-rending pity: pity at their youth, their vulnerability, their breathtaking lack of experience.

If there was underneath this pity a sense of loss, of disappointment, of squandered opportunity, it was not very compelling at the time, though it was later to color all her reflections on Frank and his marriage, until in her old age it dissolved in a general sense of weary resignation and uncertainty. The marriage survived, and as Elizabeth had to acknowledge, that in itself was no small thing. As husband and wife grew older, they came to resemble each other in manner as well as in physical appearance. In time, Maureen acquired Frank's boisterous good humor, his ready smile, and his full-bodied laugh—along with his florid complexion and plump figure. Their childlessness seemed to bind them ever closer together, and Elizabeth noticed that whenever they visited her, they hardly ever moved out of physical reach of one another: if Frank strayed to a corner of the room to look at a new magazine or to fetch something for his mother, Maureen was drawn irresistibly after him. Whether this was a sign of their deep intimacy, a sort of animal magnetism that existed between them, or simply of their fear of being alone with her, Elizabeth never determined.

Their visits were usually unannounced. They would descend upon her two or three times a year, bearing useless gifts in gaudy wrappings—hideous pieces of souvenir crockery from Niagara Falls or some Centenary Exposition, or the latest patented gadget intended to make her life easier by performing tasks she had never dreamed of performing—and presented with exaggerated gestures of jollity and goodwill, clearly meant to "break the ice." Elizabeth was almost always caught off guard by these descents and increasingly rattled by them. She would instinctively hasten to the kitchen to put together a meal of some sort, but Frank and Maureen had always "just eaten" or were "going out to dinner in town" and made it emphatically clear that they wanted to spare her the bother of "fussing." Elizabeth did indeed wonder *why* they came and continued to come regularly over the years, this increasingly foreign yet aggressively familiar couple, with their slightly vulgar mannerisms, loud clothes, and overbearing profusion of endearments. (Elizabeth had winced inwardly whenever her daughter-in-law addressed her as "Mama.") She could only assume that they came out of a vague sense of duty and even, perhaps, out of genuine if inchoate goodwill. She saw that Frank was in some small, private way proud of her and anxious to justify himself in her eyes. During the visits he invariably carried the burden of the conversation, boasting in elusive terms of important business deals and hinting of fabulous prospects for the future, while Maureen beamed cheerfully, with a distant, dreamy look on her face, as if he were telling them all a nice bedtime story. Elizabeth was never entirely clear about her son's financial situation or even about what precisely he did for a living. After several years as a salesman, first for a wholesale baking supplies firm, then for a brewery, he found (or "landed," as he put it) "a really responsible position" with something called the Harrison Express Company in Chicago. The way in which he talked about the business, tossing out phrases like "Me and Jim Harrison have decided to expand into the North End" or "I'm looking into the advisability of enlarging our fleet of motor vans," gave her reason to think that he might be something more than a simple employee, perhaps even a junior partner of the firm, but she felt instinctively that it was better not to inquire too closely on that point. It was odd, but whenever he began expanding too lavishly on his prospects, she felt prompted to offer him money! Fortunately, she had nothing to spare (a large part of her daily activity was devoted to ways of concealing her poverty); she knew that he would have been affronted and humiliated by such an offer. Like his father, Frank had a reckless faith in the reality of his dreams.

" . . . Or a nice bowl of soup?" It was the woman's voice. There was no point in Elizabeth's pretending to be asleep since her eyes were open, staring hard into her memories.

"What was that, my dear?"

"I said would you like some of your porridge or the soup I have just made up for the children's supper?"

"What sort of soup, dear?"

"A nice tomato soup, with milk in it."

"Aw, Mommy, you know we hate that!"

"Now Chuckie, that's not true. Anyway, your sister doesn't hate it. And there will be hot corn bread to go with it."

"I think, my dear, that I had better stay with the porridge. The digestion, you know. No point in taking chances."

"Can't I have the porridge, too, like Granny? With brown sugar in it. Please, Mommy?"

"You may not! Besides, there isn't enough. And anyway, you'll eat what is put before you, young man."

"It's not fair! Granny has a choice."

"Granny is Granny. Granny is ninety-six years old and has her own rights and privileges. Besides, she has a very delicate digestion and gets sick if things don't agree with her."

"Tomato soup makes *me* sick, too. I'll puke on the floor if I have to eat it."

"Red puked on the floor yesterday, didn't he, Chuckie? Only it warn't tomato soup. Daddy said it was a rabbit. He said . . ."

"Now you children stop that this minute! I won't have that sort of talk. See what you put your sister up to, Charles? I've a good mind to send you both to bed without any supper at all. And you stop that sniveling, Corrie; you haven't been hurt none and got no cause to cry. Now the two of you go off and wash your hands—and faces—and come sit down at table like proper ladies and gentlemen. And hurry up about it! Off with you!"

Buzz, buzz, buzz, thought Elizabeth, the cheerful buzzing of young voices, busily engaged in the process of living. Buzz, buzz, buzz, that is how it should be, the voices flitting here and there like bees, among the bright things of life. The words did not matter, she did not bother much with the words unless she were compelled to do so. She did not mind those voices at all as long as she did not have to attend to them, as long as they remained the murmur of daily living, around her, outside her, like distant music from the village bandstand down by the beach on a summer evening. She had other voices to attend to, voices that spoke to her alone: voices of memory, voices of the past, her past. Sometimes they were very faint, coming from far, far away, and required her full concentration; other times they were alarmingly clear, as if the words were spoken by someone right there beside her—like Miss Shaw's voice, each word ringing as if struck from a bell: "Young ladies, please! Open your books to page forty-three!" Or the voice of Mr. Smiley, the butcher, a soft, insinuating voice, heavy with meaning, addressed not to her, Elizabeth, but to Fanny, the family housemaid, to whose skirt she was tightly clinging: "Now for *you*, Miss, I do have a nice piece of mutton this morning, oh very nice indeed." Or the voice of William at the pump, lifted in song, the words wafted to her through the window as she lay there in bed, her firm, young body glowing and warm under the eiderdown coverlet:

> "Lesbia has a beaming eye,
> But no one knows for whom it beameth;
> Right and left the arrows fly,
> But what they aim at no one dreameth . . ."

Voices, oh so many voices, voices, calling out to her, jostling one another for her attention, like the voice so manly and clear of that handsome young doorman in Philadelphia (his face now entirely lost in the shadows of the night, but all the more handsome for that) saying, "Excuse me, Miss, but isn't this your glove?" And another nocturnal voice, hardly more than a whisper, but urgent, almost pleading, "You'll see, Miss Gow, things will work out somehow. It will be a new start for both of us, you'll see. . ." She could almost smell the scent of the sea and feel, yes, the warmth of young Macready's shoulder lightly pressing against her own. And now another voice intruded, coarse and jeering, "You want 'em in the kitchen, lady?" a nasty, cockney voice out of the damp cellars of the distant past, sending a sudden shock of fear and revulsion through her—*"In the kitchen, lady?"*— and making her want to clap her hands, her useless, wrinkled hands, over her defenseless ears.

Her voices, so many of them! And what, she wondered, would happen to these voices when she died? Would they disappear forever, be wiped clean off the slate? She could imagine oblivion for herself, but not for her voices, for her memories. They seemed to her now immeasurably precious, and she felt a terrible need to protect them from harm, such as a mother feels for her defenseless children. Perhaps she should rouse herself, break through this lethargy, and write them down—these voices, these memories—in her best hand, on lined paper, in a large notebook. But she was too old, too old for such a task. Besides, it was hardly likely that people would care at all about her memories or be able to appreciate them. . . . Of course they wouldn't. Better to try to take them with her into that other world. But she knew, she somehow knew for a fact that they would have to be left behind because they would not belong *there.* They belonged to this world, not the other one. They would remain behind, and she was sure that they would survive, somehow, somewhere. Oh, if only she could think more clearly, she could manage to explain to herself the reason for this certainty. She would have to husband her strength for the effort. The explanation—the luminously clear, the triumphantly clear explanation—was hovering near at hand, almost within her reach!

" . . . Here, let me help you, Granny." They were tugging at her again, pulling at her arm.

"Let me be! I'm all right . . . my dear."

"Sorry! Just trying to be of help, Granny. Your porridge is ready. Just thought I'd give you a hand to the table."

"I don't think that I'll have any porridge, dear. I'll just sit here as I am. You go ahead and eat."

"But Granny, it's your suppertime. You have to eat. Beside, I have just warmed it up for you. I warmed it up in milk, just as you like it. Here, take hold of my arm."

Why are they always hauling me about? Why can't they leave me alone with my thoughts for a few minutes? She did not see why they had to inflict porridge on her just now, as if porridge had anything to do with her memories. They were always trying to reduce the world to porridge, but who wanted to live in a world devoted heart and soul to porridge? Whatever happened to those other things—Beethoven sonatas and Alfred Lord Tennyson and her lost glove? Where have they all gone? Are they dead and buried, like Willy, like William, like Christabel, the little gray and white kitten that her father had given her for Christmas in London long, long ago? Gone! Forever! The music, the faces. She could not, try as she might, recall any of it. She closed her eyes tight and tried to see, tried to listen intently. If she could only make her way to the piano, she might bring them all back, force them back out of the dark silence. If she could run her fingers over the keys, she could fill the room with their vanished presences!

"That's it, Granny, just take hold of my arm."

I shall fall, thought Elizabeth. The woman does not know how to hold me properly. She means well, but she holds me all wrong. "Where's Fred?" She stopped herself just in time from saying, "Is he dead too?"

"Fred's at the Grange tonight. You'll have to let me take you to the table. There's a big meeting at the Grange tonight, they're electing new officers. Here's your stick. . . . That's it, you're doing just fine. Chuckie, pull out Granny's chair for her—you hurry now!"

It was no use, thought Elizabeth, she could not recall a single note. She sat there at the table, listening to the silence.

"*Do* eat your porridge, Granny. Is that spoon too large for you? Would you prefer a teaspoon? I bet that'll be better."

Elizabeth fumbled with her spoon. "Of course it isn't too big for me, this spoon is quite all right." The gathering notes had scattered, the hovering faces had receded into the shadows at the far corners of the room. The aroma of the warm porridge came gently upon her like an old sentimental tune cranked out of a barrel organ several streets away. It was so very sad and so very familiar that it almost brought tears to her eyes.

"Don't you like it? Would you like some sugar on it, Granny?"

"That would be lovely, my dear." Suddenly Elizabeth was ravenously hungry.

That evening, tucked tightly into bed, lying there in the darkness, she was finally free to gather her thoughts around her. There was still that buzz of voices in the background, but it had grown faint and sporadic, like the summer sound of moths against the window pane. . . . She could distinguish Fred's low, gravelly drawl, posing a question or, at intervals, filling in some forgotten bit of news, and Mabel's lazy, sing-song replies. Yes, as long as the voices were familiar to her and did not require her response, they were no bother; in fact, she found them comforting. When she was a small child, she had liked going to sleep with the sound of her parents' voices gently rising and falling in the next room, like the sound of spent waves lapping the shore, gently drawing her away on the tide of sleep. Now, however, it was not sleep she sought but calm, quiet, and the opportunity to concentrate her thoughts on the myriad memories that crowded about her bedside, like a classroom full of bright-faced children, waving their arms importantly in the air, eager to capture her attention.

Elizabeth sighed. People did not realize what a busy time old age was. Because you did not join in their useless chatter, had no inclination to compete in the exchange of puerile remarks, or attempt to impose your private, hard-earned opinions on ungrateful minds, people liked to assume that you were totally at loose ends. At times they almost seemed to resent your detachment, as if they half—suspected that you were indeed preoccupied with important matters of your own, felt jealous of your activity, slighted by it, and were trying to drag you back into their own world, insisting that you bestow on them and their affairs the precious little time that remained to you. Mostly, though, they simply did not understand. They did not realize what a great effort it was to detach yourself from your own pressing considerations in order to respond nicely to their needless and futile inquiries. Of course you tried to be polite, you tried not to offend or show impatience. But it was difficult to put together decently enthusiastic replies to questions that seemed like complete non sequiturs. The more time you took in framing your replies, and the more time you gave them out of your rapidly diminishing store, the more they demanded. There were moments when you were sorely tempted to feign senility, if only to be left in peace.

The voices in the next room trailed away. Fred called something to Mabel from the darkness outside, on his way to the barn, and Mabel sounded an affirmative reply from the back porch. Now she could hear Mabel moving about upstairs, in the bedroom directly overhead. Soon a great stillness would descend upon the house, broken only by the creaking of its joints in the wind and by Fred's low, rapturous snores. Elizabeth hardly slept anymore. She did not need sleep. Time enough for that later, she told herself. Soon.

She lay there wide-eyed and alert, attentive to the darkness. Her frail hands folded before her on the coverlet seemed faintly luminescent in the night-enshrouded room. Her body, she thought, would rot and decay after her death; first it would be put away in a casket and lowered into the earth: all that she had been told. *From ashes you come, to ashes you will return:* all that was easy to understand; it was part of the natural process. She had been told, too, that the body would be raised whole and intact at the Last Judgment. That she could not understand; it made no sense whatsoever. But so little made sense! She was willing to believe it because it was wholly beyond her comprehension. Besides (and this she would never whisper above her breath, even here in the darkness), the question really did not interest her very much; her belief was based on indifference as much as on faith.

Her body was but a poor tattered thing, whose final disposition was surely of little importance, a broken, near-useless thing that she clung to now like a shipwrecked sailor to the splintered remnants of his mast. Once she loosened her hold, it would float away like driftwood on the tide. The mystery, the great mystery was what happened to those *other* things. That no one had told her. Why had this important information been kept from her? Why had she been left here in the dark? Or perhaps she had been told but in the frailty of age had forgotten. She struggled to remember and in her struggle managed to rise in her bed, propping herself in an upright position with eager, trembling arms. "Please, Lord, let me remember," she pleaded in a whisper. Then, in response to the echoing silence, she said aloud, in protest, "I want to know. I have a right to know." But then, did she? She was not sure. Her conviction faltered. She interrogated the shadows with a wide-eyed gaze.

Yes, I do know what happens to this wretched body of mine, but was all the rest left in the lurch by its departure? Ashes to ashes, that she could understand, but where did that leave her memories? Were they dissipated in the great void, like mist from the lake? No, that she could not believe. Her memories were, she felt, more real than bones because more personal, because unique. They were *her* memories and must remain forever apart from the rest of the universe. But where? And how? If only she could *remember!* She closed her eyes and sank back onto her pillow. If her body were to be resurrected one day, it stood to reason that her memories, the very stuff of her life, of which the body was but the torn envelope, would somehow survive. And yet, did survival really matter that much? Why was she lying here, fighting against mere oblivion? If she could bid farewell to the body—and that she could, with good riddance—why not to all the rest as well?

After all, her life viewed by conventional standards, the standards she had been raised to believe in, was at best a drab affair, hardly worth memorializing! She had, she seemed to recall, worked hard—worried and worked hard—but she had surely made no mark on the world, or why would she find herself now, at the end of her life, remote from the world on a windswept farm, huddled here in bed, alone in the darkness? The most she had done was to survive while others had died. Survive! So much for survival. A tawdry thing, survival. Surely life had nothing to do with survival, any more than it had to do with oblivion. It seemed to her that as a young girl she had other ideas about living, that she had had intimations of . . . yes, yes, *sublimity.* She could not remember what they were; she would look into that later. What mattered for now was that nothing had turned out quite as she had planned, that life in general had proved a disappointment. She had hoped for clarity and brightness and a great suffusion of goodwill. She had hoped for strength and for the opportunity to touch other people, to touch and be touched. She had come toward people, but they had slipped from her grasp, like phantoms. And her children, where had they gone? She had clung to their warm, naked bodies, but they had fled from her, down the vast corridors of time.

Her music, her longing for beauty, for art—what of that? She had put her faith in it, practiced hard, and it too had left her and seemed now like one of those mocking, ragtime tunes that Frank had pounded out on her piano just, she felt, to annoy her. It was all, all of it, a disappointment, but perhaps, she thought, life always ended like that. Perhaps it *had* to end like that in preparation for what was yet to come. Perhaps—who knows?—her life had even been a success, and now that she had reached its end, the triumph had simply lost its savor. How could she tell? Certainly a savor of sorts remained— not perhaps a savor of triumph, but of something more private and personal, a faint lingering perfume, like the scent of dried rose petals pressed in the pages of an old book, like an aftertaste of something very like hope—not hope in the future (the future!), but hope in the past. Yes, with her eyes closed tight she could sense it, like a sharp glint of light fleetingly, but unmistakably, the fixed and immutable features of . . . what?

Had she been dozing? Why were there tears in her eyes? The darkness was all about her, vibrant with meaning. "I want to know . . ." she whispered again, but this time in a calmer, less peremptory tone, "I want to know. . ." But what did she want to know? "Have I been happy?" Immediately on framing the words and without waiting for a response, she rejected the question. After all, she had asked for happiness only when she was very young. Besides, whatever the answer, it did not really matter now. No, the question she really wanted to ask was: What had it all meant? That was a truly lovely question, a question that interested her immensely! She lay there very still, very attentive. Yes, it was meanings that she was after, of that she was now sure. But meanings of *what*? Why, of everything. There was a soft inrush of air in the darkness, as if the room were drawing a breath. No, perhaps not of everything. She must try to be reasonable; she had the impression that there was perhaps no answer to "everything," or if there were, it would undoubtedly remain outside the range of her comprehension. "Then," she asked in a confidential, almost conspiratorial voice, hoarse with excitement, "what is the meaning of anything?"

It seemed to her that the room swelled slightly now, like the gentle heave of a sleeper's bosom. Her heart was beating rapidly as she listened for the answer, but if there was an answer, she could not quite make it out in the overwhelming silence. Or was that an answer of sorts in the cough upstairs? Or in the sharp crack of the floorboards? Yes, she had the impression that the answer was very near at hand, all about her, or perhaps already within her, placed there for safekeeping and awaiting to be opened, unlatched, like the little crimson case that she had found at her bedside so long ago. How wonderful! Tears of gratitude welled up in her eyes. "I am so happy!" she said aloud, though she hardly knew what she meant or why the words came to her lips. "I have never been so happy. . ." Closing her eyes, she saw a dark form moving slowly, cautiously across her vision amidst a thin rain of stars.

New York City, 1942

THE YOUNG SOLDIER STOOD on the steps outside Pennsylvania Station and surveyed the scene with approval. His ill-fitting uniform, exposing several inches of shirt cuffs and heavy woolen socks, made him look even younger than his nineteen years; with his cap thrust far back on his head and his hands thrust deep into his trouser packets, he looked for all the world like a schoolboy on a spree. Casting a final appreciative glance at the skyline, he whistled softly to himself, gave a firm tug to the visor of his cap, and hurried down the remaining steps to plunge himself into the hurly-burly of the curbside traffic.

There was a general scramble for taxis, and after only a moment's hesitation the soldier threw himself cheerfully into the fray. Seizing the door handle of an incoming cab, he leaned toward the open window and said in a loud, firm voice, as if addressing a foreigner, "Can you take me to Riverside Drive? You know where that is?"

"Hop in, soldier."

The young man pulled open the door, then paused, still standing on the curb. "How much will it be to take me to 524 Riverside Drive?"

There was a stump of a dead cigar in the driver's mouth, and his cap, a tired tweed affair of indeterminate color, was pulled down over one eye. Unruly tufts of steely gray hair stuck out from the sides of his head. He looked up at the kid, taking in the freckled, sunburned face and the clear, sportively challenging gaze. "Hey, it's all up to the meter. I'm just along for the ride. See that little black box there? The meter. What it says, goes. Maybe a buck. Maybe a buck fifty." He removed the cigar stub from his mouth, eyed it critically, and added, "Plus tip."

The soldier smiled broadly. "OK," he said, and sprang into the cab.

He settled himself into the back seat, pulling down the armrest and stretching out his legs until his shoes touched the folded jump seat. "I've never been in New York before," he proclaimed.

"No kiddin'?"

"Been in Chicago, but never New York. It's my first visit here. It's a great town!"

"Yeah, quite a place."

"I'm from Clarksville, Iowa. I don't suppose you ever had anyone from Clarksville, Iowa, in your taxi before!"

"Hey, there's a first time for everything, soldier."

"I'd really like to spend some time here, just looking around, but I only have a few hours' layover between trains. I'm going to see my uncle now. He lives here, on Riverside Drive. Since I was passing through New York, I thought that I might just pay him a visit."

"Good idea."

"I haven't seen him since I was a little kid. Fact is, I hardly know what he looks like, except from photos. He's a professor. Teaches at Columbia University."

"Must be a pretty brainy guy."

"You said it! He has all sorts of degrees; I mean, besides the usual ones. He teaches engineering. I phoned ahead to make sure he was there."

"Yeah, be a shame to get there and find he wasn't at home."

"Actually, he wasn't there when I phoned, but my aunt said he had just gone down to the corner grocery store for something and would be right back. Guess she was pretty darn surprised to hear from *me!* She kept saying, 'Who is that? Who did you say that was?' "

"I'll bet she was. After all those years."

One entered the building through a large, bleak courtyard, flanked on all sides by row upon row of windows, most of them with their shades tightly drawn. In the center of the courtyard was a decorative circular fountain, now dry. The lobby of the apartment house conveyed to the young man's eyes an air of opulence. The marble facings and the leather sofa and armchair gave off a sumptuous sheen; the runner leading from the entranceway to the elevator savored faintly of the Orient. As his vision adapted to the dim light, he noticed that the tiles on the floor were cracked and ineptly patched in places, and the furnishings were well worn, but the place still managed to maintain some of the factitious splendor of a movie palace and imposed upon the soldier a pleasurable sense of exoticism. *This is New York!* he thought to himself.

On a plain metal folding chair beside the elevator cage sat an elderly Negro in a threadbare maroon-colored uniform. He had a pair of steel-rimmed spectacles perched on the edge of his nose and was perusing the comic pages of the *Daily Mirror.* The young man was almost upon him before he glanced up from his reading.

"I'm looking for Professor Macready, Professor John Macready. He lives here, doesn't he?"

"He does. Apartment 3B." The old man carefully folded his newspaper.

"I'm his nephew. From Clarksville, Iowa."

"Well, I'm pleased to meet you." The Negro bent down and placed the newspaper on the floor under his chair, then reached behind him to take hold of a cane, which was resting against the wall. With great deliberation he rose to his feet. He was an imposing figure, surprisingly tall, and he carried off his quasi-military regalia—the visored hat, the gilt buttons, and the epaulettes—with dignity and conviction. For a fleeting moment the soldier felt himself seriously outranked and just managed to suppress an instinctive inclination to salute.

"A bit stiff from sitting," the old man explained as he drew back the iron door of the elevator. "You get along in, young man, and I'll take you up."

It was his uncle who answered the door.

"Charles! Well for goodness sake! Come right in, boy, it's great to see you." His uncle was balding and bespectacled but did not look or sound forbiddingly brainy. His nephew noticed with satisfaction the unmistakable cast of the Macready chin.

Uncle John led him down a long dimly lit corridor lined with bookshelves and pictures. The boy caught out of the corner of his eye a passing glimpse of his mother's high school graduation portrait hanging above one of the bookshelves, the same photograph that stood on the piano in the parlor at home, and for an instant he had a troubling feeling in the pit of his stomach that the picture had been magically transported here. Farther on he encountered another familiar sight, one of his grandmother's distinctive watercolor paintings of the old Madison house, slightly different from the one that hung in Ma's bedroom. But the smell of the place was decidedly different from home—a sharp, slightly acrid smell that he took to be the odor of New York domesticity, an aromatic blend of strong coffee, steam heating, and insecticide, and underlying it all a hint of Turkish cigarettes.

The corridor opened into a bright, spacious living room, with two large windows looking down on a strip of park across the street and beyond that the slate-gray Hudson River. On the other side of the river was a large electric sign proclaiming in icy white letters JACK FROST SUGAR. With a surge of pleasure, the boy took in the room: the boldly colored cushions strewn about low-slung sofas and chairs, the profusion of decorative objects brought back from vacation trips to Mexico and the Southwest—papiermâché masks and sculptures in garish hues, small brass boxes, grotesque toys suspended on strings from the mantelpiece and shelves. Yes, this is what he had hoped the place would be like, even though his imagination had failed to supply any sort of precise anticipatory vision. It was a setting just right for a professor uncle and an artistic aunt who sent them homemade Christmas cards constructed out of bits of string and tin foil and old candy wrappers or whatnot. He wished that his ma were here to share the spectacle with him. A couple of years back the two of them had spent a joyful evening together bent over an illustrated catalog of Aunt Edith's recent work, sent to them in Iowa from a New York gallery, marveling at the strangeness of the objects and at the accompanying price list. Thirty dollars for a small, slightly lopsided ceramic bowl that looked like the sort of thing Cora used to bring home from Miss Doyle's third-grade art class! But as his ma said, you had to admire the gumption of it all; and maybe, she remarked, people in New York City had different sorts of needs than folks in Clarksville, Iowa, and they would likely enough laugh at some of the things Iowans took pride in and found downright pleasurable. His gaze latched onto a tall corner bookcase lined with row upon row of yellow-spined *National Geographic* magazines.

"See you get the *Graphic* too, Uncle John. We've subscribed ever since I was a little kid."

Aunt Edith entered the room bearing a tray piled high with sandwiches and a tinkling pitcher of lemonade.

"Is that really little Chuckie? Just look at that boy! I can't believe it."

He had almost forgotten that Aunt Edith was not only an artist, but Jewish. She was certainly exotic looking to his eyes—tiny and trim, with her gray hair cut short, almost like a boy's, and with the faintest hint of a mustache. She was wearing black pants, a sort of smock that buttoned down the front, and a large silver and turquoise necklace that she had bought from an old Navajo craftsman in his adobe workshop outside Santa Fe. She balanced the tray rather precariously on a chair and rushed over to embrace him. He had to bend down to receive her kiss.

"I thought that you would want something real to eat after all that army chow. I hope the lemonade's all right. Now that I get a look at you, it occurs to me that you might prefer a cocktail or a shot of bourbon."

"Aw no, Aunt Edith, lemonade's just fine." Then, catching sight of the twinkle in her eyes, he blushed a deep crimson, and they both burst out laughing.

Uncle John asked after his ma and the folks at home, and the boy launched into a full account of all the twists and turns of the family's fortunes over the past few years, touching not only on the past, but on hopes and plans for the future of each member of the Iowa clan. He knew as he spoke that much of this information could hardly be of interest to his aunt and uncle, who probably did not even know some of the people he was talking about, but he found real pleasure in invoking their names and faces here in this New York apartment, so very far from home. Uncle John kept nodding his head and making encouraging little exclamations, while Aunt Edith kept replenishing his plate until he had to cover it in silent protest with a large, raw, farmboy hand.

At one point the tray was carried off, and Aunt Edith reappeared with the family photograph album, which she placed in his lap. It was a large disorderly volume, with a number of its pages detached from the binding, and many photos roaming loose and threatening to escape from the book. He was shocked by the state of the album. At home the family photograph album was a treasured object, kept on the same shelf as the family Bible; his mother had carefully aligned each of the photos on the page and lovingly, respectfully fixed them in place with corner holders. This book on his lap had about it a decidedly promiscuous air, a faint aura of sacrilege. It was not, he felt, what a family photograph album *should* be. And it surprised him that Aunt Edith, who was after all a professional artist, would tolerate such an amateurish job. Yet as he gazed in bewilderment at the jumble of faces and images before him, all comparisons vanished, and he was aware of a super-abundance of life surging forth from the pages.

Uncle John was leaning over his shoulder, directing his attention to the earlier pages of the book, where together they found, with a little shout of triumph on his uncle's part and of recognition on his, a group of snapshots taken during Uncle John and Aunt Edith's last visit to the folks in Iowa, many years back. There they all were! How strange to encounter his whole family, staring out from this foreign album! There was Ma and Pa and Cora and George and Aunt Louise and Uncle Ted. . . . How awkward and youthful they looked. And there, in the corner of the picture, shielding his eyes from the light, was himself. Just a little kid. He was barefoot and wearing a new pair of overalls—the ones with the brass clasps on the shoulder straps. And right beside him was Tippy. When told that Tippy had been killed by a car, he had run off and hid in the hayloft, and the whole family had spent the entire day looking for him; he could almost hear their voices now, calling his name in the far distance. . . .

"You must have been five or six when that photo was taken. Do you remember our visit?"

"Sure I do. You had a new Ford convertible, didn't you, Uncle John? Blue with a white top. Or maybe I just heard about it."

"That's right! Only the top was black. Though there were whitewall tires! And there's the very car. We were on a trip to Arizona to see the Grand Canyon."

"Oh for goodness sake, don't inflict the whole book on the poor boy. He can't be interested in all that stuff."

"Isn't that my cousin Dan, Aunt Edith?"

"Yes, that's Danny. He must have been ten or eleven at the time. As you see, he used to play the cello. Played it damn well, and *should* have too, considering all those years of lessons. When he went off to Cornell, he left the instrument behind him. I found it in his closet. I could have strangled him, the beast! And he's never touched it since."

"I played the trombone in the high school marching band. We won the All-State competition. George plays the tuba. Ma says we are a musical family, all right. I could have gone out for the army band—they say it's a pretty soft deal. But it didn't seem right, somehow. I mean, I might just as well get my money's worth and see the whole show. What's Dan up to these days? He must be three, four years older than me."

"Two years, I think. There's a recent picture of him." She crossed the room and brought back a silver-framed picture that had been standing half-concealed among the jumble of things on the mantelpiece. It was a formal studio portrait of a young air force lieutenant, smiling back at the camera with sharply inquisitive eyes, a halo of light behind him. He looked older than his twenty-one years, and the boy was impressed by the expression of self-assurance on the young officer's face and by his Clark Gable mustache.

"Danny's in England with the Third Bomber Command. He's a navigator on a B-24. I'll give you his address, Chuckie. Maybe you'll be over there yourself, and you can look him up. He'd be as pleased as all get out to see you."

"The guys all think that we'll be going the other way, Aunt Edith. We had a long lecture last week in camp about the importance of mosquito netting."

He continued to turn the pages of the album, fascinated. Faces and more faces; people in strange hats, striking strange attitudes, and gazing out at him with airs of complete familiarity, as if he should recognize them, one and all, and know what they expected of him. It was almost a relief to come across Aunt Edith and Uncle John in the crowd, though he could not quite tell whose side they were on.

Aunt Edith intervened to take the album from him. "Enough of all that," she said soothingly. "Perhaps Chuckie might be interested in seeing the picture of his great-great-granddad. I'll bet he's never seen that before. Why don't you haul the old gent out for him?"

Uncle John went over to a large bureau, got down on his hands and knees, and started rummaging through the bottom drawer. "Know it's here somewhere," he said.

He returned with a small, square object in his hand. "Here, meet your great-great-grandfather Gow."

The case was in red leather, once crimson to judge from the corners, now a pale pink. The boy unhooked the tiny clasps and opened the lid. "What is it?" he said.

"Here, tilt it that way, to the light."

"Well, just look at that! The guy suddenly leaps out at you. It's on glass. Must be darned old."

"Actually, it's on copper. Taken nearly a hundred years ago."

"Wow. He sure is a stern-looking old geezer."

"You had to sit absolutely still for a couple of minutes or more. Usually the sitter's head was held steady by a concealed clamp or brace. You'd look stern too under the circumstances."

"I guess so." He tilted the case this way and that, fascinated by the way the image came and went, the way it was drawn forth from and receded back into the shadows. "Whose writing is this?"

"That's his. Here, as you can see, it was a gift to your grandma—no, your *great*-grandma—Macready on her birthday, when she was a girl at school, in London."

The boy stared back at the image, confronted it head-on. No, the eyes were not really stern. In fact they looked a little anxious and almost pleading. Faces! Too many faces! What did they expect of *him?* And if he smiled or frowned back at them, they would continue to regard him with the same fixity of expression, still and forever awaiting his response.

"That's real great," he said, closing the lid and carefully sliding the hooks back in place before handing the case to his uncle. Instinctively he had risen to his feet. He couldn't linger here any longer. He had to get on with things.